CLEMATIS
AND THE
QUEEN
OF THE
VOID

HIYODORI

Contents

1

Mangle rays soared overhead as our stagecoach pulled up to the town of Bittercress.

I poked Wist in the arm. She woke with a start. She stared at me as if I'd plunged a knife in her back.

Which is a roundabout way of saying that she wore the same blank look as always. Wist was the Kraken: the most powerful mage in the world. Her expression wouldn't budge for assassins, or deadly vorpal beasts, or an audience with the Board of Magi. Nor for an awe-inspiring air show put on by foreign wildlife.

She did turn to watch through the window with me. The giant rays sent slippery-smooth shadows gliding across the sea-green land outside our rattly coach.

The sooner we could escape this butt-bruising contraption, the better. The creatures pulling the stagecoach were not horses. Not by a long shot. More on that later.

It was our first time visiting this territory. A small landlocked country named—most incongruously—Manglesea. The only sovereign state on the continent that strictly forbade all magic of human origin.

That's what made it the perfect place to go on vacation.

Wist was not the effusive type, but I could tell she liked it here. She obeyed their regulations to a fault. She'd stopped magically dimming her presence as soon as we got through customs. Despite that, no one in the border cities had followed her around or fawned over her.

I adjusted the patch over my right eye socket.

"Wist," I said. "Don't forget that we're tourists. We're here to bask in the atmosphere. To splurge on gifts and food and souvenirs. To have a frivolous good time. To—"

"To see Katashiro Caverns."

She had the blackest eyes I'd ever seen, and a low toneless voice just as emotionless as her face. A dizzying mass of latent magic writhed in her torso. Those with a particular sensitivity to magic might get motion sickness if they sat right beside her. They might faint dead away.

I didn't blink. "The caves are tomorrow," I said. "Today, we're on a day-long date. Got it?"

Wist glanced at the blue bond thread on her wrist. I took that as a sign of agreement.

I wore a utility jacket and loose-fitting pants held up by suspenders, but Wist lifted me down from the stagecoach as if I were a lady from five centuries ago in robes too heavy for walking.

I didn't object; my depth perception wasn't at its best. I'd popped out my magic-laced prosthetic eye before we entered the country.

The stagecoach (along with the hungry-looking creatures hitched to it) clattered away to take our luggage to the inn. No need to worry about them going to the wrong address. There was only one place for strangers to stay in town.

We'd left the border zone hours before dawn. During our prolonged coach ride, we'd polished off a variety pack of sweet sticky rice cakes for breakfast and lunch. Now it was mid-afternoon on a warm day at the very beginning of fall. My legs ached from sitting.

If legality were of no concern, Wist could've ported us from the border to Bittercress in less than a second. But look at how little tension she held in her jaw, here in this country where magic use wasn't a viable option.

The less magic she used, the less it would pain her.

Traces of an old wall surrounded the town. The stones had crumbled all the way down to their foundation. Left to our own devices, we stepped right past the remnants of the wall. I'd asked the coach to drop us here and go on ahead, so we could start getting our bearings on our own. Before anyone took charge and started guiding us.

In all of Bittercress, there were well under a thousand residents. I might not have the greatest sense of direction, but this didn't seem like the type of place you could get incurably lost in.

Far more aerials flew here than above the plains closer to the border. Kite-shaped mangle rays. Sky nettles like jellyfish the size of cruise ships. Faraway ribbony critters reminiscent of oarfish.

We got takeaway drinks at a microbrewery and brought them to the banks of the shallow river that ran east-west through town. There we sat and watched the aerials for close to an hour.

I could now understand why airships were forbidden to pass over Manglesea. Even without any laws against magic use, human traffic would've been much too disruptive to the delicate ecology of the sky.

I sipped my mead and soaked in sunshine while Wist gazed silently up at the floaters. On the inside, though, I was brimming with triumph. This fine afternoon marked another genius plan flawlessly executed by Asa Clematis.

There was no escaping the responsibilities of being the Kraken. But Wist needed a vacation. She always needed a vacation. Yeah, I'd take full credit for dragging her out here.

While nothing ever really took her mind off her duties, the wonders of nature came close. It helped her to remember that not all magic was human in origin. Not all magic made sense to human minds. Not everything in the world was her fault.

I mentally thanked the wild mangle rays and sky nettles for coming out in full force. As far as I was concerned, this trip could already be termed a grand success.

At last Wist came out of her daze. She stretched her neck. She confiscated my empty cup of mead. Then she caught herself—she'd been about to transmute it with magic. She peered at the bottom of the cup as if hoping it might tell her what to do instead.

I reminded her that we could return our cups to the brewery.

"This isn't much of a date for you," Wist said.

"Wildlife observation is a perfectly respectable way to spend a pleasant afternoon."

"Never knew you were into birdwatching."

"Aerials aren't birds," I retorted. "More to the point—aquariums and zoos and aviaries are classic date spots."

Despite my assurances, Wist seemed to get it in her head that she owed me a proper tour of town. Ah, well. There would be plenty of time to gawk at aerials later.

In our whole trip, we had only one planned activity. Only one task that resembled actual work. I'd dangled it as bait to convince Wist that it was okay to travel for comfort, to relax in a country bereft of human magic. We'd get that one lonely obligation out of the way tomorrow. At Katashiro Caverns. Then we'd be free to do anything. Or, better yet, to not do anything at all.

Truth be told, I quite liked Manglesea, too. We'd only been in the country for a few days. Which was more than long enough to realize that they truly didn't distinguish between mages like Wist and healers like me.

Granted, it was a lot harder for mages to obtain a visa. But those who successfully passed through border control got treated the same as anyone else.

Unlike back in our homeland of Osmanthus, it didn't matter that I didn't have magic of my own. It didn't matter, conversely, that Wist was only the second Kraken-class mage in all of recorded history. As long as she didn't try to use her magic here, no one would care.

There were drawbacks to such a thorough rejection of human magic. Like how it took half a day to trundle across the countryside in an old-fashioned stagecoach. Like the fact that Manglesea had a very, very short history as an independent state. Up until just a few generations ago, it was constantly getting conquered by neighboring countries. Most often Osmanthus.

Yet the conquering forces encountered misfortune after misfortune. Despite Manglesea's dire lack of military power (magical or otherwise), no one nation managed to hold it for long. Within the past century, they'd more or less given up for good.

Naturally, it helped that Wist the Kraken had gone on the record as supporting Manglesea's right to stay independent. There were Board members back in Osmanthus who would've stopped at nothing to change her mind. To persuade her—or force her—to go on a colonizing rampage. So far, all their petty efforts had failed. But that's a story for another day.

Another thing I liked about Manglesea: height-wise, I fit right in. I was quite short compared to other Osmanthians. Here, for the first time in my life, I felt average.

(Wist, on the other hand, was tall even for an Osmanthian. She was already used to strangers getting startled by her height. In Manglesea, most people at least had the good grace to hide their reaction.)

The local innkeeper—who would be our primary hostess in Bittercress—was around the same size as me, too. Except for the fact that she appeared to be heavily pregnant. She wore her hair in thick brown-black twists with sharp metal fishhooks dangling from their ends.

It took all my self-restraint to refrain from asking if she'd ever accidentally hooked herself.

The people of Manglesea called themselves Manglelanders. During introductions, the innkeeper mentioned that Manglelanders only used their real names amongst themselves. And even then, only on special occasions.

We'd noticed this in the border cities as well, though a few people had told us to call them by nicknames. It seemed stricter in Bittercress.

"Won't cause any problems for you," the innkeeper said cheerfully. She patted her heart. "No way to get me mixed up with anyone else. There's only one innkeeper in town."

As she showed us to our room, she added: "Oh, there is one man around these parts who freely gives out his name. A real eccentric. You'll meet him later."

Manglesea had the same official language as Osmanthus. To my ear, the accent here didn't sound much different from what you'd hear in the rural Osmanthian east.

"Have a nice evening," the innkeeper said once she'd helped us settle in. "Don't be lost."

The door clicked shut behind her.

Don't be lost?

It was a generous room with an outdoor balcony and a large private bath. Random knots of wood in the walls had been painted over with crude yellow eyes, some more faded than others. Paper wards were taped in every corner and on every open surface, low and high.

"Charming," I said. "Feel protected?"

Wist reached up to touch one of the wards near the ceiling. It bore the six-spot seal: a pattern of red circles arranged like the dots on playing dice. I only knew what the symbol was called because it had shown up in the border cities, too.

"There's no real power in any of these," Wist pronounced.

"Of course not."

The inn doubled as a tavern, which was likely its main source of income. I didn't spot any other foreign visitors, although we did become acquainted with a group of Manglelander merchants staying down the hall. They'd come on a business trip from a much bigger city. They spoke to us with bombastic enthusiasm about the growing popularity of Bittercress mead and honey and cider.

That night, like every other night, I fell asleep with one arm draped around Wist.

A few hours later, I woke to find myself holding a spare pillow instead.

It was too dark to make out the six-spot seals pasted willy-nilly around the room.

An animal howled outside. Not a wolf. Not any regular mammal.

Did the flying rays and nettles and ribbon-like streamers ever make noise up near the clouds? Or might this cry come from one of the long-faced beasts that had pulled our stagecoach? Manglelanders called them primevals.

The howling died out. I touched the spot where Wist should have been sleeping. It held a dim memory of warmth.

Voices came from the balcony. I recognized Wist's voice first—a cold contralto. Someone answered indistinctly.

Wist spoke again. Couldn't make out any actual words.

My feet found slippers next to the bed. I shuffled over to the balcony doors. I craned my neck to see through the gap in the curtain.

Just one other person stood on the balcony with Wist. Someone much shorter than her.

Then again, most people were much shorter than her. Especially around here.

I only saw them for half a second before Wist moved. She stepped into just the right spot to completely block my view. As if she knew I was there.

She probably did. She'd probably done it on purpose.

By the time I slid open the curtains and stepped out to join them, the stranger was gone.

2

WIST AND I were bondmates. Magically tied together for the rest of our lives. One might even argue that we'd gotten measurably closer than other bonded pairs. Though I possessed no magic of my own, I could reach inside Wist to hijack her power—to use her magic for her.

We'd first met as teenagers. Now we were in our mid-thirties. We hadn't been together the entire time. For one thing, I'd spent seven of those years in prison for treason.

Let me tell you this, though. Even if you know someone as well as your own face in the mirror, even if you're bonded for life, even if you can speak mind-to-mind, even if sensing their unease bleeding through your bond could roil you awake in the middle of the night—

It would be foolish to think you knew everything.

Out on the balcony, a chorus of autumn insects surrounded us. Bell crickets. Pine crickets. Mallet bugs that sounded like zealous swordsmiths banging away at microscopic metal anvils.

The sky seemed clouded, its stars half-occluded. Just the usual floaters. Aerials never really came down to rest.

Wist wore one of the long belted sleeping robes provided by the inn. Her black hair was tied low over one shoulder. She'd begun growing it out again—although it had been much, much longer in the distant past.

"There was someone out here with you," I said.

She looked from side to side. If she had any concerns about being overheard, she could've clapped a hand over my mouth. But she didn't.

"Who was it?" I asked.

"A local."

"A robber? A killer? A seducer? In lieu of further details, I'm fully prepared to think the worst."

"They came to clean the balcony."

"Came?" I said. "From where?"

Wist shrugged. She tilted her head back. "The roof?"

She was lying.

Worse—she was shaken.

I only knew this because I'd known her for years. Not even the finest of machinery would have been able to detect any difference in her voice or her face. She looked as if she'd feel nothing when the world ended.

But she stood just a little too straight.

I focused inward. I traced the invisible line of the bond between us. If I wished to, I could share in what she felt. The landscape of her mind would reveal itself like echolocation returning messages out of the dark.

This time, I came up empty.

Wist always presented a neutral mask to the world around her. Now she wore that impervious mask on the inside, too.

"Let's go back," she said.

The aerials looked positively apocalyptic at night: great shadows that sometimes went too slow, and sometimes too fast. I moved to block the door.

Wist reached for my face.

I flinched. I flinched much too hard. I almost cracked my skull on the glass at my back.

Her fingers never touched me. I'd misjudged their closeness.

A breath later, she lowered her arm.

I'd removed my eyepatch to sleep. I found my chilled hand shielding the naked right half of my face. I couldn't bring myself to take it away.

"Can't blame me for reacting," I said roughly.

"No," Wist agreed. "I can't."

I wouldn't call myself traumatized. I'd lost an eye. End of story. It wasn't Wist's fault, and it wasn't mine, either.

My false eye (which was currently in storage) helped round out my depth perception. Still, it wasn't anything like my original vision. I couldn't rely on a magical prosthetic in Manglesea, anyway. I got by well enough without it.

But look—I couldn't help getting jumpy when something came at my face without warning.

Wist reached past me, this time keeping her hand near waist level. She slid open the glass door. With an arm curled around my side, she steered me back into the unlit bedroom.

We slipped into bed as if that were that. If Wist had been hurt by my cringing, she didn't show it. No distress filtered through our bond, either. She'd walled me out.

We'd only been bondmates for a few short years. Regardless—as I'd feared, bonding had spoiled me. The insensate abyss at the other end of our bond felt as wrong as a limb gone numb.

I curved myself to fit the shape of her back again. I quietly breathed in the scent of her hair.

She felt very far away.

I could've kept interrogating her about her nighttime visitor. I could've questioned her until the eyes painted on the walls tired of listening.

There were two reasons I didn't.

One: Wist could be every bit as stubborn as yours truly. If we both dug our heels in, no one would win.

Two: I could already imagine why she might not want to tell me. In fact, I could imagine a rich variety of possibilities. The difficult part would be narrowing it down to a single truth.

I hadn't personally witnessed any signs of a struggle. That didn't mean none had happened.

The visitor might have been a killer come to menace one or both of us. Wist had enemies all over the continent. What better place to target her than a country where using magic to defend herself might turn into a major international incident?

Anywhere else, she'd crush assassins and kidnappers and extortionists without a second thought. In Manglesea, she'd struggle to strike the right balance between obeying the law of the land—avoiding magic use—and keeping the two of us safe.

If hostile forces visited and warned her not to breathe a word, she might very well keep mum to appease them.

Alternatively, the visitor could have been a so-called ally. An agent from Osmanthus, our home country.

Our vacation had nothing to do with international relations. But the Osmanthian Board of Magi might see it differently. This might represent their greatest chance yet to trick Wist into becoming an avatar of war and conquest.

If I were them, I'd try all kinds of chicanery. Anything to provoke Wist into openly using magic here. Anything to turn Manglelanders against her. Maybe she'd get hurt by a Manglelander, or someone masquerading as one. Maybe she in turn might accidentally wound a civilian.

From there, the Board of Magi would find it a simple matter to concoct a pretext for military intervention. It'd be easy as—what's the saying? As easy as drowning a baby.

Also: the Board was not fond of me. Usually they knew better than to target me directly. They didn't have the guts to risk truly enraging Wist. But maybe they'd gotten greedy.

If so, Wist would try to take care of it without letting me hear a peep. Especially after all my yammering about how this was supposed to be a relaxing and mindless vacation.

The crickets singing outside took occasional breathers. My mind refused to join them.

These were all legitimate possibilities. To be honest, I was more worried about the possibilities that hadn't even occurred to me. Those were always more dangerous.

About an hour before dawn, I gave up. I moseyed out from under the covers. I removed the bell-shaped metal lids covering the stone lights on the nightstands and dresser.

Manglelanders drew a clear distinction between magic of human and natural origin. I mean—all magic is natural, when you get down to it. They used the word *natural* for magic born on its own out in the wild world, without any human intervention.

These shining lights of raw crystal were, therefore, acceptable by their standards. The stones might hold some form of magic. But they came from the earth, not from a mage.

I'd seen oil lamps burning in other parts of the inn and tavern. Guess these stones were considered a safer option for travelers from foreign lands—those who might never have dealt with lighting oil or gas.

Of course, the stones couldn't be extinguished or turned on and off with the flip of a switch. But it was easy enough to add or remove their light-blocking lids.

Wist, still sleeping, had rolled onto her stomach. Her face stayed buried in a light green pillow. Not quite sure how she could breathe like that.

I pushed up my sleeves and briskly performed my duty as a healer: sorting through the tangles in her magic branches. She had far too many branches to count.

The tangling wasn't so bad, though. Thanks to her total abstention from magic use.

When her work took her far away from me, I could heal her magic remotely. No need for that now. We'd be together constantly here in Manglesea.

"How'd you sleep?" Wist mumbled into her smothering pillow.

"About as well as you," I said.

"Sorry to hear that."

I balled up my fists and began pummeling her in the back, all up and down the sides of her spine.

This had nothing to do with correcting the flow of her magic. She just liked getting her muscles pounded. It was equally rewarding for me—I wouldn't pass up a chance to punch her. Might count as a form of massage, I suppose, if not for the fact that I was a total amateur.

"On the other hand," I added, "I was thrilled to sleep in a bed without cat hair. What a blessing."

After I tired of beating her back, Wist slithered to the floor to do a lazy version of her morning workout. Push-ups, sit-ups, squats, planks, and other maneuvers too obscure for me to bother remembering what she called them. My job was to sit back and enjoy the view.

"You could join in," Wist suggested as she stretched.

"I sure could," I replied without moving. "Want to deadlift me?"

She immediately perked up. I withdrew my offer before she had a chance to say yes. "Never mind," I said. "I don't believe in exercise before breakfast."

"How about after breakfast?"

"We'll be too busy. Boo-hoo. What a shame."

"Lift weights with me once we go home."

"To Osmanthus? Sure. If you can get your cat to stay out of the way. Oh, and if you try using a posture corrector. I don't do self-improvement for free."

I didn't normally make a point of hassling Wist about her posture. Whether or not she slouched, she'd still be annoyingly tall. Objectively speaking, though, it had to be bad for her back. With all the aching in her magic, the last thing she needed was more chronic pain. If Wist wanted me to work on my own health, the least she could do was reciprocate.

Our plans for today: go on an informal tour around town, then leave to check out Katashiro Caverns. Wist had arranged the tour herself, as if to make up for our languid afternoon the day before. Although when you got down to it, both of us would've been totally content to laze by the river every single day until our departure.

We'd strive to keep a low profile in Bittercress. Wist hadn't entered the country on a diplomatic mission, but she was nevertheless a figure of unparalleled international fame.

There was an unauthorized Church devoted to worshiping her (much to her dismay). And, in contrast, a continent-spanning ring of terrorists had dedicated themselves solely to her pursuit. Hopefully they wouldn't track her all the way to a remote town in a country that utterly prohibited magic.

Manglelanders were unique in that they wouldn't kowtow to her.

They wouldn't try to stone her, either. To Wist, that sheer indifference must've felt like a rare and priceless gift.

What about me, you ask? Great question. What about Asa Clematis?

In Osmanthus, I was a certified criminal. Technically still out on parole. I'd been exempted from wearing my parole thread in Manglesea—since, like my prosthetic eye, it was an object inextricably infused with human magic.

In exchange, Wist and I were supposed to stick close together at all times. Day and night.

I'd been abroad with her before. However, it was frankly something of a miracle that I'd gotten approval to travel to a country where I couldn't even keep my parole thread. And that Manglesea had been willing to let me in. All thanks to Wist's status and influence.

Maybe it helped that I'd only been convicted of sins against the mageocratic state of Osmanthus. No one here called me the Magebreaker. They might not care much about that stuff in Manglesea. Less so, anyway, than if I were a drug trafficker or a magic smuggler.

Our tour guide to Bittercress turned out to be the local mortician, a plump older woman in masculine garb. She looked ready to stride out in the brush and shoot partridges. She also smelled very strongly of overripe summer melon. Not a bad scent, but one so sweet that I kept expecting hungry sugar ants to swarm her, as if carpeting leftovers at a picnic.

Most of the locals we'd met so far played multiple roles. The mortician, for instance, sounded very pleased with the work she did as a hairdresser. For herself she favored a style similar to mine—very crisp and short on the sides.

She proudly showed us a pretty yellow building near her graveyard. A sign marked it as *The Preeminent Bittercress Funeral Home & Salon*.

Likewise, the town doctor was the same person as the town veterinarian.

The innkeeper did occasional work as a fortune teller. The cobbler was an accomplished dentist. The street performer who earnestly played an accordion down by the river (yesterday we'd heard him in passing) was also one of the town guards.

"Wishes he were the town *bard*," sniffed the mortician.

Meanwhile, beekeepers doubled as hostlers for the ubiquitous cart-pulling animals they called primevals.

Only a small percentage of primevals were tame. The wild ones prowled around town as if they owned the place, leaving hard egg-shaped dung everywhere they went. We saw street cleaners dutifully collecting it. Children played field hockey by pushing leftover droppings around with long sticks.

"Makes a good fertilizer once you process it right," the mortician told us. "Also works well as fuel. Low moisture content. Highly flammable."

I had no idea what to do with this information. At any rate, most primevals seemed wholly uninterested in passing humans.

We gave them a wide berth anyway. Just to be safe.

Some curled up in big scaly blobs under bridges to sleep. I don't think they counted as reptiles, strictly speaking. Their scales were large and keratinous, prone to falling off at random and growing back in ugly spurts.

One of the hostlers explained how domestication made them undergo drastic physical changes. At the peak of their docility, they sprouted patches of coarse brown hair like the fibers covering a coconut.

After a couple years of service, their hair would mostly fall out, leaving just a few scraggly remnants dangling like loose threads from a sweater. Their claws and spikes and teeth would grow back twice as sharp. No primeval could stay tame for long.

During another trip to the nearest brewery, we learned that most such facilities in town were not, in fact, breweries. Cider was made in a cidery, and mead in a meadery, and neither were brewed in the first place. Apparently brewing was different from fermenting. Oh.

We also learned that the primevals were absolute fiends for mead.

"Don't give them any," warned a server.

The mortician proved to be quite a willing source of local gossip. She knew a number of sobering stories about tourists who'd attempted to ply primevals with drink in the past.

On the way back to the inn, I leaned over and asked her when the innkeeper was due. Just curious. I would do anything in my power to avoid having to assist with a sudden birth.

"Her?" The mortician seemed incapable of lowering her voice. "She's taking her sweet time."

"You mean the baby could be coming at any—"

"She's been pregnant for three years."

"Three years," Wist uttered.

"Three years and counting."

I coughed to disguise my embarrassment. "So she's not—I'm sorry. Shouldn't have made assumptions."

The mortician chortled. "She's pregnant, all right. It's a slow one, that's all. Some children are like that. What can a mother do but be patient?"

She strode ahead past row after row of red lantern plants. Wist and I exchanged a glance.

She's got to be joking, I said in my head.

Sounded serious enough to me, answered Wist.

We'd been trying not to speak mind-to-mind in Manglesea. Out of courtesy, rather than legal concerns. Voiceless communication was a mutual ability that stemmed from our bond. Not a magic skill in the traditional sense. So we weren't breaking the law—and even if we were, who could tell? We did make an effort not to overdo it.

It's sarcasm, I decided. *Or a prank. Maybe this is the local brand of humor.*

I had no trouble accepting the unusual wildlife of Manglesea. All those aerials. All those primevals. I was pretty open-minded about our cultural differences, too. Like how none of the townspeople wanted to give us their names. Fine with me.

Nevertheless, we were all human beings. This was a town without any human magic to explain away its oddities.

The pregnancy isn't a lie, Wist said.

Then someone's got to be lying about its length.

Even if they were—that wouldn't hurt us. No harm done. What really bothered me was the mortician's matter-of-fact tone.

Was a three-year pregnancy normal here? Who was I to say it *wasn't* normal? How much knowledge did I have about human gestation, anyway? Why was I asking myself this in the first place?

Wist and I lagged behind as we conferred mind-to-mind. The mortician stopped and turned, frowning.

"Careful," she barked. She had a voice loud enough to make butterflies scatter. "Don't be lost."

3

A BEDRAGGLED MAN stared at us as we returned to the inn. His walking stick looked perfect for bludgeoning innocent victims to death from behind.

I gave him a nod. He kept staring. He kept staring even after Wist turned her flat black gaze on him. For a stranger, it was honestly kind of impressive. "We've got a fan," I said to the mortician.

Her head swiveled. "Who? Oh—you mean Lester."

"Lester," I repeated. "Is that some kind of job title?"

"Just his name. He doesn't mind visitors knowing it."

"He's got a very foreboding look on his face."

"All part of the job. He's our local hermit."

"Lester the hermit," I said, nonplussed. "A paid position?"

"Of course. Rich folk fund his salary. Same ones who own property up on the hilltop." Her voice shifted to the tone of a whisper without actually getting any quieter. "See his beard?"

"How could I miss it?" It was extraordinarily long and wispy.

"It's fake. But don't let on that you know. He'll be terribly sad. And don't act too curious around him. He'll start reciting poetry."

I felt an inexplicable sense of kinship with Lester the salaried hermit. Maybe because his hairy eyebrows gave him a perpetual look of bemusement.

It was a bright day. A shining paradigm of early fall, hot in the sun and cool in the shadows. Aerials coasting above helped soften the glaring light.

We ignored Lester, as per the mortician's recommendation, and let ourselves inside. The main doors to the inn were equipped with a pair of long handles designed to look like axes embedded in wood. Quite fun to yank open.

The lobby beyond the axe-doors was centered around a sunken hearth. Cooking noises spilled over from the tavern next door. Braided onions and drying flowers hung from ceiling beams.

Other than that, the only real decor was a plethora of empty baskets with eye-like beads peeping out from among their weave. Plus more wards with the six-spot seal. So many that I'd all but stopped seeing them.

With our rather casual tour having officially come to an end, the mortician left us in the care of the innkeeper. Said innkeeper looked remarkably spry for a woman who had allegedly been pregnant for three-plus years.

She asked me and Wist to hold our hands out over the unlit hearth. When we obliged, she stamped us with bright red ink, as if granting us permission to enter a nightclub. She'd marked us with the six-spot seal.

"Don't wash your hands till you get back from the caves," she told us.

"What's this supposed to ward against?" I asked.

"Shadows and devils. All-seeing evil."

"I see." Very specific.

She asked if she could stop by our room while we were away. Apparently the raw stone lights needed to be fed and tended like houseplants.

Sure, I said. I had things to hide, but I kept them close by. Namely, in the small sling bag over my shoulder. No one would discover anything dubious in our luggage.

The innkeeper gave us a basket of fresh-baked bread to eat on the road. She asked us to wait with her while our next escort finished prepping. We talked business; as I'd thought, Wist and I and the merchants were currently her only guests. The only outsiders staying in all of Bittercress, for that matter.

Midway through our conversation, a fresh-scrubbed young man popped out of the bathroom. The same guy we'd seen playing the accordion down by the river. The innkeeper introduced him as the town guard who would serve as our guide to the caverns.

The open-air carriage to Katashiro Caverns would, of course, be drawn by primevals. It was rather smaller than the closed-up stagecoach we'd taken from the city.

Wist and I climbed in back, beneath a collapsible leather roof. The guard and his rifle rode up front. The rifle was really the only guard-like thing about him, come to think of it.

"Don't be lost," the innkeeper called as we left.

I leaned out of the carriage and said it right back at her.

The primevals got going in earnest. The innkeeper shrank to the size of a matchstick doll. Then she and the inn left our sight.

It would take us at least an hour to reach the caverns. I chatted with the guard so Wist wouldn't have to.

"Isn't there a horn you have to play from one of the towers?" I asked him. I'd kept hearing it every couple of hours. "Will we make it back in time?"

"A friend took my shift," he said. "I was on duty yesterday morning, too, so no one will mind. You don't have to rush."

"What would happen if no one remembered to play it?" The horn didn't seem to serve any real function. Except, I suppose, to let people know what time it was.

"Disaster. Ruin. Utter catastrophe." He sounded completely sincere. "The primevals are real sticklers for routine, you see. Even the wild ones. They'll fall ill if they don't hear the horn on time. Or, worse, they might get … agitated."

"Wouldn't want that," I said.

"No, ma'am."

"When the time comes, won't you need to play a tune for the ones pulling us, too?"

He laughed. "They only expect it when they're in town. They know things are different out here. Beyond the wall."

What wall? I thought. The one around Bittercress looked as though it had collapsed back before the time of the previous Kraken.

I didn't know anyone in Bittercress by name (aside from Lester the ornamental hermit). But between today and yesterday, I'd conversed with a whole lot of people.

Both Wist and I had done our fair share of research on regional lore before coming here. We'd asked around in the border cities, too. Still, there was something to be said for hearing it straight from the locals.

The carriage bounced past hills and fields and farms that looked vaguely abandoned. The guard said there were ravenous river deer in most bodies of water outside town, and singing deer in the hills, and flat-toothed grazing wolves in the woods.

We didn't see or hear any of them. The sky stayed thick with floaters.

Without looking sideways at Wist, and without moving my body, I probed delicately at our bond.

The block was less obvious than it had been last night, when she'd masked her immediate reaction to her anonymous visitor. But she was still holding something back.

The thing about Wist was that even in normal times, she always held herself back. She downplayed her latent magic so as to avoid accidentally flash-banging innocent bystanders. She'd never been much of a talker.

There were plenty of people in the world—even some mages and healers of mages—with minimal magic perception. To them, Wist would come off as a pushover. She rarely took advantage of her height. When confronted, she would blink owlishly at her challenger. Some might interpret her silence as a sign of passivity or helplessness.

It's hard to imagine the strongest mage in the world getting underestimated. But she was—and it happened surprisingly often. She liked it that way. Which might have been partly due to my influence.

I'd always relished being able to give my enemies a nasty shock.

Sometimes even those who knew exactly who and what she was made the mistake of underestimating her. They couldn't comprehend what it meant to be the greatest mage of our time.

The difference between Wist and the world's second most powerful mage (whoever that might be) wasn't anything remotely like the subtle distinction between two champion racehorses.

It would be more like the difference between a horse and a modern airship. Or like the difference in diction between a trained human orator and an unusually unintelligent parrot.

No offense to other mages. The gap separating them from Wist was of such staggering scale that most people, through no fault of their own, simply weren't equipped to grasp it.

Which was probably a good thing for society. If Wist made her opinions and the extent of her power more obvious, people would start bending to her will without realizing it. They'd yield to the wordless threat of her magic out of a kind of unconscious animal deference.

I'd seen that happen before. But it could've been more frequent. It could've been much worse.

In all of history, there had only ever been one other Kraken-class mage. The previous Kraken had nearly conquered the world. She must've been a rather more assertive type than my Wist.

You could say, actually, that the previous Kraken was part of what had brought us here. Although she was presumably long dead.

"What's on your mind?" I asked Wist. I knew better than to expect a real answer.

"What's on yours?"

"Just reminiscing fondly about enemies we've destroyed in the past."

The town guard shot me a startled look over his shoulder. I smiled as if to say I were joking. All in good fun.

Together with the guard, we stopped and nibbled our assortment of stuffed bread before readying ourselves to enter the caves. He huffed and puffed as he hauled a towel-wrapped rock from the carriage and dropped it at the side of the road.

"An anchor," he said.

The primevals sniffed the dirty towels on the rock, then settled down nearby. He made no other attempt to tie them in place.

His rifle stayed hitched to his seat in the carriage. Guess there was nothing that needed shooting—or nothing, perhaps, that could be harmed by shooting—down in the caves.

The people of Manglesea had sworn off magic at least a thousand years ago. Maybe more like two thousand years ago. I'd come across a lot of contradictory dates.

Local legend had it that the first Kraken had come to Manglesea in the twilight of her life. She'd visited Katashiro Caverns. She faced her darkness in the caves, and she emerged with a revelation.

Human magic lays a curse on the land, and then feeds it. Human magic draws monsters from the deep, she told Manglelanders. This epiphany, they claimed, was why she'd stopped conquering the world. A single trip to Katashiro Caverns reformed her.

Now, I should mention that their Kraken myths were considered to be purely apocryphal. Not a single historian outside Manglesea took any of this seriously.

But Wist, as the ancient Kraken's successor, was extremely curious about those caves.

It wasn't merely folklore that drew us here. Every other country on the continent had its own fictitious tales of the Kraken. If you believed them all, it'd seem like she'd done nothing but run around from one obscure village to the next, alternately smashing and blessing old temples. Carving out natural stone arches. Spawning beautiful waterfalls. Digging craters in the ground. Shifting mountains to and fro. Pulling stars down from the sky. Giving starving farmers the gift of a neverending feast.

The first Kraken's rumored exploits in Manglesea were no more or less believable than any other batch of regional fables. Wist and I weren't archaeologists or anthropologists or expert historians, anyway. Far from it.

So set aside the legends for a second. Look instead at provable facts.

Vorpal holes—a type of uniquely magical natural disaster—plagued every country on the continent. Except for Manglesea.

It's not that deadly vorpal holes never spawned here. But the last recorded instance had been hundreds of years ago.

The small territory of Manglesea seemed, for reasons unknown, to be almost completely immune to a problem that caused no end of grief for more powerful nations like Osmanthus.

Some claimed that Manglelanders were spared because of their total abstinence from magecraft. Even if this were true, though, it wouldn't be a realistic solution for the rest of the world. Nothing could make other countries abandon the convenience of porting. Nor would they revert to lighting homes with gas and oil and raw natural rock.

Wist was the only living mage in any country with the ability to close vorpal holes. Normally she spent much of her time crossing international borders, erasing the worst holes in each region. She'd never had a reason to come to Manglesea, which had no such holes that needed sealing.

In the name of going on vacation, I'd convinced her to personally investigate this phenomenon. She alone could close vorpal holes. She alone might be able to discover the real reason why they hardly ever appeared in Manglesea.

(As further bait, I brought up all the stories about how the previous Kraken had experienced a dramatic change of heart in Katashiro Caverns.)

As for me, I was just here to have a good time. Was poking my nose around in an isolated cave system my idea of a good time?

Well, not really. But I'd needed a compelling hook to get Wist to set aside her other obligations and travel to Manglesea. I didn't mind devoting a few days of our trip to cave exploration, if that's what to took to make her commit to a real vacation.

I'd come wearing sturdy hiking boots and a utility vest. I didn't have much in my pockets. I kept all my secrets in my khaki sling bag—which looked low-key, but was actually the single most expensive item in my possession.

It was an import, you see. Of Jacian make.

Jacian bags were renowned for their ability to camouflage magical contents.

I'd done my best to conceal its origins. Bringing this bag into Manglesea had nevertheless been a headache and a half. You can get away with a lot of shenanigans when your partner is a modern-day Kraken.

At a glance there was no way to distinguish it from a normal bag manufactured in any other country. I kept some innocent things in there, too. My bond thread, for instance. An extra eyepatch. Spare bandages. A tiny tube of disinfectant.

Forbidding mountains rose up behind the entrance to Katashiro Caverns. The guard pointed us past a skewed wooden signpost with letters too faded to read.

Steep stone stairs led into a corridor with framed informational posters tacked haphazardly to unfinished walls. Each poster was lit by the cold white glow of raw crystal fragments screwed into the rock above. For the most part, they seemed to reiterate the old stories about the original Kraken's time in Manglesea.

"Tour groups ever come out here?" I asked.

"Not often," said the guard.

I was surprised at its state of maintenance. All the lights still worked, and none of the frames had cracked or fallen. Someone must've been tasked with periodically trekking over to check up on the entryway.

The locals didn't appear wealthy, but a lot of money flowed into Manglesea. Foreign nationals owned all the most desirable real estate in their cities, and even in Bittercress.

Said foreigners might only stop by once every other year or so. It was considered quite a sign of prestige for Osmanthian mages to keep vacation homes in Manglesea, though many found life here too inconvenient to visit for long. Even the Shien clan had bought up a bunch of property near the border. (Wist evinced no interest in seeing their holdings.) It could very well be foreign patrons who'd established a fund for the caverns' upkeep. Just like how they paid for a picturesque hermit to wander around town and read poetry.

The ground inside was rather too slippery for my liking. We went slowly. Here and there, pale blue glowworms spangled the ceiling. They seemed too dim and sparse to impress sightseers from faraway lands.

The deeper we got, the cooler it felt. I was glad I'd worn long sleeves.

The guard stopped to light a handheld oil lantern. No more crystals dotted the walls. The only sounds were our damp footsteps and the tense rattling of two keychains: one dangling from my bag, and the other from the bond thread Wist wore around her wrist.

The cramped corridor opened up into a soaring chamber full of snowy limestone formations. Parts of the floor turned out to be pools of perfectly reflective and perfectly motionless water. It could've been an inch or an acre deep. No way to tell.

The guard passed us a handwritten map, along with a piece of shining rock meant to serve as a flashlight. Perhaps he didn't trust us with his oil lantern. Or perhaps there was some sort of taboo against carrying fire any deeper in the caverns.

"I can't go any further," he said, apologetic.

"Yet we're allowed to?"

"You aren't bound by the same rules. You received official permission from the town. I do wish I could join you."

He sounded like he meant it.

Ordinary tourists wouldn't be permitted to roam freely, either. For all practical purposes, Wist was the equivalent of a visiting foreign dignitary. Being a Kraken-class mage got her all kinds of special exceptions. Even in a country where no one used magic.

"You like caves?" I asked the guard.

"These caves have an incredible history. Look deep enough, and you'll be surrounded by artwork and artifacts from people of the ancient past. Might uncover archaeological sites like nothing else in all of Manglesea. No one's ever properly gone in there and studied—"

He had forgotten to breathe. He spluttered briefly, then said—in all sincerity—"Enjoy your time here. It's priceless. To see what the Cressians saw—to inhale this same sacred air...."

I squinted at the map of the caverns. After about thirty seconds of silence, Wist reached over and rotated it ninety degrees counterclockwise.

Oh. Now I understood where we'd come from, and what lay before us.

The guard cleared his throat. He proceeded to read off a long list of safety disclaimers. It all sounded quite terrifying. There were innumerable ways that explorers could die—and had died—in these caves.

Still, I wasn't inclined to worry. If our lives were really in danger, Wist would save us with magic. We might have to resign ourselves to getting deported afterward, but we'd been through much worse in the past.

The guard said he'd wait at the entrance. (He also begged us to move as carefully as possible if we stumbled across fossils or human antiquities or other such treasure.)

The flickering light of his lantern retreated back down the smaller corridor. I caught him peeping wistfully over his shoulder as he left. Surely not all town guards were such ardent disciples of history.

I glanced around at the great columns and icicles and skinny carrots and termite hills of lumpy limestone. They came in every hue of ivory and yellow and watered-down brown.

At last we could speak freely.

"So," I said to Wist. "Is this just a regular cave or what?"

"I wish it were."

"You feel something?"

"You don't?"

We looked at each other.

Wist was the Kraken, a mage of inimitable stature. I wasn't a mage at all. But when it came to sensing magic, usually we were just about even.

Imagine us as two sommeliers doing a blind wine tasting, or as perfumers battling to identify scents. If we made a competition of it, I'd have a good chance of beating her.

I struggled to think of other times when Wist had picked up on traces of magic—be it human, natural, or otherworldly—and I, standing beside her, hadn't noticed a thing.

"There's something strange about this town," I said. "Maybe there's something strange about Manglesea as a whole. But Bittercress seems way more off-kilter than the border cities."

"Because the strangeness comes from there."

Wist pointed deeper in the caverns.

4

I offered Wist the map. She already seemed to know where she was going.

My gaze returned to the cave floor. It had no paving, no railing, and no set path. I gripped Wist's sweatshirt and concentrated on not tripping.

I wouldn't have attempted to navigate these caves alone. Not without my prosthetic. I missed its assistance for judging distances, although it wasn't the same as having my right eye back.

The cave roof soared dizzyingly high, but many stalactites hung low. Wist kept bumping her head. She wasn't one to mutter curses or otherwise comment on her woes. I almost didn't notice: I was too busy glaring at the rugged ground.

Suddenly she pulled me toward her, one arm tight around my back.

"Wist?" I said, muffled. Couldn't see a thing.

She shifted me forward. No explanation. No monsters swooped to attack, either. I blinked, squished against the warmth of her sweatshirt.

I understood once I peeked over my shoulder. Water dripped from a fringe of spindly stalactites, beading like liquid at the end of a hypodermic needle. Those drops would have fallen very close to my face. Right at the edge of my blind spot, near where I used to have a working eye.

I might have severely overreacted. Or I might not have reacted at all. Impossible to guess until it happened.

I curled my hand around Wist's forearm. My fingertips sought out her bond thread.

"You know," I told her, "this is a quasi-historical site. Not a place of worship."

"And?"

"No one's watching."

"Are you—"

"Don't think it'd be sacrilegious to stop and make out for a bit."

"Caves don't put me in the mood," Wist said with finality.

Other people had warmer eyes than her. Other people were better at smiling. Other people knew how to deliver a quip with real zing, and not sound like they were reading off a speech at a state funeral.

But somewhere along the line, I'd lost my ability to see the appeal in anything other than this dark unmoving gaze, this frigid face that no one except me could possibly interpret as being solicitous or tender or loving.

Wist passed me the stone light. She raised her arms to retie her hair.

She'd loosened the tourniquet around our bond. Cavern-heightened wariness circulated between us. It was a closed system, hermetically sealed, our shared anxiety bouncing back and forth from her to me to her like a trapped moth fluttering wildly, hitting wall after wall.

This was one of the risks of taking a bondmate. Some might find it all too easy to get sucked down into a spiral of mutually exacerbated panic. Fortunately for us, it took a lot to rattle me—and Wist was the very definition of phlegmatic.

The guard's map indicated how to make a pilgrimage following in the old Kraken's footsteps. She was said to have visited a grotto in the deepest known reaches of Katashiro Caverns.

The caverns extended much further beneath these uninhabited mountains. But none of the passages beyond the Kraken's route had ever been explored. Dotted lines and rueful question marks littered the section of the map that marked her alleged final stop.

Calcified protrusions hung down in rippling curtains, in pale strands like hanks of ghostly hair, in cascading shapes like frozen waterfalls. No matter how far we went, the air remained perturbingly scentless. I leaned over and sniffed Wist to make sure my nose wasn't broken.

"At least there aren't any bats," I remarked.

For that matter, we hadn't observed any signs of life since the wan colonies of glowworms back near the entrance.

Was it normal for a cave system to feel so sterile? I was no naturalist, but shouldn't there have been a smattering of pale blind fish or newts or arthropods or worms or snakes?

I kept an eye out for movement, for water bugs and sightless crustaceans and other colorless ancient critters. No luck.

The passage of time folded in on itself like the pleated rocks all around us. We could've been strolling for minutes or for hours. Why did I have to be such crap at reading maps? We were near the Kraken's grotto—I knew that much—but how near?

My right foot hit something that went skittering off into darkness. A pebble? It sounded inordinately loud for its size.

Then came a noise like tiny bones crunching under the soles of our shoes.

It felt very cold now.

"Wist, you see that?"

"...Socks," she said.

"A mismatched pair, at that."

Once we left behind the posters and lighting near the entrance, the caverns had been rigorously lifeless. Sparkling clean, you could say. No discarded straws or receipts or coins or gum. Right up until here, where all that began to change.

Wist tapped the map. We'd arrived at the part filled with question marks. It took the shape of a towering cavity of dark glossy rock. Wavy surfaces reflected hints of our own movement back at us, slippery funhouse shadows that made me seasick.

More notably: garbage lay scattered from wall to wall, coating the floor like shells at a beach. On second glance, it bore more of a resemblance to a lost-and-found than to an overturned dumpster. I'm talking old train passes from foreign cities, wooden toys for small children, bicycle locks, cheap pens, spare buttons, that sort of thing. Not eggshells and orange rinds.

The thing I'd kicked earlier had probably been one of those pens. Or maybe someone's lost set of keys.

"That guard didn't mention anything about people coming to trash the place," I said.

"If no one's explored here for generations, he might not know what it's like."

Hence the question marks. "You think it's all from decades ago? Way before his time? Some stuff looks pretty recent."

I crouched down. Having said this, I soon spotted much older artifacts. Potsherds, arrowheads, a dull metal disc that might once have functioned as a primordial mirror.

"Maybe people didn't wander in and drop these of their own accord." I turned the heavy disc about. Couldn't quite see my face in it. "Maybe some force in the caves sucked this junk down here like a magnet. Or maybe we've got a giant monster crow living over in the next cavern. A creature that loves collecting random trinkets."

Wist murmured something inaudible.

When I looked over, she was gone. I lurched upright.

The glazed-looking walls must've bamboozled my one-eyed sight. Wist had just wandered over to the other side of the cave. The place where the first Kraken had supposedly ended her descent.

There was nowhere else to go. The chamber terminated in a single six-sided door without any visible seams or hinges. Stylized eyes were carved in its surface. Rather than watching us, they gave an impression of seeing nothing.

I joined Wist in front of the door. "Legend has it that the first Kraken descended into the caverns to confront her darkness," I said. "Whatever that means."

"Sounds metaphorical."

"Assuming she actually came here—what do you think she confronted?"

"......"

I leaned forward to look her in the face. "Wist?"

She clutched at her chest as if trying to reach her heart through her clothes.

My breath drained out through the bottoms of my lungs. "Wist?"

I heard growling. The crystal light shook like the flame of a torch on a windy night. Stone ground on stone, the turning of a slowly awakening cog.

No—there was no growling. Nothing but pressurized silence. The light had not flickered. If it seemed unsteady, that was entirely the fault of the hand that held it.

"We have to leave," Wist said.

"What?"

"Quickly."

"Is—"

Before I could get another word out, she picked me up and sprinted out of the room with the hexagonal door.

I gulped. I threw my arms around her neck and tried to make myself as small as possible. She'd already grazed her head countless times on our way in. Dashing like this, she might careen straight into a shadowed pillar and knock us both out in a two-for-one special.

I clenched my teeth. I didn't try to look where we were going. I prayed fervently for higher powers to keep our skulls intact. Meanwhile, Wist made it all the way back to the passageway dappled with glowworms.

Her chest heaved against me. Her breath was harsh on my shoulder. She kept up the same jolting pace till we both flinched at the unbearable light of the entrance.

She lowered me. Her arms shook. Then she sat down hard on the ground by the unreadable signpost, her head in her hands.

My good eye watered at the brightness of the open world. Peppery wild grass gave off the stinging scent of horseradish. It got much stronger now that we'd trampled it.

A lone aerial circled like a vulture, its shadow sketching huge rings around the lonely plain at the base of the mountains. I wiped my eye. Surrounded by his docile primevals, the guard waved to catch our attention.

I crouched next to Wist. "My turn to carry you?"

"You'll break your back."

"Rude. I might surprise you."

She got up on her own. "Just needed to catch my breath."

"Want more of a challenge?" I said. "Next time you carry me, do it with one arm only. Like a lapdog in the city."

Wist seemed to be seriously considering how to make this happen.

I lowered my voice. "What spooked you back there?"

I'll tell you later.

The guard was walking over.

Tell me on the way back, I suggested. *It'll be a long ride.*

No. Later.

The guard asked, in his chipper way, if we'd found what we were looking for.

"Yes," I said. "Probably." Then, in lieu of further elaboration: "Your country really is full of wonders."

He beamed.

I kept him busy with conversation during the ride home to Bittercress. In my usual charming fashion, I described the various glorious sights we'd encountered. I praised the scintillating natural beauty of the caverns.

Once I got down from the carriage, I couldn't remember a single word I'd said. Although I was pretty sure I'd refrained from mentioning anything about the cave with the six-sided door.

I'd been ill at ease in the caverns, sure. I would not have recommended attempting to wrench open that ominous door. Not on my life. But I couldn't begin to guess what had alarmed Wist—Wist the Kraken!— enough to make her grab me and flee without another word.

5

I TIPPED THE GUARD handsomely for his services. Then I dragged Wist over to the riverbank.

Parts of the path were paved in stone. Parts were simple dirt and gravel. Wagtail birds bobbed among the reeds, and hundred-eye ducks coasted placidly in the water. (Their feathers formed a pattern of countless shapes like yellow eyes.)

I spotted a few people crossing distant bridges, but down here we were alone.

"I've been patient," I said. "What'd you sense in the caves?"

Wist's answer: "Something I don't want to provoke."

We kept walking. "A vorpal beast? A buried monster? An old deity sealed behind that door?"

"Something less tangible. Something without a name."

"The door looked thick. Downright indestructible. Didn't see a way to open it, either."

"It's meant to stay closed."

"Why'd you run?" I asked sharply. "Is it really that dangerous? How can you tell?"

Wist was not a rapid-fire speaker even at the best of times.

"Imagine if a rat died in our walls," she finally told me. "You'd recognize the scent of rot. Even if you couldn't see it. Even if you'd never smelled it before in your life."

I attempted to expand on this. "Some seventh sense of yours picked up on an unknown threat. One more fearsome than any number of hired killers or mages or vorpal beasts. You genuinely didn't know if you could defeat it. You decided not to risk it."

She didn't nod or murmur in agreement—with me, she knew she wouldn't need to. I'd read her correctly.

We climbed the stairs leading from the riverbank to the street. Wist was quite talented at spotting the bizarre tracks left by primevals. We stepped around their dung, and made sure not to lock eyes with the wild ones.

We kept passing below water towers. They were strangely—almost oppressively—common. This town had erected far more water towers than seemed necessary for a settlement of under a thousand people.

Most of the older stone-clad structures were long defunct. A few comparatively newer towers served as a venue for the guards on duty to toot their horns.

Wist had not previously remarked on the prevalence of these water towers. Now she watched them as if she knew they all teemed with spyglass-carrying strangers.

Everywhere we went, we saw the red husks of lantern plants. Dandelions seemed to be having their fall resurgence, too. The locals called them devilsmilk.

We paused in a neighborhood of mansions, each four or five times larger than any other house in town. The architecture was markedly different, too. No open windcatchers on their grand roofs.

These buildings bore an eerie resemblance to the urban estates of Osmanthian oligarchs. Like they'd been air-lifted straight from Osmanthus City. In a way, that's exactly what they were: manors built to the dictates of foreigners. (Mostly Osmanthians.)

Manglesea had a rather temperate climate all year round. Yet in most seasons, these mansions stood empty.

Some had remained empty for decades.

Despite being all but abandoned, they didn't look haunted. They weren't crumbling. Their wealthy owners hired townspeople to faithfully clean and maintain them, day after day, year after year.

A couple Osmanthian mage clans, upon catching wind of our travel plans, had invited Wist to stay in various high-end local properties. After all, no one else was living there.

We'd considered taking them up on it. In past decades, more than one foreign mage had vanished while visiting Bittercress. If there were something shady going on here, an ostentatious empty manor might offer more clues than the inn meant for common folk.

Now, if this trip were just a matter of kicking back, there'd have been no need for us to leave Osmanthus. We could've spent a nice weekend at a mountain resort, or on one of the barrier islands off the western coast.

But Wist would be restless. She'd get hopelessly distracted by thoughts of all the vorpal holes she could be closing, all the people who might need the Kraken to save them.

I wanted her to commit to a longer vacation. Two or three weeks. Or more. That's why I—we—chose Manglesea. It's also why we ended up in Bittercress. Here lay fragments of a mystery that might be very much relevant to her as the Kraken.

Three mysteries, in fact.

One: legends of the previous Kraken.

Two: the dearth of vorpal holes.

Three: rumors of vanishing mages.

Were those past disappearances the reason people kept telling us *Don't be lost?*

Wist immediately knew which mansion belonged to which family up here on the highest hill in Bittercress. She recognized the telltale signs from her upbringing as part of the snobbish Shien clan. (There were a few she couldn't name, but they didn't seem to have been built by Osmanthians.)

We slowed our pace. Gardeners snipped at bushes and pine trees inside a nearby walled garden. Fallen leaf matter littered the ground around their metal ladders.

They weren't quite close enough to eavesdrop. And the sound of their shears would cut through any hints of our conversation.

I tugged at Wist's tied-back hair. It was long enough to wrap three times around my fist.

"That thing you felt in the caves," I said. "What'll happen if no one disturbs it?"

"Hopefully nothing."

"It'll stay sleeping? Or locked up? Nothing will change?"

"I'd like to believe that nothing will change," she said carefully.

"So if it's a volcano, so to speak, there's a chance that it'll stay dormant forever. There's a chance that it's already dead."

"There's a chance, yes."

I released her hair. "What if someone disturbs it on purpose? As a form of sabotage."

"Might not end in disaster," said Wist.

"Really?"

"As long as the person who goes there isn't me."

"And you know that by pure instinct."

"I can't prove it," she said flatly.

We completed our circuit of the hilltop neighborhood. These empty mansions had the best view in all of Bittercress.

Come late in the evening, and you'd see wild primevals parading to their resting spots. You'd see the ritual lanterns that went streaming down the river after the final trumpeted tune of the night.

Only a few golden lanterns ever made it to the grate at the other end of town. Most capsized against grass-choked silty sandbanks or the huge turtle-shaped stepping stones (stepping boulders?) that bisected the water at its shallowest points. Lantern-herders would comb the river every day before dawn to collect them.

I linked arms with Wist. "About that mysterious stranger you saw on the balcony."

"The housekeeper?"

"Your so-called housekeeper, yeah. Were they someone we've met around town?"

"Probably."

"What makes you think that?"

"They spoke like they knew me."

She was choosing her words with far too much care, damn her. "Would you know them if you saw them again?"

"They had a mask on." Wist gestured in the air by her face to illustrate the pattern on the mask. "Six circles. Three on each side. Red on black, I think. It was hard to see in the dark."

The same mark stamped on all the paper wards around the inn. The six-spot seal.

The stranger couldn't be a mage. I'd gotten a brief glimpse of their silhouette through the glass balcony door. I'd have seen the light in their torso if they possessed any magic whatsoever. If they weren't a mage, neither Wist nor I would be able to identify them by their unique internal configuration of branches. Wist couldn't use forensic magic to trace them, either—not so long as we planned to continue relying on Manglelander hospitality.

"Did you witness your cleaner doing any actual cleaning?"

"No," Wist admitted.

She had a world-class poker face. She knew when to shut up, too. She wouldn't incriminate herself by babbling. But improvisational fabrication had never been her strong suit.

"What else did they say to you?" I inquired. "Besides claiming to be a housekeeper."

"They praised me—us—for planning to visit Katashiro Caverns. They said: *Don't be afraid of the caves.*"

"They climbed up to our balcony just to give you a pre-cavern pep talk?"

"Seems that way."

"When will you tell me the rest?"

I still had her arm in mine. I felt her stiffen.

"You'll know everything in time."

She spoke neither heavily nor lightly. Her voice gave me nothing to measure, nothing to weigh.

"While you're making promises, make me one more." I tipped my head sideways, nudging her shoulder. "No more ditching me to chat on the balcony. Especially not in the middle of the night."

"It won't happen again."

"Better not. Don't make me jealous."

Wist hadn't been this secretive about anything since back when I was fresh out of prison.

I'm as nosy as they come. I won't deny it. It kills me to get left out of the loop. At the same time, I trusted her. More than I should have, maybe. If leaving well enough alone meant we could have a leisurely time here and then depart the country in peace, without any unplanned trouble—frankly, I'd be content with never learning the details.

Therein lay the biggest difference between me and my younger self. In the past, I would've sacrificed everything just to scratch open the bloody scabs of my own curiosity.

That said, if I ever found out who or what was forcing Wist to keep secrets from me, I'd make them pay. I didn't care if they hailed from Osmanthian intelligence or the Extinguishers or a local religious cult or what.

I'm not a forgiving woman. Never have been.

As we descended the slope leading away from the foreign manors, the landscaping began to go noticeably downhill as well. Heh. Weeds the height of my waist burst from every spare scrap of earth. I wished I had half their vigor. Spider lily stalks sprang out of nowhere, too, their slender buds still fused shut.

Six-spot burnet moths fluttered about spiky purple wildflowers. They looked like living incarnations of the six-spot seal. Each metallic black wing was stamped with brilliant blots of red.

I'd never seen these moths outside Bittercress. The mortician had called them a sign of good fortune—a summer moth that could linger well into fall. But only in Manglesea.

Like the six-spot moths, Wist's mystery visitor was almost certainly a local.

When I said this, she looked askance at me. "Why?"

"It's simple."

"Is it?"

"No one from outside Manglesea assigns any importance to Katashiro Caverns. No one from outside Manglesea thinks the first Kraken really went there. Only a Manglelander would bother cornering you just to talk about the caves."

"Mm. True."

"The question is—who?" I put a flat hand on my head. "Was your visitor about the same height as me?"

"Close enough."

"We could snoop around for locals who fit that description. Won't narrow it down much, but every bit helps. Of course—that's only if we decide to keep digging."

"As opposed to what?"

"Let's get out," I said crisply. "End our trip early. Let's leave as soon as tonight, if we can."

"But you—"

"I would've liked a nice long vacation. But I know when it's smarter to fold." I touched my eyepatch. "This town is kind of obsessed with eyes, in case you haven't noticed. It's starting to bug me. I've only got one left to lose."

"A stranger appearing on our balcony isn't the oddest thing that's happened here," Wist said slowly.

"No kidding. I'm a lot more disturbed by the innkeeper's neverending pregnancy. Anyway—so what if we take off? Your nemesis in the caves will keep sleeping. No?"

"More mages might vanish," said Wist.

"Maybe someday. We don't know what's causing it. The last recorded disappearance happened—when was it again?"

"Fix or six years ago."

"At this point," I declared, "it doesn't matter to me if the whole town is secretly part of some big devil-worshiping sex cult. Good for them. They haven't harmed anyone that we can see."

"That we can see," Wist echoed softly.

I pointed toward the ruins of the ancient town wall. "You already know better than to try going back to the caves. Leave soon enough, and we can still leave with a clear conscience."

I let Wist stew over this for the next few minutes.

Truthfully, I didn't think my argument would hold water with her.

Here's how it would usually work. Wist would agonize over the risks. She would consider a long list of pros and cons. Ultimately she'd decide that no one could deal with the cave-bound menace and the (possibly related?) missing mages except for her. The Kraken.

Once she saw it as her responsibility, she'd insist on seeing it through to the end.

A side note about those mysterious disappearances. Before coming to Manglesea, we'd only heard of a handful spread out over the past half-century.

Older records were difficult to come by, due to Manglesea's long history of getting punted back and forth between avaricious neighboring countries. It hadn't always been known as a peaceful and rustic vacation spot.

Anyway, the disappearances we learned of during our research back home were all Osmanthian mages.

For instance: an elderly man who'd planned on spending his retirement years in his clan's newly renovated Bittercress mansion. He'd used stressful magic all his life—for work, for politics, for prestige. No fate more restful than to stay in a country where he would never have to use magic again in his life.

But he was old, and he was alone. He didn't associate with the townspeople. It took some time to notice that they'd stopped seeing him on his daily walks. Most believed that dementia had made him walk past the fallen town wall and out into the wilderness, never to be seen again.

Another vanished Osmanthian mage had been a schoolgirl on vacation with her family. Some thought she might have fallen in the river on a rainy night. In that case, you'd expect to find a body. The water was slow and shallow, with plenty of blockages along the way. Yet she never turned up again, dead or alive.

There was always a somewhat plausible—if unsatisfying—explanation. Suspicions of foul play quickly faded. And the disappearances were rare enough to be viewed as a sad coincidence. Which was why Osmanthians seeking a taste of a quainter lifestyle kept coming to spend holidays in Bittercress, and in other parts of Manglesea.

But. After crossing the border, Wist and I discovered that there were more missing mages than we'd thought. Many, many more. All the rest were native Manglelanders. Nearly all had disappeared as young children.

(As soon as they grew old enough, most Manglelander mages would enroll in special exchange programs to study in Osmanthus or other neighboring countries. They often ended up staying abroad for the rest of their lives.)

It wasn't just the people of Bittercress who had a weirdly lackadaisical attitude about these disappearances. No one in the border cities wanted to discuss the topic of missing mage children, either.

They took it as an unfortunate fact of life. A natural phenomenon. Like the vorpal holes that tormented every other country on the continent. Like how women in past centuries used to be much more liable to die in childbirth.

If you were a Manglelander with a mage child, your child might one day vanish. If they vanished, all you could do was accept it.

No one would attempt an official investigation. There was nothing to discover, nothing to investigate. Their classmates would quickly learn to pretend that no one had ever occupied that one empty seat.

6

"You're right," Wist said.

"Hm?"

"Let's leave town."

We'd made our way past a tiny lending library, a lone schoolhouse, two rival cideries, and an assortment of one-story homes topped with chimney-like windcatchers. Dense vegetable plots grew out back.

"We could spend the rest of our trip in the border cities," I said.

Her taut awareness of our surroundings pressed at me through our bond. Aerials in the sky. Primevals in the roadside brush. Empty-looking water towers and hollow windcatchers. An old-fashioned windmill.

She kept her magic branches coiled obediently inside her. They twitched as though longing to investigate the area like exploratory whiskers. I hadn't seen her on such high alert in a very long time.

"I think it'd be better," she said eventually, "to leave Manglesea altogether."

In a true emergency, she could've pulled me close and ported us straight to the border. Or even all the way home to Osmanthus. But she didn't propose that, and neither did I.

Using magic in Manglesea would necessitate explaining why she'd used it. No matter her excuse, it'd greatly heighten diplomatic tensions—and cause extra headaches for everyone who'd supported our trip here. Like my long-suffering parole officer.

"All right." My turn to be useful. "You go meditate or something. Keep your cool. I'll find us transportation."

Over by the inn, Wist folded herself into a hammock hanging in the shade of old trees. Deeper in the garden, a hand-drawn sign warned visitors to beware of killer hornets. (We had yet to see any.)

I left her there drowsing. I eradicated lingering thoughts of the sealed door in the caves, all those abandoned human objects, the cold luster of minerals untouched by sunlight.

Let those mysteries sleep undisturbed—as they'd already slept for decades, or centuries, or who knows how long. I had more practical matters to attend to.

I spoke to everyone I could get a hold of. Hostlers, storekeepers, woodworkers and other craftspeople, guards and lantern-herders, the town blacksmith, the doctor, a tailor, a baker. I even inquired with Lester the salaried hermit.

They were quite amiable. Easy to talk to. But no one could offer us a ride to the city. Not today, and not tomorrow, and not the day after. Not until the planned end of our weeks-long vacation, and maybe not even then.

Almost as if they'd formed an unspoken pact to trap us here.

I took this in stride. Next I went in search of our fellow guests: the traveling merchants who'd taken rooms down the hall from us. They hadn't been planning to stay for long.

"We're leaving tomorrow morning," one merchant said.

"After a hearty breakfast," said another. "No rush."

"We can easily fit two more. You'd like to come?"

I'd found them clad in borrowed beekeeper suits, taking a tour of the apiary by the mead brewery. Sorry, sorry—the meadery. Having no particular affinity for bees, I kept my distance until the merchants reemerged in plainclothes.

I thanked them profusely for promising us a ride, then trotted back to give Wist the good news. I didn't call out to her in my head. If she were still napping, I'd let her rest.

Daytime crickets and squeak bugs chirped in the garden next to the inn.

Wist's hammock hung empty.

The late afternoon light was too diffuse to form distinct patches of light and shadow on the ground. Everything melted into shade.

Shrill shouts rang out from the street at my back. A gaggle of children were attempting to careen around on miniature unicycles.

I ignored their yapping. I shut my mouth and silenced my inner voice, too. A lukewarm breeze riffled the leaves above. One of the unicycles kept creaking incessantly, a sound like an unused swing in an empty park.

My bond with Wist was not a homing beacon. But I could sense her approximate distance. She hadn't ported to another country. Nor had she slipped away to the opposite side of town.

She was somewhere very close. I stepped deeper into the shady garden.

My magic perception detected her before my sight did. Like an amateur spy, I shrank behind a tree trunk.

Wist stood with the stranger from the balcony.

Now—I had no actual proof that this was the same person. Last night had been much too dark to notice details.

The stranger faced away from me. They looked very small compared to Wist, but then, so did most people. Especially locals.

This time there was enough light to make out a pair of skinny androgynous legs. Definitely not a bodybuilder. They wore a hooded black jacket decorated with six large red circles, three on each side of their spine.

The six-spot seal.

Wist's mouth moved. Whatever she said came out too soft for me to hear.

Her eyes went to my tree.

Before I could step out to make a suitably dramatic entrance, someone grabbed me and hauled me in the opposite direction.

The heavy-set mortician.

I dug my heels in. Unfortunately, the mortician had a lot more leverage.

"Heard you were trying to leave town."

As usual, she spoke with the undiluted volume of an announcer at a magesports match.

I made another futile attempt to shake free. Somehow she'd already yanked me past the garden hammock, past the inn and tavern entrance, past the children faffing about on unicycles.

"We secured a ride," I said. "Look, I'm a little busy with—"

"How soon are you leaving?"

I stared at the meaty hand on my arm. "Not immediately," I said. "Not tonight."

Wist, I hissed in my head, *I'm getting kidnapped. Feel free to come do something about it. Any moment now. When your schedule allows.*

I craned my neck. Wist and the stranger were already well out of sight. The mortician had frog-marched me right up to her cemetery. Bushy vines of blue plumbago framed the open gates.

Had the cemetery always been this close to the inn?

The moment the mortician released me, I lunged to make a hasty exit.

I didn't get far. Townspeople clustered outside the cemetery, blocking my path. They didn't budge. They might not have budged even if I'd kept running at them full tilt.

I pulled up short. The crowd didn't inch any closer. The mortician had begun orating about graveyard weddings, about her storied career, about how I absolutely needed to bask in the funereal air here one last time before I left.

Whatever their intentions, it didn't feel like these people were about to shove me in an open grave. Or rip me limb from limb and feed me to the nearest primevals. (There were a couple sleeping in a far corner of the graveyard.)

If this gathering had a purpose, it was to give the stranger in the six-spot jacket a chance to speak longer with Wist.

I didn't accuse them of being in cahoots. I forced my shoulders to relax.

All sorts of strangeness might lie beneath the surface of Bittercress. So what? In less than a day, it would no longer be any of our concern. Until then, I'd rather appease the townspeople than provoke them.

We didn't need to understand them. We wouldn't linger to dig up local secrets. All we needed was to catch our ride with the merchants tomorrow morning.

I—very politely—asked the mortician why she'd brought me here. She, in turn, started showing me around the graveyard as though I'd specifically requested a private tour.

Bare spider lily stalks grew everywhere, mysteriously straight and leafless, still not ready to bloom. Some were topped with red buds; others looked creamy white.

"They're extremely poisonous," said the mortician, as though she suspected me of longing to make a spider lily salad.

I knew that. I'd grown up in a family of avid gardeners.

The gravestones were vertical. Some stood taller than I did. The mortician collectively called them stelae. They had actual names inscribed on them, although the lettering was so idiosyncratic that I couldn't read more than a few stray syllables.

"Of course we carve their real names," said the mortician. "They're dead."

She wasn't just a funeral director (and part-time hairstylist). She was the town coroner, too, and the sole caretaker for all these graves. Did she drench herself in melon perfume to chase away the scent of death? Did she always speak at such high volumes because the dead were hard of hearing?

She was also, it seemed, a wedding planner. She lectured me extensively on the traditional Manglelander marriage ritual, which involved lying together in a specially designed coffin.

You and your spouse were supposed to treasure that wedding coffin for the rest of your lives. It wouldn't go to waste once you died.

The crowd of townspeople trailed soundlessly in our wake. No one spoke up except the mortician.

There were children among them, all far more docile than the ones who'd been playing around on unicycles. They studied me with limpid doll-like eyes. A few of the youngest were mages. Just one or two magic branches apiece. These were the kids at risk of disappearing next.

Even if Wist and I decided to stay, there was no guarantee that we'd be able to save them. Besides, they might end up being lucky. They might not ever need saving in the first place.

We should never have left the border cities. These small towns were much too intense for me.

I was glad I'd dyed my hair fully black before crossing the border. Everyone else here had dark hair, too. If only this weren't the sort of place where every single resident already knew every other fellow resident by heart. If not for that, Wist and I might actually have succeeded at blending in.

The mortician droned on. I strove not to let any of the listening townspeople creep into my blind spot. At least none of them carried rifles or butcher knives. I stepped around spider lily stems. I tried to subtly steer a path back toward the cemetery gates.

"Where are you going?" asked the mortician.

Her tone made me feel like a student accused of cheating.

"Nowhere, I guess," I said pitifully. I resigned myself to spending the rest of the day learning about the gradual historical evolution of Manglelander burial rites.

Seconds later, the town horn blared from a distant water tower. Everyone in the cemetery simultaneously looked up. Humans and primevals alike.

The sky had turned salmon pink—raw, with fleshy striations. Some of the aerials coasting above were reduced to solid black silhouettes. Others looked wispy. They became twists of traveling shadow.

The evening horn sequence seemed to go on forever. It was not a terribly melodic instrument. It almost sounded as if the aerials themselves were wailing.

The townspeople kept their heads tilted up the entire time.

The music stopped. And then, without further ado, the crowd scattered. They chatted amongst themselves like a gang of parents who'd come to collect kids after school.

One child tripped next to a pair of tall gravestones. He promptly began screaming. An adult scooped him up and carried him briskly out through the flowery gates. No one glanced my way.

The mortician slapped me on the back hard enough to wind me. "Don't be lost," she said in the matter-of-fact tone of a hard-driving sports coach.

She trundled off, leaving me alone in the dimming graveyard with its wide-open gate. About half of the primevals followed her out.

I stood there dumbfounded.

After the mortician left, Wist leaned around the side of the entrance. I saw her black ponytail swaying before I saw her face.

"Took you long enough," I said.

She slipped inside the graveyard to join me.

It felt even more expansive now that it was all but empty. Graveyards in Osmanthus City were usually much more compact. Land prices out here must've been dirt cheap in comparison.

"What was that all about?" Wist asked.

"That's my question."

"You don't know why the mortician brought you here?"

"Maybe she wanted to give you more private time to flirt with your secret admirer," I said sourly.

An indecipherable look crossed Wist's face. "It was the same person who came up to our balcony. They—she—came wearing a mask again."

"She," I repeated, even more sourly. "What'd she have to say for herself?"

"Tried to persuade me to go back to the caves again."

"That's it?"

"I told her I couldn't," Wist said. "I refused. She ran away when I reached for her mask."

"How long did you keep talking after the mortician accosted me?"

"Almost until the evening horn. She had a lot to say about the wonders of the caverns."

"And you just stood there nodding blandly?"

"For the most part."

"While I sent you desperate pleas about getting kidnapped."

"You didn't mean it as a serious cry for help."

I sniffed. "You should've come running to save me anyway."

"Thanks for the feedback," Wist said dryly.

Purely by accident, we'd acquired proof that the masked stranger wasn't the mortician in disguise. Nor could they be any of the other people who'd popped up to gawk at me in the cemetery.

That still left hundreds of suspects. Pretty much the entire rest of the town, in fact.

Dinner lay another couple hours away. In the meantime, we tackled the extremely important business of last-minute shopping. This would be our final chance to find souvenirs.

On my list of recipients: my parents. My famous duelist friend. Wist's assistant. A smattering of more distant acquaintances. Plus my parole officer.

(Wait, would that count as a bribe? I felt like I owed her something extra nice. Before we left, I'd teased her way too many times about the fact that her name rhymed with Manglesea.)

Family aside, I had little contact with anyone who'd known me before my time in prison.

Wist examined jars of local honey while I sifted through an eccentric selection of clothing. Many appeared to be used items imported from Osmanthus.

Fashion here lagged a few decades behind Osmanthus City, come to think of it. Maybe that was why the town felt vaguely nostalgic.

I steered Wist over to a shelf of earrings and necklaces. She hadn't packed any jewelry for our trip. Our bond threads didn't count—those were just a piece of symbolic string.

She dutifully stood still while I held a series of quilled paper earrings up to her face. Would her earlobe piercings close if she kept neglecting them? I didn't really know how it worked—didn't have any piercings myself. Wist didn't seem too worried, though. I put the earrings back.

We'd already gotten plenty of presents for others. We could hold off on buying more for ourselves. Anyway, the store one door over had already closed up for the evening. It was getting to be about time for us to go grab seats in the tavern.

Two steps down the road, I did a double-take. I went back to gape at the dark shop window.

A black jacket hung there, its back facing the glass. It bore a pattern of six huge red circles.

"Wist!" I pointed at the jacket in the window. "Your masked friend wore this."

"Might be a common design here," she said.

"We haven't seen anyone else wearing the exact same jacket. Have we?"

As I spoke, my eye went to the price tag. Took me a few extra seconds to mentally convert it from the local currency.

"Oh," I said faintly.

The jacket looked more like a mocking target for evil than a humble attempt to ward it away. If they were selling it openly in a store like this, it probably wasn't the official uniform of an underground cult or an ancient secret society. Too bad.

We moved on. By the time we settled down for dinner, the six-spot stamps on our hands had completely washed off. It felt like half the town had squeezed into the tavern adjoining the inn, although in reality the population wasn't quite that tiny.

Out of everyone I'd been introduced to, the only person I noticed conspicuously missing was Lester the hermit.

"He takes his hermit duties very seriously," said the baker seated across from me. "It's a demanding job."

"Poor guy," I said vapidly. I fluffed a bowl of millet with my fork. Like much of the food here, it was exquisitely plain.

We drank the requisite Bittercress cider—most of it made not from apples, but from crisp round pears. Everyone wanted us to try more local mead, too.

Somewhere in the midst of all this, I asked what the town primevals ate. Just trying to keep the conversation going, you know?

"Mageflesh," said a woman to my left.

I choked violently on my cider.

Wist passed me a napkin as I attempted to recover my dignity.

"But only in stories," added the smiley baker.

"Ever heard the Ballad of Ninny the Hostler?" someone asked.

This was around the time when Wist rather wisely excused herself.

Our dinner companions regaled me with a twenty-verse song about a slow-witted woman and the ravenous primevals in her care. They devoured her many, many children one furtive bite at a time.

I think it was supposed to be a light, comic tune. Half the lyrics sounded like vulgar double entendres—although they only worked if you sang with an overexaggerated Manglelander accent.

Several real-life hostlers pulled up seats at the end of our table. They explained that if a primeval got too aggressive toward humans, other primevals would band together to put it down. It only ever happened with the very oldest specimens, who sometimes developed a form of animalistic dementia as they aged.

Tame primevals came to crave a pacifist diet, but the wild ones were thorough omnivores. They ate everything from fish to weeds to the corpses of fallen aerials in the plains outside town.

They also consumed an incredible volume of insects. Hence their long faces and tongues.

"Do aerials ever fall in town?" I asked.

The table went silent. Several people simultaneously uttered a quick prayer. If you were lucky, I gathered, you might never witness such a crash in your lifetime. But only if you were very, very lucky.

Wist returned from her breather just in time for dessert (lucky her). At last we lumbered out of our seats, weighed down by all that bountiful food and drink. I could no longer taste anything except the sticky residue of sweet cider.

Wist stopped near the door leading from the tavern to the inn. I contemplated leaning my head on her arm and falling asleep right then and there.

"That mask," she uttered.

A black cloth mask dangled from a rusted nail high on the wall. Naturally, it had a pattern of six bright red spots.

"Let me guess," I said fuzzily. "This is the one your admirer wore."

"Oh, we all have these," the innkeeper said from behind us.

I gave her a skeptical look.

"We use them for festivals. You'll see everyone wear them tomorrow."

"What's tomorrow?"

"The fall equinox."

Was it? I hadn't been keeping track.

"Did anyone tell you what we call this motif?" The innkeeper motioned at the spots on the mask. It was getting hard to hear her over the drunken noise at her back.

"The six-spot seal?" I said.

"We call it the Six Eyes."

Six Eyes. Hundred-eye ducks. Eyes painted on knots in timber. Eye-shaped beads woven into baskets. Jackets, masks, paper wards, protective stamps, six-spot burnet moths.

It felt like high time for me and my one good eye to begin developing a persecution complex.

7

Wist and I took a late-night bath together. I figured we'd go to sleep right afterward, damp heads moistening our pillows. But Wist wrapped her arms around me as if she were trying to crush me.

I flicked a look at the bond thread on her wrist, still dark and wet. One of us needed to reach over and put a lid on the last remaining stone light.

"You trying to start something?" I asked.

In response she bit the back of my neck.

"Wist?"

"Don't be lost," she said very quietly.

I sat bolt upright. "That's not funny."

"Just wondering where it comes from."

"For a second there, I thought you were flat-out possessed."

"You've seen me be possessed before," Wist said.

I grimaced. "In a manner of speaking, yeah."

"Don't be lost," she echoed once more. "Are they telling us not to get lost in unfamiliar places? Not to lose ourselves?"

"Maybe it's a roundabout way of saying they hope we don't get spirited away. Like the other vanished mages."

"You'll be safe, then," Wist concluded. She relaxed back into her pillow.

I stuck the lid on the final stone light. Plush darkness enveloped us. "You better not get lost, either," I said. "I won't allow it."

Wist pulled me down and kissed my shoulder. "Then I won't."

"Want to pull an all-nighter?"

"We're getting a little old for that."

"The mighty Kraken can't handle a day or two of sleep deprivation?" I made sure she could hear my disappointment. "Pathetic."

"You told me that the mighty Kraken deserves rest more than anyone."

"I'm just saying—no one can snatch us in our sleep if we never sleep."

"I don't think anyone's coming to snatch us in our sleep," Wist said.

"You never know. Think back to that meat they served us tonight."

"It was delicious."

"Did anyone ever explain what kind of meat it was? No. Who's to say it wasn't the meat of abducted mages?"

Wist's eyes drifted toward the wards on the ceiling. With all the lights hidden, they looked like mottled splotches of pale mold. They appeared to shift minutely in position whenever I stopped paying attention.

"Wasn't the last mage disappearance almost six years ago?"

"Isn't aging meat supposed to make it taste extra fancy?" I countered.

"You can't age meat for years on end." She paused. "Can you?"

I shrugged dramatically.

I loved these dumb conversations of ours. And I loved Wist's willingness to play along. Although cannibalism might not have been the best topic to bring up right before bed.

Just as I started drifting off, an awful screaming pierced my sleep.

My heart rate skyrocketed. I shook furiously at Wist's shoulder.

"Feral cats," she said drowsily.

"What?"

"That's the noise cats make when they mate."

"Sounds more like a child getting murdered by our window."

"Want me to check?" she asked.

No need. I chose to believe her. At last—well past midnight—the cats settled down.

Before I knew it, I was dreaming.

My dreams had always been violent. For most of my life, they'd been singularly focused on death. My own death, to be specific.

In recent years, my dreams had begun to diversify. When I did dream of death, though, it was always Wist killing me.

Her face and voice never changed. They remained true to real life: unreactive, unemotional, unwavering. For all that, she murdered me with remarkable cruelty and creativity.

I usually tried not to mention any of this upon waking. She hadn't done it on purpose, after all. She hadn't done anything wrong to begin with.

On the dawn of our departure from Bittercress, the first thing I did after escaping my dreams was lie there like a beached corpse. I struggled to master my racing breath.

I was still alive. I still had my body. I still had one eye.

I reached for Wist.

My hand touched dry empty sheets.

There was no warmth left on her side of the bed.

8

I DIDN'T PANIC. I didn't panic because even if I couldn't see Wist, even if she mentally blocked me, our bond would tell me if something truly irrevocable had happened.

It would snap if she died. No hiding that.

Maybe she was just hanging out in the bathroom. Or on the balcony.

A feeble whitish light spilled in when I whisked the curtains apart. I could hear crickets chirruping even with the balcony doors closed.

An insect hit the glass. It bounced away, buzzing, then rebounded to hit the glass again. It was longer and thicker than my thumb, a mix of shocking orange and black, its surface as smooth as plastic.

A giant hornet. A so-called killer hornet, though they were more prone to killing honeybees than human beings.

It kept coming back, ramming the glass right at eye level. The balcony looked otherwise empty. I pulled the curtains half-shut again. I listened distantly to the hornet's furious buzzing as I turned to the bathroom.

No light leaked out from under the door. I knocked and called Wist's name. I let myself in.

Empty.

She wasn't in the closet or under the bed, either.

I slowly got dressed, discarding the boxers and borrowed robe I'd used as sleepwear. My head still felt heavy from last night's mead and cider.

The merchants—our saviors—planned on taking a full sit-down breakfast in the tavern before their departure. I still had time to find her.

Under normal circumstances, the bond in me could serve as a kind of compass. Follow it long enough, and it would always lead me to Wist.

Yet now it felt as if the compass were constantly spinning. As if Wist were in this room with me—and simultaneously on the other side of the river. Or at the edge of town, overlooking the ancient fallen walls.

Ambient magic tickled my perception, too. Far more than I'd ever sensed elsewhere in Manglesea. It was a full-body itch like phantom mosquitoes on my skin.

I couldn't perceive it with enough precision to determine if it were human or wild magic. It might be a natural burst of pure directionless power like a gas leak from the ground. Or it might be a series of controlled skills carefully executed by a gifted mage. The sort of mage capable of orchestrating elite magic in the way of pyrotechnicians setting up for a centennial fireworks show.

A mage like Wist.

The only other mages I'd seen in town were untrained children.

My ability to pick up on this ambient magic would exponentially decrease with each passing minute. Like becoming nose-blind to a once-powerful stench. Twenty minutes with the mortician, and her melon scent had stopped making my eyes water.

Wist, I thought. *You better not be hiding on purpose.*

If she wanted to, she could use magic in such a way that even I wouldn't be able to identify it. She could be right here, invisible and imperceptible. She could be touching me, and I wouldn't know it.

She'd never played games like that before, though. Not with me. And after all her efforts to avoid using magic in Manglesea, why go wild on our last morning?

My skin crawled. As I wracked my head, I picked irritably at the wall.

Eventually I looked down and realized I'd peeled off three or four paper wards. They lay curled like old bark on the floor. I tried to stick them back up where they belonged. Not enough adhesive left.

I abandoned the wards. I got up. Wist was still somewhere in Bittercress. I could tell that much, despite the bleariness fogging my mind and bond and senses. All I had to do was hunt her down before breakfast.

I plunged a hand in my Jacian sling bag. At the bottom of it lay a curved shape in a velvet pouch: my magical prosthetic eye.

I'd brought this Jacian bag to Manglesea specifically for the purpose of smuggling in magical objects. Just a couple. I wasn't looking to get in trouble.

My false eye—slathered in custom magic cuttings produced by Wist—did more than just supplement my depth perception. Some of its magic was defensive in nature. Basic protections would activate if I got attacked in Wist's absence.

She'd wanted to layer on way more defensive magic, but I'd asked her to hold off. Make it any denser, and I wouldn't be able to pass through magical security detectors back in Osmanthus. Trying to attend a stage play or a magesports match would turn into an enormous hassle.

More pertinently, this eye had a function that I could use to summon Wist instantly and forcibly from anywhere in the world. Even if she were in the middle of closing a vorpal hole or battling brutal mercenaries or parting the waters of a catastrophic flood.

Which was why I'd never used that function before, although Wist encouraged me not to hesitate. I saw it as my absolute last resort.

After all, using it might make a bad situation much worse. If I couldn't get in contact with Wist, maybe it meant she was busy grappling with something she couldn't afford to stop fighting. Something that posed an actual threat. Even to the world's one and only living Kraken.

I thought of Katashiro Caverns. I thought of how Wist had turned her back on the depths of the caves. She'd seized me and fled as if she were running for her life. For both of our lives.

Nothing had followed us through the tunnels. Nothing had pursued us out past the stalagmites and reflecting pools and glowworms and the brightness of the cave entrance.

Or had it? The confused killer hornet kept bashing at the balcony glass. For a brief deranged moment, I wondered if I ought to let it in. Had Wist, for obscure reasons, decided to transform into a hornet? Had she sent this angry insect as a messenger?

I was at least lucid enough to discern that my bond didn't lead straight to the hornet. How would it leave a message for me, anyway? By tattooing words on my skin with its stinger? No way.

Sometimes a lost wandering hornet was just a lost wandering hornet.

I did a quick inventory of the other contents of my bag. Past the bandages and the tangle of my bond thread lay several pointy transceiver pins.

We occasionally gave these out to people we met during our travels. Anyone who we might want to contact us on short notice. I couldn't picture them being terribly useful right now, though. I'd be confessing to a crime the moment I showed one of these magical pins to anyone in town.

I left my prosthetic packed away. I put on a fresh eyepatch, slung my bag over my shoulder, and slipped out of the too-quiet bedroom.

Despite my best efforts, the hallway floorboards creaked lustily underfoot. It was earlier than I'd thought. The merchants might still be sleeping. I tiptoed apologetically past their room.

I had to open a number of paper-screen sliding doors to get down to the main reception area. The taut creamy paper let in ample morning light. A few minor rips had been pasted over with eye-shaped patches. Of course.

Clinking sounds came from the tavern next door as I slipped outside. The innkeeper (or a hired cook) must've been preparing for breakfast.

I checked in the garden. The hammock was empty. I took a peek at the nearby cemetery, too.

Distant chickens squawked on and on as I walked down to the river. Primevals slept like rocks on silty islands in the middle of the water. No sign of Wist. No sign of anyone else, either.

For the first time since we'd bonded, I couldn't tell if I were getting closer to her or drifting further away.

The morning air tasted sweeter than in the city, but I wasn't in the right frame of mind to enjoy it.

Something looked different. Something other than the emptiness of the streets and the delicate post-dawn light. I couldn't put it into words.

Wist often had to leave without warning. Whether to subdue a disastrous vorpal hole or to save lives threatened by something less magical.

We'd discussed this before traveling, in fact. It was prime typhoon season back on the Osmanthian coast. I'd known and accepted that there were all kinds of reasons Wist might need to cut our trip short.

If she'd ported to another country, our bond wouldn't be making it feel like she was still here in town.

If she didn't seem so close, I'd suspect her of having snuck back to Katashiro Caverns alone.

She'd been surprisingly vehement about staying away from the caves. She'd been fully on board with my plan to leave town and never set eye on the caves again.

But I still didn't know what, exactly, the masked stranger had said to her in the garden yesterday.

My search outside proved fruitless. Upon returning, I caught the pregnant innkeeper wiping tables in the empty tavern.

I asked her if she'd seen Wist.

"Who?" she inquired.

"My partner," I said. "My companion."

She unfolded and refolded her damp white cloth. It was hot enough to emanate little tendrils of steam.

"Not quite sure who you're talking about," she said politely. "You came here alone. You booked a room for one."

I bit back my retort. I reminded myself that this was a woman who had been pregnant for years—without anyone thinking strangely of it.

Was pranking strangers one of their equinox traditions? Would everyone I spoke to start feigning amnesia?

Over in the tavern kitchen, pots and pans clanked. Liquid bubbled. I couldn't see who was cooking.

Rather than argue, I began describing Wist. "She's very tall." I raised my hand to demonstrate. "Much taller than anyone else in town. Black eyes. Doesn't smile. She's a mage. Not just any mage—a Kraken-class mage."

The innkeeper stopped wiping tables again. She dried her hands on her apron. "No new mages have come to Bittercress in a very long time," she said.

"Lady, I can swear on any deity you bring me that—"

"This woman you're looking for," the innkeeper continued, unruffled. "She sounds a little bit like the Queen."

"The who?"

"The Queen."

Manglesea was not a monarchy. No one would mistake me for a political scientist, but I knew that for a fact.

The governmental structures of Manglesea were notoriously impenetrable to foreigners. Unintuitive. Inefficient. Full of roles and concepts that had no proper analogue in other continental countries. I nevertheless remained solid in my confidence that they'd never had a queen.

When I said this, the innkeeper smiled vaguely. She gave me the smile of someone who couldn't be bothered to argue with a paying customer.

Today, like every other day, ornamental fishhooks capped the ends of her hair twists. About one in four were rough and dull with rust. Most others were shiny and new. They looked keen enough to cut her neck open if she swung her head too hard.

I didn't get worked up. I didn't waste time insisting that Wist was real, and we'd come here together, and we'd fallen asleep together last night. It wouldn't convince her.

The innkeeper had her version of the truth, and I had mine. I didn't know why our truths had diverged. I would find out—but not by stamping my foot and caterwauling about how wrong she was.

As long as I could feel the bond in me, Wist was still around somewhere in this world. No matter what happened, I'd track her down eventually.

I cleared my throat. "Your Queen," I said. "Do you mean there's a queen chosen for the equinox?" Some regions had a tradition of crowning symbolic monarchs to reign over special seasons or holidays.

"Not a bad guess," said the innkeeper. "We do have a lot of festivities planned. But the equinox is tomorrow."

"You mean today."

She shook her head gently. Somehow she managed to avoid getting lacerated by her own fishhooks.

The look on her face said it all. *Silly traveler. Well, vacationers often lose track of time. No big deal. Should I show her a calendar?*

I was having trouble letting this one slide. "Last night, you said the equinox would be tomorrow. Which means today."

"I'm quite sure I wouldn't have said that." A wary note entered her voice. "Perhaps you misheard me? It can get awfully loud in the evening."

I looked for the mask Wist had shown me. The red-spotted mask hanging from a crooked nail. Didn't see it.

I relented. "Okay. The fall equinox is tomorrow. Clearly I'm very confused. Must've enjoyed that famous Bittercress cider a little too much, if you know what I mean."

We shared a few seconds of pained laughter.

"Sorry to put this on you first thing in the morning," I said, "but could you help refresh my memory?"

"Anything for a guest."

"How'd I spend my time yesterday? What'd I do all day?"

She pressed her hands to her lower back as she thought. "A meadery tour, I believe? You also attended several tastings."

No mention of the caves.

"How long ago did I first arrive?" I asked. "The days—they really blur together."

"A couple weeks ago."

"Weeks!" I blurted.

It came out a lot louder than I'd intended. She blinked at me, startled.

If anyone spied on us from afar, it'd look like I was bullying a pregnant woman. Cornering her in her workplace. Yelling at her for stating facts.

I took a step back.

"My bad," I said sheepishly. "One last thing. We—I was planning on riding out with the merchants."

"The merchants?"

"The guys staying down the hall. When they come for breakfast, can you tell them I'll be right back? Need to do a few quick things around town first. Don't let them leave Bittercress without us. Without me."

"But they've already left," said the innkeeper.

"What?"

She wrung her cleaning cloth. Only a few drops of liquid came out. She immediately wiped up the new drips.

"They left in a hurry," she said. "Late last night. They had pressing business back at the border."

The equinox was tomorrow, not today. Wist didn't exist. (Not as a guest of this inn, at any rate.) I'd come to Bittercress weeks and weeks ago, not just a couple of days ago. I'd come alone.

What else?

I hadn't spent yesterday at Katashiro Caverns. In the innkeeper's version of reality, I'd probably never been to the caverns at all. The merchants had broken their promise.

If anything, the merchants taking off early was by far the most believable part of this whole mess.

9

Be Wist, I told myself. Implacable. Unreadable. Show no outward reaction.

I thanked the innkeeper for her time. I'd already gotten enough information from her to upend all my plans. Better go seek out other sources.

"You removed them," the innkeeper said to my back.

I turned.

She was no longer pretending to smile. She gestured as if scratching a film off the air with her fingernails. "You removed the Eyes of the Queen."

I swear I felt my heart stutter. I kept up a calm facade, of course.

Her nails kept picking at empty air. Like she was trying to peel away gunk left behind by an invisible sticker.

The wards. I'd ripped a couple off the wall in a fit of absentminded pique. Just before coming down here.

I could've asked how she knew. I could've asked why she'd switched to calling that symbol the Eyes of the Queen.

I wasn't sure I wanted to hear the answer.

Her accusatory gaze lingered on me as I stammered out some pretext for leaving. I might've said I'd forgotten my bag in my room. (The same bag I currently wore on my shoulder.)

The fishhooks in her hair snared bits of morning light, gleaming. She didn't move a muscle when I fled.

I left her behind in the tavern, crossing back over to the inn. I climbed the stairs again. I knocked at the merchants' door. I pressed my ear close to listen. No one came to let me in.

As for the bedroom I was supposed to be sharing with Wist—

I'd only peeled off a few wards. Just a few out of many. If you didn't know what I'd done, it wouldn't look like any were missing.

The curly paper remnants had vanished. Something new had appeared on the nightstand instead. A metal keychain—a perfect match for the one that hung from my bag. Together with it: a vivid blue string wound in wrist-sized loops.

Wist's bond thread.

I picked the thread up, keychain and all. I don't know why I expected it to be warm to the touch. It wasn't.

I put it in my Jacian bag for safekeeping. In the same compartment where I kept my own bond thread.

These textile threads were something completely separate from the mechanics of our actual bond. They were just a tradition. An ornament. I rarely wore mine in public.

Wist was different. Once Wist started wearing hers, I'd never seen her remove it.

I closed my eyes. I cleared my perception. I scoured the room for new traces of Wist's unique magic.

There were fingerprints of her presence all over the place. On the sheets, by the bathroom and balcony doors, on the impenetrable lids meant for covering stone lights. No such fingerprints seemed any fresher than last night.

I left the inn again.

I knew for a fact that this wasn't a dream. My dreams were invariably much more violent.

There were more people out on the street now. They watered flowers; they rinsed the pavement in front of shops and houses. (No dog-walkers, though. It wasn't safe to take pets outside with so many wild primevals in town.)

Everyone I spoke to reacted much like the innkeeper. If they knew me, they knew me as someone who'd come to Bittercress all on my own.

They thought I was joking when I said I'd come with a mage. They definitely didn't believe me when I referred to Wist as the Kraken.

They didn't even acknowledge the existence of a second Kraken. Not anymore. To them, there had only ever been one: the historical Kraken from thousands of years ago.

Sometimes, when I told them more about Wist, they nodded and began muttering about a nameless queen.

"Where's this Queen of yours?" I asked.

"The Queen is in your heart," they said glibly.

Great. Thanks.

Others suggested that my Wist—the Wist I claimed to have come here with—was in fact the Queen's living ghost.

"That's quite a blessing," they told me.

Manglesea was filled with stories of ghosts of the living. Some seemed modern enough to be categorized as urban (or rural) legends rather than outright folklore.

The way they saw it, you didn't have to die to become a ghost. Your spirit might slip out for hauntings while you slept, or daydreamed, or lapsed into a coma.

An old woman with shockingly good teeth—bluish-white, large, and eerily straight—waxed eloquent about living ghosts while the morning horn blared its tune. I couldn't tell which tower it came from.

After parting ways with the toothy lady, I had two revelations. I finally understood why the scenery felt so different. I finally understood what had changed.

First: aerials swarmed much thicker in the sky. Despite the fact that many had semitransparent bodies, their flocks had grown dense enough to dilute the sunlight more than ever before. It did seem noticeably cooler down here on the ground.

Second: the town was surrounded by walls taller than any water tower.

No such barrier had been there yesterday. The historical town wall had crumbled to the point that anyone could step across without effort. In some places, you couldn't even see it there. Weeds and soil and wild grass covered the disgraced stone foundation.

I drifted toward the new wall as if mesmerized, as if falling slowly down a long straight hole. It must've risen overnight.

In the shadow of the green-gray wall, a young hostler with a threadbare mustache stooped to collect old dung. I asked him to point me toward the gate.

He straightened up. "The gate?"

He didn't appear particularly interested in or surprised by the sudden walls. I didn't bother questioning them.

"The town gate," I said. "The portcullis. The drawbridge. The door. Whatever entrance you use to get in and out of these walls."

He gaped at me as if my Osmanthian accent rendered my words incomprehensible. I said the same thing again.

"There is no gate," he said cautiously.

"Then how do you pass through?"

"You don't." He adjusted the sweat rag draped around the back of his neck.

"I did," I argued. "I came to town just a couple of days ago."

He looked me up and down. "No, you didn't."

"There were no walls like this when I first arrived."

"The walls have always been here. So have you."

"Look—even the innkeeper said I've been here for weeks. Not forever."

He shook his head with the world-weary air of a man five decades his senior. "Women say strange things when they've been pregnant that long."

Great heavens above. I wanted to go fling myself in the river.

I left the poop-gathering hostler behind. He was probably glad to be rid of me, anyway. Once I could no longer see him, I proceeded to examine the wall on my own. If push came to shove, I'd need to walk a full circuit of the town perimeter. I'd need to search for holes, for cracks, for crumbling sections, for hidden gates.

I'd save that lengthier investigation for later. For now, I focused on the section of wall right in front of me.

It wasn't impossibly tall, but I had no confidence in my ability to climb it. The green-gray stones fit together like a seamless puzzle. No mortar. When I touched them, they had the slippery texture of snakeskin.

Wist didn't feel any closer here. Nor any farther.

I mined my brain for scraps of knowledge about the historical walls surrounding Bittercress (which may or may not have been the same as this uncanny new wall that had sprouted while I slept).

The historical walls—the fallen walls—were said to be remnants of a much older culture. The Cressians. They predated even the first Kraken.

Modern-day Manglelanders were purportedly descended from different stock. They spoke of the Cressians as a lost civilization—never as their ancestors. In some legends, Cressians weren't human at all. They had wings. They flew with aerials.

Legends aside, archaeological evidence suggested that they'd worshipped the now-extinct elder aerials. They'd even built their own airships for sky hunts. Yet they'd left little imprint on Manglelander society, with one crucial exception.

The ubiquitous six-spot seal came from the Cressians.

I turned my back on the flawless new wall around town. Time for a different approach.

I passed the shops Wist and I had looked at last night. They were all open, but the black jacket in the window was gone. Had someone stopped in to buy it this morning?

I asked people where the Queen was. I asked them to take me to her. Most gave me inane answers about how the Queen was always with us. The Queen was everywhere.

I didn't lose my temper. I didn't lash out. I set my teeth—it wasn't their fault. Something was wrong with them. Something was wrong with Bittercress as a whole.

Time felt both slow and sickeningly fast. For all my running around, I seemed no closer to finding Wist.

Did I have any grand theories about what was going on? Sure. Of course. Honestly, though, I was trying not to think too hard about it. In some ways, the answer felt painfully obvious.

Only magic could cause a vast distortion of this nature. The fall equinox getting put off another day. Walls rising where no walls had been before. Yes, magic deserved the blame for this—magic powerful enough to outwit my ability to perceive it.

Only one person in the world could work such magic.

Innumerable aerials churned and churned overhead. Down below, my gut churned in response.

I jogged to the lower part of the riverbank. Lester the hermit stood there in long layered rags, holding his signature walking stick.

He smelled much better than he looked. Which is another way of saying that he didn't smell like much at all.

"You saw me with a mage the other day," I said. "Remember? You kept staring at us outside the inn."

He stroked his long thin beard, which petered out near his waist. He'd tied the ends off in a single firm knot.

The strands looked curiously similar to the coarse strands of a horse's tail. Or perhaps they were more like the stringy hairs grown by certain primevals.

If he changed his clothes and peeled off that fake beard, he would've found it easy to blend in with the hearty young hostlers or town guards or street cleaners.

"I remember," he said. "I remember both of you."

I'd called out to him before. This was my first time actually hearing his voice in response. He made some attempt to imbue it with dignity, but it wasn't nearly as grave or wizened as the rest of him.

"No hard feelings," I answered automatically. "Everyone else forgot her, too."

"I remember her. I saw you together."

"Wait—what?"

"I remember her," he repeated.

"You do?"

I sounded embarrassingly overeager. Nothing could make me doubt that my bondmate was a real living human being. But it sure helped to know that one other person in Bittercress still recalled her existence.

"Are you looking for the Queen," he asked, "or your mage?"

I would've liked to tell him I was looking for Wist and Wist alone. Unfortunately, there was a very high chance that she and the so-called Queen would turn out to be one and the same.

"Speaking of which," I said, "is the Queen a mage?"

He immediately nodded. No need to think it over.

"And she gets to use magic freely, does she? How come? Human magic is supposed to be verboten here."

Lester the hermit rotated his stick in his hands as he pondered this. I awaited his response with bated breath.

There were shiny traces of dried-up spirit gum around the edges of his beard. He should've powdered his skin to hide the adhesive.

"The Queen is the Queen," he said at last.

"So magic use is okay as long as it's only her using it? That's no fair."

He furrowed his hairy eyebrows. "She uses magic so we don't have to. The Queen absorbs the curse."

As I attempted to process this, something black zoomed through the air at my face.

I reeled. I caught blindly at a nearby signboard. It was the only thing that kept me from falling.

The moth never touched me. It flitted away, changing direction at random.

My breath felt stoppered up in my throat. I kept clinging to the sign for support. The moth alighted on a thorny flower the height of my shoulder. It had six gory red marks on each wing.

I'd thought the moth was flying straight at me. In retrospect, it hadn't actually gotten anywhere near my face. The emptiness behind my right eyelid twinged all the same.

Lester the hermit made no attempt to intervene. Which was fine by me. I wouldn't have panicked any less if he'd caught me.

I released the sign that had saved me and, for the first time, actually looked at it. Parts were too sun-faded to make out. It appeared to warn the reader about the risks of rapidly rising water. Hard to imagine now, with most of the Bittercress river being no deeper than your average bathtub.

Lester gave me a look of philosophical concern.

I pulled myself together and asked him to elaborate on what he'd meant by *the Queen absorbs the curse*.

This ended up going nowhere. Eventually I realized that all his attempts to answer were drawn from obscurely translated scraps of Cressian poetry. (Which was widely thought to have been written many years after the fall of the Cressians, and falsely attributed to them by literary pranksters. But no matter.)

"None of you townspeople know where to find your Queen?" I asked.

"I'm not a townsperson," he said. "I'm a hermit."

"Right. How could I forget."

"You don't know where to find your mage?" he asked in turn.

"Yeah—you've got me there. I'm lost."

With surprising earnestness, he suggested searching wherever Wist would be most likely to go. I scoffed. "If I knew that, I wouldn't have wasted all this time running in—"

...Where *would* Wist be most likely to go?

I couldn't begin to guess at what had happened to her—and to the town as a whole—late last night. I had no idea why she still refused to show herself.

If I ignored all the mysteries that I couldn't possibly solve on the spot—

If I thought solely of my Wist, and what parts of town she'd be most drawn to—

"The water towers," I said. More to myself than to Lester. "But it'd take forever to check every single one of them."

10

Wist had a predilection for rooftops. For high unreachable places where no one would show up to bother her. If she wasn't in one of the water towers, she might be at the top of the town wall. But I had no idea how to get up there.

I'd start with the towers.

Water towers may have been a misnomer: many no longer held water. Some might never have stored or pressurized water in the first place.

I climbed the riverbank, brushing past the papery husks of old lantern plants. I motioned for Lester to follow.

One far-off tower had a tank painted like a giant summer melon. Another spherical tank on stilts was allegedly meant to resemble a naked eyeball. The iris pointed directly at the sky, so no one would notice it from the ground. Only aerials could make eye contact.

In the opposite direction stood a water tower shaped like an octagonal lighthouse. This one was mildly famous for its beauty. It claimed to be the only lighthouse (albeit an imitation one) in all of landlocked Manglesea.

On the other side of the river squatted a stubby tower of brownish stone masonry. About the height of an old grain silo. It used to double as the town jail, though it had room for just a couple small cells. Sometimes those cells got put to use as bare-bones accommodations for stranded travelers.

Lester himself lived in one of the more remote defunct water towers, far on the outskirts of town. Right by the wall.

How did I know all this?

Why had I so quickly identified the eyeball tower from below? For that matter, how had I been able to recognize Lester's Cressian poetry? I wasn't exactly a student of world literature.

I looked with alarm down at the riverbank. At the blank reverse side of the sign that warned of rising waters. I clutched my tight-closed bag.

No wild dogs nipped at my heels. No primevals clambered out of the water in hot pursuit, claws digging furrows in the earth as they tracked me. The landscape couldn't have been more tranquil.

It didn't reassure me. Something was seeping up into my brain. Something that didn't belong there. A highly contagious infection of the mind. I remembered more than I should have—as if I'd lived in this town all my life.

Was this what had happened to Wist? To the townspeople who claimed I'd been staying here for weeks or years, and that they'd never seen or heard of a mage named Wisteria Shien?

For the time being, I still had a name of my own. I still knew myself as Asa Clematis.

I scanned each roof and tower in sight.

There was one in particular—located high up on the hill of empty mansions—that induced a reflexive wiggle in my bond. Not a purposeful pull, reeling me in like a fish. Something jerkier, more subconscious, closer to the fitful way your body might kick on the verge of falling asleep.

Lester raised his gnarled stick.

"The Queen favors that tower," he said.

He was a professional hermit. A fake hermit, arguably. He had no obligation to interact with anyone, much less me. Despite this, he'd already helped me more than anyone else in Bittercress.

Makeup artists would despair upon seeing how sloppily he'd applied his beard. But it wasn't my place to criticize how well he played his part. Besides, he was the only person in town I knew by name.

I dug through my bag. I took out one of the silver transceivers Wist had made for me. All the pins were shaped like clematis flowers; each had six long, pointy petals.

"Take this. It's got the Queen's magic," I said, hoping he wouldn't ask me to prove it. "So it's fine for you to borrow. Tell me if you see my mage. You know what she looks like."

I showed him how to activate the magic cuttings grafted to his pin.

He didn't make any promises. He kept the pin, though.

I let him go back to meditating on the riverbank. I began ascending the long hill leading up to the finest houses in town.

The tower I aimed for was, in fact, a genuine water tower. Probably still in use. It was by no means one of the oldest buildings in Bittercress, but it did date back at least a few decades.

It wasn't just a tank mounted on scaffolding. It was much wider and taller, with a thick base built around enormous vertical pipes.

The door bore a sign that warned sternly against trespassing. But it wasn't locked. The hinges didn't even creak. I stood there dumbly for a moment before slipping through. Quite anticlimactic.

An uncomfortably steep staircase—open risers, all plain unpainted steel—clung to the curved inner walls of the tower's hollow base. It formed a jagged, angular spiral up to the top. Nothing held the stairs there except a series of spindly metal buttresses.

No elevator, sadly.

Every step I took echoed far louder than it should have. I climbed grimly, determined not to look down.

There were a *lot* of stairs, mind you. I wasn't in nearly good enough shape to charge straight to the top without breaks.

That being said, stopping on the periodic narrow landings didn't do much to ease my strain. The railing was minimalistic, with gaps large enough that I could've gone sailing through them in an instant. I kept thinking I'd sensed the whole staircase swaying.

I avoided touching anything overtly industrial. Past the peak of the stairs, I shimmied my way over to a caged-off viewing platform.

Not one designed to lure tourists. After all, the staircase I'd ascended was definitely meant just for workers. But the narrow outdoor catwalk did offer a spectacular view.

It took me three tries to force open the entrance. The change in air pressure made my ears pop. As soon as I stepped outside, a sharp gust sucked the door shut at my back.

I looked out through the lattice of the cage at patches of private and communal farmland. At windcatchers topping buildings all over town, old and new alike. I took in the glimmering river. The perfect walls.

A constant current of cool air streamed past my face. I could imagine how the town's many windcatchers might work to alleviate summer heat.

I couldn't see Wist. Not out there, and not in here.

I have many great virtues. But I've never been especially renowned for my patience.

The top of the water tower spread much wider than its base. Like a mushroom cap. The platform I stood on jutted out just below the edge of the cap. I'd have struggled to spot it from the ground.

The chain-link fencing around the platform was the only thing stopping me from getting blown down to a terrible death. At the same time, it felt like a cage meant to display prisoners in the olden days.

My own prison tenure seemed as distant as a memory from a past life. Then again, it had taken place in an entirely different country.

"Wist," I said. Both out loud and in my head. "Show yourself. Or I'll make you. I'm getting lonely."

I reached in my bag and withdrew the pouch that held my prosthetic eye. I was very, very careful not to lose my grip. If my eye slipped free, it'd fall straight through the gaps in the floor.

I could use the last resort she'd given me. I could use the eye to summon her. I could do it right now.

I couldn't tell what kind of situation I'd be calling her out of— but no matter what, she would come to me. That I knew for a fact.

I sat down gingerly, my back to the tower's solid outer wall. The cage was by no means soundless. It vibrated whenever the wind stroked it with idle fingers, testing for weakness.

I removed my eyepatch and tucked it away in my bag. I rubbed disinfectant all over my hands and waited for the breeze to dry them.

I extracted my prosthetic eye from its specialized pouch. It was lustrous with magic. But only if I focused on it with my magic perception. I could no more *see* that magic than my ears could smell an omelet.

I pulled up the eyelid of my empty right socket. I nudged the prosthetic in, then adjusted the skin of my lid gently around it.

It felt gut-wrenchingly strange during insertion. It bulged and squeaked. It wasn't anything close to a perfect sphere, either. It subtly changed shape to fit the empty hole in my face. The same material that had felt as hard as a seashell in my hand gained a springy—almost rubbery—quality once I put it in me. Not unlike a squishy real eyeball.

As soon as I blinked, magic stopped me from feeling the prosthesis. No more than I consciously felt the presence of my organic left eye, at any rate. It was a remarkable little object. Yet it didn't restore my sight. The most it did was flesh out the depth in my existing field of vision.

Standard prosthetic eyes were a two-part affair, with a permanent ocular implant deeper in the socket to replace lost tissue. The removable cosmetic prosthesis—usually shaped more like an oval bird egg or a curved shell than a round ball—would connect to the surgically attached implant.

My eye socket stayed hollow. Doctors warned that leaving it empty might lead to the socket itself minutely changing shape over time. I wore my prosthesis almost constantly, though. Except here in Manglesea.

I'd opted out of getting an implant because Wist had personally developed the magic for numerous aspects of my prosthesis. She still tinkered with it in her spare time. I didn't want to get stuck sitting there like a patient in a dentist's chair while she fussed over my ocular implant (if I had one).

I told her she could do just about anything she wanted with my eye, but it needed to stay completely removable. So I could toss it at her and go off to do my own thing while she tweaked it.

Naturally, I set certain key limits. I didn't want Wist to waste decades of her life trying to synthesize a false eye with perfect sight.

She could've done it. She could've done anything with magic, given sufficient time.

Self-centered though I may be, even I would sleep more poorly at night if my private needs kept the Kraken too busy to close vorpal holes, put a stop to burgeoning wars, rescue innocent civilians from raging wildfires, and so on. I know my place.

My right eye had settled in nicely. I closed my bag.

Up here near the top of the tower, I felt like an insect clinging furtively to the wall of a stranger's room. Hopefully no one would come by to squash me.

Summoning Wist would involve using magic. Not my own, as I had no magic to speak of. It was all hers—intricate trimmings pruned from her branches and affixed to my prosthesis, awaiting activation.

We'd argued quite a bit over what sequence of actions to use as the activation key. Above all, it had to be something I would never do or say by accident.

Wist wanted to use this as a pretext for making me utter something incredibly sappy. She had a point: normally I'd never get caught whispering sweet nothings out loud. I countered her by protesting that I might be hiding when I called her. I might not be in a position to safely speak.

(I could envision far worse situations, too. I might not be able to use my hands freely. I might not have access to my false eye, either. But not even the Kraken could account for every single danger under the sun.)

I held my breath. I thought—as clearly and with as much irony as I could mentally muster—our agreed-upon passphrase.

Don't keep me waiting, snookums.

I reached for my right eye. All that remained was to spin it like a globe.

"You don't have to go that far," said a voice nearby. "I was with you all along."

11

My hand stopped before touching my eye.

I was still hunched on the cold grated floor. She stood on my right. In my blind spot.

She must've ported in. The door to the platform was far to our left. But I'd been much too focused on the summoning sequence to detect any burst of magic. Either that, or she'd attained godlike levels of magical stealth.

I twisted to see her. She wasn't slouching. She wore a loose shirt with long sleeves. On me it would have fit normally. On Wist, it turned into a stomach-baring crop top.

She regarded me with what I could only describe as heartfelt disinterest.

Her eyebrows and lashes were as dark and straight as ever. The rest of her hair, tied back in a long ponytail, had turned the color of the clouds half-hidden by aerials. An unreachable and flavorless white.

My first thought:

This wasn't my Wist.

But she wasn't an impostor or any kind of lookalike. She wasn't being puppeteered.

I recognized the irreproducible pattern of her inner magic: the legion of vein-thin branches swarming throughout her body.

On top of that, I could still feel our bond. Unbroken. A cord stretched from me to her—then hit a wall stronger and higher than the walls around town. She wouldn't let me invade her head. But she was there on the other side of that wall. She was there.

You can't steal a bond, or pass it off to someone else as if handing off the reins of a primeval. My bond led straight to her. Thus proving that she was my bondmate.

This was a Wist I didn't know yet.

"Thought you were more talkative," she said.

She didn't speak in her usual monotone. She traced the average expected inflections for each word as a diligent student practicing penmanship might trace model letters on a page. Beneath it was still the same inimitable deadness.

"Wist." I rose shakily to my feet. The platform let out a metallic whine. "They've been calling you a queen."

"That's not my full title."

"Then what is?"

"It's cramped up here," she said, ignoring me.

The sides of the cage fell away like metal fences flattened by a storm. They dangled there in open air, squealing at the slightest touch of wind.

I pressed myself flat against the hard wall of the water tower. One slippery step, and there'd be nothing to stop me from lurching off the edge. My blood pumped as if it were about to explode.

Wist, in contrast, seemed wholly relaxed.

If she fell, her magic would catch her. If I fell, her magic would catch me, too. Under normal circumstances, anyway. But now? Would this Wist lift a finger to save me?

I couldn't tell.

"Flimsy screens," she murmured. "They never offered much protection to begin with."

"That's no reason to—"

"All I did was remove the illusion of safety."

"Thanks," I croaked, gripping my bag for dear life. "Really appreciate it. What the hell happened to you?"

Slowly, infuriatingly, she spread her hands. She shrugged. Without opening her mouth, she spoke in a voice that ground right up against the underside of my skull.

What do you think?

I winced. Wist laughed quietly.

She wasn't a perfect avatar of human virtue—no more so than I was—but she'd never been openly sadistic. She'd never toyed with me for her own amusement.

Except once. I'd seen multiple mages go berserk before, Wist among them. She'd been frightening then. And also frighteningly affectionate.

This was something altogether different. She still had control. Her magic hadn't consumed her.

What do you think?

The colder I got, the more sweat poured out of me. I huddled against the too-smooth wall as if my clamminess could paste me there like a safety belt. The back of my mouth made several abortive attempts to swallow before I spoke.

"The stranger in the coat," I said. "The coat with red circles. They wanted you to go back to Katashiro Caverns."

"When you started speaking just now, I thought you might beg for your life." She sounded disappointed.

I refused to get thrown off course. "You listened to the stranger. Even though you claimed you wouldn't. You went back there alone last night."

"Interesting theory. And then?"

"You met the—the thing in the caves that you were so worried about. The thing you acted so determined to stay away from." I drew myself up, indignant. "No—you tell me!"

She held out her long cloud-white tail of hair, then let it fall.

"Yeah," I said. "There's the proof that something was done to you. Or you did something to yourself. Your hair was still black when we fell asleep last night."

"You change your hairstyle all the time," Wist said reasonably.

"We're talking about you, not me."

"Seems like a double standard." Her fingertips touched the short bristles just behind my ear. An icy frisson shot down the side of my neck. "You've gone from black hair to white hair and back again. Sometimes you've got a mix of both. Is it so strange if I follow suit?"

That was ... exactly the sort of thing I'd say if I were her. This felt disturbingly like arguing with myself.

The platform groaned.

"It's tilting," I squawked. "Wist—"

"No, it isn't."

I tried very hard not to glance at what lay below us. Treetops. The roofs of abandoned mansions. The steely river. Bobbing shadows cast by aerials. The faraway curve of the town wall. A dizzying drop.

I stared at Wist instead.

She looked utterly detached—but hey, that was nothing new. We'd had worse ups and downs than this. Once upon a time, she'd kept her distance while I languished in prison for seven years.

The bond was still safely anchored in each of us. She still smelled like herself. The same scent I'd breathed while dozing off at the inn just last night.

What had changed in her? Was it something I could undo on my own? Could I pick it apart like a knot, the way I always unraveled painful knots in her magic?

Right. I was a healer. I was *her* healer. She hadn't needed much healing in Manglesea, but only because she'd refrained from using magic. That, too, had changed overnight.

"Someone's been throwing around a lot of magic," I said.

"Someone?"

"The Queen," I snapped. "I mean you, Your Majesty. You must need healing."

"Does it look like I need healing?" she inquired.

I studied her magic.

It wasn't tangled at all.

This was so deeply strange that for a few moments I forgot the precariousness of my footing, the pushiness of the treacherous breeze. I no longer heard the keening that came from the dangling sides of the cage, the fencing she'd burst wide open.

We were bondmates. I could still heal other mages—not that I had much interest in doing so. I felt no great personal passion for the art of soothing ornery magic branches. Even if I happened to be incredibly good at it.

Wist, however, could no longer accept healing from anyone else. It simply wouldn't work.

"Perhaps I've ascended to new heights of glory," she said coolly. "Perhaps I've overcome my need for healing from external sources."

The backs of my shoulders ground into the wall. I realized belatedly that she was pressing me there. My body made no attempt to get away. Partly because it knew this was Wist. Why would I flee her? Partly because she was the only barrier between me and the unprotected edge of the platform.

"You must be confused," she said. "I can help with that."

Her hand touched a spot very close to my prosthetic eye. My throat rasped all on its own, a sound below the level of words.

"I don't like this," I choked out.

"Hold still."

This was not a request. It was more akin to a bland statement of fact. A voice reading off stage directions. I remained still because I had no other choice. Her magic froze me in place.

I don't know you, I thought. It was the one and only coherent thought that managed to surface, again and again, from the storm in my head. *I don't know you.*

Without any further preparation, she held me against the wall and popped out my prosthetic eyeball as if she'd done it a thousand times before.

My tear ducts watered. It stung as though she'd inserted needles in them, hair-thin needles deep in my face. I heard the sound of my bag being unzipped, then zipping back up again. She must've tucked my prosthetic right back where it belonged. Such a courteous Queen.

She stretched open my sagging empty eyelid, the one with nothing behind it. It was a brisk and clinical touch. Neither painful nor loving.

Panic surged. "Wait," I gasped. "Wist—"

She didn't wait.

She released my face. She pulled away for a second. I thought— hoped—she was done with me.

Then she grabbed the back of my head.

I saw her other hand coming. I saw it coming too quick to scream. Nothing would've burst out if I'd had the breath to scream, anyway. Beeswax clogged my vocal cords.

Her finger went deep into the hole that used to hold my eye.

It didn't hurt. It didn't feel like anything at all. I wished it would hurt—at least that would've given me something to drown in, something to cling to other than this penetrating sensation of old betrayal.

Magic ignited at the very back of my hollow eye socket. The platform trembled underfoot. It moved like soil liquefying during an earthquake. Wist kept a merciless grip on my hair.

At last her finger left the hole in my face. The magic she'd planted there guttered down to the dimness of old coals.

I must've teetered on the border of blacking out.

The next thing I knew, it was very quiet.

Whether through porting or simple pushiness, she'd moved us back inside the water tower. We were at the very top of the long crooked-spiral stairs, the stairs with wide open risers. I sat slumped in a daze, my small khaki bag in my lap. My right hand cupped my eye socket.

"You know"—what was the point of saying this? But I couldn't stop myself—"you know how much I hate it when stuff comes rushing at my face."

She lounged above me with her hip against the unreliable railing. "Could've been worse," she said, unmoved.

Her palm landed on the crown of my head. An idle, paternalistic gesture.

"Shall I take your other eye?" she asked.

It sounded like a genuine threat.

My heart felt so unsustainably small and fast that I could've sworn someone had replaced it with the heart of a rabbit.

"You—"

"Tell me," she said. "Did I ever promise not to hurt you?"

This was the closest the Queen had come to speaking in the same flat naked voice as my Wist.

I felt the hard shape of my prosthetic eye when I clenched the bottom of my bag.

"Doesn't matter whether or not you ever made a word-for-word promise," I snarled. "I mean, it was definitely sort of implied! Stop making me doubt—"

"Can you love this?" The white-haired Queen pointed at herself. Her tone turned mocking again. "*Do* you love this? Of course not. You already understand that you don't know me."

Suddenly it became much easier to speak. "Give me back my Wist," I said. I grabbed the railing and rose to face her.

12

"I HAVE NOTHING left to give you," said the Queen.

We shared space on a small landing, one just as cramped as the platform outside the tower wall. The interior felt like a slice of a completely different world. A world without wind.

The plain metal steps connected to a bare rounded room. A gallery of obscure certificates and inspection notices. In the middle, new stairs—these a bright enameled blue—corkscrewed up to the meager outer platform, and other facilities I hadn't dared to poke at.

Wist had always been very tall. She seemed taller still as the Queen. She'd stopped hunching to diminish her own presence. Magic aside, I had no hope of physically wrestling her into submission.

"My eye socket," I said, pointing. "What'd you do to it?"

I didn't ask this with any expectation of getting an actual answer.

Yet the Queen replied immediately, and without further urging. "I granted you the ability to see what I see."

"That tells me nothing."

"To see what the townspeople can't. Not even your friend the hermit."

"To see the truth?"

She glanced at my humble brown bag. "Wear your prosthetic if you like—the locals won't complain. You can't block the sight I've planted in you. Not by damming it up with a false eye, and not by wearing an eyepatch. Cover the right side of your face, and you'll simply notice more with your left eye."

"Notice *what*?"

She didn't answer.

In my defense, I wasn't just standing there hoping for her to crumble in awe of my dastardly interrogation skills. Back in Osmanthus, certain people called me the Magebreaker. I'd earned that nickname for a reason.

The fact that we were bonded ought to have made her particularly vulnerable. I could use our bond as a direct line to heal her myriad magic branches, without any need for physical closeness. I could exploit it to perform the reverse of regular supportive mage healing, too. I could snarl and mat her branches, torture her, drive her mad.

Or I could use the bond as a set of reins to seize total control over her body and her magic.

On a practical level—before we even get into the ethics of it—there were several problems with this. For one thing, I'd made Wist train very hard to resist me. It'd be much more difficult to turn her into my marionette than it would've been a year ago.

Besides, the Queen hadn't left herself exposed. Though our bond remained intact, she'd cut off my access to her with ruthless totality.

When and how had she learned to protect herself like that? Sure, Wist could prevent me from invading her head or picking up on her moods. She'd never presented me with fortifications so impeccable that I didn't know if I could break them by force.

She stepped off the landing and into the room dotted with an irregular smattering of fist-sized windows. All frosted glass—no outside view whatsoever.

I trailed after her, hands clasped behind my back. Feigning a sort of wounded innocence.

The floor was worryingly damp and uneven. In some sections, the moisture almost formed puddles.

The Queen stopped by one of the tiny windows. As if she could actually see what lay on the other side of the thick clouded glass. I stopped next to her, my head bumping her shoulder.

"Haven't you wondered what makes you special?" she asked.

"I've always been special," I said drolly. "I'm a genius healer."

"Does your genius explain why you alone remember what date it's supposed to be, and your own origins, and the name Wisteria Shien? Everyone else in Bittercress forgot."

The words themselves seemed vaguely jeering, but there was something off about her tone. As if her heart wasn't in it. As if her heard wasn't in anything.

Not everyone forgot, I thought. Lester—the full-time hermit—had remembered who I came to town with.

"Like it or not, we're bondmates," I said. "Guess that gives me some kind of exemption."

"No."

She said it quite plainly.

As she said it, I reached for her back. I moved as if to slip an arm around her waist. Soft and affectionate. Her short-cropped shirt meant she had nothing there but bare skin. A bold choice for a mage.

The greatest concentration of magic lurked near the small of her back. Act deftly, and I could seize magic threads in my fist as if grabbing that long hair of hers right at the roots.

It would hurt her if I balled up her magic in my hand, if I yanked it. It would hurt her profoundly, and overwhelm her, and hopefully disable her. I could hobble her magic in half a second if she were just a little bit too slow to react.

She wasn't.

My fingers never brushed skin. She caught my wrist before I came anywhere near the source of her magic. She held my hapless arm high in the air as if denouncing a pickpocket before an invisible crowd.

"What was it that people used to call you?" She sounded thoroughly unimpressed.

I couldn't free my arm.

"The Magecracker?" she said.

"The Magebreaker," I muttered, embarrassed by failure.

She released me. I lunged for her back again. This time the air itself halted me, stretching and pulling like a sheet of unbreakable plastic wrap.

I came very close. But I still couldn't touch her magic.

"Are you done yet?" asked the Queen.

In my mid-thirties, I was a tad too old to let the threat of mere humiliation deter me. I also knew when to acknowledge that I wasn't getting anywhere. I stopped flailing.

"You have three days," she said.

"Until what?"

She ran a dispassionate finger along my bag. The same finger that had violated the empty gap where I used to have an eye.

"The only reason you still know who you are," she told me, "is because your prosthesis protects you. Even when you don't have it inserted. Keep it near you, and it'll keep you sane."

"That's entirely your doing," I pointed out. "You made the damn thing. If it protects me, you have only yourself to blame."

"I know." She didn't crack a smile. "Three days from now, if you're still here in Bittercress, I'll come to take it."

Her hand briefly cupped its light shape at the bottom of my bag.

"You're telling me to flee?"

"You can't get away," said the Queen. "But you can try."

"What'll happen to me without my prosthetic eye?"

"Think of everyone else you've met in town."

Would I be fully assimilated? Would I gain a local job, or two, or three? Would I surrender my name, and my identity as the notorious Magebreaker, and my memory of having crossed international borders to come here on vacation? What a terrible decision that was turning out to be.

Would I forget what Wist had been like before her hair turned white? Would I forget what she'd meant to me?

Other questions pressed at me, too. Foremost among them: why would the Queen let me have those three days in the first place? She could take my prosthetic eye away right here and right now. She could vaporize my entire bag with magic.

I didn't want to encourage that, obviously. I kept my mouth shut.

As if reading my mind, the Queen said: "I've been sorely lacking in entertainment."

"You want me to run around and try to escape because everyone else in town is too dull? It's your town now. It's your own fault if they bore you."

"After three full days," said the Queen, "your escape attempts will begin to feel stale."

She seemed supremely assured of victory. Where's the novelty and entertainment value in a situation where you already know the outcome? I wondered. Why sit there watching a horse race if you've already seen how it ends?

I didn't say this out loud. The Queen answered anyway.

"Would you skip a stage adaptation of a famous old story because you're familiar with the ending?" she asked. "Would you throw out a book about the first Kraken because history has already happened, and your school lessons spoiled all the drama? I appreciate your concern, but there's little else you can offer me."

"Except the picture of a bug scrambling not to get crushed," I said. "Got it. You think I'm a cockroach? Watch me scurry."

I backed up toward the unpainted steel stairs. The Queen followed at her leisure.

"How're you counting the days?" I demanded. "The equinox hasn't come yet. Three days from now might never get here. Maybe I've got all the time in the world to mess around with you."

"The days are passing," she replied. "Time isn't. If you think you've found a loophole, why not wait to see what happens?"

I gripped the cold top of the railing and stood as tall as I could. I still had to look up at her. My neck hurt.

"I've been your enemy before," I said. "I can be your enemy again."

Her eyes were unmistakably Wist's eyes, hopelessly black, devoid of anything resembling color or light. "You've never been enemies with me," she said obliquely.

I scoffed. "With you as a magical monarch? You've already been the Kraken for years. Practically mythical. Collect all the extra nicknames you want. I can still handle you."

Her face didn't change.

Her fingers tensed in the air just above my clavicle. For a moment I found myself absolutely convinced that she was about to push me down the stairs. All it would take was the slightest nudge of magic.

The bottoms of my shoes had gotten distastefully wet from the industrial floor that by rights ought to have remained perfectly dry. The ridged steel stairs felt slippery even when I strove not to move a muscle. Wist—the Queen—remained so still that she might not have been breathing.

"I could spare you the trip to ground level," she said softly. "But I don't think I will. See you in three days, Clematis."

The Queen vanished.

13

Going down the tower was much, much worse than going up.

The stairs had gone all wobbly. I paused to put my prosthetic back in. This only made me feel slightly better about my ability to judge the distance to the next step.

Black shapes like lizards skittered across the featureless curved walls—walls the color of yellowing old teeth. It always happened right at the boundary of my one-eyed vision. Turn my head, and I'd see nothing but the long descent to the bottom of the tower shaft.

How much water was held in reserve in the chamber at the very top? The imagined weight of it bore down on the back of my skull, willing me to trip and go somersaulting violently down the rest of the stairs.

As before, I sensed the Queen through our bond. She was still somewhere around town. I couldn't guess where.

I was with you all along.

My hand spasmed on the metal banister. At the periphery of my vision, more sinuous dark lizards scattered without a sound. I whipped around to look up the jagged stairs.

She wasn't there. Or if she was, I couldn't see her. The other end of the bond felt like a string hanging slack, trailing down into an unlit well. Like the drifting deep-sea chain of a broken anchor.

On a surface level, Wist never came off as being particularly empathetic. People thought of her as cold and robotic.

To be fair, even if she put on a show of being warm and gregarious, everyone would still regard her first and foremost as the Kraken. The greatest mage alive. Not even S-Class mages would dare consider her a true peer. She was as different from them as a normal mage was different from a magicless healer like me.

Not to belabor the obvious, but Wist did have emotions. She cared for others, though she had never cared very much for herself.

I didn't know if I could still say that about the Queen.

Three days, I reminded myself as I trudged the rest of the way down the tower. That meant three new dawns and nights, right? Surely it didn't include today.

The door to the base of the water tower banged shut behind me.

The townspeople sounded disturbingly loyal to their Queen who had come out of nowhere. They spoke as if both she and they had lived here forever, always one day before the autumn equinox.

Then again, they weren't openly hostile. They merrily added every imaginable expense to my hotel tab. At least I didn't have to worry about running out of funds for food, drink, or shelter.

Not that I had much of an appetite. In a bistro without any other customers, I ate just enough peppery goat meat stew to keep from fainting.

Afterward, I set out to explore the town perimeter.

Every citizen I met claimed the walls had no flaws, and the town had no gate. Yet they also spoke casually about primevals foraging in the fields beyond the walls. They perceived no contradiction in the fact that primevals (which had no wings) possessed some sort of ability to pass back and forth.

Perhaps parts of the walls were illusory. Or perhaps there was a secret door meant exclusively for use by animals.

If nothing else, the local river neither started nor ended in Bittercress. I might not have time to comb over every inch of the walls in person, but I could at least examine the places where they intersected with the river.

I kept a suspicious eye out as I crossed town. I still couldn't articulate what the Queen had done to the deepest recesses of my right socket.

So far, nothing looked overtly different. I observed cabbage patches covered in an infestation of white moths. Autumn-blooming trees swarmed with uncomfortably large bees. Elsewhere, tiny birds like white balls of fluff darted from branch to branch, followed by greedy honeyeaters.

Magic had descended over Bittercress in a single night. Not the uncontrolled magic of a human berserker. Not a natural outburst of wild magic like a geyser erupting.

The magic at work here was both too all-encompassing and too imperceptible.

All human magic could be broken down into specific skills assigned to a specific magic branch of a specific mage. If the magic that had infiltrated town were made up of individual skills, it must've been a pastiche of far too many to count.

Wist alone possessed enough branches that she'd never need to worry about running out. Wist was capable of inventing strange new skills on her own, too. But not in an instant. Unless she went fully berserk. However, the Queen I'd met was very clearly not a berserking mage.

How to explain it, then?

Last night, Wist had slipped out of bed. For reasons of her own, she'd set all her fears aside and gone back to Katashiro Caverns. Without me.

At that point, perhaps she'd stopped caring about the laws of Manglesea. Perhaps she'd ported straight to the cave entrance. No need to arrange for another carriage.

She'd encountered something down in the caves. Something that unlocked in her the power to instantaneously brainwash an entire town. To revive the ancient Cressian walls. To warp the passage of time.

Maybe the thing in the caves had given her the ability to access all the benefits of a berserker-like state—without facing any of the usual drawbacks. Maybe it had indeed liberated her from the most fundamental burden weighing down any mage, no matter how powerful: the crippling pain their magic caused them. Their need for lifelong healing.

Maybe the thing she met in the caves had simultaneously empowered and corrupted her.

Why, then, would she stop at mastering a single rural town in a small and historically powerless country?

Had she stopped at mastering a single town? Was the entire continent—or the entire world—stuck repeating the day before the equinox? Did they, too, know her as their Queen?

Only one way to find out.

I didn't like doing as my enemies told me. But none of my usual tricks seemed likely to work against the Queen. I'd already missed my chance to hobble her magic. Now I was racing against an artificial deadline—one entirely of her making.

If I wanted to see what was happening in the world outside, if I wanted to avoid getting turned into Townsperson C, I'd better follow her script for the time being. I'd better try my damnedest to escape.

<h1 style="text-align:center">14</h1>

My deadline was three days from now. That made this Day 0.

I stopped briefly back at the inn. I contemplated what I could do in the event of failure.

I almost started leaving notes for my future self. The room had plenty of paper, what with all those six-spot wards pasted high and low. Someone had seamlessly replaced the few I'd peeled off earlier.

In the end, I opted not to scribbled down secret messages. They weren't likely to stay hidden from the Queen. Not to mention the sharp-eyed innkeeper. I couldn't expect true privacy anywhere in Bittercress.

I wouldn't waste time trying to hedge against an uncertain future brought on by unfathomable magic. Better focus all my energy on escaping.

I still had a couple clematis pins left in my bag. I could've attempted to call outside help, although I suspected that no messages would go through. Wist the Queen was savvy enough, surely, to block her own transceiver magic.

I didn't even try, though. So what if I reached the Osmanthian ambassador to Manglesea—or my parole officer, or other allies back home?

Let's say they chose to believe my word (the word of a convicted criminal). Let's say Manglesea welcomed in the Osmanthian army and let them assault the walls of Bittercress.

Would it make any difference? Wist was an army unto herself. As the Queen, she'd seemingly reached grand new heights of power. The military wouldn't stand a chance. Besides, with international politics gumming up the works, no meaningful rescue mission could possibly come rushing over in less than three days from now.

That afternoon, I hired a rickshaw to take me all the way from one end of the river to the other. It intersected the wall in two places, east and west.

In both locations, a dungeon-thick metal grill blocked the gap where the river flowed beneath the wall. The water ran much deeper and darker and faster than in the middle of town.

Passing through would require either tunneling down in the riverbed, or somehow detaching the grate itself.

Sadly, I didn't know how to build a sufficiently powerful bomb. Even if I did—that water looked like a great way to drown. There was probably another such grate at the far end of the passage under the wall, too.

I parted ways with the friendly rickshaw runner and proceeded on foot to the town library.

The building had no sign. A keening chime rang when I opened the door. It still felt like walking uninvited into a random stranger's living room.

A fossilized-looking elder hunched behind the reception desk, busily sharpening knives. The blades already looked plenty sharp to my amateur eye. I kept my distance.

The grating sound of it followed me as I stepped between suffocatingly narrow shelves. An occasional high-pitched squeal rent the air—the sort of noise that would do wonders for dispelling feral cats and other garden pests. It nearly dispelled me straight out of the library. The toothless woman grinding away at her knives appeared completely unbothered.

I started looking up information about aerials. Maybe I could tempt one to come grab me and carry me away over the walls.

This, the books told me in no uncertain terms, would be an extremely bad idea. Oh well.

I also skimmed quite a few volumes about the Cressian civilization. They'd supposedly had a culture of sacrifice. Especially mage sacrifice.

They would periodically choose a mage as their symbolic sovereign. They'd sacrifice numerous other mages to make their chosen one stronger. Eventually they would sacrifice their sovereign, too.

A sovereign, huh. Like some kind of queen?

The dreadful music of sharpening knives droned on and on in the background. Despite her skeletal arms and cataract-clouded eyes, the woman up front showed no sign of tiring.

The more I read, the more I began to suspect that the Cressians were just a distraction. I found no end of books full of Cressian speculation. But I couldn't find a single local guide or map.

I stopped in at a souvenir shop, too, just to be sure. There were no pamphlets summarizing the history of Bittercress and its walls, risen or fallen. Nothing about Katashiro Caverns or other regional natural wonders. Nothing but booklets of old Cressian-attributed poems for the dead.

I asked around to see if I could borrow a ladder. Preferably the tallest ladder in town.

None seemed tall enough to take me anywhere near the top of the wall.

If I could cobble together some kind of paraglider or hang glider, perhaps I could send myself coasting off the roof of a well-positioned water tower. Some of the towers looked just high enough to launch a trip to the top of the town wall. From there I could fly my way outside. But that was about as realistic a prospect as figuring out how to communicate with far-off aerials.

I sat on a bench near a bright green bridge. A child dashed across the street, small and quick as a stray cat. Much too quick for its size, actually. No toddler could run like that.

I missed Wist.

It felt like half my brain was absent when I couldn't narrate my thoughts at her. It felt like I was overlooking something of vital importance.

This fatal dependence was why I'd remained ambivalent about bonding. Even after it was already a done deal, and we'd found ourselves tied together for life.

I was at a severe disadvantage here, and not just because I couldn't consult with my bondmate. My options were limited by the fact that I needed to assume this town and its people were real.

I had yet to catch anyone dissolving in mist after turning a corner. None of the locals were see-through. They cast shadows. Their feet touched the ground when they walked. Besides, they'd been here since long before Wist and I showed up.

This wasn't a mere dream or illusion. If even one townsperson among hundreds of well-made puppets might be a real human being, I couldn't gleefully murder random bystanders.

I leaned back. I was alone on this bench. Just me and a praying mantis the size of a well-fed rat. It tilted its head to look at me with protuberant eyes.

I bounced my leg furiously. The mantis seemed unperturbed.

I pictured Wist as the Queen. To be quite frank, white hair looked aggravatingly good on her. Her imperious air made everything seem to suit her, from the long snowy ponytail to her incongruous crop top.

I'd never been attracted to mages who couldn't hide their arrogance. But this wasn't any old mage. This was—at least on some level—Wisteria Shien. You'll have to forgive me for getting a little mixed up.

My core problem was that I didn't know what motivated the Queen. What she cared about, if anything. What I could use as leverage. I couldn't afford to make careless assumptions based on what I knew of my Wist.

I got up from the bench. It was still Day 0. This was a time to test (and eliminate from consideration) my wilder escape plans. Like stacking every ladder in town, or tying myself to a homemade kite. This was a time to gather information.

Down by the river, long-necked turtles rested on rotting logs. Beard-like strands of algae trailed from their shells. Kids threw balls of primeval dung into the water until an adult rushed out to scold them.

Every ten feet along the riverbank were posted signs that said *BEWARE OF______*.

I'm serious. No matter how far I walked, each sign said the same thing. Two words. No punchline. No image. Just a pale blank space. The most crucial part of the warning had been strategically whitewashed out of existence. I caught a street cleaner and asked them what the signs meant. They looked at me as though wondering which asylum I'd escaped from. They couldn't see any warning signs.

I granted you the ability to see what I see, the Queen had told me. *To see what the townspeople can't.*

I touched one of the blanked-out boards. It felt real enough to me, if not to anyone else.

I already had a lot to beware of. What good had this gift of sight done me? None whatsoever. In fairness, she hadn't claimed she was trying to help me.

Maybe she'd enhanced my vision to subtly torment me. To make me doubt my perception of reality. To drive me that much closer to losing my mind.

Whatever the case, I couldn't let it deter me. I kept exploring.

Late in the evening, I stumbled across a church.

Not a place for worshipers to gather. More of a storehouse. A shrine. A sacred vault.

At first I mistook it for yet another obsolete water tower. It was a hexagonal stone building, about four stories high, with a prominent windcatcher jutting out like a very tall chimney.

The facade bore carvings of descended aerials and mutated primevals and winged Cressians, all with morose human faces.

The hard-packed path up to the entrance was marked with a series of deep dried-up footprints.

I knocked at the door. Someone called for me to let myself in.

Inside the vault, I found a nail-strewn floor. The innkeeper sat on a stool and dug through the contents of a wooden chest that looked large enough to hold multiple bodies. She was barefoot.

I'm not terribly proud of this, but the moment I saw her, I wondered if I could use her as a hostage.

No one would mistake me for a trained combatant. She, however, was ponderously pregnant, and right around the same height as me. I could take her. All I needed was a simple weapon. A knife or a nightstick or a candelabra. Or one of those long nails lying in a corner. Or a pointed crystalline light.

Don't worry. I didn't threaten the pregnant woman. Mainly because I didn't know if the Queen would care enough to intervene.

In any case, the locals had been letting me do my own thing, no matter how eccentric I might seem to them. They'd even been so kind as to ignore my overtly magical prosthetic eye. Although it's possible the Queen simply prevented them from recognizing the magic on it.

It'd be a lot harder to maneuver if I made the townspeople turn on me. "Need help?" I asked. I figured the innkeeper would shoo me out if this storeroom were too sacred to be tainted with my secular presence.

She shook her head. She sighed. She rubbed fretfully at her lower back. A couple of her fishhooks glinted like tinsel.

She looked me dead in the eye and cried—loud enough for it to echo off all six walls—"My—my water's breaking!"

"Your *what*?"

"Just kidding." Now she spoke in a tone so normal that, by way of contrast, it seemed wooden.

"Great joke," I said weakly. "You, uh, really got me with that one. Whew."

She didn't giggle. "This shed stores a lot of our supplies for the equinox festival tomorrow," she told me. "I was getting some of it organized. Almost done now."

"Are you a..." How to put this? "...A religious figure?"

She spread her hands humbly. "For now I am, yes. I'm the priestess of the past. Also the priestess of the future. Most of my duties end after the equinox."

Yeah. No big surprise. I knew there had to be some kind of cult here.

"Shall I read your fortune?" the innkeeper asked.

"For the past or for the future?"

"Does it matter?"

"Er—yes?" Now she was making me doubt myself.

"There's only one priestess for the past and for the future," she said. "I can only read one fortune."

I bought a few moments to think by making a show of looking around. A stone light rested on an empty stool beside her. Moonlight leaked in through miserly windows.

This was no vault of riches: it held no gold-plated regalia. Several gigantic barrel-shaped drums rested on horizontal stands in a corner. On the wall above hung musical horns made of various material ranging from literal animal horn to old brass.

Other walls bore polished metal mirrors and hanging banners dyed with a more elaborate version of the six-spot seal. Lengths of ceremonial rope—parts of it thicker than my waist—lay draped over a table, complete with enormous iron thorns that stuck out at intervals like shark teeth. There were elaborate eye shapes woven in the middle of each rope.

"Looks dangerous." I nodded at the table.

"We'll hang the ropes across the river early tomorrow."

"When the equinox comes."

"Exactly."

"I'll pass on getting my fortune told," I said. "Thanks for the offer. Those horns over there—are they what the guards play?"

"Good guess. These are spares."

I asked, delicately, if she and the other townspeople would pray to their Queen.

"No," she answered at once. "We demand nothing of the Queen, and the Queen demands nothing of us."

"Healthy boundaries," I said. "Sounds like a great relationship. What's she the Queen *of*, by the way? You told me before that she's not just a queen for the equinox. Is she the Queen of Bittercress? Of Manglesea? Of the ancient Cressians?"

The innkeeper pivoted slowly on her stool to face me. She looked troubled, as if she couldn't understand why I wouldn't know.

In the moonlight, I realized that she was much older than me. Much older than I'd originally thought. I'd bet she had twenty-plus years on me and Wist.

Why hadn't I noticed till this precise moment? Because I kept getting distracted by the fishhooks at the ends of her hair twists? Because it would strain belief for a woman in her late fifties to be walking around happily pregnant?

"Our Queen is the Queen of the Void," she said.

"The Void?"

"The Void."

What was a void, anyway? A sky without aerials? The deadly space on the other side of a vorpal hole? A locked safe without any treasure inside?

Or the hollowness, perhaps, of a forbidden cave.

"Is your Void an entity?" I asked. "Or is it the name of a place, like—"

The innkeeper groaned. It was extremely convincing. Enough to shut me up, and almost enough to make me think she'd started having contractions.

But she'd been joking about her water breaking. And tomorrow—like today—would not yet be the equinox.

She lifted herself up from her seat. The fishhooks in her hair swung gently as she moved. They looked as though they ought to make a sound like tinkling bells.

The innkeeper told me it was about time for us to leave.

I didn't press the issue of the Void. Further questioning might inspire her to pop her baby out right then and there.

She put a pair of clogs on before walking around on the nail-strewn floor. I helped her carry out stacks of festival supplies to bring back to the inn. A box full of cloth masks decorated with the usual crimson circles. A bundle of long necklaces strung with shiny imitation coins. Sheafs of blank paper cut for use as slim rectangular wards.

She took a key ring from her apron pocket to lock up the storehouse after we left. I stood close enough to see exactly which key she used.

It appeared to be a disappointingly ordinary jagged-edge variety, shorter than her thumb. I'd have expected a long fancy skeleton key, one worthy of being passed down for centuries. Maybe that would've been too much of a hassle to carry.

<h1 style="text-align:center">15</h1>

I borrowed sleeping pills from the innkeeper.

I'd weighed the merits of prowling around town all night, but ultimately decided against it. My brain would work better if I got some rest. Drug-assisted or otherwise.

I did wonder what would happen if I refused to sleep one wink. Would morning still come? Would the dammed-up passage of time be forced to divert even further from its natural course?

I wouldn't risk it. The Queen was already less than impressed by my efforts to identify a time-related loophole. No reason to think I could dodge her deadline.

Sprinkling rain woke me near dawn. It would've been nice to find Wist there, all back to normal. But I was alone in bed—no such luck.

By the time I left the inn, the rain had ceased.

Outside, I met a guard strolling to his post. The peppy accordion player who'd driven our carriage to Katashiro Caverns. He wore a black satchel. Just the right size for storing one of the horns I'd seen in the storehouse yesterday evening.

We exchanged a cheery greeting. I asked him if today was the equinox.

"No, ma'am," he said. "The equinox is tomorrow."

"Of course," I agreed. "Have a wonderful equinox eve."

This was Day 1 out of 3. At least going by my count. I kept wearing my prosthetic eye out in the open. No one seemed troubled by its dense web of magic.

As the guard's footsteps retreated, an inky liquid glistened in the gaps between cobblestones. Too dark to be plain water. The back of my right eye socket ached, albeit with something closer to hunger than pain.

I went over to the graveyard and found the gates already open.

The mortician used a broom with a crooked handle to sweep up periwinkle blossoms. Her plumbago bushes never stopped shedding. She also caught a smattering of fallen leaves. Despite the overnight rain and damp streets, the leaves looked dry enough to crackle.

The spider lily stalks still hadn't bloomed yet. They grew like asparagus spears all over the cemetery.

We tossed around small talk as the mortician hustled to and fro, soaking the air with her signature melon scent.

My nonexistent right eye panged when I glanced at the grave stelae behind her. Each stone bore stacks of multiple names, all crossed out. Like tasks on a to-do list.

No—like targets on a hit list. There was a violence to the horizontal lines obscuring the names. They could've been frenzied claw marks from a mythical beast.

Last time I came here, I hadn't been able to sound out any names. But only because the text itself had been illegible. I didn't remember seeing these slash marks.

The primevals seemed different now, too. Several clustered in a corner of the graveyard, feeding on a corpse of indeterminate species. A creature too small to be one of their own, and too large to be a feral cat.

I took a step closer.

"I wouldn't do that," the mortician said calmly.

The more I looked at them, the more monstrous the primevals appeared. Those long distorted faces and anteater-skinny tongues, blue-black tongues that could hang from their mouths like leather whips. Those keratin scales, larger than my hand, and mangy patches of fibrous hair. Their giant back legs and claws. Their multiple sets of forearms, squashed and useless-looking, fat as the truncated front legs of a caterpillar.

No one in Bittercress acted scared of primevals. They coexisted with human beings like fellow citizens of a different species.

They hadn't bothered me all that much, either. Until the Queen touched the empty hollow of my eye socket.

Except—I'd passed plenty of primevals yesterday, too, without noticing anything unusual. Was her influence on my sight getting worse over time? Day by day, would the town begin looking increasingly warped?

I didn't understand what she was trying to show me.

The oddest thing I'd run into so far were the half-blank signs lined up along the riverbank.

BEWARE OF_______.

Perhaps the scratched-off parts were supposed to show a primeval in silhouette. Beware of the local beasts. It would make sense, wouldn't it? Especially now, as they gathered to slurp at something sprawled helplessly in the cemetery grass.

Or perhaps the signs weren't damaged at all. Perhaps the blank sections were intentional. A complete message. No guesswork needed.

Beware of empty spaces.

Beware of nothingness.

Beware of the Void.

In the Queen's voice: *Beware of me.*

"Know what they're eating?" I asked the mortician.

She stopped sweeping leaves. She looked at me as though puzzled about why I would ask something so basic. "A body."

"I can see that. What kind of body?"

"A dead one."

"That's a relief. What species?"

"A human body, of course," she said tartly. "They dug up one of the graves."

I almost gagged on her clouds of melon-sweet perfume. "Shouldn't you, uh, do something about that?"

"It's a great blessing to be exhumed by primevals. Their living family will rejoice."

"Oh. Wonderful."

From here, the chosen corpse looked more a dirty rag than a human being.

"I thought you buried people in coffins," I said, remembering her long spiel about Manglelander traditions. "Same as the fancy coffins you use for marriage rites. How can primevals get them open?"

"Have you seen their claws?"

"Is that ... natural behavior?"

The mortician squinted at me. Regardless of her more advanced age, this was a woman that I had absolutely no illusions about being able to hold off in a fight. (Unlike the innkeeper—though all three of us were similar in height.)

With or without her broom, the mortician would pummel me in a matter of seconds.

"Must be some sort of vital nutrient in human hair or bones," she said. "Something primevals crave. Like deer licking salt, or birds eating rocks."

"When was the last time you buried anyone here?"

"A very long time ago."

"What's that mean? Years ago? Decades ago? What kind of nutrients could possibly be left?" I bent my head at the nigh-unidentifiable corpse. Felt like it would've been rude to point with my finger.

"A metaphysical nutrient," the mortician said, unruffled. "Don't ask me—I'm not a primeval."

I turned my back to give the primevals some privacy as they chomped. The mortician wouldn't hesitate to shoo me away if she got sick of my presence, so I figured I could hang around a little longer.

"Do you happen to have a town map?" I said. "Or a map of the whole area. Can't seem to find one."

"A map of the area," the mortician echoed. "What do you mean?"

"You know. One showing the main landmarks in town. Plus what lies beyond the walls, too. The hills with singing deer. The uninhabited mountains. Katashiro Caverns."

"Katashiro Caverns?" She snorted. "They're right below us."

In the silence that followed, I could've sworn I heard ravenous primevals suckling away at the hollow parts of bones that used to hold marrow.

"I've been to Katashiro Caverns," I said. "Rode there in a carriage. Took over an hour."

"The caverns are under Bittercress," she said stolidly. "Everyone knows that."

I collected myself. No point in arguing with the Queen's new reality. "Even better. Could you show me to the entrance?"

"Are you lost?"

"Not lost, exactly, but—"

"Only lantern-herders go in the caves." Her tone turned dismissive. She took up her broom again.

I didn't care if she found me annoying. Being annoying is my specialty.

I began wheedling her for help—or tried to, that is. The morning horn starting playing as soon as I opened my mouth.

When the melody ceased, the feasting primevals got up. They abandoned their corpse. They filed out through the open gate of the cemetery, polite as you please. The mortician and I moved aside so they'd have plenty of room to pass.

A gamey odor lingered in the air as the line of primevals ambled away. It went very poorly with the mortician's sugary melon scent.

"Where are they going?" I asked, half-expecting her to once more say *Don't ask me—I'm not a primeval.*

"Whenever the horn plays, some leave town," she said. "And some return."

"Leave town? How? Do they climb the walls?"

"Animals have their own paths."

That made up my mind for me.

I'd already planned on trying to track primevals at some point. If they timed their movements to the horn played every few hours, might as well hurry up and get started.

I gestured vapidly at the mangled human remains they'd been picking at. "Guess you've gotta do something about that. I'll let you have some peace and quiet, yeah?"

The mortician made no effort to stop me from leaving.

The primevals were not small or subtle animals. They would tower over other land-bound creatures in the wilds outside Bittercress: the singing deer, the flat-toothed wolves. To me they looked larger than draft horses, too, although I was admittedly not an equestrian.

They hadn't been moving quickly on their way out of the graveyard, either. Even if they got a minor head start, it should've been impossible for me to lose them.

I dashed down an alley to chase after the ends of their tails—and then they were gone. Couldn't even hear the click of claws on cobblestone.

This felt like a promising lead, though. I had other plans in store for the evening, but during the day, I could focus on stalking primevals.

After a hasty late breakfast, I chatted up a bored hostler. This reminded me that primevals had a terrible weakness for mead. Maybe later I could buy some and tempt them to do my bidding.

I'm a genius healer. I habitually overestimate my intelligence in fields unrelated to healing. Still, even I knew better than to try wrangling giant animals on a whim. I observed the primevals from a sufficiently safe distance.

They were quite sedate, all things considered. They didn't go stampeding across the river. On the whole, they didn't move around much more than your average middle-aged house cat. Their most thrilling activity (aside from grave-digging) appeared to be dropping neat ovoid clods of dung.

If I waited a couple more hours, the town horn would resound through the air again. And at least some of these primevals would go on the move.

Meanwhile, I had a lot of time to brood. I leaned on a lamppost near a tower with numerous bodies hanging off it. Hopefully effigies, although they were infinitely more convincing than the typical scarecrow. From a distance, it looked like a macabre version of the merry swing ride you might find at a carnival.

No other passersby took note of the dangling bodies. Maybe this was an everyday occurrence in Bittercress. Or maybe I was the only one who could see them. I didn't bother asking.

This morning, the tap water at the inn had run clear. But it smelled powerfully of blood—a stench so distinct and unmistakable that I couldn't help but laugh. While brushing my teeth, I'd quivered with the effort it took to stop giggling.

Clouds of tiny flies had filled up the window at one end of the hallway, as dense and dark as thunderclouds in an angry sky. I ignored them until they flew at me—with the perfect synchronization of a school of fish—at which point I'd clamped my mouth shut and endeavored not to inhale any.

Afterward, I ended up wiping numerous dead specimens from my ears and nostrils and the corners of my eye. Gross.

I didn't want the Queen to up the ante. But she had to realize that this would hardly suffice to make me lose it. Wist herself had always been way more squeamish about bugs than me, anyhow.

I'd felt genuine horror before. Horror of a more existential sort. Mostly in my younger days. It crept up on me at an age when I'd never seriously dreamed of setting foot outside Osmanthus. I'd thought I would spend my whole life in a single country. A country that, unlike Manglesea, had long been ruled by mages.

I was a healer. I would always be a healer. True horror seized me once I realized I could never change that. Neither with hard work nor genius. Neither with courage nor guile nor dirty tricks.

Nowadays I lived very comfortably, and I got away with a whole lot. Much more than I deserved to, really. Only because of my affiliation with Wist.

This led to some discomfiting thoughts about what might happen if I did escape Bittercress all alone. I could make a beeline for the Osmanthian embassy near the border—but how would they treat me if I showed up on my own? How could I get anyone from Osmanthus to believe me without Wist there to back me up?

Stressing over it wouldn't help, though. I needed to get away regardless.

I discovered a fallen primeval scale near the riverbank. It lay nestled beneath a bush covered in purple berries as small and hard as peppercorns. I tossed it from hand to hand as I watched dusty primevals slosh in the shallows. The scale had the heft and rough texture of a big washed-up clamshell.

An accident of birth and talent had sentenced me to my life as a grudging healer. Whether or not they realized it, everyone in Bittercress was locked into their respective roles, too. I felt especially bad for the innkeeper, who might end up forever pregnant—frozen in time together with the rest of them—unless I managed to knock some sense into Wist. Or otherwise unravel whatever twisted force had crowned her Queen of this peculiar town.

16

Once stores began opening for the day, I ducked into a couple to hunt for maps. Still none to be found.

Instead, I settled for shoplifting a box of matches. Didn't want anyone to know I had them. To clear my conscience, I bought a couple cans of fruit and fish, along with a colorful kit of street chalk meant for children. I told the cashier to keep the change. Problem solved.

The touristy information boards I used to glimpse around town had vanished, too. In all honesty, though, it was impossible to get lost in here. Even for me, and even without a map. Walk far enough, and I'd hit the wall or the river. Follow the river in either direction, and eventually I'd reach someplace familiar.

So it wasn't that I needed maps for navigation. I was primarily interested in seeing how they might've changed, now that the walls had risen. I wanted to trace the shape of the Queen's world.

When the midday horn sounded, the primevals I'd been studying went on the move. I watched with mounting dismay as they squeezed one after another into the mouth of a dried-up old well. The sort of well that ought to have been lidded with concrete to keep rambunctious children from diving in.

Primevals had no wings to fly. They wouldn't fit through the metal grates filtering both ends of the river. They didn't seem quite magical enough to walk through solid walls. Nor were they built to scale vertical surfaces like a slender skink.

If Katashiro Caverns now lay below Bittercress, it stood to reason that these local primevals would go underground to leave town.

They weren't the only ones who used the caves. Lantern-herders supposedly knew the way down there, too. Did they really climb in and out of this dark well, day after day, wrestling with bundles of lanterns balanced at the end of long sticks?

I'd met a couple lantern-herders in the tavern. Hadn't spotted any of them out and about since the Queen took over. But someone or something still dropped lanterns in the river at night, and came back to collect them early each morning.

Lanterns....

Lantern plants grew in a cluster near the base of the abandoned well. From a distance, their heart-shaped red-orange husks resembled ripe fruit. The primevals had assiduously avoided trampling them, stepping sideways as if they were fatally poisonous.

Bittercress had been crawling in lantern plants before the Queen took over. Where'd they all go?

I found more back in the graveyard. Down by the river. Behind a decommissioned water tower. I made a mental note of each location, then returned to the old well.

The well was completely bricked off.

I walked a full circle around it. No secret openings. I knocked at the bricks. The mortar was brown with age in some parts, lichen-stained in others.

I was beginning to get the hang of this. My theory: lantern plants grew near each potential cavern entrance. The entrances opened only when the town horn played, and only for a short time.

I borrowed scrap paper and a pen from the innkeeper. I made my own crude map, one focused mainly on the caves. I marked down all my theoretical points of ingress. I'd use one safer than the black vertical shaft of the well.

I wasn't planning on making a break for it just yet. First, I had a couple bones to pick with the Queen of the Void.

Willingly or not, consciously or otherwise, Wist the Queen had done the one thing she'd surely sworn she'd never do again.

And she was still doing it. Right here, right now. All throughout town. While I stared at drooling primevals and rubbed the sore bones around my right eye socket.

I'm not talking about hurting me. She was breaking one of the great taboos of magic use. One of the taboos proclaimed by the previous Kraken.

Never change the flow of time.

There would be consequences. Maybe right away, or maybe much later. They might turn out to be the same unspeakable consequences she'd brought on the world the last time she shattered one of those great taboos. Or her punishment might end up as something completely different—something beyond my ability to imagine.

Was she already being punished?

I wasn't so optimistic as to think she'd tell me just because I asked.

This thought—the prospect of Wist violating another taboo—was much more likely to keep me up at night than all the peripheral horrors that had begun infecting daily life here. The stink of blood in water.

The illusory naked blades I saw sliding in and out of every ceiling. The spider crickets that had taken over quiet corners of the inn. The mirage of long withered strings trailing from the backs of town denizens, making them look like puppets in search of a master.

These were minor irritations. I could sleep them off. I'd survive. Likewise, I could probably survive Wist breaking any number of taboos.

But if she reverted to the Wist I knew, if she realized what she'd done, if she saw yet another world forced to live out the natural repercussions of her unnaturally powerful magic—

She'd decide this world, and all worlds, would be better off without her.

Our neglected bond felt like a stitch in my stomach. My breath came short. I pressed haplessly at my prosthetic eye as if I could reach her through it, as if I could force her to come to me, as if I could force her to listen.

I'd already tried summoning her, again and again. In the privacy of the inn. Out on the balcony. In the middle of a wooden bridge without any paint left to protect it. The wood had felt very soft underfoot. Soft and rotten.

The summoning magic didn't activate. That stupid passphrase reverberated hollowly in my head, a joke failing to land. My prosthesis refused to revolve in its socket. No answer came except the dead silence of an unsmiling audience. She'd stripped me of my power to pull her like a magnet.

It would take much more than a heartfelt plea to make the Queen grant a hearing with a mere peasant.

Once dusk fell, I accelerated my preparations. While tracking primevals throughout the day, I'd assembled quite a collection of dung. I wore rubber gloves when picking lumps off the street to add to my sack. They were hard and dry and surprisingly light for their size.

After lugging my dung-sacks up the hill at the far end of town, I traipsed back to the inn. It took longer than expected to find an oil lamp I could pilfer without anyone watching. They'd glowed and flickered everywhere when I didn't need them. Now that I actually wanted to take one, they felt incredibly scarce.

I got my lamp in the end. I kept it unlit. I also brought several bundles of scrap paper (I'd asked the innkeeper for way more than I'd needed just to make a single map). Plus my stolen box of matches.

Under the cover of darkness, I crept back up the long hill to the neighborhood of empty foreign-owned mansions. Housekeepers and gardeners and other caretakers only worked there during the day. No one would loiter around at night.

Nocturnal crickets peppered me with accusing chirps. Hopefully they'd be smart enough to flee before they burned.

It got surprisingly cold after sunset. Granted, I didn't possess much in the way of fleshy insulation.

I'd compensated by borrowing one of Wist's sweatshirts. The one she'd worn when we went to Katashiro Caverns. Like much of her wardrobe, it was a bit ratty. And far too big on me. But it hadn't lost her scent yet.

The sky was laced with broken veins of stars. They only showed up in the cracks between massive flocks of aerials. They'd be even harder to see once I finished my work here. No one would think to stop and gaze fondly at the heavens.

Now, I would never claim to be a survivalist. I'd be in real trouble if you asked me to start a fire with flint and steel. I wouldn't know how to choose appropriate firewood, either.

I put on my dirty rubber gloves again. I began laying dung out on the porch of the largest mansion. I crumpled up balls of paper and wedged them in the pile, too.

I repeated this procedure at two other neighboring houses. Between the stars and a few distant gas-burning street lamps, there was just enough ambient light to see by.

Keep in mind that I was operating based on the vaguest of knowledge. In my twenties, I'd been convicted for crimes against the state of Osmanthus. But I'd never been sentenced for arson.

The mortician had mentioned offhand that primeval dung was highly flammable. I figured bits of paper might help. For the same reason, I wrestled with the oil lamp until it came apart, nearly spilling on me. I poured its reserves over my mountains of tinder.

It was a dry night, thankfully. Early autumn. Mild wind. I tossed my used gloves on one of the dung mounds.

Then I rolled up the sleeves of Wist's sweatshirt. I took out my pilfered box of matches. I lit a fire right up against the front door of three empty houses.

I'd imagined the lumps of dung heating gradually. Similar to coals in a grill.

I was dead wrong. My amateur mounds of makeshift fuel lit up like an alcohol-soaked flambé at a showy restaurant. I scrambled back before the heat could singe my hands.

A couple minutes after I ignited my bonfires, flames started seeping up the front of each house. My eyes watered from the sheer piercing stink of it. Yes—my right eye, too. I no longer had the eyeball I'd been born with, but my tear ducts still worked just fine.

Second by second, the reek intensified. A rotten fermented aftertaste coated my sinuses. Much worse than plain old ammonia.

The mortician had claimed that primeval dung worked well as a fuel source. Really? Maybe it'd smell less deadly with proper processing.

I could barely see anything through my tears. The world broke down into crude blotches of flaming orange light and fluctuating shadow. I retreated clumsily away from the growing heat, the noxious smoke. I circled around to the darkness of the trees behind the burning houses.

Fire engulfed the nearest mansion, unfurling into a writhing mat of red-hot vines. Glass shattered.

I no longer knew how to make sense of what I heard now. Air gusting with a vengeance. A popping like a thousand knuckles getting cracked in succession.

I'd chosen these manors for a reason. They were empty, if not abandoned. They stood apart from the rest of town. The blazing hill (or at least an eerie redness lighting up the lower part of the sky) would be visible to anyone who looked outside.

Also—I'll admit I couldn't pass up a chance to vandalize real estate owned by some of the richest Osmanthian mage clans. I'm not that mature.

Anyway, if there was one thing this town had plenty of, it was fresh water. Just look at all the towers. They could quench a fire of any size. No way it would burn too fast for them to tame it.

Right?

Counting from the moment I first dropped a lit match, about twenty minutes passed by the time the town horn blasted a warning. Compared to the usual horns, its pitch was low to the point of being borderline toneless. They might've switched to a different instrument altogether, so as to avoid agitating sensitive primevals.

Bells jangled. The deeper horn grunted its urgent call again and again. I felt it more as a rumbling in my body than an actual sound in my ears.

I breathed through the sleeve of Wist's sweatshirt. I retreated deeper into the shadows.

I couldn't tell how the Queen would choose to handle continuity from one day to the next. If everyone still remembered this fire tomorrow, it might not take them long to find the arsonist. The last thing I needed was to get thrown in the dinky town jail. I hadn't done a perfect job of covering my tracks, but I could at least attempt to avoid getting caught in the act.

A thundering sound thumped the ground, as if dozens of panicking primevals had begun stampeding away from the flames. Hoarse shouts penetrated the crackling air. I licked acrid-tasting teeth as people climbed up the hill, dark wavering silhouettes. They yelled instructions at each other. They were coming dangerously close.

I smelled like fire from head to toe. Dung-infused fire, no less. Maybe I ought to dunk myself in the river before slinking back to the inn. Or should I pretend to have just arrived here? Should I run over and offer my help? Surely it was too frenetic a situation for anyone to keep tabs on whether my story made sense.

I edged back around the side of the estate.

The wind and flames and bells and horns and voices went silent. So silent that for a few befuddled seconds, I thought something had exploded. I thought my hearing had blown out.

I raised my arms and waved at the nearest figures, willing them to notice me.

No one reacted. They stopped running. They turned around, as precise as soldiers doing an about-face. They walked serenely away, their backs to the burning mansions.

The three-house fire winked out like a stone light getting lidded.

I wiped searing wetness from my real eye and my fake eye. The sudden erasure of the flames left me blinded. The moss-carpeted ground beneath my feet looked the same as the inky sky.

But I felt her there. Her irritation needled at me like a mosquito bite. It was the first emotion she'd let bleed through our bond since becoming the Queen.

"You do care," I said.

A hand on the back of my shoulder turned me around. It wasn't gentle. "About what?" asked the Queen.

"About preserving the town in a certain state of upkeep. About not disturbing the populace."

This was extremely useful information. My only regret was that I couldn't get away with using the same trick twice. So much for my career as an arsonist.

"You could have killed them," the Queen said. "You *would* have killed them."

"I targeted uninhabited houses."

"Fires spread."

"But you came to stop it," I said innocently.

"You had no guarantee I would—"

She didn't continue.

She had her hair tied loosely over her left shoulder. It took on a pearlescent quality in the dark. Almost luminous. The way white flowers shine in moonlight.

I couldn't make out much of her face, but it was easy enough to imagine her expression (or the lack thereof).

"Do I smell?" I asked sweetly.

She reached down and pinched the hem of my dress-length sweatshirt. (Well—technically it was her sweatshirt.) She stretched it out to one side, then the other, forming a shape like the wing-flaps of a flying squirrel.

"Please wash this," she said.

"If you want your laundry done, do it yourself."

"You're the one who drenched it in smoke."

I shrugged, unrepentant. "How else was I supposed to get your attention?"

"You set the town on fire to get my attention?"

"Would anything less drastic have worked?"

The next time she spoke, there was an edge of contempt in her voice. That alone set her apart from my Wist, whose impassive tone wouldn't have shifted even in the face of wanton arson.

"That's the thought process of a teenage delinquent. How old are you? Certainly over thirty."

Was she joking? "You can't have forgotten," I said.

She always celebrated my birthday even while refusing to do anything for her own. It'd be my birthday in just a couple of days, assuming the equinox ever came. She knew that. We'd talked about spending it together right here in Bittercress.

"It's been a while," she replied.

"It's been a day since you last saw me."

I rubbed the skin around my prosthetic eye. The reek of smoke had left the air. Blasted away by magic, I suppose, together with the soaring flames.

"Listen," I told the Queen. "Have dinner with me tomorrow. It's not like you've got anything else to do, right?"

Irritation pierced through our bond again.

"You don't enjoy spending time with me?" I said plaintively. "Like it or not, we're still bondmates."

"If you're trying to escape, you're going about it very poorly."

I pressed my palms together. "I promise to make dinner entertaining. If you don't agree to come, I'll just keep setting new fires all night and all day."

"Is this how you usually get dates?" the Queen inquired. "With arson?"

"You tell me. You know our history."

(Did she, though? I was beginning to wonder.)

The Queen's long tail of white hair rose like an uncoiling snake.

I quailed. She arrested me with a couple light fingers on the side of my neck. Her hair landed on my other shoulder, much heavier than the touch of her hand.

She stooped and said in a voice so even that I could've believed I was with black-haired Wist again: "No more fires, Clematis. You'll regret it."

I swallowed. Couldn't stop her from feeling it.

"Don't forget about our date," I said feebly.

She laughed at me. Not out loud. Harsh amusement vibrated down the length of our bond. Then she was gone, spirited away by a magic so deft that I could hardly detect it.

I let out a shaky breath. I had my prosthetic in, but my orbital bones ached with a sensation of emptiness.

Normally, with perception as good as mine, observing magic at work was like watching a play from backstage. I'd have a clear view of the ropes and fog machines, the flatness of the backdrops, the choreographed changes of costume and scenery.

When a mage ported in front of me, I wouldn't just watch them physically disappear. I'd see their magic threads go off with the bright snap of a firecracker.

Wist was no exception. She knew how to disguise her magic branches while they lay dormant, but not when she actively put them to use.

The Queen, on the other hand—she made me doubt my most powerful sense. She'd extinguished an entire conflagration with a glance. I only saw the outcome of her enchantment, the darkness and chilly air after the fire came to an unceremonious end. I hadn't actually perceived the raw blast of magic she used to make it happen.

This felt far worse, in a way, than losing half my physical sight.

A gifted mage could deceive my eyes and ears and nose and tongue and skin with artful hallucinations. But even when I couldn't trust anything else, I'd always been able to trust my magic perception.

I was a healer, incapable of fighting back with magic of my own. But if an enemy used magecraft on me, at least I would know what was happening.

Was this why they called her the Queen of the Void?

Looking at her did give the impression of gazing into a void. A black box. I sensed her overwhelming web of magic branches. For the most part, I couldn't sense when or how she used them.

Wist's magic—so easily tangled, so prone to torment—had always been more expressive than her voice or her stance or her face. Her magic writhed and creaked and contorted itself even when her eyes remained blank of either pleasure or pain.

In contrast, I had no clue what the Queen felt. What she was thinking. Or how far her mastery over her magic extended.

Compared to my Wist, she feigned more emotion when she spoke. She let her annoyance with me drip down the fragile thread of our bond. But all of that was wholly deliberate. Her walls remained stronger and higher than the resurrected walls around town.

17

Day 2. I made it through the night with the help of more sleeping pills. The innkeeper had lent me a generous supply.

As I drowsed off, little feet rushed by my door. Small and scampering.

I got up to check the hall. There was never anyone there.

I'd believe in a ghost that had enough moxie to come right up to me and announce itself. These pitter-pattering footsteps from invisible children didn't count.

Day 2 was still the day before the equinox. Three days before my birthday.

Early in the morning, I went to peek at the mansions on the hill. No damage. No ashes. No evidence of malicious arson. I asked if anyone remembered a fire. Only Lester the hermit had any idea what I meant.

I found him in the process of extricating himself from a pack of bored children. After ripping off half his fake beard, they tired of harassing him.

Lester and his pint-size bullies were on a verdant green walkway, one of many that crisscrossed all over town. A wisteria trellis grew overhead, ungroomed tendrils stretching every which way, seed pods dangling.

The kids didn't care for his wisdom. They showed more interest in the rocks that lined the path, which were carved with a variety of stylized faces. Gaping grins, turgid anger, comic disgust.

Lester put a cloth mask over the mangled remains of his beard, protecting his modesty. It was a black mask with six red circles.

Which didn't necessarily mean he had anything to do with the stranger who'd come to see Wist. Everyone had access to these masks. I'd hauled around boxes of them for the innkeeper.

His audience rapidly diminished. They scattered, as unpredictable in trajectory as foraging beach crabs. They hopped over the emotional rocks. They darted off to catch bugs with handheld nets, or to practice tromping around on sets of child-sized wooden stilts.

Lester maintained a bracing grip on his grand walking stick. He kept reciting poetry at their backs, undeterred. This might have been his secret technique for shooing them off.

"The sky ships sail from land to land, across the mangled sea.

"There's a hole in the ground that no one has found. The sky ships sail for me.

"The sky ships sail from land to land, across the mangled sea.

"The crossroads are bitter, the crossroads are sweet. The sky ships sail for me.

"The sky ships sail from land to land, across the mangled sea.

"Aerials fall like stones in a siege. The sky ships sail for thee."

No one clapped. A kid in a blue shirt vaulted past Lester as if he were a piece of furniture, yelling incoherently. Additional shrieks erupted in the distance. More kids—or perhaps just a particularly noisy group of birds.

"Come up with that yourself?" I said once the children had dissipated.

"It's a Bittercress nursery rhyme."

"Charming. One of the classics?"

"People in other towns wouldn't know it."

"You remember it from childhood?"

He shook his head gravely. "I'm not originally from around here."

"Is that why you're the only resident willing to give out your name?"

"Perhaps." He pivoted, preparing to stump away alone. All this human interaction might be threatening his hard-won status as a hermit.

I quickly moved to block the way. "Most adults wouldn't end up learning new nursery rhymes by heart. You must have quite a good memory."

He pointed at his (confusingly smooth) forehead. "Used to have more of a scholarly bent."

"How about now? Been losing your touch?"

"I still keep archives in my mind." He sounded mildly miffed. "I've memorized all the classics of Manglelander literature."

I asked if he recalled anything unusual from last night.

He frowned. Now he looked more like a properly old and wrinkly hermit. "Parts of the sky went light. I smelled smoke. Nothing came of it in the end."

Satisfied, I let Lester resume his solitary walk. The kids never did return to give him back their stolen handfuls of his mutilated beard. They'd kept the hair as a trophy—or just dumped it in the dirt somewhere, forgotten.

I wasn't sure how much I could count on his memory. But it might prove useful someday.

It was still morning when I finished preparing to explore the caverns in earnest. Some of the entrances I'd found (like the old well) were easily ruled out. I ended up selecting one located behind the water tower shaped like a lighthouse. This was an entrance favored by lantern-herders. As such, I figured it had to be reasonably hospitable to human passengers. It also attracted a lot of primeval traffic, which was important for my purposes.

I'd hunted down a few lantern-herders. None seemed willing to let me shadow them. They didn't approach the caverns much during the day; they got most of their business done before dawn and after dusk. Besides, they had no interest in leaving town.

In lieu of a human guide, I'd follow primevals through the caves. They knew how to get in and out of Bittercress. All I needed to do was keep up.

Hopefully their paths wouldn't be reliant on powerful hind legs and claws. I'd never fancied myself much of a rock climber.

The faux lighthouse towered near the eastern end of the river. It was a coquettish white structure, stunning from a distance. On closer inspection, it turned out to be badly in need of a good powerwashing. Wind and rain had coated the base with a fresco of powdery brown dust. Lantern plants spilled from grimy pots lined up in front of the decorative tower door.

The now-familiar town horn rang out from somewhere to the west. That instant, the rocks around the tower yawned soundlessly open, revealing a staircase studded with stone lights.

Three primevals slipped down the stairs, one after another, as if sneaking into a castle basement. I hastened after them.

I couldn't afford to lose sight of their thick scaly tails. My sense of direction was nothing to boast about. Without anyone to follow, I'd get lost in no time.

I'd brought my multicolored chalk kit—the one I'd bought at the general store—so I could mark the cavern walls as I went. Spend too long on this, though, and the primevals would outpace me.

Halfway down the stairs came a wide landing. Almost a room unto itself. Semicircular walls bowed away on either side. River lanterns rested in cubbies and hung in bundles from racks.

They appeared to have been deposited rather hastily. I could imagine a lantern-herder sprinting down the steps earlier this morning, unloading lanterns they'd collected from the riverbank, then dashing away again in hopes of making it out before the entrance closed.

The primevals kept descending. The stairs beyond the lantern depository had no radiant stone lights. Just empty sockets. A terrible tripping hazard.

I'd brought a stone of my own from my room at the inn. I wedged the base in my Jacian bag. Part of the crystal stuck out to light my way.

It barely fit, and the weight strained my shoulder. Unlike the handheld light we'd carried during our original trip to the caverns, this was essentially a nightstand lamp. Not meant to be portable.

Something crunched at the bottom of the stairs. The corridor was very narrow—the primevals' artichoke-like scales scraped both sides. The ceiling rose unsettlingly high.

The stuff I kept stepping on felt too soft to be bits of stone. Once I'd caught up with the primevals, I risked looking down.

Old dry wisteria petals covered the path all around me. They'd curled and faded to a much bluer color than the purple everyone knew them for.

They looked exactly like a scattering of blue-gray gravel. In fact, with each subsequent step, they grew as hard as gravel under my shoes.

I could've questioned where the petals came from, and why they'd lingered so long out of season, and if they'd ever been petals at all. I was definitely treading on rocks now.

Then again, my mirror back at the inn had gotten in the habit of weeping fragrant oil whenever I attempted to look in it. At this point,

I'd shrug and accept whatever peculiarities came my way. Bittercress was a strange magicless town ruled by a strange and magical Queen.

I'd hoped the geography of the cave interior might bear more of a resemblance to the original entrance. The one rife with glowworms. The one an hour's ride away. I suppose that would've been too much to ask.

If I could get my bearings, I would've liked to search for the part of the caves that Wist had fled on our first visit.

The part of the caves she'd secretly gone back to see without me.

The part of the caves that had made her a queen.

The passageway began widening. The primevals thumped ahead faster. I trotted to keep up. No time to mark the walls with chalk.

Then—as the primevals loped with heavy steps into the darkness—I stopped.

For the first time in days, I could sense where the thread of my bond led.

Dawdle any longer, and I'd lose the primevals. I could follow my bond instead, trace it like a string meant to guide me through a labyrinth.

The primevals would lead me out of Bittercress.

The bond would lead me to Wist.

If I followed the bond, I'd have to come back later and do this all over again. I'd have to jog after a different set of primevals to find out how they circumvented the town walls. Wist—the Queen—might throw more obstacles my way in the meantime.

But my ultimate goal wasn't simply to escape Bittercress. It was to do something about the Queen herself. If I escaped right now, how could I devise an effective strategy from outside the walls? I'd learned nothing about what drove her. What had become of her down in the caves. Even if I succeeded in rallying Osmanthian help, would it ever be enough to defeat or save the woman they all revered as their Kraken?

More than anything, I *wanted* to follow the tautness of the bond between us. Above ground, I hadn't been able to trace it anywhere. I'd been lost.

I couldn't hear the primevals anymore. My feet were already moving toward a side passage. Well, that decided it.

In the space beyond, rock undulated to form elaborate hanging curtains. This portion of the caverns felt excruciatingly familiar. As if time had folded back on itself like an accordion. As if Wist and I had never left the caves after our seemingly truncated first trip.

The only difference now was the weight of my bag, laden down by the stone equivalent of a small desk lamp. And the fact that I walked alone. No one would catch me if I tripped.

I went slowly. I reluctantly clutched at shiny-wet stalagmites for support.

Not everything was the same as before. The bond pulled me through drier, smoother-walled caves covered in a dense matrix of stenciled hand shapes. Splayed fingers outlined by a shadowy spray of red-brown paint.

Other chambers were caved with intricate reliefs. Some looked as though they'd been damaged in battle—faces bashed in, brutal claw marks marring the scenery. I wondered if primevals were to blame.

The temperature dropped. I kept thinking I'd seen my breath. I hugged my heavy bag closer, though the stone light gave off zero warmth. My footsteps sounded too quiet, or too loud—never sure which.

I found her in a cave full of water.

18

I HAD NO IDEA what kind of rock I was looking at here. Dark and slick as ice, with a surface like chipped flint. Definitely not limestone or dolomite.

My bond with Wist drew me toward a jagged crack in the glassy black cave wall. It looked just wide enough to squeeze through sideways. There would be a very real risk of getting stuck in the middle.

I peeked through the crack as if trying to use an apartment peephole. My poor left eye strained and strained to no avail. If I wanted to see the other side, I'd have to climb through.

The problem was my bulging bag. I adjusted the strap to make it as long as possible, then laid it across the stony threshold of the vertical crack. After shimmying through—rocks pinching me in all sorts of places—I crouched down to grope for the strap again.

My fingertips almost couldn't reach it. I had to wedge my shoulder against the opening as if attempting to dislocate it. But I succeeded in the end. (At retrieving my bag, not dislocating my shoulder.) With the stone light back in my arms, I could finally see where I'd ended up.

It was a breathtakingly humongous cavity. A natural cathedral. A smattering of dim glowworms—or something more sinister disguised as glowworms—lurked in crevices of the far-off ceiling.

The cave floor curved down like a water-filled basin. A rocky shore ringed the edges of the central pool. Or lake.

That meager stone shelf was where I stood now, my back to the cave wall.

The Queen was waist-deep in the middle of the water.

She faced away from me. She wore soaking white clothes—from the looks of it, the sort of button-down shirt that Wist would pack for a trip but never actually use. Her hair fell loose, trailing into the silent pool.

Was it inky black water, or clear water reflecting the darkness of the rock dome overhead? Was it even water at all?

No need to announce myself. She had to know I was there. Our bond went both ways. If I could feel myself approaching her, then she could feel me too. Besides, I'd made my fair share of noise as I wiggled through the opening.

I might not have been able to call out to her even if I wanted to. My voice withered in my throat.

The black water was moving. It climbed her in ropes like fire climbing the facade of a house. It pierced her back. It sought out her core.

The water healed her magic.

Correction—a dark substance healed her. It was a solid that moved like a liquid, or a liquid that moved like the wind. With its currents, it separated the fine threads of her inner magic. It pressured her branches into bending the other way, squeezed them almost to the point of breaking. In the process, it undid every last hint of tangling.

This was like a physical therapist ruthlessly breaking bone after bone in order to fix your alignment. Like a cardiac surgeon cutting out a patient's heart and then congratulating them on being free of disease.

In other words—it worked, after a fashion. But it looked so cruel that my head spun to see it, and I didn't even have magic of my own. I'd never felt that particular pain for myself.

Even if a human healer were terribly sadistic—even on the off chance that they figured out how to use their abilities to cause pain—they wouldn't do it like this. Such rare prodigies might try to hurt instead of heal. They wouldn't hurt a mage in the name of healing their magic.

This pool of shadow healed Wist with the innocent efficiency of a heartless machine. It bulldozed its way down the most brutally direct path to straighten out her crooked branches.

Wist didn't say a word. She didn't cry out for anyone to come save her. The bond stretched between us like an invisible clothesline—thank god that the water ignored it—but no tinge of agony or emotion trickled across it.

My brain still felt like it was in a centrifuge. Time slowed as my dizziness gathered speed. Dazed steps brought me to the brink of the shore.

That's right: we were bonded. She shouldn't have been able to accept healing from anyone other than me. They could try, but it wouldn't work. It wasn't supposed to work.

Could I stop the water from healing her?

When I came up to the water's edge, I realized she wasn't as still as I'd thought. She held herself—her fingers gripped the sides of her shoulders. She held herself as if she were about to crumble.

For an instant, something in my missing right eye glimpsed an inconceivable abyss of pain. I saw it in the space behind my prosthetic. Magical pain that would never leave a mark on her body, and that no one else would ever witness. Pain more crushing than the inherent burden of having that much magic in the first place—the burden of being the Kraken.

This was many times worse. Like the difference between diving a hundred feet deep and plunging all the way down to the alien realm of the ocean floor. Like the difference between purgatory and hell.

If she wasn't screaming, it was only because she couldn't. If she remained standing, it was only because she had nowhere to fall.

I broke. I'd wade into that cursed-looking water if it were the only way to reach her.

"Wist—"

"Stay back!"

Her voice resounded like a blow to my head. Inside and outside me. I actually staggered.

She'd half-turned to glare at me. The vast dark water—although it definitely wasn't water—began to drain.

It swirled heavily around her, making a distant roar akin to wind or thunder. It swirled *into* her, absorbing through her pores, streaming like reverse tears up through the corners of her eyes. It jammed itself under her fingernails. Black slugs of inky material climbed in her ears, her nostrils, her mouth.

It was all over before I could catch my breath.

She stood stranded at the center of a bone-dry hollow. An empty lake with no indication that water had ever filled it. The cave floor around her bulged with twisted rock formations. Shapes reminiscent of old, old vines. Or loose-spilt intestines.

Her veins briefly looked as black as the stone beneath her. Feathery lines like buried tattoos showed through the skin of her wrists and hands and neck and face.

Then that, too, faded—a fleeting afterimage.

I'd stumbled and landed on my butt, though I couldn't remember when. My legs must've given out. Sharp edges of rock pressed dents in my palms.

I strung my ungainly bag over my shoulder and lowered myself to the dry lake bed. It took a combination of clambering and sliding.

Before I could approach Wist, she ported in front of me. She trapped me with my back to the steep slope of the shore.

She was still very much the Queen, white hair and all. I should've stayed up on the stony bank so I could look down at her.

"That thing you absorbed," I said. "Was that the Void?"

She tilted her head by half a degree and regarded me as if the answer were obvious. I suppose it was.

"Is this how you first … met it? You found a black lake deep in the caves? What'd you do, drink from it?"

"It isn't black," said the Queen. "The Void has no color."

"It looked like liquid ink."

"It looks dark because we're in a cave. Because it's always been in the caves." She gathered her hair, tying it into a low tail. "The Void has no inherent appearance of its own. It doesn't look like anything until someone perceives it. Think of it as a mimic."

"Is the Void mimicking you?"

"I took it in. Not the other way around."

"Did it steal your hair color? Did it want to match your eyes?"

"You shouldn't be down here," she said.

"No one forbade me."

"I could."

"Will you, though? I thought you wanted me to make things interesting."

The Queen let out a very small sigh.

"Take a seat," I said. "You seem exhausted." Just calling it how I see it. I gestured at the strange ropey rocks as if this cave were my living room.

She didn't take me up on my offer. Her once-crisp white shirt was still wet enough to stick to her skin. The pitch-black water of the Void hadn't left a single stain on it.

Had I been able to sense her location due to something unique about the caves? Or because she'd been too weakened by the Void's merciless healing to keep throwing off the figurative compass needle of our bond?

I didn't ask. Instead, I said: "Never thought my job was at risk of automation."

The Queen blinked.

"Mages can't heal themselves. Bonded mages can only take healing from their bondmate. How do you explain"—I gestured wildly—"whatever just happened? Didn't look pleasant."

"The Void is part of me." She sounded too tired to deflect. "But not entirely. It isn't a mage, and it isn't a healer. It isn't human."

"So you've threaded your way through some kind of one-in-a-million loophole? Congrats on making history. You've certainly suffered for it."

"Did you enjoy watching?"

That right there was the voice of my Wist. No emotion whatsoever.

"Yeah," I bit out. "Enjoyed it so much that I almost dove into the water for a closer look. Can't imagine why you stopped me."

"You always did like making me break down and cry."

"Two problems with that statement," I said. "For one thing, you weren't breaking down at all. You held it in."

"What's the other problem?"

"It wasn't my doing. You think I'd like seeing some kind of eldritch monstrosity torture *my* mage?"

"It was healing me."

"Even worse!" I cried.

My voice echoed. The Queen gazed down at me without further comment.

"I'm not jealous," I added stiffly.

"Of course not."

I hoisted my bag up to better light her face. "I've seen the Void for myself now. Don't you think it's about time to tell me what it is? And where it came from?"

"I won't answer without compensation."

"I mean, I don't really have anything to offer you except my feminine wiles." I motioned at the intensely uncomfortable-looking rocks. "Do you really want to—"

She ignored my innuendo. "Don't just ask. Bring a theory or two of your own, Clematis. Use your brain."

"Sounds like something I would say," I remarked. "Well, if you insist. I can spin theories in my sleep. I'll cough up a smorgasbord of hypotheses right on the spot. Watch me."

I tilted my head back. Glowworms winked down from the unreachable ceiling.

The cold made me fidgety. This deep in the caves, my utility jacket didn't do much to keep me from shivering.

When I looked at the Queen again, she was in a chair.

An office chair.

A very nice one, no doubt. The sort that might cost the equivalent of a month's rent for a spacious urban apartment. But still very much an office chair.

"Is that your throne?" I asked.

"Don't worry about it."

"Do I get one?"

"No."

She crossed her legs. The tip of her naked toe touched my shin. She was barefoot, yet as clean as if she'd just stepped out of a bath.

"Right," I said. Wouldn't let her distract me. "Theories on the origins of the Void. They say the first Kraken came to Katashiro Caverns toward the end of her known life. Maybe she died here in this very cave. Maybe the Void formed as she faded from our world. Like the black hole left by a dying star."

"Is that how black holes form?" the Queen inquired.

"I hope so. Don't poke holes in my metaphor."

She flexed her ankles as though stretching after a long day of office work. Her toes landed on my leg again.

"Or," I said, trying not to look down, "it could be related to the Kraken—without being related to her death."

"How?"

"Supposedly she faced her personal darkness in Katashiro Caverns. Maybe she shed something. An overwhelming hunger, or power, or some other inner demon. She left it here to fester and roil without her. That's what I saw bending your magic. Streaming back inside you to hide beneath your skin."

"You think my predecessor left a parasite in the caves," said the Queen, "and now it roosts in me."

"Something along those lines."

She looked bored. "Anyone could think of an explanation hinging on the original Kraken."

"Pretty good for something I whipped up ten seconds, no?"

"It's the obvious assumption when you're looking the second Kraken in the face."

"Sometimes obvious is right." I tapped her knee until she stopped tickling me with her foot. She might not have been aware she was doing it.

Her chair creaked as she shifted her weight. It was, in all fairness, an extremely refined and expensive-sounding creak.

"Very well," I said haughtily. "Want something different? Forget the first Kraken. Go further back. All the way back to the lost civilization of Cressians."

"Hard to know what's true about them and what's a fable."

"Sounds like they sacrificed mages." I pretended to stab the air. "A lot of mages. Who's to say they didn't sacrifice them—or at least dispose of them—in these handy-dandy caverns?"

The Queen examined her nails. "Not sure what you're implying."

"The Void could be a millennium's worth of pent-up mage resentment. Or Cressian malice. The ghost of all those sacrifices. The ghost of an entire civilization. Is it a coincidence that mages keep mysteriously disappearing around these parts? Even in recent decades."

"You think the Void has been taking them?" the Queen said in undertone.

"Maybe the Void is the last living remnant of the Cressian culture of sacrifice. It keeps going and going long after every single Cressian vanished from the earth and skies. It mechanically snatches mages, without any feeling or thought behind it. It mechanically latched on to you, too."

"Is that all?"

I hesitated. I did have other theories. There were some topics, however, that I didn't necessarily want to broach deep underground, trapped in this basin of nameless stone together with the Queen of the Void and maliciously glimmering glowworms.

"Look," I told her. "The Void seems like something very strange and very powerful. Something we have no proper name for, and no way to categorize. Something almost as singular as the Kraken."

"There've been two Krakens," she reminded me.

"Let's just hope there won't be two Voids to deal with, huh? Anyway— it might be connected to all of the above. The first Kraken's life and death. The ancient Cressians and their dead mages. Et cetera."

"You're essentially correct," the Queen replied. "The exact origins of the Void may not matter much in the end."

"So we could've skipped that entire conversation. Thanks."

She leaned on the right arm of her office chair, unrepentant. I'd have been freezing in damp clothes and bare feet, but she didn't appear to feel the cold. Her toe traced a reproachful line from my knee down to the top of my ankle.

"You tire me as much as the Void does."

"Wow," I uttered. "Stab me right in the gut, why don't you?"

"You don't sound hurt."

"You aren't the only one who's good at putting on a brave front, Your Highness."

I scooted to one side and crouched near the arm of her fancy chair. I'd had enough of getting poked by her foot.

"If being everyone's Queen is what drains you," I said, "you can stop acting like a queen around me. Let down your hair, so to speak. I won't badmouth you to the townspeople. I won't start a movement to guillotine the monarchy. You think I've got time for that?"

She didn't roll her eyes, but I could tell that some part of her very much wanted to. I'd consider that a victory. Although I would've preferred to make her laugh.

"Do you have a plan for getting out of here?" she asked in a tone of foreboding.

"I always have a plan."

"The caverns close shortly after each horn plays."

"I know that's how it works up in town. Decided to see for myself if it would work the same way on the inside."

"You're content with being stuck here for hours?"

"If you'll keep me company, yes," I said brightly.

"I refuse."

I made a show of clutching my heart. The Queen acted as if I hadn't. "Remember how to get back to the entrance?"

"………"

Her right hand left her armrest. She touched my head, a priestess giving absolution.

"Don't do this again," she said in an empty voice. She sounded exactly like my Wist.

19

I crouched alone on a bridge. The shadows of swooping mangle rays formed strange dappled patterns. Very different from the sun falling through leaves.

Strains of music wafted from the riverbank. Not an accordion. This time it sounded more like someone plucking at a lyre.

Magic had banished me from the caverns so smoothly that I'd failed to sense the transition. I would see the Queen again tonight—assuming she was one to keep promises.

Every bridge in Bittercress had a name inscribed on both ends of it. Sometimes on an ornate metal placard. Sometimes carved directly into heavy stone pylons.

This bridge occupied a position roughly halfway down the river. It was thus called (most unimaginatively) the Middle Bridge. Across the street stood a small post commemorating the true midpoint of town. Dead center.

It was so much warmer here, compared to down in the caves, that I began to sweat from sheer confusion. I walked off the bridge and strolled a bit to reorient myself.

Every day was the day before the equinox. Yet it was never the exact same day as yesterday. Time neither moved forward nor turned in a circle, recycling. The weather and temperature fluctuated. People's actions changed subtly, though not drastically.

This morning, I'd wandered through the first floor of the inn before taking off to start my day. In the sitting room with a sunken hearth, I'd seen boxes of black cloth masks and piles of coin necklaces and stacks of blank wards. The supplies I'd helped the innkeeper carry over from the holy storehouse.

Some things did change from one day to the next. Almost enough to make me wonder if time *was* advancing. The only evidence I had to the contrary: the verbal testimony of all the townspeople. Everyone here insisted on every day being the same date.

Wouldn't it be better if the Queen had only fiddled with their sense of time, and not with the flow of time itself? Not an admirable use of magic, to be sure. She'd definitely be in violation of the international Mage Conventions. Still, at least it would mean she hadn't broken another one of the great taboos.

But the spider lilies never bloomed, though they kept looking ready to pop any day now. My black-dyed hair showed zero sign of growing out, either. Maybe it was too soon to know for sure. Or maybe time really had come to a standstill, avoiding action like an army bound to a truce.

I spent the rest of the afternoon preparing for dinner. Unexpectedly, everyone believed me when I said I had a date with their Queen. They filled my arms with fresh-picked vegetables. More than two people could eat in an entire week, much less a single meal.

In the middle of gathering groceries, I got hold of the town doctor. I did a bit of prying about how they'd treated past cases of food poisoning, bad mushrooms, and the like.

"Not that I'm planning on doing any foraging," I lied blithely.

Later, I snuck past the mortician and dug up several spider lilies from the cemetery. Stems and bulbs and all. None had actually bloomed yet. I picked dandelions (aka devilsmilk) too, in case anyone asked what I'd been rummaging around for.

All the while, my mind lingered down in the caverns.

I'm a healer of unprecedented skill, if I do say so myself. And I do. Frequently.

It had been equal parts humbling and unnerving to watch the Void treat Wist's magic. To watch it take over my job.

For all my resentment of the Osmanthian mageocracy, I wasn't interested in torturing mages in order to heal them. I wasn't interested in healing any mage except Wist, if I could help it. So I couldn't see myself replicating the Void's approach as-is. But it had given me a lot of ideas for (less painful) new techniques.

The innkeeper helped me cook dinner. Once she saw my excess of vegetables and learned that I'd be dining with the Queen, she insisted on coming up with a menu.

Rather than work in the tavern, we used a smaller kitchen in the inn. She let me book a private dining room on one of the upper floors. She hummed blissfully as she hung dry flowers and pasted fresh paper wards on the walls.

We—well, she—prepared simmered sweet taro, salty broiled river fish, a salad of crisp cider pear and pale thin-shaved roots, squash of various colors, and meat wrapped like a present in other types of thin-sliced flesh.

I'd never been adept at distinguishing between different types of meat, whether cooked or raw. I tried to think of critters I'd noticed around town. "Is it duck?" I asked. "Goose?"

"It's not poultry," the innkeeper answered absentmindedly. She sliced purple radishes with incredible speed and accuracy.

"You don't slaughter primevals for meat, do you?"

"They taste extremely unpleasant."

"Don't think I've seen typical livestock anywhere in Bittercress," I said. "But no one passes through the walls, either. Including suppliers. Do they?"

Her knife never stopped. "The Queen provides."

I really didn't like the sound of that. I shut my mouth and decided to leave well enough alone. For now.

Eventually the innkeeper apologized and excused herself. She had her own job to attend to; soon the tavern would need to open for dinner. I graciously sent her on her way.

Once she was gone, I rolled up my sleeves. I got to work on my hidden stash of spider lilies.

I washed them as best I could, then shredded their stems and buds and bulbs into a semblance of a salad. Together with my dandelion leaves. I drowned it all in an excess of sweet creamy dressing. Plus a handful of toasted pine nuts. Just to make it look more like an actual dish.

I didn't taste it as I went. I chose to trust in my epicurean instincts.

The kitchen and private dining room had been on their best behavior for the innkeeper. As soon as she left, though, the walls started bleeding backwards.

In the kitchen, this took the form of white grout turning red-brown. Bloody lines traced a path between clean square tiles like rats trying to find their way out of a scientist's maze.

I pretended not to see anything.

In the dining room, meanwhile, blood (or something trying very hard to resemble blood) seeped out of seams in the wood-paneled walls like sap from a tree. It inched in lines toward the ceiling in lieu of streaking down toward the floor, and moved with all the haste of your average garden slug. On the plus side, it didn't seem liable to drip on our plates. Nor did it dye any of the innkeeper's crisp new paper wards.

The Queen appeared right on time. Not only that, she ported her office chair in with her. It was a poor match for the rest of the furniture.

I spared her my complaints about her chair. Instead I pointed at the fresh-stained walls. "Is this how you set the mood?"

"Do you want more?"

"It's fine just the way it is," I said. "Very tasteful. Enough blood to be noticeable. Not quite enough to overwhelm the smell of our food. Mm-mm."

She surveyed the crowded array of mismatched serving dishes. "You made this yourself?"

"Kind of," I answered humbly. "You could say that."

"Was that the best use of your time today?"

"Anything to please my Queen."

She made a quiet noise of distaste. I acted like I hadn't heard a peep. I snatched her empty plate out from under her nose and began filling it. I'm such a great hostess.

"I did have a question about the meat, though," I said.

"The meat?"

I pointed with a pair of tongs. "What is it? Rather, what *isn't* it?"

"What are you asking?"

"Blood crawling up the walls. Plates painted with patterns of fingerprints. Makes me worry a little, you know? I don't want to become a cannibal. At least not by accident."

"We've had this conversation."

"That was before you became the Queen."

She studied the platter of meat for a long moment. "It isn't human flesh."

"Then what kind of meat is it?"

"Venison patties wrapped in bacon."

"Why wouldn't anyone just say that? They never tell me what meat they're serving at the tavern, either."

"Maybe the entire town likes watching you squirm."

"You made this town the way it is," I muttered.

"Your presence shapes it, too."

"Don't blame the victim, Your Majesty. It isn't becoming."

She'd arrived after sunset. Crickets trilled through open windows. Occasional bursts of good-natured noise spilled from the tavern, too. Earthen belly laughs; snippets of song.

The Queen didn't have much of an appetite, but she dutifully ate one bite of each item I'd put on her plate. Then she went back for a second bite, all in precisely the same order as her first round. I wondered if she could taste it.

She glanced up. I'd made no effort to hide my staring.

"You coerced me into coming to dinner," she said.

"Still mad at me for starting fires?"

"What's your real objective?"

"Thought we could enjoy a nice date," I said virtuously.

"I never promised to stay for long."

I'd been imitating her, sampling bite after bite of each different dish. The spider lily salad was nothing to write home about, but it did a good enough job of blending in with the rest.

"Tell me what you want," I said.

"I want you to impress me," she replied.

"Am I not impressive?"

"You don't seem any closer to escaping than you were two days ago."

I raised my chin. "Wouldn't be much of an escape plot if you could already see through it. Where's your trust in me?"

For the next few minutes, we ate in silence.

The Queen stopped first. Every utensil on the table—the large spoons and forks and tongs stuck in serving plates, and the spare cutlery framing our place settings—had begun shaking as though in the throes of a one-room private earthquake.

She gave them a look of mild reproach. They ceased their rattling. Then she turned that same look of reproach on me. It felt odd to see such emotion on Wist's face, however muted.

"Spider lilies are incredibly toxic," she said.

"I'm surprised you know that."

"Why are we eating them?"

"Wonder how long the poison takes to kick in," I mused. "Just a couple more minutes? Or will the wait last for hours?"

The slow-moving blood on the walls suddenly fled. It vanished through cracks in the wood like the Void spiraling back inside the Queen's body. A faint undercooked scent of iron still hung in the air.

"I can understand why you would poison me." The Queen chose her words one by one. "This was a poor attempt."

"Hey. I didn't ask for criticism."

"What I can't understand is why you would poison yourself in the process."

I leaned forward. "You saved a bunch of empty burning mansions," I said. "Clearly you care about some things. I'm not about to set myself on fire, though."

"You planned this dinner solely so you could eat poison in front of me."

"Not *solely*."

"To see if I would save you."

"Actions speak louder than words," I said, with maximum smarminess.

I didn't like the way she glanced at her steak knife.

"When you put it like that," she murmured, "I suppose I'll let you suffer."

"I might die."

"I'm sure you made prior arrangements with the town doctor."

"Maybe," I admitted. "But do you really want to watch me go through violent indigestion? Or give up on escaping before the deadline?"

She clammed up.

"This is turning out to be a pretty depressing date," I said mournfully.

"You poisoned me, Clematis."

"You can counteract it with magic."

And she did. For both of us.

For once—straining my magic perception to its limits—I saw her do it.

A thread of her magic cast itself at my stomach like a fishing line. It went straight through me, painlessly, then retracted back inside her.

"That's awfully nice of you," I said sweetly. "Our Queen is such a merciful Queen."

She pushed the remainder of her toxic salad to the edge of her fingerprint-pattern plate. She didn't appear inclined to eat anything else, regardless of whether it had come in contact with the delicately shredded spider lilies.

I dragged a paper bag out from beneath my seat. I plunked its contents down on the table one by one: sealed cans of overly sweet fruit and fancy fish. Part of the haul I'd bought while shoplifting matches. Asa Clematis always thinks ahead.

"There you go," I said. "I know your taste. Knock yourself out."

She looked at the cans without moving.

"Want me to open them for you?" I asked. "Want me to act like a proper serving girl? I may not know how to curtsy to royalty, but—"

"Spare me," said the Queen.

She tapped a can of peaches as if ringing a desk bell to call a receptionist. The lid neatly peeled itself open.

She stabbed the top slice with her dessert fork. "Did you want any?"

"No, no," I said. "All yours."

"Are you trying to get on my good side?"

"Are canned peaches all it takes to get on your good side?"

I didn't expect her to answer. I contemplated the bluish dusk outside the open windows. Large flying insects kept bouncing off the screen.

I wasn't concerned about eavesdropping. The Queen wouldn't let any townspeople overhear things they shouldn't.

"There might be another explanation for the Void," I said.

She stopped eating her peaches.

I had my hands on the edge of the table. My fingers curled into my palms. "Every magical taboo has a consequence." I sounded almost as flat as my Wist. "No one can predict the exact consequences, because no one has the power to go around breaking those taboos in the first place. No one except a Kraken-class mage."

"Is this new information?" the Queen inquired.

"You've broken the taboo against deforming the flow of time. You're still breaking it. I don't know why. But maybe the consequences took the form of the Void. It's attached itself to you. It burdens you. It's changed you."

"Does this theory make sense to you?"

"No," I said. "It's paradoxical. If you bent the flow of time, you did it after leaving me alone in bed that night. After going to meet the Void. That means it birthed itself. That means the consequences appeared before you broke the taboo. The order of events is all messed up."

She stretched a napkin between her hands. I envisioned an assassin readying a garotte.

"A lot of things stop making surface-level sense once you trail your fingers in the river of time," she said.

I snatched her napkin away. Her fingers opened and closed midair as though puzzled to find themselves empty. I dropped the stolen napkin like a shroud over my remaining stack of canned food, all still sealed.

I glared at her until she met my gaze.

"Wist," I said. "Your Queenliness. Did we die when we visited the caves together?"

"...What?"

"Did we die there? Are we dead now? In reality, are we still down in the caves below the mountains an hour away? Have we been there all along?"

"No one died that day."

"We aren't ghosts, then? This isn't purgatory."

"You could call it purgatory," the Queen said, "but we aren't dead."

I released a loud sigh. "I can't speak for your queenly self, but it would take a lot to make my Wist violate one of the great taboos again. More than I can imagine. You were never proud of it. You deeply regretted the outcome."

"One small correction," she said.

"Yeah?"

"I did break the taboo about time."

"I know."

"That in itself didn't produce the Void."

"Oh, fantastic. Not only is there a Void to grapple with—we've also got other unknown consequences lying in wait for us."

"Those are much further away. Those will come in a different time."

"Have you been stopping time to avoid it?" I snarked. "That's a lovely bit of trickery. Right up my alley. No punishment can ever reach you if time never moves forward, huh?"

She let me rant without interjection.

I slumped in my chair, tuckered out. "All right," I conceded. "You broke a taboo. You claim it's not what created the Void. Sure. Heck, it could've spawned back when the first Kraken broke one of her own taboos. Or during the time of the Cressians. Maybe they were more powerful than anyone knew—powerful enough to bump up against the same set of taboos.

"Whatever. You said its origins aren't the important part. I'll buy that. So tell me. What the hell did the Void do to you?"

"Turn your question around," she said detachedly, "and you'll be closer to the truth."

What did you *do to the Void?*

My stomach began to feel as if the spider lily toxins were kicking in. As if she hadn't cured me at all. Acid at the back of my mouth reacted corrosively to the rich scent of still-hot food.

"I thought it forced itself on you. I thought it forced itself inside you." My right eye socket throbbed to the same tempo as my heart. "You chose to make the Void a part of you. You chose to—to become what you are now. Why?"

She rose, as though signaling an end to dinner. Her fine office chair rolled back an extra foot or two before stopping. She wore the same white button-down as in the caves, this time looking spotlessly dry.

"Will those questions help you find a way out of Bittercress?" she said. "Tomorrow is the third day."

"Worried about me? You're so sweet."

In the next moment, there was no one in front of her chair at all. I didn't see her move.

A beat too late, I realized from her shadow that she was now behind me. Behind me in the worst possible spot: a little to my right, where I'd struggle to see her even if I turned my head.

Her hand came down over my eyelids.

"Is this a guessing game?" I kept my voice light. My pulse was already going a lot faster than it had when the walls started creepily leaking blood. I won't try to claim that I've never been afraid of Wist.

"I won't guess wrong. I know who you are," I continued into the silence.

"Do you?"

She stopped blindfolding me with her hand. As she let go, my eyelids came open and stayed that way. Like she'd glued them in place. Both my eyes began to water with a vengeance.

Her right hand still touched the right side of my head. I thought she would stroke my hair as if petting a dog. Instead she reached around and pressed the teary surface of my prosthetic as though pressing down on a single piano key.

I sort of saw it coming. Her finger emerged from my blind spot, and my prosthesis had almost no sight of its own. But my left eye caught a hint of movement before she touched me.

I jerked against the hard back of my chair. If I were alone, I might've tipped over. But she stood behind me. There was nowhere to go.

My lids strained with the agony of being unable to blink. Her fingernail tapped the firm surface of my false eye. I thought of revelers tapping wineglasses. I thought of anything I could come up with to avoid making noises that would abase me.

I didn't know if she'd actually locked me to my seat with magic, like how she'd locked my eyes open, or if it only felt that way.

"This eye is the only thing anchoring you to yourself," said the Queen. "Without it, you'll forget everything. You'll forget to fight back. You ought to be terrified."

I wet my lips. My hands were claws on the wooden arms of my chair. "Well. Pissing myself won't help much."

She flicked my prosthetic, as if in retaliation. She flicked it quite hard. My throat gurgled.

"Please," I said uselessly. "Please let me blink."

Through blurry vision I saw her in her chair again. Like nothing had ever happened. My eyelids cringed shut.

I blinked many more times. I offered ardent thanks to the nonexistent gods of Manglesea.

I dried my face off with a napkin. I looked across at the Queen.

"You don't mind if I forget you, too?" I asked.

"You won't forget me as I am now. You'll forget the person you think of as Wisteria Shien."

"It won't come to that." My voice wobbled. I kept going regardless. "You might force me to assimilate as one of your townspeople. You might bury my memory. But you won't fully erase it. You'll leave me a way out."

She rested one ankle on the opposite knee. She leaned back and regarded me with the air of a displeased king.

"You're very sure of yourself," she said icily. "Why?"

I pointed at my face. "I've run into a lot of weird things around town since you planted magic at the back of my eye. Primevals feeding on corpses. Razor-sharp blades and open scissors lying around in dangerous places. The smell of dank sweat rolling off inanimate objects, and handprints on my pillow, and human hair growing from between floorboards like the world's most disgusting moss."

"I wasn't inviting you to file complaints."

"Gives me a little jolt each time," I said. "But nothing has outright harmed me. Nothing has chained me up or slashed my leg tendons or cut out my tongue."

The silverware had started trembling again. It vibrated until the Queen laid her fingertips on the table. For half a breath, all sound and motion ceased. Even the crickets lapsed into silence.

"I can hurt you," the Queen said.

"Sure you can," I agreed. "You gouged my eye out way before anyone ever called you their Queen."

I would not normally have said this to my Wist. But she was not my normal Wist.

Even if I loved her, it felt unbelievably cathartic—almost euphoric—to hit below the belt. The lower the blow, the bigger the spike in adrenaline.

I guess that's why I end up in situations like this. I kind of deserve it.

I almost got her, too. I sensed her wavering, though her face didn't show it. She teetered right on the edge of taking my bait. Go on, I would've told her. Prove how cold you are. Prove you can hurt me. Do it for real.

In the end, the Queen didn't say another word. She and her favorite new chair evaporated from the dining room.

I rubbed my face. I eyed her abandoned yellow peaches.

I used her little dessert fork to eat the rest of the can. In purging the spider lily poison from my system, it felt as though she'd eradicated all other evidence of dinner, too. I was ravenous.

Then I got up to begin cleaning. There would be a lot of leftovers to share with the innkeeper.

20

Allow me to clarify. There was another reason I'd been enthusiastic about cooking in close quarters with the innkeeper.

Accomplishing my goal took a long time, and multiple bouts of poorly feigned clumsiness. I spilled half-stirred sauces all over both of us. I knocked over a mortar and pestle full of freshly ground spices. I nearly cut myself on the fishhooks in her hair.

I'm not a trained pickpocket, okay? I made a fool of myself in the process, but eventually I pulled it off.

I stole the key ring out of her apron pocket. I slipped off the key she'd used to open the storeroom. I put her key ring back without it. So far, she was none the wiser.

Please do note that I exercised some restraint. I didn't knock the innkeeper into counters or other hard surfaces. And of course I never let her fall. I have standards, you know.

After the Queen unceremoniously ditched me, I packaged up our leftovers for the innkeeper (minus the spider lily salad, which I discarded). I washed a bunch of dishes. Then I took my stolen key and left the inn. I went creeping over to the sacred storehouse.

I didn't spend long in there. I examined the spare horns hanging from brackets on the wall. I selected a couple more modern variations, both made from dull spotty brass. I had to stand on a stool to take them down.

I locked the storeroom up behind me. Back at the inn, I mulled over how to return the key. I decided against pretending to have found it fallen in a corner.

Instead I wiped it thoroughly with the Queen's dinner napkin—not sure what kind of fingerprinting technology they had here, but best not to risk it—and tossed it under a serving cart. The innkeeper would find it eventually.

I retreated to my room.

I now had a milk crate full of unopened mead bottles sitting in a corner. I'd bought it earlier today, after one of the higher-ups at the biggest meadery gifted me a sack of taro from their personal garden.

I'd asked for an assortment with both alcoholic and nonalcoholic drinks. The staff rattled off a list of options—fruity melomel, cider-mead and mead-beer and cider-beer blends. I could hardly be bothered to remember all their proper names. Oh, but I did recall that a mead-beer hybrid was called a braggot. Heh.

That night, I curled sideways under the covers with Wist's pillow in my arms. The same question kept ringing in my head like a gong. Over and over.

Why?

Taking in the Void had boosted Wist's magic. It sure looked that way, anyhow.

If she were anyone else in the world, the answer would be obvious.

If she were anyone else, I'd say she'd accepted the Void because of the greater magical power it promised her.

But Wist—Wist alone—had never been drawn by the promise of power. That, to my mind, was her most unique and unfathomable strength. Far more so than her ridiculous natural abundance of magic.

Wist was the one person on the continent I'd trust to resist such temptation. (Way more than I'd trust myself.)

My question lingered unanswered. Why?

All I could imagine was that we'd unknowingly ended up in a dire predicament. One she couldn't solve in any other way. Hence my attempts to interrogate her about whether we'd died during our first trip to the caves.

If we'd ventured too deep—if we were getting half-devoured by the Void—then yeah, I could picture Wist bargaining with it to save us.

But she'd shut down that line of inquiry without hesitation. I didn't think she was lying, either. Her first meeting with the Void hadn't played out like that. This wasn't the afterlife.

So—why?

The thoughts wouldn't stop. I took another tablet from my stash of borrowed sleeping pills.

After that, the night passed with startling speed. Morning birds squeaked in unbridled excitement out by the balcony.

Day 3.

I reached blearily for the water glass I'd left on my nightstand. Good thing I looked inside before taking a swig: a frog the size of my thumbnail was busy doing laps in it. I stepped out to the balcony to decant him in a potted plant.

I had less than a full day left now. I was rapidly running out of time to escape.

Yet after a night of dreamless sleep, I woke up convinced that nothing was as it seemed. For whatever reason, the Queen couldn't actively help me. She made a great show of doing the opposite. She looked and sounded threatening enough. She claimed she'd given me a chance to flee town just so I could entertain her by running around and flailing and failing.

She'd touched the back of my eye to warp my sight. As a result, I'd been forced to witness a whole lot of gross shit. During a recent chat with the sweet-smelling mortician, stark white maggots had begun plopping out of her sleeves. They crawled down her meaty hands like they owned her. No one noticed except me.

But consider this. By the same token, my changed sight had revealed the town primevals to be much more grotesque than I'd previously thought.

The Queen—Wist—had made me see them that way. She'd wanted me to study them, to fixate on them. She'd wanted me to follow them.

She'd wanted me to find the caves.

I had a nasty feeling that merely escaping town wouldn't solve a damn thing. Not by a long shot. But getting out of here had already proven to be difficult enough in its own right. I wasn't yet in a position to plan beyond that.

Yesterday, I'd entertained wild thoughts of using primevals to trace a path for me. I still had plenty of chalk. I could tie or glue it to their scales. As they scraped their way through Katashiro Caverns, they'd automatically leave guiding marks. So even if they moved too fast for me, even if I ran into trouble along the way, I could follow their chalk-streaks to navigate toward the exit on my own.

It wasn't the worst idea I'd ever had in my life. But there were plenty of ways it could go wrong. I'd had a hard enough time lifting a single key off a pregnant lady.

I opted to respect my own limits. Especially when I had limited time to work with. Besides, some of those primevals looked awfully mangy and hungry—scales falling out in patches, coconut-brown hair growing in long bedraggled hunks. The last thing I wanted was to lose even more body parts.

I set my hiking boots by the door. I put on a pair of durable overalls. I went to the ensuite bathroom to rinse my face and scrub my teeth.

I halted in the doorway.

The bathroom floor was littered with nail clippings.

Clicking noises echoed from the shower stall, as regular as the ticking of a clock. With each telltale click, more crescent-shaped clippings would bounce up out of the teeth-colored tiles like popcorn popping.

It was just keratin. The same substance that formed big brown scalloped primeval scales. And it wasn't like these fragments belonged to anyone in particular. They were immaculately birthed toenail bits. Nothing to fret over.

I grimly swept them aside and set about my business. Let me tell you, though, it wasn't much fun to feel sharp new clippings erupt into being right under my feet.

At least the mirror looked less oily than the other day. For the sake of her dignity, more so than mine, I sure hoped the Queen wasn't individually engineering all these petty feats of surrealism.

With any luck, I'd never have to use this bathroom again.

I got my bag—once more stuffed to the brim, this time with brass horns as well as my chalk kit. No room to add a stone lamp. I'd have to buy a flashlight from one of the stores further downtown.

As I left the inn, I wondered how to drive out a parasite without medication. You could use combs for lice, or shave all your hair off. If you got bedbugs—well, might be best to burn it all down.

Would ants or termites flee a flooded nest? Would a human parasite flee a dying host?

I had other things to worry about first. Foremost among them: my lack of an accomplice.

Over these past few days, I'd made friendly small talk with too many different residents to count. They were nice enough to my face.

But I didn't think I could convince them to break the fundamental rules of this town. Their undying faith in the Queen and their rock-solid acceptance of everything that transpired here, no matter how bizarre, made them very slippery to deal with.

My only real candidate was the only one among them with a name. Lester the false hermit. The thing is, I had nothing to use as leverage against him, either.

No time left to go about this politely. I tracked him down in his designated hidey-hole. A remote water tower, long out of use, surrounded by pomegranate trees. Its wide stone base had been rebuilt to emulate a picturesque hermit's grotto.

I found him reading a book. No—a scroll. And not one of the modern living scrolls commonly used in Osmanthus. The type made from a big old roll of regular paper. Or parchment, I suppose. Incredible.

His magnificent walking stick leaned against the grotto wall. His false beard appeared to be in much better shape than yesterday.

Few hints of sun made it past the entrance. The only real light came from an oil lamp. Much of the interior had been spray-painted with a fuzz of powdery ash-gray dust. Yet the academic books stacked by his cot looked quite new.

Lester stared at me, clearly at a loss. The other townspeople would know better than to barge in on a hermit.

My sight remained unaccustomed to the dimness. Still, I managed to parse out a few phrases on the spines of his books. *The Fall of the Cressians. Aerial Commerce. Sacrifice in Antiquity. Ancient Civilizations of the Continent. Collapse.*

Okay. This might give me something to work with.

"Say," I blurted. No apology for walking in on him without an invitation. "You had a life before Bittercress, didn't you?"

I couldn't tell if he understood me. Still, I kept going. Better get it all out before this dust made me sneeze my head off.

"Did you study to be a hermit?" I asked. "Did you become a hermit so you could study more? Did you choose Bittercress because of its proximity to Cressian ruins?"

I felt a touch sorry for him. He got paid to be a decorative hermit, not to hold conversations with random strangers.

"How about this," I said. "I've been down in the caves. I'll be going back down there today."

His eyes widened. They'd already been pretty wide to begin with. Understandable. For all he knew, I'd come to rob him.

His fists tightened around the straggling ends of his beard. "Only lantern-herders go in the caves."

"I'm kind of a lantern-herder," I said. "I'm—uh, an apprentice. I've got the right to go there. You're not allowed?"

"I've never … I've never set foot in the caverns."

He sounded uncertain. Maybe he'd visited Katashiro Caverns back when they were located under distant mountains. Before the town walls rose anew. Before Wist became Queen.

"I saw Cressian artifacts down there." A bit of exaggeration wouldn't hurt. "All kinds of wall paintings. Chamber after chamber, just full of them. And the most incredible carved reliefs. I'd be happy to tell you all about them later. Could even try to make some rubbings. If you could just do me one favor.…"

His hands wrung fitfully at his artificial beard.

By the wall behind him stood a thoroughly modern metal laundry pole. Several copies of his hermit robe hung on wooden hangers. What looked like foul stains and years of dirt were in fact their original coloring. Each garment was identical to its neighbor, right down to the placement of strategic rips.

"I would like to hear more about the caves," he said. "I can repay you with a poem."

"One you wrote yourself?"

"One of the old epics. About a man who thought he was a primeval."

"My request is something much simpler. Much less poetic."

I dug out one of my spare metal horns and passed it to him.

He held it warily, the way a civilian might hold a grenade. "The guards carry these."

"Yeah. So do I," I fibbed. "Yet another lantern-herder privilege. About that favor—it won't be difficult. Not to brag or anything, but I'm good friends with the Queen." I leaned in, hands cupped around my mouth, and added: "Way more than friends, really. I want to play a little prank on her."

I asked Lester if he still had the clematis pin I'd given him. He took it out of a carved wooden box. Wouldn't do me much good if it festered away in his grotto.

"Keep it on you," I instructed him. "Just for today. Just between now and high noon."

He began pinning it to the front of his robes.

I made him conceal it behind an extra fold of fabric. A healthy dose of discretion never hurts.

"Perfect," I said. "I've got a pin of my own. I can use it to speak to you. I'll send you a code word." I looked around the ill-lit room. "If your pin says *collapse*, go outside and play your horn as loud as you can. Right out in the open."

"It won't sound pleasant."

"Don't worry about playing it beautifully. You don't need to know how. Just blow a bunch of air in. Make some noise. How hard can it be?"

"I know how to play the town horns."

"No problem, then."

He turned the old horn about as though examining a wounded animal. "This one is in terrible shape," he said. "More than that—the primevals will be agitated. Very agitated."

"Good. That's the prank."

"Do you understand what will happen?"

"Do you?" I shot back.

"No," he acknowledged. "All I know is that the primevals will hate it."

"That's hearsay, isn't it?"

"Stories from the past. Passed down for generations. No one still alive has ever played a horn at the wrong time."

If there were too big a ruckus, I figured the Queen would be forced to smooth it over. Like she'd done with my fire.

"Don't worry about getting blamed for it," I said. "The Queen is a generous monarch. I'll make sure she understands."

He didn't seem especially reassured.

"If the pin doesn't make a peep between now and noon, then forget about it," I continued. "We can pretend the whole thing never happened."

He gave a doleful nod. But he brought the tarnished horn up to eye level as though earnestly analyzing how best to play it.

Nothing I'd uttered had been a blatant lie. (Except for the part about working as an apprentice lantern-herder.) Lester had a deep and genuine interest in the Cressians. We'd made a perfectly fair deal.

Not my fault if I vanished from town before completing my end of the bargain.

I'd promised to regale him with tales of what I'd seen in the caves. I hadn't said a word about when.

21

I STUCK MY HEAD back inside Lester's grotto approximately four seconds after leaving.

He twitched like a deer who'd heard a gunshot.

"Sorry," I called. "Could I borrow a flashlight?"

If Lester had nothing else to offer, I'd requisition his little oil lamp. The only real light he had in here. Look—I was pressed for time. If I'd judged correctly, one of the official morning horns would play in less than half an hour.

Lester seemed puzzled about why—being a self-proclaimed lantern-herder—I couldn't use one of the river lanterns. Good point. I did still have a supply of spare matches.

"You know what," I said, "I think I'll do just that."

"Don't be lost," he called as I left again.

I hustled over to the water tower that looked like a lighthouse. Primevals lay all around it, making the grounds resemble a poetic rock garden. Perfect for a hermit to wander through. But Lester wasn't available to set the scene.

According to the clock posted outside the tower, I had a few minutes left to catch my breath. I munched on a strip of fruit leather. I asked the primevals to go slowly when they traversed the caves. Please.

"Your legs are much bigger than mine," I said to them. "Don't leave me behind."

They gave no indication of hearing me. Nor, on the bright side, did they appear interested in gnawing on me. They preferred digging up dead people.

At last the morning horn rang out through the skies of Bittercress. The primevals lounging about like brown boulders got up all at once, perfectly synchronized. They formed a neat line to file down into the entrance that now gaped open at the foot of the tower.

I brought up the rear. Once more I trotted down the same stairs as yesterday, the ones with stone lights embedded on either side.

I had a lot of crap to juggle, and I couldn't waste time. The primevals wouldn't stop to wait for me. As we passed the room full of river lanterns, I ducked in and grabbed one off the nearest rack.

It was startlingly light, with a six-sided metal frame. Light enough to stay afloat, I suppose. The material stretched through the six panes of the frame looked like pale textured paper. It must've been reinforced, though. I got the sense that, unlike the paper-screen doors at the inn, it would be impossible for my fingers to accidentally punch holes in it.

I hastily struck a match. I stuck my wrist through the open top of the lantern to light the candle within. Afterward, I shook the match till it lost its flame and tossed it over my shoulder. Sorry for littering.

I had to scramble to catch up with the last of the primevals, but at least now I could see past the bottom of the stairs. As I went, I unrolled my sleeves one by one, tucking the lantern into the crook of one arm and then the other as I worked. With their cuffs fully unfolded, my sleeves were long enough to pad my hands like oven mitts.

The metal parts of this lantern weren't designed to stay cool to the touch. Normally no one would carry it for long while it burned: it was meant to drift down the river all on its own.

Unlike the last time I'd come here, my bond didn't pull at me. I interpreted this as meaning that the Queen wasn't currently haunting the caverns. Great.

I had a stick of chalk protruding from the top of my bag for easy access. I'd start marking walls if the primevals' path became overly complicated.

Not once did I find myself reaching for my chalk. Now that I kept following the ambling primevals—instead of getting distracted by the Queen—the road they chose began to look decidedly different from the rest of the caves.

If anything, it seemed more akin to a series of man-made tunnels. Occasional raw holes in the wall indicated the possibility of other passageways. But it was easy enough to stick to the primevals' intended route.

Did they always walk this road in total darkness? Thankfully, they didn't act disturbed by my light. I stared at the swaying of their pendulous tails until it started to make me queasy.

The only sounds were the grating of their scales on stone (in narrower segments of the tunnel) and a forlorn, irregular dripping.

The lantern grew uncomfortably hot to the touch, even with my sleeves pulled down to protect my palms. It illuminated more murals made of outlined hands and feet of all sizes. Then a study of various cloud patterns. Line art of sky nettles and mangle rays, improbably wide-winged birds, singing deer and river deer and grazing wolves with their too-flat teeth.

The caverns were so considerate. They'd made my words to Lester more truthful. Although this artwork might date back to either before or after the Cressians. There were stretches where some mischievous latecomer had doodled judgmental white eyes in every open crevice.

How much time had passed? The lantern's light metal frame began to feel as though it would blister my skin through my clothes.

When I couldn't bear it any longer, I set the lantern on the ground. Then it occurred to me that I might no longer need it at all.

I crouched to blow out the candle sheltered inside the open-top lantern. I left it there in a tunnel covered in hand shapes as dense as summer leaves. (With a mental apology to the real lantern-herders of Bittercress, who'd lost a perfectly good piece of stock through no fault of their own.)

There was still a vestige of light even after my river lantern went dark. Now it came from the opposite end of the tunnel.

I hurried onward. The primevals had far outstripped me. They shrank in my view, black shapes silhouetted against unbearable brightness. They vanished, swallowed by the exit.

I too would leave. I wouldn't miss my chance. But I wavered over whether to implement any last-minute precautions.

I repositioned the contents of my bag, shoving the chalk down lower. I took out a spare clematis pin. The petals pricked at my palm like a blunted throwing star.

I'd brought along my second stolen horn, too. I wouldn't try tooting it unless Lester failed to respond. No guarantee that it'd have the same effect when played down in the caverns.

There'd be no need to trigger untold havoc if I knew I could slip out of town unnoticed. So far, so good—but the Queen might show up to block me at any moment. Gotta be prepared.

I was definitely getting closer. Still, I couldn't see anything beyond the exit. It looked like a mass of glaring unbroken light. Just had to wait for my eye to get used to the transition. Almost there now—

Gravity buckled as if a giant had squeezed it like a sponge. The tunnel tilted, then reoriented itself.

I hit the ground—or a wall that had temporarily turned to ground—and scrabbled for purchase. I lost hold of my pin for half a second, then frantically scraped it back to me.

The tunnel stopped moving. My knees bled inside my overalls. My hands must've gotten scraped, too. My palms were very hot. I stood dizzily.

There was magic behind this. Like all the magic in town, no matter how powerful, I had to fight to sense it. It was embedded too deep in the rocks for my perception to warn me.

The exit was in the floor now, surrounded by a hip-high stone wall. It still leaked light.

I leaned over the wall.

All I could see was a wide, wide hole of uncertain depth that led to a cloud-dotted sky.

A blue sky peculiarly empty of aerials. A sky blocked by a thick-barred grate. One very similar to the grates blocking both ends of the river. Except that this one was covered in a forest of lance-like metal spikes.

No sign of the primevals who had preceded me—and who had presumably exited the caverns without incident.

Let me preface this by stating that I had to make a potentially life-changing decision with less than zero time to think.

The instant I made eye contact with those horrible long spikes, the bond inside me leapt and twisted like a startled fish.

I knew she was there before I turned to look for her. I didn't dither. She might already be reaching for me. She might stop me by sealing me in a coffin of magic, and then I wouldn't be able to go anywhere.

Ghostly white hair. A too-calm face. The Queen stepped forward out of the lightless part of the tunnel. Her cautious bearing suggested that she would attempt to talk me down from the edge. As if I stood on the railing of a high infamous bridge, threatening to jump.

Before our eyes met, I'd already brought my bloodied clematis pin to my lips.

"*Collapse*," I croaked.

I backed away toward the far side of the ring-shaped wall, working my way around the hole in the floor. At a glance, it could've passed for an industrial-size well.

The Queen watched me go without moving. Was she weighing just how harshly to interfere? Or debating whether she cared enough to interfere at all?

Letting a single rat escape won't make you any less of a queen.

I hadn't meant to think it *at* her. It came out all the same, a mental slip.

She raised her head. Her magic stirred.

Then we both heard Lester's horn.

Somehow I hadn't expected its sound to reach us. But of course it would. These horns had the miraculous ability to resound throughout Bittercress, all without deafening the one who played them.

The hole in the cave floor might point somewhere beyond town, but no one had ever said the walls were soundproof. Primevals grazing outside needed to be able to pick up on the daily music, too.

Lester's horn had no melody. Its sheer awfulness must've shocked the Queen into stillness.

She recovered her composure. "Don't step any further," she warned me.

I'd clambered on top of the wall around the exit.

She didn't get a chance to utter any other straight-faced threats. A horrendous screeching followed Lester's horn. All the noise came from below, as if the caves were simultaneously under Bittercress and above it.

It sounded like a pack of monsters sarcastically imitating the cries of a dying human.

As soon as the screams started, I stepped off the edge of the wall.

I glimpsed her face—mask-like rigidity—the instant I fell. I glimpsed her magic shooting like tree roots through the caverns. And perhaps all through town, where the entire primeval population must've been on the rampage.

I hadn't wanted to put Lester or any other residents in real danger. If they were, though, the Queen would save them. Hundreds and hundreds of them, men and women and elders and children. All over town. All at once.

Her magic reached everywhere. But not for me. The Queen wasn't infallible. She couldn't perform infinite amounts of magic all at the same time. Even the Queen had to do triage. Or maybe she just wanted to see me impale myself on the consequences of my own actions.

I made a split-second gamble as I jumped. A twofold gamble.

The best case scenario: the bottomless sky and the grate and deadly spikes might all be illusory. A final test of courage. I might tumble down two feet, uninterrupted, and land blinking in a meadow of seedy autumn grass.

If the spikes were real, on the other hand, I had some hope of minimizing my exposure. I'm a small woman. I could leap in vertically, feet first, and aim like the dickens for the space between spikes. I could at least avoid getting skewered like a piece of chicken.

Frankly, I don't know where that confidence of mine came from. I'm not a trained diver. I barely have any experience with jumping in pools or lakes, much less murderous traps.

It wasn't a logical choice. I threw myself off the stone wall because I knew right down at the base of my bond with her that this was my last and best chance to escape the Queen.

It happened in less than two seconds. My traitorous body twisted midair. Utterly against my will. Fear rushed up to meet me like an open mouth filled with ravenous teeth all the way to the back of its throat.

I belly-flopped onto the lattice of spikes.

I felt them punching through me. I felt that long, long before there was anything remotely resembling pain. In how many places had I gotten spiked? Beats me. I lay tangled against the grate like a fly caught in glue.

More screaming erupted below me. So many screams. I hadn't realized that primevals possessed such powerful lungs.

I got confused. I mistook it for my own screaming. Maybe it ought to have been my screaming.

Eventually it cut off, though. If it were me, I wouldn't have stopped so easily.

I had the curious sense of being marooned alone on an island. I strained to see the opposite shore. My pain awaited on that shore. It stretched from horizon to horizon, enormous beyond measure. But it wasn't here yet.

Among other things, I'd horribly misjudged both the spacing of the spikes and the distance of my fall. Should've known better than to rely on my damaged depth perception. Even my magical prosthetic didn't make it perfect.

The shore moved closer. As if the sea were shrinking, or my island had become a drifting boat. It was very quiet without anyone shrieking now. My breath devolved into a delicate whistle, the sound of air squeaking out of a deflating balloon.

The spikes were much girthier than they'd looked from above. Maybe anything would seem thicker than expected once it gored a hole straight to the other side of you.

I couldn't go anywhere, and I knew better than to try. It still felt bizarrely as if my body were moving, tilting this way and that, sliding on its spikes. The slightest twitch of my fingertips reverberated through the rest of me like an earthquake.

A shadow fell across my face.

The Queen stood on the very tip of the spike impaling my right forearm. This put her high above me. The spike was as long as a javelin, and I'd sunk all the way to the bottom.

She didn't wobble. Nor did the spike stab through her foot, as it should have. She wore a look of intense concentration.

In a ghastly act of stating the obvious, I attempted to tell her I was dying.

She perched there like a hawk with her hands in her pockets. She watched me quiver below her, gelatinous, gushing fluids like a broken faucet, trapped against the unbending grate. Trapped above an empty sky. Trapped there as pain rushed from nowhere to fill me like my wayward soul rushing back to my body. I would've preferred to remain a living ghost.

It may have only lasted a millisecond in total, but she watched me for what almost ended up being the rest of my life.

22

The grate beneath me crumbled like dried-up mud. The spikes vanished. As I started falling, I missed how they'd anchored me. It was like someone had stuck their hands in and wrenched my bones out.

Wist caught me.

This ought to have been excruciatingly painful. As bad as getting run through in half a dozen different places.

Invisible magic trussed me up like a spider's prey getting wrapped for storage. That magic muffled my senses, stopped my too-hot blood from gurgling like a skinny waterfall past her arms and all down the front of her body. Before she snatched me out of the air, I must've been bleeding freely into the endless sky.

I'd dropped like something rotten tossed down a garbage chute. Wist didn't fall: gravity would not sabotage her the way it had sabotaged me.

I couldn't tell if we were still suspended by the cavern exit. I couldn't tell how long she carried me in that false empty sky. The magic swaddling me made everything sound like the languid curl and collapse of small ocean waves.

Eventually, she ported. My swollen left eye got a blurry glimpse of new scenery. A proper sky filled with motion, with implacable aerials. Water towers and wind catchers on one side, and green hills on the other.

We were on top of the town wall.

Every last barrier—the metal spikes and bars—had disintegrated. I'd followed my guiding primevals all the way to the end of the line. Only to land right on the wall itself. I'd never actually set foot outside Bittercress.

A long braid curled around me, pressing me to her like a binding sling, soaking up blood like white cotton. Only then did I remember she was the Queen.

"No one can leave," she said to the top of my head.

A steady wind blew past us as she held me. I heard the sound of flowing water.

When I came to, my entire body felt as though she'd dragged me behind the tavern and systematically beaten me up from head to toe.

I was not lying on a soft bed. No one tenderly held my hand. No cool compress on my brow. No IV drip. No gift baskets full of expensive fruit.

Nor did I have numerous gaping wounds retching blood all over the floor like sailors bailing out a sinking boat. I was alive. I could see.

I knew this place. Kind of. We were at the top of the water tank painted to look like a skyward-facing eyeball.

"You have a sick sense of humor," I said.

"And you don't?"

The Queen still wore my blood in her hair. It looked much drier, though. A rusty hue.

The pupil of the great eye held up a disc-shaped platform surrounded by a nominal guardrail. Discreet stairs snaked sinuously out of sight down the curve of the tank.

I sat up, my back to the railing. The bars were distressingly similar in diameter to the spikes that had bored now-sealed holes in me.

"Figured you would rescue me," I said. "Even as the Queen."

"You screamed and cried for me."

"Yeah, right. Think I had any energy left for that? I was hallucinating about remote islands. I was about to kick the bucket."

I looked down at my overalls. A sorry sight indeed.

"Is the town okay?" I asked. Couldn't tell from up here.

"No one died."

"Guess everything's peachy, then."

"Every single primeval ran wild. There were countless injuries."

"I count myself among them."

She appeared to be reconsidering her decision to remove me from the spikes. "No one forced you to jump off. I specifically warned you to stop."

I laughed deep in the back of my throat. "Remember our deal? You ought to know how far I'll go to win a game. You're the one who wanted me to try to escape in the first place."

"I didn't tell you to traumatize the entire population in the process."

"So?" I said. "You'll make them forget tomorrow, won't you? It'll be like it never happened. You'll make me forget, too."

My sling bag rested next to me, the strap draped loosely over my wrist. I pulled it closer and started sorting through my things.

She'd confiscated both of our bond threads—the symbolic woven ones we were supposed to wear for show. Also gone: our matching keychains. All my extra transceiver pins.

I opened my mouth to say something sarcastic, then caught myself. There was still a chance that she hadn't tracked down the pin I'd given

Lester. For starters—and I'm not trying to brag here—my death throes would've been an extremely effective distraction. Pretty sure I didn't actually die this time, but I must have come close enough to make her sweat.

On top of that, the entirety of Bittercress was so deeply steeped in her magic that she might not notice one pitiful stray pin. It was a minor magical object of limited utility. The overwhelming omnipresence of her power could serve as an inadvertent form of camouflage. In a dust-choked attic, who would fixate on a single hidden grain of sand?

Best not to mention my clematis pins, then. Instead I showed her a handful of bandages and my travel-size tube of disinfectant.

"I came prepared, see?" I said self-importantly. "You could've used these."

"Let's try that next time," the Queen suggested.

"Yup. When my organs get ripped asunder, slap on a little boo-boo bandage to make it better."

She didn't chuckle. I closed my bag. "How long was I knocked out?"

"Is that relevant?"

"Of course it is," I insisted. "I'm working on a deadline. Has it been a full three days yet?"

She bent before me, moving her hair out of the way, and held her palm cupped in the air near my face. The way you'd extend your hand when ordering a possessive pet dog to spit out a toy.

My prosthetic eye lurched out of my right socket all on its own. It plopped neatly, glistening, in the middle of her waiting palm.

"You lost your chance," she said simply.

She curled her fingers shut. When she opened them, the eye was gone.

"I still know who I am," I said.

"Not for long."

I couldn't muster up the will to panic. My flesh had gotten perforated by spikes that would've fit nicely in a museum of ancient torture devices. The Queen might have forced my wounds to close—similar to how Wist would travel around closing vorpal holes—but I still felt like a tube of extruded jelly.

A last-ditch effort to escape would require crawling past the Queen's legs and scrambling down the narrow steps leading to the underbelly of the tank.

No, thanks. I'd already come close enough to breaking my back today. Who knew what the Queen would do if I fell again?

"How'd I do?" I asked, resigned to my fate. "Were you entertained when I impaled myself?"

Her fingertips twitched. Nice to see that I hadn't lost my gift for annoying her.

She drew back and told me to choose a job. Every proper adult townsperson had a career, I suppose. Right down to Lester the hermit.

When she spoke, the inside of her mouth looked darker than it should have. As if black water filled her up to the top of her throat. As if she'd become more Void than human.

With each word she uttered, more shadowy hints of the Void filtered out into the air like smoke. They darted craftily back inside when she inhaled.

"You're leaking," I told her.

"You made me overexert myself," the Queen said coldly.

Didn't take me long to select an occupation. "I'll be a hermit," I declared. "Seems like a pretty sweet gig. And maybe I can keep my name, too?"

"That position's taken."

"How stingy. Your monarchy can't afford to support two measly local hermits?"

"Would you like me to off the current hermit? Would you like to depose and replace him?"

"No, no," I said hastily. "Fine. I'll be his manager."

"His manager?"

"He's a kind of entertainer. You get me? He adds to the scenery. I'll be an agent—I'll take a cut of his earnings. I'll make him the best damn hermit to ever do a tour of duty in Bittercress. I'll double his aura of wisdom and mystery."

"That's not a legitimate—"

I didn't let her finish. "Most people have multiple jobs, right? I want to be a lantern-herder, too."

"Why?" asked the Queen.

"I like cleaning things up."

"...Do you?"

"You ordered me to choose a job," I retorted. "Didn't realize you were gonna be so picky about it."

I started to lug myself up off the textured steel floor. I immediately had second thoughts. I flopped back down like a drunkard tossed out of a bar. "All right, then," I said with irrepressible dignity. "Make me a stripper. Or a high-end escort. You want a sideshow? I'll give you a sideshow. Watch me spice things up around here. This town is sorely lacking in nightlife."

"You?" the Queen said. "A high-end escort?"

"I may be about as voluptuous as a piece of string cheese, but that never stopped you from wanting me. If you've got a problem with it, give me the jobs I originally asked for. This was your idea, you know. Don't be prissy."

She eyed the aerials as if seeking their sympathy.

Then she took my hand and pulled me up. The moment she touched me, I rose without difficulty. I all but floated to my feet.

"Why do you think nothing changes here?" she asked. "Why do you think no one can leave?"

"You really want me to answer that?"

"You'll forget what you've said in a matter of minutes."

Viewed from a sufficient distance, the green-gray rock of the town walls took on a misleading silvery hue like a mirage of water in a desert. The walls seemed to breathe, to ripple, to coil tighter like a world-choking constrictor snake.

"The walls aren't there to lock us in," I said.

Just a hunch. I couldn't prove it. But I said it anyway.

"The walls are there to keep *you* contained. Time doesn't stand still because you like it better that way. Time refrains from moving forward because nothing good would come of its passing."

She let go of my hand. My body instantly reverted back to a sack of disintegrating meat. I braced myself on the cold railing.

"You're protecting us from what's inside you," I continued. "Those of us in Bittercress, and those outside it. You're protecting us from the Void you picked up in the caves. If nothing changes, and no time passes, it can never get the best of you. If no one leaves here, it can never touch the rest of the continent."

The Queen said nothing.

My right eyelid cinched open as if pried apart by tiny hooks. The rounded bars of the railing ground into my back.

The Queen of the Void took one deliberate step closer. The metal-plated floor rattled wanly.

She reached for me.

It was still light out. Clean wind flowed in a tireless stream from one side of town to the other. Aerial-filtered sunbeams poured down on the water tank painted with the pattern of an isolated eyeball. The afternoon should have been nowhere near over.

Yet this day—whichever day it might be—ended the moment she touched the back of my empty eye. It ended as if with the press of a kill switch.

23

I was a lantern-herder, and I had two eyes. I could only see out of one. The other was just there for decoration. But I did have two eyes.

On second thought, I don't know why that seemed noteworthy.

Here in Bittercress, we uttered each other's real names so infrequently that my own had slipped my mind. Luckily, this didn't cause any issues during the course of everyday life.

I lived alone in a rented room on the second floor of the inn. I had everything I needed, plus a number of things I didn't. For instance, I kept finding patches of cloth with strings attached. Not at all the right size or shape to wear as a face mask.

Lantern-herding was not an easy job. Only a fool would think lightly of it. Of course, there were no such fools in Bittercress.

Retrieving washed-up lanterns from the river could take hours and hours. Then they needed to be inspected and mended as necessary, or else discarded and replaced.

There were a number of us lantern-herders, so our duties rotated from day to day. Those who restocked and repaired lanterns. Those who sent them gliding down the river at night. Those who retrieved them early the following morning.

We all balanced these duties with other jobs. Like assisting with minor tasks of town governance. Or tilling community gardens. Or, in my case, tending to the hilltop mansions that no one lived in.

My housekeeping duties were not frequent. I stepped in as a substitute every now and again, so the more dedicated cleaners could take an extra day off. Most were decades older than me: I often got called in because someone had thrown out their back or experienced a flare-up in a bad hip.

This was the sort of life I'd always longed for. Wasn't it? Here it didn't matter that I'd been born as a talented healer. There were no mages to serve. No mages to rule over the rest of us.

Well, it wasn't perfect. A mage *did* rule over us, if you wanted to get technical about it. But our Queen felt more like a mythical being or a demigod (or a child's imaginary friend) than a human mage. She didn't interfere with our daily lives. None of us were forced to heal her. That made it very different from how things had been back in—

Back where?

The sort of life I'd always longed for?

That's weird. Forget I said anything. I'd always lived here. Why long for what I already had?

Anyway. The other townspeople dearly loved the Queen, though they rarely saw her in person. I couldn't relate. I found their reverence confusing.

But it wasn't worth arguing over. The Queen didn't bother anyone—I'd give her that much. And she did keep us safe.

When the Queen saw fit to show up, no one kowtowed or sang hymns to her. They kept their worship on the inside. They treated her like any other customer. Everyone recognized that she didn't care for attention.

I did have one thing in common with my neighbors. I was deeply content.

Except sometimes I had the illusion that there was a string trapped in my body, a string that would one day destroy me. Like I'd swallowed a length of floss, and it had wandered out of my stomach to tie knots around every other organ. Like a careless surgeon had dropped a scrap of dirty twine next to my heart before stitching me up. Very itchy. I wished I could dig it out.

Sometimes my mind fogged up with a maddening sense that I had a forgotten nemesis. It haunted me with the vagueness of a dissipating dream. There was someone out there I wanted to take down. Someone I wanted to break into pieces. Someone I wanted to demolish, to stand over in triumph, to laugh at, to step on, to—

But I didn't feel that strongly about a single person in town.

In any case, I was much too busy to dwell on it. Lately, half the town seemed to be laid up with mysterious injuries. The few healthy rickshaw runners worked themselves to the bone hauling around those too feeble to walk long distances on their own.

As for me, I'd been pulling double shifts to cover the more active lantern-herding duties. Namely, putting lanterns out on the river at night, then painstakingly retrieving them the following morning.

I wasn't on the schedule today—for the first time in a very long time. I could've dived into the hammock behind the inn and treated myself to a mindless day of napping.

But a lot of tasks had been neglected since we got reduced to a skeleton crew. During my free time, I figured I'd help chip away at the backlog. It'd make my own life easier in the long run.

I woke before the sound of the first morning horn. As usual, I had breakfast with the innkeeper. Just as we were cleaning up, one of the tavern regulars came by to gift her a giant haul of fresh-caught river fish.

I slipped away once they began discussing what to do with it. In a small town, you have to be real quick on your feet to avoid getting roped into doing people favors from sunrise to sunset. I don't think anyone saw me as standoffish, but I was a natural prodigy at figuring out when to conveniently vanish.

I took a roundabout path toward the river. Still had some time to waste before the next horn would play.

I didn't wear a watch. There were public clocks posted in various places around town, some comically inaccurate. I rarely looked at them. None of us needed them.

We knew what time it was from the quality of the light. From long experience. As if our bodies had learned exactly how to account for the days getting longer or shorter with the turning of the seasons. Or as if the days never got longer or shorter at all.

I passed a hostler on crutches. He looked like he'd just come of age, with a meek mustache that consisted of a grand total of about six individual hairs.

He gazed mournfully down at a roadside arrangement of primeval dung. Someone—probably a kid with nothing better to do—had put the lumps in a triangle formation. As if setting up for a game of billiards.

"Don't stress about it," I told him bracingly. "There's been poop all over the place since everyone in town decided to get hurt all at once. Well, almost everyone."

His face fell.

"Just focus on recovering," I said. "Then we can all clean the streets together."

He sniffled and mumbled something I didn't quite catch.

All the hostlers had been depressed lately. The recent epidemic of injuries did have something to do with the primeval population. No one blamed any hostlers, though. And nowadays, the local primevals were extremely docile—tame and wild alike. Even with fewer workers available to watch them.

I left the scantily mustachioed hostler. He continued contemplating his piles of abandoned dung.

The good thing about primevals was that their droppings didn't smell much. As long as they weren't freshly laid, that is. As long as you didn't set them ablaze.

Aerials crowded the vast autumn sky. They formed flocks thicker than ever before, thick enough to noticeably dim the morning sunlight. Maybe that's why it felt colder now.

Had something changed about the air over Bittercress? Why were there so many more of them, compared to—

Compared to when?

I forged onward in a state of befuddlement. My destination: the base of Cutting Board Bridge. (I wasn't the one who named it. But it was indeed a very flat, straight bridge.)

A tangle of red lantern plants sprawled across the slope of the riverbank, hiding the eroded dirt path down below.

When the next horn played, one of the bridge pylons crumbled inward. This entrance had always been a touch overdramatic.

I picked my way across the rubble and into the caverns. No primevals joined me. After a brief descent—slippery, but with a lifesaving banister bolted to the cave wall—I reached the lantern graveyard.

Fresh-picked lanterns went first to the part of the caverns by the lighthouse. Once they'd been inspected and sorted, the hopeless specimens got carted here. It was more of a dump or a mass grave than a proper graveyard, to be honest.

Might seem inconvenient for us to insist on keeping them in the caves. By different entrances, to boot. I will say, though, the caves were great for making sure that shifts never ran too long or too short. You couldn't start work till a guard's horn opened the door. You couldn't leave till the next horn played, either.

Behind me came the grumbling of the bridge pylon rebuilding its broken parts. Sealing me in semi-darkness. I managed to ignite an oil lamp before it closed completely.

It wasn't so bad down here. The air had a way of remaining mysteriously clean. Even when we burned fuel for light.

We had a portable toilet in a nook at the top of the stairs, too. What more could you want?

I rubbed my hands to keep them limber. I'd be warmer once I got to work. I'd hunker in the graveyard and methodically break down condemned lanterns into their respective components.

Metal bits would get lumped in a box to pass off to the town blacksmith. She'd find a way to repurpose them.

The remnants of burnt-out candles would go to the chandler, who could pick out old wicks and melt the wax down for reuse.

The specially treated shades—water-resistant and eye-poppingly robust—would get peeled off and bundled for the papermaker. He'd reprocess our lantern waste into other types of paper, like the sheets we'd slice into rectangular strips to make wards with the Eyes of the Queen.

Recycling all these elements required expertise and craftsmanship. Taking apart the broken lanterns? Not so much. Heck, even I could do it.

I set my fresh-lit lamp in an alcove. I took a few steps into the graveyard. Abandoned scrap lanterns formed piles like snowdrifts. Large labeled bins—mostly empty at the moment—waited to be filled up with dismantled parts.

Handwritten signs on the cavern walls proclaimed *SAFETY FIRST, LAST, AND IN BETWEEN* and *CLEAN WORKPLACE, CLEAN SOUL.*

Our souls might be in trouble, then.

For the most part, I looked at my feet. My vision wasn't the greatest to begin with. All these tumbling lanterns might turn out to be a real tripping hazard.

That's why I didn't see her till I reached the center of the room.

First I noticed something dark at my feet. A black puddle. Unlike any liquid ink I'd ever witnessed, it was intensely matte. It let no light in. It reflected nothing whatsoever.

The puddle filled the open space where I'd planned on performing my disassembly work. In the middle of the puddle rested an expensive-looking office chair.

It wasn't empty. A long-legged woman sat there, eyes downcast, head lolling slightly. Sleeping?

She had white hair loosely bound to one side. The tie on it seemed about to slide off at any moment. She wore a transparent raincoat over sleek athletic gear, as though she'd just come in from a run. In the same outfit, I'd have been shivering and whining nonstop.

I couldn't remember the last time I'd seen our Queen up close.

24

She wasn't sleeping, actually. Her eyes were only half-closed.

I stared, wondering what to do next. Couldn't get much work done with all this muck on the floor.

At last she noticed me. She clapped a hand over her left wrist. Covering up something.

Something blue?

"I'm not about to steal your watch," I said.

When the Queen moved her hand away, the blue thing on her wrist was gone.

The ink on the floor whirled up inside her clear raincoat, draining away into her. Hard to tell exactly where it went. The rock under her chair looked dry now, as if it had never seen a drop of moisture in all its life.

I hadn't officially been scheduled to work at the lantern graveyard today. Maybe she'd assumed she could come here to be alone. The

Queen of the Void was a humble queen. At least according to everyone else in town.

I made my way over to a rickety workbench flanked by stacks of stools. I fished around in the workbench drawer, seeking safety gloves and basic tools.

I used a shopping basket to fetch ripped, dented, and otherwise ruined lanterns from the nearest heap. I put on my gloves and set about dismantling them one by one.

The Queen's chair rotated to face me.

"Need more light?" she said.

My hands paused. I'd moved my oil lamp to a nook behind me, close enough to warm the backs of my shoulders.

"Do I look like I'm struggling?" I asked. Did she think she could strip these lanterns for parts any faster?

I got up to toss metal in the bin for metal, paper in the bin for paper, wax in the bin for wax, and so on. I brought over a larger batch of lanterns to tackle next.

The cavern felt oppressively hushed.

If I were alone, I'd have lapsed into a trance as I took apart lantern after lantern, my mind drifting like a lofty aerial that would never make landfall till it died.

But the Queen's presence made my stomach itch.

I didn't look up from my work. "You come here to rest?"

"There is no rest," said the Queen.

I didn't encourage her to elaborate. Apparently she didn't require an invitation.

"Bittercress is like a fish tank," she continued. "The largest tank in the largest aquarium you can possibly imagine."

"Huh."

"It's difficult to maintain the correct pH. To cultivate a healthy population. I'm constantly making adjustments to keep the town alive and well, to clean the water, to stop it from spilling over the tops of the walls."

"The metaphorical water," I said. "Indeed. Of course."

"I've got thousands of magic skills active below the surface. They interact in ways even I can't begin to predict."

She pulled off her hair tie. She stretched it in her fingers as if she were about to flick it at me like a school kid with a rubber band.

"It's been particularly difficult to manage the progression of everyone's injuries. What does it mean for time to stand still? Would an open scratch never naturally heal? Will hair and nails never grow? There's no correct answer. Because it's not a natural state. Everything has to be manipulated in minute detail with magic."

"I understand perfectly," I said.

"You do?"

"I was being sarcastic, Your Highness."

I had no clue how to interpret her rambling about time and fish tanks. I mean, really. Had the Queen of the Void just started complaining about her job to me, a lowly lantern-herder?

"Sounds like a pain in the ass," I appended. "Don't know what you expect me to do about it, though."

"Nothing."

"Good. That's well within my capabilities."

"Carry on with your duties," the Queen said generously. "Don't mind me."

I reluctantly resumed my lantern autopsies.

The Queen scrutinized me as if I were the star attraction at a human zoo.

Was this some kind of test? Was she lingering to make sure I didn't slack off? I wouldn't call myself lazy, but I'm something of an expert at cutting corners. Er—optimizing workflows, that is. Improving efficiency. Slap that on my resume.

"Are you happy here?" she asked.

"What, in this cave?"

"In Bittercress."

"Have I ever been elsewhere? I've got no basis for comparison."

Belatedly, it occurred to me that she might've been fishing for compliments. It was her town, after all. Maybe even the Queen of the Void craved praise from time to time.

I picked up the naked metal frame of a former lantern. The safety slogans on the wall glared down judgmentally as I lobbed it at the appropriate bin. It went in like a charm: I had pretty good aim.

I wouldn't toss parts around if I were together with coworkers. I was the only employee present at the moment, though. Our illustrious Queen wouldn't be susceptible to workplace injuries. Perish the thought.

"Are you happy here?" she asked again.

"Sure," I said. "I'm happy as a primeval with an old body to chew on. There's no misery in Bittercress. No poverty. No caste system. No change. No insiders or outsiders. No forced mage healing. No mageocracy—well, present company excepted."

Didn't know where I was going with all this, to be truthful.

When I raised my gaze, the Queen was right on the other side of my workbench.

She'd left her empty office chair. It continued to occupy the rocky clearing at the center of the lantern graveyard.

Her fingertips grazed the workbench surface. Her clear crumpled raincoat played confusingly with the yellow lamplight.

She was very tall when she stood. Much taller than anyone else in town.

"What's your name?" she said to me.

"I'm a lantern-herder."

"Is that your name?"

"I don't think…" My voice stumbled over nothing. "We don't know each other well enough to be on—on such intimate terms. You haven't given me your real name, for one thing. I wouldn't dare presume to ask."

"You wouldn't?" She made it sound like a challenge.

"I'm not an eternal rebel," I said in a huff. "I know how to behave myself. I know how to read a room."

She held her left hand out as if expecting me to kiss it.

She wore no rings or other such royal jewelry.

I slid off my stool and onto my feet. My mouth was quite dry, parched by performance anxiety. Took me a couple dread-inducing seconds to work up any semblance of saliva.

I bent forward obsequiously and spat on the back of her hand.

The Queen remained rigid. She didn't slap me. She didn't snatch her hand away. She didn't even wipe it clean. Instead, my pitiful glob of spit sank below her skin like water sinking into cloth.

In less time than it had taken me to conquer my desert-dry mouth, she erased all evidence of my efforts.

Her hand came down to rest on the table again.

"You said you knew how to behave yourself."

"I said I knew how to read the room," I corrected.

"You thought I would want to be spit on?"

"Some people like that. I don't judge."

I quailed at the look on her face. It wasn't much of a look at all, to be precise. Her eyes reflected as little light as the black soup she'd been surrounded by when I first found her here.

She couldn't have cared less. She'd look the same if I vaulted over the workbench and spat at her cheek instead. She'd look the same if I shot forward like a snappy lapdog and left teethmarks on her skin. There was absolutely nothing I could do to fluster her.

"Thought you might prefer to be surprised," I confessed.

"Why?"

"My biggest flaw is—"

"Hubris?"

"No," I said, offended. "It's my self-destructive streak. Aren't you supposed to know everything there is to know about me, anyway? You're our one and only Queen."

She studied my half-finished lanterns. "You like breaking things down."

"That's why they call me the—"

"The what?"

"The...."

I drew a blank. How very embarrassing.

The Queen, for reasons inconceivable to a mere peon like myself, seemed quietly satisfied. The blankness of her eyes didn't change, though.

"I'll help," she said with a nod at my broken lanterns.

"With magic?"

"With my hands."

"I didn't volunteer to be your on-the-job trainer, Your Majesty." I tossed her a pair of safety gloves. "I won't coddle you."

"Will you spit at me again?"

"Sounds like you want me to."

"No, thank you."

She came around to my side of the workbench. I shoved a spare stool at her.

We methodically separated paper, wax, and metal.

The base of each lantern locked into a shallow hexagonal tray to help it float. I tasked the Queen with the simplest part of the process: popping off the trays. She stacked them in a column like used dishes at a busy restaurant.

The prickle in my stomach grew stronger now that she sat next to me, puzzling over lanterns too warped to come apart easily.

This had to be a natural adverse reaction to her closeness. The Queen was meant to be a distant figure. She wasn't meant to become a tangible part of our lives.

The lamp behind us didn't shed a very large pool of light. It wasn't like we'd started huddling with our shoulders together for no reason.

I considered scolding her for failing to bring an outfit suitable for manual labor. Her workout gear showed way too much skin, and that see-through raincoat didn't count as personal protective equipment. Not in my book.

Rest assured that I knew to keep my mouth shut. I'd have gotten in trouble if I wore the same thing as her, but she was the Queen. She made the rules.

She'd tied her hair up in a high ponytail. It was still long enough to tickle me when she leaned my way to ask questions.

I grew snappish. What about her figurative fish tank? Didn't she have better things to do than brush up against me while prying lanterns off their trays?

I hadn't sought help, anyway. I could take care of my duties perfectly fine on my own.

Every so often, a sudden cramp stopped my hands. Not a normal muscle cramp. More like a red-hot boil bursting open inside me. Between my kidneys. Deep in my thigh, and in the meat of my lower legs too. In my shoulder. My forearm.

It hit me in a rapid series of pops, one random body part after another. It felt the way gunfire sounds. I'd look at myself expecting to see blood and exposed fat and bone—but I wasn't injured at all. The pain winked out of existence, mocking me.

Each time, the Queen stopped to watch me from the corner of her eye.

Finally I had enough. I dropped my latest lantern and ripped off my gloves. My hands felt weak and hot.

"Are you doing this?" I demanded.

"Doing what?"

"How should I know? Stabbing me with your mind. I guess."

"Not on purpose," she said, with zero change in tone.

I was incredibly irritated to find that I believed her.

I wiped sweaty palms on my sides. I tried to stay positive. It didn't come naturally. "At least I'm not bedridden. Don't know how I managed not to get hurt when the primevals ran wild."

"You must have been very lucky."

I couldn't recall what I or anyone else had been doing at the time. This didn't bother me. Why would it?

In Bittercress, today was today. A relatively fine day. A day that fell at some mysterious point right before the fall equinox. Soon, tomorrow would also be today. Nothing else mattered, before or after.

Between criticizing the Queen's amateurish approach to lantern deconstruction and enduring debilitating attacks of inexplicable pain, I soon lost track of time.

I knocked my stool over when I heard the cavern entrance crumbling open in the distance.

"That's the afternoon horn," said the Queen.

I cursed. I came very close to throwing an outright tantrum. No way I could put everything back in its place and dash up the stairs in time. Before I got there, stones would pile up to fill the hole again.

The Queen, sedate as ever, acted like she couldn't hear me squalling.

She retrieved more damaged lanterns for our workbench. I could've rolled on the floor like a pill bug, and she would've stepped right over me.

Perhaps she was waiting for me to ask a favor from her. Never.

"I work long shifts," I told her, pulling myself together. "You sure you can keep up?"

If she didn't want to say anything—if she was too proud to offer to end this—then I wouldn't surrender, either. I'd work her to the bone.

25

AFTER THE FIRST evening horn, the Queen stopped me from bringing more discarded lanterns to the table. She pulled off her safety gloves. She reached over and plucked mine off, too.

"I'm sending you out," she said.

I crowed in triumph. "So you're giving up. Too tired? Can't take it anymore?"

"The innkeeper will worry if you miss dinner."

"Sounds like an excuse to me. I could do this all night."

If she were indeed worn to the bone, it wouldn't be from a single shift spent picking at old river lanterns. It would be the inevitable price she had to pay for serving as our Queen. For deploying magic on our behalf, so none of us would ever have to—and thus drawing the evil eye to herself alone.

I wasn't enormously sympathetic. We all had our own roles to play. I had colleagues currently laid up with multiple fractures in both legs.

The Queen's metaphysical burdens might be crueler than broken bones. But it wasn't my responsibility to weigh them.

She laid her head in her arms on the workbench. The clear glossy texture of her raincoat made it look as though she were clothed in water.

"Don't be lost," I said.

For once, I was just trying to act polite. Yet the Queen winced. She closed her eyes. Like she wished she could unhear it.

Her magic shoved me out of the caves.

She'd shown more of a reaction to those three rote words than to me spitting on her hand.

If I'd known how easy it was to get to her, I'd have said it much earlier.

She'd banished me straight from Katashiro Caverns to the middle of the Middle Bridge. I stood there watching the sun sink behind the town walls. It would be gone in less than a minute.

A sensation of having been through these exact steps before—bickering with the Queen, getting dumped alone on the Middle Bridge—gripped and released me. Like the tide going out.

A town guard stood on a turtle-shaped rock in the shallow river, playing the same phrase on his accordion over and over.

Now, I knew a thing or two about the basics of magic. Which made me wonder why the Queen wouldn't use magic to take apart lanterns. If she were to insist on helping, why not do so with maximum efficacy?

Sure, she'd need specific preexisting magic skills to put to work in the lantern graveyard. Your average bumbling mage might not possess any applicable magic—but she was the Queen of the Void. She'd own an encyclopedic number of preset skills to combine and choose from. There had to be something in her repertoire that could've let us skip a couple steps.

I recalled her strained talk of nonexistent fish tanks. The black substance she'd spilled all over the cave floor. She'd sucked it back up inside her like a hostess rearranging cushions to hide an ugly old stain from her guests.

All that time, she'd been actively using other magic. Magic on a scale I couldn't possibly comprehend. Magic inextricably enmeshed with the soil and walls and people of Bittercress. While she fiddled with broken lanterns. While her stiff crackly raincoat brushed my arm.

Maybe she couldn't stand the thought of deploying a single skill more than she absolutely needed to.

Or maybe it was similar to how certain intellectual types chose to take up physical hobbies in their spare time. Sewing and baking and woodworking and the like. Maybe the tedium of picking paper out of metal lantern frames was exactly what she needed for relief from the mental load of her magic.

Need this be any of my concern? No.

Days passed as they always did. The lantern plants never lost their crimson husks. Spider lily stems kept sprouting all over the riverbank, but their sleek buds stayed firmly shut. Many local stores remained closed, too, while shopkeepers recovered from their wounds.

The mortician had been bedridden—half-dead, I'd heard—but she was also one of the first to pop up again. One morning, on my way to pick up stray lanterns from the lower end of the river, I spotted her hobbling resolutely around her salon.

Most everyone knew her best for the work she did as our local undertaker, but I guess hairdressing was her real passion. Good for her.

I got irritated whenever the Queen came to mind. I got irritated when I saw her—which was almost never—and also when I didn't.

The closest I came to exchanging greetings with her was at night, when I went to put lanterns on the water. And before dawn, when I came back to bring them in. Sometimes I'd spy a figure perched atop a water tower. A silent sentry.

Could've been one of the town guards, I suppose, but my gut knew the difference. I could tell it was her.

Anyway, she favored places where regular guards would never go. (For safety reasons.) The chimney-like rims of tall windcatchers. The roofs of empty mansions. The curved domes of high water tanks without any visible guardrail.

No matter how you sliced it, the Queen had done nothing objectionable. She hadn't personally wronged me. She was just doing her job as the Queen. Whatever that entailed.

Yet each time I caught sight of her—which I'll admit wasn't nearly often enough for my liking—I got the urge to bound up there and drop-kick her off her lofty perch. I wanted to drag her down to my level. To wash her down the river with my lanterns.

I was a menace. I'd be the first to acknowledge that. Clearly I had congenital problems with authority.

My dreams, too, came across as glimpses into a troubled psyche. I'd fall from the sky onto a bed of iron spikes, each fully as thick as a human femur. Some nights, I trembled there like a pinned bug until I expired. Some nights, the Queen showed up to perform a mercy killing.

Every other sensation would vanish when she put her hand on my neck. The pain of irreparable mutilation got purged from my nerves so fast that its very removal felt like a violent flaying. Like everything I knew being stripped away from me.

It was an ecstatic experience. Nothing left—no thoughts, no fear— except the Queen's fingers at my throat. I think she snapped my neck one-handed.

Not very realistic. I suppose dreams don't have to account for realism. If it were real, she could've done it with magic.

Day to day, I went about my usual business. I helped the innkeeper chase out spiders the size of rats and centipedes the size of snakes. All such creatures would cease appearing in random closets once it got cold enough, but true winter still lay a long way off.

One by one, my injured neighbors started appearing in public, though an incredibly high percentage were still on crutches. Local carpenters—professional and amateur alike—pulled long hours to craft custom sets for everyone who needed them.

Whenever something out of the ordinary happened, people murmured quiet prayers for the Queen.

A woman digging in a community farm plot found a stash of chewed-up bones. Human bones. The mortician and several older hostlers put their heads together. This must be the work of a wild primeval, they decided. Or several primevals.

The families involved would be greatly honored—if only they could figure out which graves the remains had been looted from. It seemed to be a mix of multiple people all jumbled together.

Fall was usually quite dry here, with occasional light rainfall. One day, however, brought a torrential downpour. It started before sunrise and kept going after sunset. The river flooded its banks that night, washing away old warning signs.

We lantern-herders nearly drowned when we went to put lanterns on the water. We did it because we always put the lanterns out—every night without fail—and because no one told us to stop.

We watched spots of golden light chug downstream, tossing wildly, soon extinguished. We murmured to each other that they'd all be ruined when we went to find them the following day.

The next morning, we convened before dawn. The banks had been miraculously restored. No hazardous debris, no muddy landslides. Every faded sign with warnings about rapid flooding stood in its original spot, undamaged.

Then, all at once, we remembered that we hadn't given any lanterns to the river last night. Of course not. Far too risky. We'd put safety first, last, and in between. There was nothing to pick up, because no torrent of lanterns had gone sweeping down the churning river at all.

By noon, no one spoke of the rain anymore. It hadn't left any lasting scars. Besides—had it truly come just yesterday? It could've been two weeks ago, or a year ago, or before any of us were born. No real difference. The days all averaged out in the end.

Still, curious incidents seemed to be increasing in frequency. There came a night when no one in the entire town got any sleep: mysterious animals howled from dusk to dawn. They sounded wounded, outraged, insatiable. Like a mob in search of a sacrifice.

Some claimed that it must've been primevals shrieking. That they were mourning all their wild brethren who'd drowned in the flood. ("What flood?" we asked, and no one could answer.) Others insisted that primevals never made any noise to begin with.

Days later, one of my housecleaning jobs got canceled on short notice.

Rather, I canceled it. Because there was no house left to clean.

As I climbed the hill up to the empty mansions, a full-grown mangle ray came plummeting out of the sky. It landed right on the four-story building I'd been slated to tidy up next.

The ground shook as if the caverns below town had jumped a furlong lower. My ankles folded up beneath me. I sat in the dirt, winded, with six-spot burnet moths darting about overhead.

The mansion had not been flattened. But it definitely looked a good deal shorter than four stories now. The mangle ray was huge enough to cover the entire roof and then some, its wide fins draping down the sides of the broken house like a shroud to cover the face of the dead.

It emanated a scent unlike anything I'd ever smelled before. Neither good nor bad—just purely alien to my nose. The only familiar element was its piercing mustard sting.

The ray's long tail drooped down the length of the house and stretched across the ground far enough to brush the wall of the next closest mansion.

Its entire translucent body—and the visible parts of the wreckage below—shone as though painted with lacquer. Some sort of glossy goo dripped in globules large enough to drown anyone who ventured too close. Its texture looked reminiscent of the clear gelatinous glaze on a fruit tart.

Other people began limping their way up the hill behind me. They'd heard the ray fall from all over Bittercress.

We decided to keep our distance. Only the Queen herself could handle a disaster of such megalithic proportions.

Sure enough, she ported into the air by the mansion seconds later. She stood there on nothingness, her back to us, at eye level with the dead ray.

Mysterious gray creatures, mice-like in their swiftness, came circling down in whirlwind flocks. They took passing bites out of the fallen ray with the practiced movement of seabirds diving for prey. I couldn't tell if the Queen had summoned them, or if they would've come to scavenge the ray regardless.

At that point, every last rubbernecker turned in unison and walked away. Me included. The Queen would take care of it.

I'd gone all the way back to the river by the time my hypnotic calm wore off. Searing fury rose to replace it.

That was her magic at work. She'd made us depart the scene like well-trained dogs.

I was tempted to go marching back up the hill. But I didn't. The same thing might happen all over again. Or she might have already disposed of the fallen ray.

Instead I chucked angry pebbles at the water. Wild primevals lay motionless on a sandbank, attempting to sunbathe despite the relative weakness of the aerial-filtered light. I took care not to hit them.

Something silver-white bobbed along the surface. A dead fish, belly-up. Death was a part of Bittercress, too.

Was it, though?

I guess that would depend on our Queen of the Void.

Children in yellow hats and ladybug-pattern cloaks ran screaming joyfully down the opposite bank.

I mulled over what to do now that there was no house left for me to clean. All the neighboring mansions had adequate coverage.

In case you're wondering why we tended so diligently to vacant houses: even locked buildings without anyone living there would deteriorate over time in the absence of care.

We dusted. We checked for pests and water damage. We opened windows to let in fresh air and chase out mold.

Granted, vandalism wasn't a concern in Bittercress, but houses didn't need help from vandals to begin falling apart on their own. That's what common sense told us, anyhow.

Would these foreign-owned houses actually suffer if we stopped tending to them? What if the ambient temperature never changed much? What if fall never turned to winter?

Such questions kept floating to the top of my mind like dead fish. So did images of the Queen's magic. The magic core that shone brightest near the small of her back, and the endless branches that filled her body like veins.

There was something achingly familiar about the shape of the magic in her. Down in the lantern graveyard, I'd kept compulsively peeking at it. She'd probably thought I was ogling her bare waist beneath her raincoat.

But of course it would feel familiar. Poignant, even. Her magic was interwoven with every citizen of Bittercress. Myself included. Of course it would ensnare us like the scent of a childhood home. She and her magic meant that much to all of us. Not just me.

She was our Queen. Not *my* Queen. I was no more special to her than the mortician or the beekeepers or the badly overworked town doctor. If she remembered me for anything, it would be for my insolence.

26

I FOUND a different job for the day.

First I took a long lunch at the tavern, grumbling to all and sundry about my ruined housekeeping shift.

Once I finished eating, the innkeeper gave me a stack of blank paper wards and told me to paint them with the Eyes of the Queen.

I wasn't very good at it. The six red circles always looked obscurely out of whack.

It didn't help that every other tavern customer kept stopping by to critique my symmetry.

The always-smiling town baker—who gave my artwork more encouraging comments than most people—mentioned that the hermit had been seeking help with his grotto.

"What, he wants it deep-cleaned?" I asked. "Does housecleaning fit with the whole hermit ethos?"

The baker shrugged and offered me a free spinach pie.

I made the trek over to the hermit's grotto. An old stone tower standing in the shadow of the town wall.

The wild garden out front currently resembled a flea market. Shelves and desks and other rustic furniture rested topsy-turvy among crushed beds of bewildered spiky weeds and sad herbs.

In the space between stunted pomegranate trees, a spindly orb-weaver spider had strung a web large enough to snag primevals. It rested in the middle of its fine nest and observed the proceedings below with a critical eye.

The hermit was on his hands and knees, his long beard tucked inside his clothing so it wouldn't drag on the ground. He appeared to be shifting dusty stacks of books out of his dim rocky grotto. His entire body convulsed as he stopped to release a very loud and unmystical sneeze.

I asked him why he'd felt compelled to start cleaning. "Aren't hermits supposed to be free of worldly concerns?"

His wild eyebrows didn't usually look quite so pasted-on as his beard, but one of them had begun to slip dangerously low. "I'm looking for something," he said.

"For what?"

"Something sharp."

I picked a pointy twig off the ground. "Like this?"

He pointed behind him. "Something in my hut."

"You can't even name it?"

He nodded mournfully.

"You don't know what you're looking for?"

He nodded again.

This was a tad more interesting than merely tidying up. I informed the hermit that I would be delighted to help. I swept into his grotto before he could utter a word of protest.

The satisfying part about a job like this was that he lived in such a small space, with so few possessions, that examining every last cranny was fully within the realm of possibility.

We hauled his cot into the garden. While he rifled through books (none seemed to have been secretly hollowed out), I crawled around indoors to inspect the floor stones. Some were loose enough to remove. I found no treasures stored beneath them.

"You sure you left this thing at home?" I asked. "You couldn't have dropped it outside?"

He scratched the skin around the perimeter of his grizzled beard. Bits of dried adhesive peeled off. I did him a favor by pretending not to notice. Polite fictions are the lifeblood of polite society.

"Just checking," I continued, "but where do you wash your hermit gear? At the laundromat? At the dry cleaners? In the river? That seems more authentic. Do you look in your pockets first? Have you asked around at the mortician's lost and found?"

"Pockets," he repeated. He patted himself quizzically.

I couldn't tell at a glance if he had pockets in the traditional sense. But his brown-stained robes, dyed in numerous shades of old tea, were made up of neverending folds and pleats.

The breeze around us bore the scent of crushed herbs. We turned to his laundry pole, which he'd put to use as a kind of closet on wheels. Five identical copies of his hermit costume hung evenly spaced, their hangers smelling of cedarwood.

One by one, we stuck our hands in the folds. We shook out the garments, turned them upside down and inside out, squeezed the fabric to check for foreign objects. Sadly, no gold coins came jangling out.

"What are you looking for?" asked the hermit.

I leaned around the rack to glower at him. "Is senility part of your hermit shtick? I'm helping you look for your—"

No one cut me off. I stopped speaking on my own. The slippery-looking town wall loomed behind the hermit's short tower, covering us in cool-toned shadows. Couldn't see anything on the other side of it except teeming skies.

What was I looking for?

Long white hair, always far away from me, always alone.

The hermit let out a soft exclamation, as if he'd been stung by a passing bee.

"Found something?" I said.

"Two things."

"So it really was just stuck in your clothes."

He held out both hands. On one rested a rusty and diseased-looking blade. Its hilt must've completely rotted away.

On his other hand was a silvery metal brooch. A pinwheel-shaped flower with six broad, pointed petals.

"I got lost in my own archives," he said. "I remember now. I was asked to tell you something important."

"By who?"

"Your name is—"

"Clematis." I lifted the pin off his palm. It was mine. "Asa Clematis."

An Osmanthian name, in the classic Osmanthian order. Family name first. Asa Clematis.

I'd never been from Bittercress.

I held the pin by its sharp edges. It left dents on the ends of my fingers.

I recalled little other than my name, and the fact that I hadn't always been a Manglelander. I hadn't always been a lantern-herder. Other forgotten things started simmering to life inside me, breaking up and melting and clarifying. They just needed to cook a while longer.

I pocketed the clematis pin. "Hope you don't mind me keeping this."

"Keep the knife, too."

It looked like a surefire way to get tetanus. "Not so sure about that," I said.

"It's a Cressian blade."

"Really? An authentic artifact?"

"One hundred percent authentic," he said emphatically.

"Just sitting around in your personal hermitage? Didn't realize you had such an impressive collection."

A conflicted look came over his face, padded though it was in hoary artificial hair. Maybe he'd taken his love of the Cressians a little too far. Maybe he hadn't cleared his amateur archaeological activities with the proper authorities. Maybe he or a past hermit had smuggled treasure out of the caves without permission.

I wouldn't snitch. I was beginning to suspect that I hadn't lived the most aboveboard of lives myself.

"If it's truly a knife from Cressian times," I said, "its historical value must be way beyond our reckoning. Priceless. Very nice. You'll appreciate it more than me, though. Don't see why I should take it."

He laid the blade across my palm. "Cressian knives are rumored to be able to cut through the flesh of any mage."

"Doesn't even look like it could cut a soft block of butter."

"The rumors might not be true," he allowed.

I accepted the knife anyway. If he really wanted me to have it, far be it from me to refuse. Between the two of us, I was more likely to need it.

"You have a name, too," I said as I fought to fit his other spare costumes back on their hangers.

"Do you remember it?"

"Keeps slithering out of my head," I admitted. "Feels like I knew it before."

"Lester," he told me. "I'm just an ornamental hermit."

I helped him heave his furniture back indoors before leaving. I kept blinking, squeezing my right eyelid shut over and over. Trying to reset my right eye.

It felt wrong. It felt like having multiple fallen eyelashes trapped somewhere out of sight. It felt like the tactile equivalent of tinnitus—a buzzing along the rim of my eye socket.

Why did I have this eye?

Why did I still have this eye?

It filled a hole in my face. But I couldn't see with it.

I covered my right eye with my hand as I rushed back to the inn.

I lived in the inn because I was a guest, not a resident. I lived in the inn because I had no home in this town. I didn't belong here.

The bathroom mirror was a mess of chalky soap marks and moldy-looking black spots where the backing had worn off. I put my clematis pin and the Cressian knife on the counter.

No way to tell what color the knife had been originally. It was rough-textured all over now, a dessicated orange-brown hue. Unlike the pin, it bore no magic cuttings of human origin.

Any Cressian magic would have died together with the Cressians. That didn't necessarily mean it had no power whatsoever—it just wasn't a type I knew how to parse.

I imagined wrapping a hand towel around the part that used to have a hilt. I imagined aiming it at my right eye. The impostor eye.

But that knife was only meant to cut mages.

I went downstairs and borrowed a paring knife from the innkeeper, who was spreading small brown beechnuts on a table to dry. I pretended I'd bought some persimmons to cut up in my room.

She told me in passing that the beechnuts would need to cure for at least a few weeks before roasting. I wondered if they would ever be ready.

I returned to my quarters and thoroughly washed my hands. I washed the paring knife, too, for good measure. I looked in the cloudy bathroom mirror.

I pointed the paring knife at my right eye.

I couldn't do it. My hands wouldn't push the blade any closer. It wasn't a last-second reflex, either. I hit a wall before the sharp point came anywhere near my cornea.

The buzzing in my eye got worse. It felt like a full-grown hornet trapped in there, squished behind my eyeball—behind this piece of flesh that didn't belong to me.

I laid the paring knife next to a stone light and flung myself down on the bed. Wards on the ceiling leered at me. Wards painted with the Eyes of the Queen.

It wasn't primal fear or squeamishness that stopped me. It was more of a simple physical block. Like a dog coming up short at the end of its leash. I couldn't even test if I had the guts to go through with it.

I knew better than to ask for assistance. Bittercress residents could take just about anything in stride, and we all liked to pitch in. But I didn't think I'd find any willing volunteers to gouge my eye out.

If I couldn't do it myself, and I couldn't get help, then my best hope would be to trip into the innkeeper and snag my eye on her fishhooks. I couldn't risk being too forceful, though. I couldn't risk hurting her.

Was the Queen controlling my body? The same way she'd made us all leave the scene of the mangle ray crash? Was she consciously monitoring the magic she'd attached to me like marionette strings, or had she unleashed a complex sequence of automated emotional undercurrents to nudge each of us this way and that, sight unseen?

If I asked her, would she help me stab my own eye?

I was too proud to ask.

Perhaps the problem lay in my intent. I rolled over and plucked the paring knife off the nightstand. I sat up, my left hand splayed flat on the bed.

I raised the knife as high as I could. I readied myself to plunge it through the back of my hand.

I missed point-blank. The knife didn't puncture me: it punctured the poor innocent mattress.

I'm not trying to hurt myself, I thought. I clenched that thought very hard—in my fist, in my jaw.

I would not hurt myself. I was at peace. I was content. I was a model citizen of Bittercress. I loved our autumn days inside these walls. I loved the golden light of six-sided lanterns wafting down moody dark waters at night. Nothing was wrong with this town, and nothing was missing.

As best I could, I embodied a completely different sort of intent. A lack of intent. A bland absence of desire or anger or hunger.

I managed to move the knife across the surface of my skin. Not hard enough to draw blood, or leave any kind of mark. But I did succeed in lulling myself enough to make contact.

Time for another experiment.

I let go of the paring knife. I laid my hand on the right side of my face, very near the rim of my eye.

I wasn't trying to hurt myself.

I wasn't trying to hurt it.

I was utterly sincere. This eye wasn't part of me. I didn't believe it was a thing that could suffer.

My fingertips met the surface of my eye. It felt subtly springy. Like a little bouncy rubber ball. I squeezed gently, as if trying to remove an ephemeral contact lens.

I looked up, toward my own forehead. I used my left hand to open my eye wider. I probed along the lower curve where the rest of the orb vanished behind the damp inner flesh of my bottom eyelid.

A basic false eye would have a detachable front part, a shell you could pluck out if only you managed to hook your fingers around its hidden edge. (I couldn't recall why I knew this.) That lower edge was what I sought now, almost rolling my eyes back in my head in my attempt to expose it.

Instead, as I prodded ever so tenderly at my eyeball, the entire thing came plopping out of my face without any further resistance.

For a few addled seconds, I couldn't understand what had happened. My fingertips kept patiently sweeping about the perimeter of my eye socket. Except now they touched nothing. My eyelid drooped, sagging.

I turned to see what had come out of me. It nestled unassumingly in the bedspread. An untethered eyeball, too impeccably spherical and white in back to be real. No visible damage, no artery, no optic nerve trailing like a severed umbilical cord.

I reached for it. My left eye—my one good eye—blinked.

The thing I picked off the bed was not a real human eye, or even a prosthetic eye. It was not a bouncy ball or a marble or some other child's toy painted to look like a body part. It was more of a misshapen lump than a sphere. A grayish river rock, eroded to smoothness, without any outstanding features whatsoever.

I felt like a befuddled folk hero. The butt of a joke played by a traveling god.

The cloth scraps I'd kept finding in random corners had been mine from the start. My eyepatches.

My arm shivered with the urge to hurl this rock through the balcony window.

I exercised a modicum of self-restraint. I got out my utility jacket. It had pockets generous enough to hide Lester's decrepit Cressian blade as well as the innkeeper's paring knife.

I fastened my clematis pin near my shoulder.

Alone in my room, I touched one of the magic-laced metal petals. I used the pin to send my voice to the Queen of the Void.

"Come here," I said. "Come right now."

She had all my matching pins. She'd confiscated them before burying my memory. She would hear me.

27

THE QUEEN ARRIVED without a sound. She wore an artist's smock that left her forearms bare, with perplexing smudges along the bottom hem. This room felt very different when the number of occupants went from one to two.

"You smell like dead mangle ray," I told her.

She didn't. But I derived some satisfaction from watching her pause and inhale.

"The corpse is gone," she said. "I repaired the house it fell on. In case you still wish to clean it."

"I'll pass. You and the mangle ray gave it a good airing out. Thanks for doing my job for me."

"You're welcome." The Queen's voice contained exactly as much gratitude as mine had.

Behind her, wind pushed at hanging plants on the balcony as if helping a child on a swing.

"What's your name?" she asked.

"Asa Clematis."

"You remembered." She didn't sound particularly touched.

"I remember your name, too."

"Tell me."

"Give me my eye back."

"Your right eye? It's gone," she replied. "Destroyed in a stabbing. Not lost like a kid in the woods. Did you forget?"

"Don't play dumb," I said. "That's my job. Stop taking my jobs away."

I took my hand out of my pocket. In it I held the rock that used to be part of my face. The rock she'd slotted there to make me think I still had a right eye. I bounced it in my palm as I spoke.

"Give me my eye back," I said again. "The prosthesis. The one Wist— the one you made for me."

I kept jiggling the stone at her like a palmful of change.

She'd forgone shoes again. She left dark watery footprints on the floor, as if the Void begun seeping out through her soles.

The bare footprints multiplied even when she made no move to approach me. They circled around her like the silent pacing of a ghost. They walked sideways along the walls, too.

"Did you think I would dispense your eye upon request?" she inquired. "Like a vending machine? You haven't even asked nicely."

"No," I agreed. "I'm not asking nicely."

The tinted afternoon light made her rogue footprints take on a color like old bloodstains. But they were very fresh in their wetness. They came faster and faster, growing agitated, blotting out paper wards and rustic painted eyes. They ran across the ceiling and then across the floor again, shooting past me. The more they spread, the more the room began to look like pox-infested skin.

At the center of it all, the Queen never moved.

My memory remained imperfect. I knew who we were, and who we were to each other. I remembered our first trip to Katashiro Caverns. I remembered everything we'd done in Bittercress with a kind of fevered clarity.

Our lives before that remained clouded. Only a few key facts stayed with me. I couldn't picture where we lived in Osmanthus. I couldn't remember the name of Wist's cat.

(Did she really have a cat back home? Would it recognize her now, changed as she was? Could I identify what, precisely, had changed when she became Queen? Her hair, sure. What color had her hair been before it went white?)

She regarded the footprints with disinterest. Their desperate pattering slowed.

Then she turned that same look of disinterest on me.

I entertained fantasies of flinging my rock at her. I'd fire it off hard enough to bury it like a bullet in *her* right eye. See how she liked that.

As she reeled, I'd leap across the distance between us, across the seething throng of reddish-black footprints. I'd whip out the paring knife or the Cressian knife—heck, why not both—and immediately have her at my mercy. Somehow.

She'd become very obedient with my rusted Cressian knife at her neck. If it really could cut mages, a blade that dull and dirty would be unimaginably painful.

This was only a fantasy. I'm no combatant.

She was moving toward me now. She might take the rock from my hand and jam it back in my empty eye socket. She might rebury my dug-up memories with another landslide of magic.

If she tried any funny business, I'd have to fight back.

The Queen halted just out of reach. "What's in your pocket?" she asked.

"My hands." I balled up my fists in my jacket. My knuckles tented the fabric.

"A fruit knife?" she guessed. Correctly.

"Who would use a fruit knife to fight a mage?"

"Seems rather small," she concurred. "Did you call me here to stab me?"

"So what if I did? You came anyway."

"I see you already stabbed the bed," she said.

"Just once." I was surprised she could see the wound in the mattress. It wasn't obvious unless you knew what to look for.

"You can stop bristling like an angry skunk."

I sniffed. "Maybe I like bristling. Ever thought of that?"

"I won't make you forget yourself right away. You'll forget on your own by tomorrow. Everything reverts to the mean."

"Unless you give me my prosthetic eye back."

"Find it yourself."

"No," I said immediately.

"Then you won't be getting it back," the Queen informed me.

She came up to the bed and reached down to straighten the covers. That wasn't the first, second, or even third thing I'd have imagined my Wist doing in her place.

Beyond the glass doors to the balcony came a sound like air whistling through a narrow canyon. No wind reached us indoors.

"I'm not about to tear up the entire town on a wild hunt for my eye," I said. "If I've only got the rest of the day before I start forgetting who I am—that's not nearly enough time."

I grabbed the bedspread she'd just fixed. I flung it backwards with a vengeance. "I already followed your orders last time. I tried to escape. I gave it my all.

"Escaping was a logical move. It made sense in the moment. Looking for where you've hidden my eye—before I forget it exists—would be a logical move, too. A reasonable next step. But that's not really what I ought to be doing now, is it?"

The Queen was on my left. We stood side by side without touching, facing the unmade bed like divers at the edge of a pool.

She had her hair tied back in a low, practical ponytail. Between that and her smock, it wouldn't have been surprising to see her whip out a paintbrush and start dabbing more eye motifs on the wood of the walls.

Her forearms were stippled in bruises shaped like smudged fingerprints. Someone could've grabbed her, I guess, though I couldn't conceive of who. (Did the Void have fingertips?) To my amateur eye, they looked more like marks left by her own two hands.

Weightless inky footprints appeared on the sheets, one after another, as if the Queen's ghost had walked straight across to the other side.

"We slept here together," she said to the bed, as if wondering how that statement could be true. "Long ago."

"Before you were Queen. How long ago is that?"

"I don't count the days. They aren't going anywhere."

A lifetime's worth of lantern-hunting packed every last empty space in my head. A lifetime spent belonging inside the Bittercress walls. Some of those memories had to be false. Most seemed much too real to tell the difference.

I could stab her now, if I wished. She'd entered striking distance. She seemed less wary of me than before. Or perhaps just more preoccupied with the Void inside her.

I had two knives in my jacket. Neither would impress a professional assassin. One was meant for skinning fruit, and the other belonged in a museum of ancient history. Still, I had a chance. With luck, I might wound her at least as much as I'd wounded my own bed.

And then?

What should I be chasing, if not my stolen eye? I didn't know how to solve the mystery of the Queen and her Void and the sealed-up miniature world of Bittercress. But the more time I spent in close proximity with her, the better my odds of finding out.

I made my fingers uncurl. I sidled half an inch sideways. Right up against the Queen's arm.

Her reaction was lethargic at best. She glanced at me as slowly as a cold-blooded animal winding down for winter.

I didn't meet her gaze.

"Wist," I whispered in the voice I'd have used if she were the very same unchanged Wist who'd slept next to me in this bed.

She laughed.

It was brief and unamused, but real enough that I felt her shake.

"Clematis," she said, almost fondly. "What are you doing?"

Okay, so she definitely wasn't in the mood for that. Duly noted. Guess the Queen had loftier things to concern herself with than matters of the flesh.

I changed course. "Need a deputy?" I asked.

"...............?"

"Must be lonely, being a queen without a court. Or a palace. Or an army. Or a treasury. Or a throne."

"I like my chair," she said, deliberately missing the point.

"Well, your chair can't hold a conversation. Listen—I'm saying I'll be your little minion." I nudged her for emphasis.

"You'll lose your memory again overnight. If not sooner."

"So? Let the rest of the town keep living in peace. I'll do your dirty work. You're a queen. You need a gopher."

"Why would I choose you when you won't even remember who you are?" asked the Queen.

"Yikes," I said, heartfelt. "That stings. I'd like to think you'd choose me anyway. Don't tell me you've got your eye on the mortician or something. Nothing against older women, but—"

A most peculiar look came over her face. Maybe the Void was giving her cramps. Surely it couldn't be that I'd accidentally hit the nail on the head. Right? Right?

Like all her expressions, it only lasted half a second.

If this were the Wist I knew, I'd wrap my arms around her waist and keep bugging her till she gave in and explained herself. I'd head-butt her like a hungry (yet affectionate) goat.

If I tried that with the Queen, she'd turn me into a coat rack. She'd give me to the innkeeper as a surprise present.

I put a cautious hand on the sleeve of her smock. She eyed it the way she might've eyed a flying ant.

"All that aside," I said.

"All that aside?"

"Don't I deserve a reward for clawing back part of my memory? Even if it won't last long. I knew you wouldn't outright erase it."

"Are you going to ask for your eye again?"

"Nope. I won't ask you to set me free, either. I'm so undemanding."

"Mm."

That didn't seem like a sound of agreement.

However, Asa Clematis was nothing if not incorrigible. "Take me to the top of the walls again," I said. "The walls around town. Let me see what's on the other side."

"We went there before."

"Yes. When I was a bleeding mess. Couldn't exactly savor the scenery."

"Does it hurt?" she asked.

"What?"

"Where the spears mangled you."

"No," I said. "Thanks to...."

I trailed off. She regarded me with a tinge of disappointment. Like she wished I could still feel those spears. Like she still stood nonchalantly balanced on the point of a blood-slick spike. Looking down at me as though I'd dissolved into a filthy roadside puddle.

She took my hand off her sleeve. She ported me—ported both of us—without touching me.

28

BEFORE ANYTHING ELSE, I heard flowing water. The top of the wall held a stream as wide as the river.

I'd expected there to be parapets—but the area between them formed a water-filled sunken moat. Wholly invisible from the ground.

The bottom of the rushing moat looked just like the river, too. Muddy and rocky and uneven, not tiled like a swimming pool.

The wall appeared level, with no variation in height. The moat carved inside it didn't follow a slope. Yet the clear burbling water constantly rushed to our left. As if something were chasing it.

The Queen's magic had placed us on a wooden boardwalk. It had no protective railing, and its path followed no discernible logic.

It hugged one side of the moat or the other, flush against the nearest parapet. Then it veered to cut right down the center, with water on both sides. In other parts, two boardwalks ran parallel. Scaled-down footbridges spanned the gap.

Fish battled the current below: sleek silver fish, fat mud-colored fish, shoals of tiny minnows clustering like clouds of underwater gnats.

I crossed over to the parapet facing away from Bittercress.

The top of the parapet was strangely unfinished, covered in warty organic growths. Burls on an old tree.

"Do you see what you wanted to see?" asked the Queen.

There had never been other towns visible from Bittercress. From this vantage point, it might as well have been the only settlement on the continent.

I saw no smoking battlefields, or new cities full of devils, or flocks of fallen aerials. Nothing to suggest that the apocalypse had come while our time kept turning in circles.

At the edge of the sky, hills grew into mountains. The same mountain range we'd gone to visit before Katashiro Caverns moved much closer, taking up residence right below town.

Closer to the walls moved slow brown shapes: primevals gone out to forage. Herds of svelter creatures grazed near the shade of a forest. The rumored singing deer?

"I might need glasses," I said.

"Or a monocle," the Queen murmured.

The far-off reaches of the sky and plains lost their color, fading precipitously. Like the gods of creation had run out of budget for high-quality paint. I suspected it wasn't just an issue with my eyesight.

Even parts of this walltop water garden felt off. The turtle-shaped stepping stones positioned further upstream were an exact copy of the ones down in the river that ran through town.

"You're recycling pieces of the scenery," I accused. "Talk about lazy."

"No one comes up here," the Queen replied, unbothered.

Tiny sky nettles—some no larger than dandelion fluff—fluttered hopefully about her hair.

"She's not your mother," I told them.

They paid me no heed. They seemed to think she might feed them. I couldn't begin to guess at what baby aerials normally ate.

One landed on her fingertip. She casually reached out and, before I could dodge her, transferred it to the crown of my head.

I went very still. The young sky nettle felt weightless. Its arms (tentacles?) caressed my scalp like glass noodles made of ice.

"Wist," I squeaked.

She waited an unnecessarily long time before lifting the sky nettle off me. It bobbed away as the wind picked up, unharmed.

"You were never troubled by insects," she said.

"I'm plenty cautious when they're dangerous! I don't go around hugging hornets." The skin below my hair still felt borderline numb with cold. "I don't know anything about aerials, anyway. These look like jellyfish. What if they sting? What if I'm allergic? What if human contact kills them? That sure would put a damper on things."

"You won't kill them," the Queen said blandly.

She turned her back on the world outside Bittercress. She gestured inside the walls—at the water towers from bygone eras. Some much higher than others. All constructed in different styles and from different material. There wasn't a single matching pair.

"Most of those towers weren't built for human use," she said. "They've been repurposed."

"What were they built for, then?"

Her eyes rose to the bustling sky. "The oldest water towers were like giant birdbaths for aerials. So they wouldn't fall in droves during seasons of drought. Stopped being much of a problem once the aerial population thinned out."

"There used to be more of them?"

"Much, much more," she said. "More in the time of the first Kraken.

Even more in the time of the Cressians. As long as we live, we'll never see skies like that."

Behind her, a wide section of the outward-facing parapet dropped away as if caught in a rockslide. She didn't turn to look.

It made a sound when it crumbled. I never heard the stones hit the ground. Water streamed over the broken lip of the wall. It streamed and streamed without any sign of running out. River fish wiggled frantically to avoid that part of the current. As if they knew a waterfall had formed, and knew something terrible awaited at the bottom.

If I stuck my arms out, I could push the Queen over the edge. Nothing blocked her now. There was just the boardwalk and the river running beneath it and that huge missing chunk of parapet. Hell, she might fall on her own if the wind played a little trick on her.

"Intrusive thoughts?" she asked.

"What? Me? Never."

She beckoned. "Step closer. The view is better."

"I can see just fine from over here," I said primly.

She put her hands back in her pockets. Her hair looped around me like a pale rope for catching cattle.

Struggle too much, and I'd pitch myself over the broken precipice. Assuming the Queen didn't fling me off herself.

With no apparent effort, her hair dragged me next to her. It tied me to her side like a prisoner to a chair.

Water kept pouring down the vertical wall below our feet. With so much of the parapet missing, the rim of the boardwalk jutted out into nothingness.

"I see the ground," I announced. It was not a comforting sight.

Lustrous sky nettles orbited the Queen like nectarivores around a butterfly bush. I stretched my hand out and gripped the side of the sheared-off parapet. I held on for dear life.

"Maybe you do deserve a reward for becoming yourself again," she said. "However briefly."

"Do I have to fight you for it?"

"No."

"Do I have to answer a riddle, then?"

"No."

"Oh. Hmm. Will you give me an impossible task? Shall I bring you the marrow of the moon?"

"No."

"I'm stumped," I told her.

"This is a gift. Freely offered."

"I don't get what you're offering."

She pointed down. Straight down at the misty green ground.

"I'll die if I jump," I said.

"You won't fall in the way you're imagining," she said distantly. "You might never be the same. But you won't die. When you land—"

"I'll be outside Bittercress?"

The rope of her hair slid off my shoulders.

It was like being in two places—two times—at once. Here I was pressed against her, gazing companionably at the long and deadly drop. All the while, something rigid in my body remembered how I'd first met her as the Queen. The rickety tower platform. The threat of a fatal fall.

She'd offered me a chance to escape before, too. But only in the sense of a cat toying with its prey. She'd known it was hopeless. She'd never really intended for me to leave her.

This seemed different.

As I stared, the wall grew higher. The ground retreated. To an immeasurable distance.

"Did I succeed in making you sick of me?"

"Think what you like," said the Queen.

Sky nettles the size of soap bubbles did laps around her wrists, her neck, the air above her head. As if weaving her a halo—as if forging her a crown.

She'd needed me here before, and now she didn't. Or she'd needed me before, and she still needed me, but she'd given up on me. She was ready to go it alone. Possibly forever. Whatever happened in the outside world, nothing would change inside Bittercress.

She'd wanted me to resist, but she'd refused to let me out. She'd wanted me to fight, but she'd refused to let me win.

What was the point, then?

Entertainment?

She hadn't seemed terribly entertained.

Killing time?

She had infinite time to kill. I could no more make a dent in it than a flea could suck blood through a primeval's hard keratin scales.

I could only conclude that she'd wanted me to surprise her. To vault three or four steps beyond the surface-level goal of escaping.

Did she secretly hope for me to usurp the throne? To hold her down and drag the Void out of her? That was a lot to ask of someone without any innate magic.

When I peeked at her, I could see hints of the Void in the veins all along her neck and the side of her face. Veins of blood and veins of magic. The Void was a thing of shadow, but it had its own radiance all the same.

There were things she could say and things she couldn't. But in her indirect way, she was telling me more than ever before. Which suggested that change could happen even in a town frozen in time.

The Queen herself had changed. Think back to our first few encounters. She now seemed less invested in intimidating me.

Because she'd already won. Or because the Void had begun to consume more and more of her attention. Or because she'd grown comfortable in her alliance with it. Too comfortable, even.

It might get harder and harder to discern who or what was really in charge here.

"This is a limited-time offer," the Queen said.

I scowled. "Trying to upsell me? Limited by what?"

"My whim."

"Oh, great."

"And your ability to remember yourself."

"I don't like it here," I said, meaning the brink of this newborn waterfall. "I won't decide under pressure. Let's go for a walk."

She didn't budge. "Make your choice."

"I'm not so tiny that I can't climb over the parapet. If I need to fling myself off on short notice, I'll figure something out. Trust me."

Her hair had stopped trapping me. I set off on my own. It was a relief to leave the gaping hole in the wall.

I resisted temptation: I didn't look over my shoulder.

A second set of footsteps followed me down the boardwalk, muffled by the sound of ever-moving water. I crouched to watch a pair of hundred-eye ducks. They nestled moodily in the shadow of a reedy sandbank.

"How far are you planning to go?" asked the Queen.

"As far as I like. You're in no rush, are you? You've got all the time you could possibly want."

The boards quivered underfoot as we strolled.

"There's nothing up here that you can't see down by the river," she pointed out.

"Except the other side of the wall."

"Except that."

"And those jellies of yours."

She pointed skyward. They streamed away into the distance like puppies chasing an invisible ball.

"We haven't been trapped here for the equivalent of years," I said, probing. "Not yet. But it's possible, isn't it?"

"What are you trying to ask?"

"How much time has passed on the outside? *How* is time passing on the outside?"

"Not enough time will have passed to concern you."

If I had to pick a label, I'd call myself a realist. But I'm still human. Part of me kept hoping that she hadn't spoiled the natural flow of time.

Hear me out. Yes, she'd already confessed to it. Once I accused her, she no longer made any attempt to hide it.

A confession, however, doesn't necessarily have to be true. The whole thing could have been a giant ruse. Everyone in town thought the equinox hadn't come yet, but they might be wrong. It might already have passed.

She could've been faking it. A mage of her caliber could create the illusion of every single day being as long as the next. She could forbid spider lily buds from blooming. She could manipulate local temperatures to make it seem like the seasons never crept forward.

That might sound insane. It would still be much easier than meddling with time itself. Even just for a single rural town.

That possibility crumbled to dust at the back of my mind as we walked together along the top of the wall.

I didn't stub my toe on fresh evidence. The aerials didn't send down a new epiphany from the heavens. The seeds were already there. An unasked-for conviction took root in me, and I could no longer chase it out.

She'd really done it. The one thing she'd promised herself she would never do again. She'd broken another great taboo. I wouldn't waste time hunting for alternate explanations.

I spoke to fill our silence. "You seem less guarded. Because you think I'll be leaving soon?"

"Less guarded compared to what?"

"I basically had to blackmail you into coming to dinner. Remember?"

"Yes. You tried to poison me."

"I also poisoned myself. No harm, no foul."

She made a skeptical sound.

"Or," I added, sweet as treacle, "has Your Highness been getting lonely? Just as I thought. Well, can't blame you."

"I could strangle you," she said emptily.

"I try my best to be inspiring."

I had to turn my head to see to my right. The town revealed itself with much more clarity than the view on the other side of the wall. People and primevals, roads and bridges, the wide shallow river. Rooftop windcatchers like chimneys riddled with holes. Thriving green farm plots. The water tower made up like a muskmelon. Stately manors built to suit the architectural taste of foreign owners.

Beneath it all, unseen: Katashiro Caverns, the bowels of Bittercress. Or else its hidden heart.

While I studied Bittercress, the Queen studied me.

She began talking without preamble. Her voice was calibrated to hold no more emotion than the clear water running past our feet.

"The Void can't see. It can't hear. It can't touch. It can't smell. It can't taste. It only has one sense."

There was only one left to name. "Magic perception," I finished.

"The Void took many mages over the years," she said.

"Everyone who got spirited away?"

"It didn't wish to harm them."

I had to scoff at this.

"It doesn't wish to harm me, either," the Queen went on. "A virus has no real desire to harm its host."

"But it *is* harming you," I said.

Her legs were much longer than mine. Her strides carried her further. "The mages it took—it consumed them by accident. It wasn't trying to kill them."

"I see. No offense meant. Yeah, that makes everything better. Water under the bridge."

"All the Void sought was a living vessel. The caverns surrounded it like a shattered eggshell. It craved a body of flesh to call home."

I had to walk as fast as I could (and then some) to stay with her. "So all those vanished mages died to the Void."

"None could withstand it. But the Void doesn't understand life and death. It doesn't even know what a mage is."

"What?"

"The only reason it takes mages is because it can't perceive anyone else."

"Because ... the Void only has magic perception." My pulse thumped a sickly beat. "The Manglelanders of ye olden days were right, then. Avoid using human magic. Avoid drawing attention. Avoid it at all costs."

"Manglelanders never knew what they were hiding from," said the Queen.

"Has the Void left the caverns before? Has it ever done anything worse than snatch occasional mages?"

"There are a lot of debates over what ended the Cressians."

"Is it like ... a ten-thousand year flood? How bad is it?"

Silence answered me.

I tugged the Queen to a halt.

The gray-brown stains on her smock could've been old paint—or blood from a legion of fallen foes.

"Explain why you took my magic eye," I said.

"You can extrapolate," she replied evenly.

I cupped a hand over my empty lid. "The eye protected me from getting swallowed up by all the other magic you use to control Bittercress. But the eye itself is plastered with powerful cuttings. If I keep it, the Void can see me. If I keep it, the Void will notice me."

I was a healer. I had no magic core. I would become a ghost without my prosthetic. Invisible to the Void. Might as well not exist.

"What about my pins?" I asked. "No, not just my pins. You left something behind when you stole my eye. You planted extra magic at the back of my socket like a piece of old gum."

"That magic is nothing compared to your prosthesis. It's the difference between a single firefly and a burning house." She looked up. "Aerials have a kind of natural magic, too. The Void keeps luring them closer. Most of the time, it lacks the magnetism to pull them straight down out of the sky."

Most of the time, huh. "What about our bond? That's a form of magic."

"To the Void, our bond looks like a flashlight pointed down a dark tunnel. The beam of light goes on and on, and eventually peters out. It goes nowhere, and illuminates nothing."

Was it just me, or was the Queen quite a bit more eloquent than my usual Wist?

"You've become awfully talkative," I said.

"Would you prefer me to remain silent and mysterious?"

"That's nice in its own way, but I'll take all the information I can get." I moved my hands to hint at the shapelessness of the Void. "It—er, your eldritch friend doesn't mind you telling me all this?"

She took a while to respond. I didn't push her.

Some patches of reeds growing in the wall-riding river were completely flattened. Submerged. They ran parallel to the current, streaming like underwater ribbons.

I'd wondered if the flow would weaken as the river poured itself out through the hole in the parapet. Thus far it showed no sign of abating. That hole was well out of sight now, in any case. The Queen's magic might already have seamlessly rebuilt it.

"The Void does not know human language," she told me. "The Void does not have conscious logical thoughts. But on some level, it comprehends human emotion and intent."

Neither of us moved now.

There was nothing suppressed behind, under, or in the middle of her voice. There was no hidden plea in her eyes. She spoke as if reading off the gravestone of a long-dead stranger.

"The Void understands that I welcome it," she said in a monotone. "I cherish it." The words were just syllables. Just a string of different sounds. "I absolutely don't want to be rid of it. The Void understands that I will never abandon it. It understands that I don't want to be saved."

Compared to the totality of her mask, I felt naked.

The Void inside her looked straight out through her unwavering black eyes, her skin, her unearthly hair.

And it really didn't see me? It really didn't hear me?

From the perspective of the Void, the Queen stood here all by herself, dropping dry facts word by word into empty air. Like a fishkeeper idly sprinkling pond salt. Perhaps that would not strike it as seeming odd or suspicious. Perhaps the Void had no preconceived notions about normal behavior.

The Void didn't know what a conversation was supposed to sound like. It couldn't listen to anything except whatever echoes of speech filtered down through her mind and her magic.

I reached tentatively for her left arm.

When my fingers closed around her bare wrist, I felt the texture of her bond thread. No matter how I looked, I couldn't see it. But I felt it.

My chest clenched.

The thread itself was just a piece of string. In other countries, she might graft on convenient magic cuttings, but she would've stripped them all before entering Manglesea. So she could wear it openly. Despite the fact that I didn't always wear one myself.

The Queen had grown more tolerant of my presence over time. Why?

My guess—because experience had made her better at masking for the Void. During our initial encounters, she must've been intensely focused on curating her inner face. On eliminating every wayward longing the Void might absorb from her.

Wist was uniquely well-suited for this. And not just because she happened to be the only living Kraken. She'd trained half her life to hide what she felt. Self-taught, yes. She still did it better than anyone. She interred every last egotistical impulse as if burying murdered bodies on a night with no moon. Then she calmly tilled the flat and expressionless soil above them.

The habit was so ingrained that even as an adult, she almost never cracked a smile. When I startled laughter out of her, she'd laugh with a straight face. Downright unnerving, if you didn't know her.

Famous though she was, few people truly knew her. At least—I didn't think they did. Most everything before Bittercress stayed opaque to me.

I recalled the stone she'd stuck in my face to make me forget my missing eye. Magic had stopped me from stabbing it. I'd managed to pluck it out after hushing my thoughts, telling myself I harbored no harmful intent.

Wist would've been much better at that. Wist would've been able to carry out my original plan. She could've put a blade through her own eye without betraying any premonition of violence, either to herself or to others.

I let go of her wrist. I'd made up my mind. The Queen wore my bond thread again, although no one would know it but us. That was more than enough.

29

"I'll take you up on your offer," I said to her.

The entire parapet disintegrated. Water poured down the unguarded face of the wall, free and abundant.

"Don't be hasty, now," I cautioned. "If I leave Bittercress, I might not see you again for a very long time. Or," I added, guessing at the contours of the Queen's unspoken response, "in your opinion, never."

She waited for me to finish.

"Do me one last favor. Come back to the inn. Come back to our room."

She answered without saying a word.

"Don't look at me like that," I retorted. "I'm not demanding a night of passion here. I assume that's not on the menu."

She studied her fingernails. Not without reason. The Void had begun to dye them a deep bluish black.

"I'm your healer," I said. "Let me heal you. For old times' sake."

She didn't turn away from the missing parapet. "You should leave while you can."

"We've got time, don't we? You claimed my mind could hold out for the rest of the day."

"I don't guarantee it."

"If I leave Bittercress, I'm coming back with reinforcements."

"You can try," said the Queen.

"My point is, I won't be gone for good. But I don't know how long it'll end up being on your side of the wall. Don't want you to forget how it feels when I heal you."

I kept going, although she hadn't said no yet. I pointed at the discolored wilderness beyond the town wall.

"You offered to let me go. It's a gift, right? My choice as to how I accept it."

"You can only take that so far," she said. Barely above a whisper. Her voice melded with the shushing of the water.

And it melded with me. An echo of the spikes clanged through me. As if her quiet, quiet voice had struck my flesh like a gong. I swayed and clutched at the now-vanished parapet. My fingers swiped empty air.

She extended an arm to stop me from falling.

She didn't have to say anything more. She could put me back on those spikes. She could make time eat its own tail. She could make it so I'd always been speared there, bleeding without dying. For all I knew, I *had* always been there, and every moment since was merely a hallucination of escape.

The Void didn't make her sound like that. The Void didn't make her frightening. My Wist was inherently terrifying. She just chose to rein it in.

Maybe I'd been looking at this all wrong. If the Void had fundamentally corrupted her, I would've felt some hint of it in our bond. I didn't understand the Queen, but on the deepest possible level, I still recognized her as Wist. At her core, she didn't seem tainted.

What could have changed her—literally overnight—if not the power of the Void? A power that, unlike human magic, required no delineation to exert itself.

I backed across the nearest low bridge, away from the missing parapet.

"On the subject of parting gifts," I said, "you may as well give my eye back. Since I'll be leaving town anyway."

"I just warned you not to be demanding."

"You sure did."

"I'll preserve it as a keepsake," the Queen said, laconic.

"You don't want a lock of my hair?"

"Is your hair long enough to give away chunks of it?"

I felt my head. "Maybe not."

Eventually she heeded my pleas to get us down off the wall and back to the inn. (The only way I could've descended on my own was by jumping off. Now wasn't the time for that.)

I didn't have any intention of leaving Bittercress, by the way. Not on my own. I just needed an excuse to bring her back to our room.

When she ported us in, all the Void-stained footprints on the walls and floor and ceiling and bedsheets were gone. Thank goodness I wouldn't have to explain them to the innkeeper.

I slid the balcony doors wide open and ushered the Queen outside. I dusted off the patio furniture, then pushed her into a chair.

"Make yourself at home," I said. I'm such a great host.

With anyone else, I would slap on an eyepatch rather than walk around empty-lidded. With her, I didn't bother.

I bustled about to remove the bell-shaped lids from every stone light. There was still plenty of sun out, but the crystals gave off an extremely flattering glow.

"You wanted to heal me," the Queen said from the balcony.

"Be patient. Let me set the mood."

She twisted to watch me lug out my milk crate full of various mead and cider blends. I'd been hanging onto this since our dinner date. I'd let it occupy a corner of the room even after forgetting when and why I'd gotten it.

"Don't judge me," I said. "Look—they're all full. Half of this is nonalcoholic, anyway." I made a shooing gesture. "The sky's turning pretty colors. Sit back and enjoy your scenery."

I grabbed two bottles of nonalcoholic cider. Pear for Wist, and crabapple for me.

I brought them to the bathroom, where we had clean drinking glasses—and which was at the moment plagued neither by toenail clippings nor plump pearly maggots nor an aggregation of long-legged harvest spiders. The mirror wasn't sobbing, and the counter hadn't melted into vanilla ice cream, and there weren't any dead rats stuffed in the drain of the tub like gauze in a wound. I'd take that as a win.

I still had a few sleeping pills left. Not enough to a kill a grown woman. I didn't want to poison her, anyhow. Not this time.

I dropped an oblong yellow tablet in her glass and stirred furiously until it looked fully dissolved.

This was why I'd picked alcohol-free drinks, you see.

I wouldn't count on it being able to fully knock her out. Even if she drank her whole glass, an hour might pass before the drug took effect. If she caught herself getting sleepy, she could use magic to clear her mind.

We clinked our glasses out on the balcony. (Rather, I bumped mine into hers and pretended she'd been a willing participant.)

The Queen made no comment on how long it had taken me to emerge with our drinks.

"Lovely, isn't it?" I said of the burgeoning sunset. "Very atmospheric."

"The sky won't heal my magic."

"Give me points for effort, Your Majesty."

She drank as if she were trying to get it over with as quickly as possibly.

"Hey," I protested. "Can you even taste that? Slow down."

"So you can interrogate me?"

"How'd you guess?" I curled sideways in my chair, hugging my legs to my chest. "What would've happened if you never went back to the caverns? If you never met the Void?"

Late afternoon light shone through her amber glass. "...I only know this because I did meet the Void. Because I made it part of me. Until then, I didn't understand."

"Understand what?"

"Its roots started in Katashiro Caverns, but its influence extended throughout Manglesea. That's how it snatched mages from all over the country. In time, it would have spread across the whole continent."

"There are mage children here in Bittercress," I said. "You won't—it won't hurt them, will it?"

She touched the base of her throat. An oddly proprietary gesture. "Once the Void takes root in a vessel, the last thing it wants to do is leave."

"Makes sense. You're the most powerful vessel around. Why downgrade?"

"Doesn't matter," she said. "I could be a branchless mage, and it still wouldn't leave me. I can tell now."

I leaned back, folding my arms behind my neck. "The Void doesn't like being a void without form. It wants to stay in a single host for as long as it can. The local mage kids are safe, then."

"It's too late for them."

"You just implied it wouldn't snatch them."

"It already has."

"How? When?"

"Not everyone in town is strictly alive." Her tone brooked no argument. "Any mages you thought you saw were in truth taken by the Void. Long, long ago."

The balcony's hanging plants cast a tangle of shadows.

It was that time of the day when even the most transparent of aerials took on a solid silhouette. Black shapes coruscated like insects crawling across the vivid sunset.

I pictured round-eyed children staring in the graveyard. Was it me they'd been looking at?

The first evening horn started playing.

Once it finished, I asked her to tell me exactly what had happened down in Katashiro Caverns.

"When?" She didn't sound drowsy. But her eyes were half-lidded.

"The first time you came face-to-face with the Void."

"I opened a vorpal hole," she said plainly.

"You *what*?"

I had second thoughts as soon as I yelped this. Half her job was to travel around closing vorpal holes; I remembered that much. In theory she would be capable of opening one, too.

Did I already know that? Was it something we'd discussed outside Bittercress? Maybe yes. Maybe no. Learning the answer wouldn't do much to help me here and now.

"Er, never mind," I said. "You opened a vorpal hole deep in the caves. Got it. Why?"

"There's a reason vorpal holes don't spawn in Manglesea."

"A reason ... you think the Void's been suppressing them?"

She nodded. "I thought the Void must have some kind of primal aversion to vorpal holes. A deep-seated phobia."

"Hold on," I said. "Opening a vorpal hole can't have been easy. Why bother? Wasn't the Void starved for a living host? If your goal was to assimilate it, all you had to do was open your arms and wait."

"The Void was afraid of me, too," the Queen said wryly.

"Oh."

"I hadn't known to hide my own wariness. It sensed enmity in my magic. But it feared my vorpal hole too much to attack me."

"It fled into you out of sheer terror."

She finished her glass. "I needed every advantage on my side in order to master it. In a world where I confronted it without using a vorpal hole—"

"Would you still be the Queen of the Void?"

"Yes." Zero doubt. "But there would be very little left of Wisteria Shien."

It wasn't the sleeping pill or the artisanal cider that made her so forthcoming. She must've grown confident in her ability to deceive the Void inside her. To remain utterly serene and colorless. To refrain from feeding it any tinge of revulsion, rejection, hostility. To embrace it with her whole heart no matter what sounds came tumbling out of her mouth.

I welcome it. I cherish it. I will never abandon it. I don't want to be saved.

I ushered her inside and onto the bed. She lay on her stomach, head turned away from me, unexpectedly pliant.

She must have been striving to avoid sensing danger. To avoid second-guessing my requests. The mind-dulling effect of the pill might have helped with that.

I kneaded a spot between her shoulders. "How will the Void react to me healing you?"

"It'll surge out and gobble you whole."

"Answer seriously."

"To the Void, it'll be as if my magic is moving around on its own."

Human magic branches wavered and wove together and twisted into knots all the time. Anyone could tell the difference between that natural oscillation and the purposeful movement induced by a healer.

"The Void must be pretty gullible," I said.

"The Void doesn't reason like we would." Half the Queen's voice got absorbed by her pillow. "It won't suspect outside interference unless I point it that way with my desires, my fears, my anticipation."

"Can you take healing from me without reacting?"

"I won't have feelings of a sort that would alarm the Void," she said sleepily.

I pulled up her smock to expose her lower back. I moved the long white coil of her hair to one side.

"That cider really didn't have any alcohol?" she asked.

"Quite good, wasn't it?"

I still wore my utility jacket. I got up on the bed and sat on the backs of her thighs.

She stiffened. "Is this necessary?"

"I'm the expert, aren't I?"

"You don't sit on me every time you heal me."

"Want me to back off?"

She shook her head against her pillow.

I didn't touch her skin directly. I plucked the air above her lower back as if playing the strings of an invisible zither. Her magic branches quivered and turned in response, quick as fish flocking to fallen crumbs.

"Thought you'd be happier to be relieved of your duties," she said, face hidden.

"As a healer?"

"Mm."

"I have my pride." I sent reproachful ripples through the length of her magic. "I won't be outdone by a parasitic mass of—whatever it is. A civilization's worth of human folly."

The Void had kept her magic in good working order, with few burgeoning tangles. She didn't particularly need extra healing. *I* was the one who needed her lying here, outwardly vulnerable. Concentrating intensely on presenting a perfect blank face to the Void.

"What would the Void make you do to me?" I asked. "If it recognized my existence. If it perceived me as a threat."

She mumbled something in refusal.

"I'm just trying to understand the risks."

"I can't say it." Now her voice came out clear and flat. "I can't say it out loud and still control myself enough to fool the Void."

I kept my mouth shut. I healed her thoroughly, and much more slowly than usual.

The layout of her magic seemed both familiar and strange. The more closely I examined it, branch by branch, the more profoundly this struck me. Like getting nostalgic for a city you've never visited.

She strained to push certain branches to the forefront. One bright thread floated higher, again and again, reaching out for me. A baited fishing line.

"This is taking a while," she said.

"My work is always meticulous."

"Trying to prove yourself superior to the Void?"

"Of course I'm superior. I'm your bondmate."

The Queen yawned quietly.

I was working one-handed now. I had my right hand in my pocket.

"How's your pain tolerance nowadays?" I inquired.

She was slow to answer, as if she'd started drifting off. "...Better than ever."

"You're setting high expectations," I said.

I kept stroking the silken threads of her magic with my left hand. I never stopped.

I mentally took stock of my tools. The clematis pin stuck to the front of my jacket. A shiny fruit knife. A rusty Cressian knife. I'd wrapped a washcloth around the metal stub it had in place of a handle.

My other pocket hid the malformed pebble I'd plucked from my face. All this junk made me wonder why I didn't carry a bag.

I didn't wonder for long. The paper wards on the wall had started smoking like incense sticks.

Too bad I hadn't equipped myself with a more impressive weapon. Like a rifle or a shotgun. I'd seen a couple around town. Although I had no proficiency with firearms, my knife skills weren't anything to brag about, either.

Enough regrets. I redoubled my focus on the Queen of the Void.

I took my right hand—still empty—out of my pocket. There were other things I could try before knifing her in the back. That one overtly luminous branch of hers winked at me like sunlight striking water.

I rambled directionlessly as I dug deeper into her magic. Didn't really listen to my own words. Just threw together some idle patter to lull her.

Somehow this turned into me listing off each townsperson I'd met—though I couldn't say their names—and speculating on whether they were technically alive or technically dead. Living ghosts or dead ghosts.

I waffled over how to categorize the perky guard who'd brought us on our outing to the caverns. That day felt like ages ago.

On the one hand, his contribution to our travels seemed rather too real to count him as a trick of the light. On the other hand, his wistful riverside accordion playing did seem like the sort of thing a ghost would do to while away the hours.

"Him?" the Queen sounded bemused. "But he—"

Before she could finish, I grabbed the roots of her magic.

I twisted the bundle in my grip as if trying to rip her branches clean out of her core. They didn't separate from it. They didn't need to separate. The pain would last longer if her branches stayed attached.

It must have hurt her deeper than anything else. Deeper than the sensation of metal spikes nailing inch-wide holes in you, in one side and out the other.

She made a muted noise through closed lips. I scrabbled to trigger that one bright, taunting, and slippery branch. A branch imprinted with a magic skill of dazzling complexity.

A branch that, if I forced it to activate, would open a vorpal hole.

I'd make it open a hole inside her body.

I still knew how to hijack her. I could force her magic to use itself. Like making someone blink by touching their cornea. Like pouring water down their throat to make them swallow.

All this happened in the space of a second.

She was sluggish, drugged, malleable from having her magic massaged to limpid smoothness. She wasn't unwilling to help me—she just couldn't do so openly. Or admit it. Even to herself.

I should've won the instant I got my fingers in her magic. I didn't miss a beat. I manipulated it with peerless finesse. No other living healer could do this.

The wards on the walls and the ceiling crumbled away in a ragged snowfall of hot ash.

I listened for the grating shriek of a vorpal hole peeling open.

Instead, we ported.

30

My hands were still under the Queen's smock, glued to her back.

She wasn't beneath me anymore. We stood on the edge of the river. Not the one that ran through town—the one that ran atop the imperious walls.

The parapets dissolved like wet sand. Water rushed to overflow on both sides of us, curiously muted, never stopping. In the streets of Bittercress, people and primevals stood as still as toy figures. The town looked like the face of a broken clock. But the wind kept moving without a care in the world, and so did the aerials circling above.

I hadn't lost contact with Wist's magic. I should've been able to slip inside her, to seize control.

The Queen sounded bored. "You can't hijack me. We already established that."

My palms came unstuck from the skin of her back. I hid my hands in my jacket.

I didn't quite let go of her magic. I stayed close enough to prod at her branches. They showed no interest in obeying my touch.

"Did you expect me to doze off while you turned my power against me? While you opened a vorpal hole in my belly?"

"Can't fault me for trying," I said. "You dangled that branch right in front of me."

"If you thought I was going easy on you, you thought wrong."

No kidding. I could grope her magic all night, and I'd never get any further. Every time, I'd fail to make her my puppet.

The sky was frozen in a rictus of a hot pink sunset. It hadn't gotten any dimmer since we toasted each other out on the balcony. By now it should've been dark.

"Sheer arrogance," the Queen said.

"That's my middle name."

"You could hijack your Wist. You'd need years of practice to hijack me."

"If you're done criticizing my tactics—"

She motioned at the endless waterfall. "No more stalling, Clematis. Make your choice."

I gave her my best pleading eyes. She stood tall and impassive, her colorless hair dyed curious hues by the livid sky.

If I thought too hard about this, I'd keel over at her feet. I might vomit. So I didn't think at all. I delegated my response to the part of me that could keep talking glibly in any predicament, whether at the knees of a god or in the sewers of hell.

"I'll leave Bittercress," I said.

But I wouldn't leave alone.

I heaved with all my might on her magic—and on our bond.

It was a dumb, crude trick. Nothing so sophisticated as magical hijacking. The sort of brute-force gambit that would only work once.

She stumbled into me. We were already very close.

She stumbled right into my Cressian knife.

It had no edge to speak of. It looked about as sharp as a hunk of tree bark.

It cut her like a stick stabbing half-melted snow. It cut her so deep. And so fast. I thought my entire arm would get sucked into her torso and come sliding out wetly on the other side.

For the barest of seconds, it cut through the illusions in the air around us.

Without that concealment, the town seethed with such a blaze of magic that I couldn't perceive anything else. Not the wind on my skin. Not the Queen's gasping. She clenched at me like she was trying to choke me.

If she pulled me closer, the knife would sink deeper. And deeper. Until there was nowhere left for it to go. Didn't she know that?

The raging magic all over Bittercress began to dim again. It stopped blinding me. It hid inside itself like an animal changing color to blend with the scenery.

We grappled. The knife moved in her. Wist was much stronger than me—but not, perhaps, while getting her insides carved to shreds.

I staggered backwards. We stayed locked together.

We tottered over the outer edge of the boardwalk. Down off the watery town wall.

The drop tore an earsplitting screech from my soon-emptied lungs. I clasped her tighter as we plummeted.

We didn't land on back-breaking rocks or hard soil. Nor did we land on water.

Nor did we land anywhere outside town.

We—no, I—landed face-down in bed. My bed at the inn.

I was alone.

I rocketed up. The sheets were drenched in blood—not my blood. Absolutely unsalvageable.

My right hand shook.

I still held Lester's Cressian knife. The white washcloth bundled around the missing hilt had transformed. It was scarlet like blood decanted from fresh-cut arteries. Velvety matte black like the stuff of the Void.

I wanted to drop the knife. I wanted to snap it in two. Instead I wedged it back in my pocket, complete with its soaking wet cloth. This jacket was already ruined.

I wouldn't find the Queen by wallowing in puddles of blood.

I trudged numbly to the door.

I didn't consider what I'd say if I ran into the innkeeper. Or any other townspeople. I'd become the spitting image of a serial killer. But that, quite frankly, was the least of my worries.

With each step, curls of ash from scorched wards wilted underfoot. They didn't yield the crunch of a dried-up leaf. They ground to dust without a sound.

I opened the door to the hall. Beyond it shone a ceiling of glowworms. Limestone columns gleamed with ridges and pleats like piped frosting.

My room at the local inn led straight into Katashiro Caverns.

I hadn't been wearing shoes to climb on the bed and heal the Queen, and I wasn't wearing shoes now. I stopped to pull on boots.

I took the smallest stone light off a side table, too. It would be cumbersome to haul through the caves. If only I had a more convenient way to carry it....

I held the stone light two-handed, as if preparing to present an award trophy. I stepped across the threshold.

The ambient glow behind me died like a candle getting snuffed. When I looked back, the door was gone. Nowhere to go but forward.

A black milky substance coated the ground, making my footsteps sound wet. I strove to quiet my body, inside and out. I listened to the whisper-thin pull of my bond with Wist.

On a practical level, our bond had been useless ever since she became the Queen of the Void. Yet some aspect of the caves seemed to rejuvenate its call.

My bloodied clothing hung cold and heavy. I followed the tug of the bond past sticky colonies of glowworms, past reflection pools, past stalactites and stalagmites that reached for each other like wrinkled yellow-brown fingers, straining to meet.

My route closely resembled our first trip to Katashiro Caverns. At least until pale limestone gave way to a dark glassy rock. It was rife with ridges that looked as though they could slice you open before you even knew what had hurt you.

This brought to mind the place where I'd seen the Void healing the Queen. These passageways were much more cramped, though. Anyone taller than me would've been at constant risk of putting an eye out on various protrusions.

Some entrances ground open and shut like broken automatic doors. I darted through as fast as I could, so as not to get crushed.

The scenery recycled itself with sufficient fidelity to create the illusion that I'd been walking in circles. Here I was once more surrounded by glossy caramel flowstone. Puddles littered with shiny cave pearls. Needle-fine crystals sprouting in shapes like sea coral. Regal calcified draperies. Long dripstone as slender as drinking straws.

I disregarded any repetition. I kept pursuing the call of the bond.

I was shivering by the time I found her. But once I found her, I forgot the cold.

It was a cave similar to the one where the Void had healed her, only much smaller. A bower of black alien stone. A hidden nest.

The stone light felt very heavy, and my hands felt very weak. I set it on the ground by my feet.

The Queen did have a throne, although it wasn't a chair. More like a nook in the rock. One that happened to be the perfect shape to contain her. There the Void embraced her. She dripped with it as if she'd bathed in it. But most of its bulk defied gravity, free-form liquid climbing up her legs again and again, as natural as smoke rising.

Her face was blank.

I don't mean that in the usual sense. From afar, it looked as though she had no face at all. Just a mask of seamless skin.

I stepped closer.

She wasn't entirely featureless. An extra membrane stretched over her face like the wall of an egg sac. I could see her eyes plastered shut beneath it, her mouth pressed tight, the holes of her nose and ears sealed over.

I came near enough that I could've leaned forward to kiss her. Or at least the starched surface of her sheltering membrane.

The Void ignored me. So did the Queen.

Her front was still torn and gory from my borrowed Cressian knife. I'd stabbed her right above the navel.

The wound didn't spit blood. It breathed as slow and gentle as a deep sleeper with parted lips. A skin-like membrane stretched across it, thinner and fresher than the one sealing her face.

She was ... nominally alive.

My hands fled inside my jacket. I squeezed fitfully at the sodden cloth that cushioned the gripping end of the Cressian knife.

I forced myself to stand back and observe her. She wasn't slotted into the wall like a human relief. The throne that held her might be described as a hollow in a huge column. She sat there like an owl who'd found a hole in a tree.

The hollowed-out part continued all the way to the other side of the column. I circled around behind her.

Then, at last, I understood what was happening.

With every passing second, the surging Void devoured more of her magic. It attacked the small of her back in streams and waves, gobbling up entire skeins, eating each branch right down to its root.

She was a Kraken-class mage. No matter how many cuttings she took from herself, she wouldn't run out. Her branches grew back from pruning with the forceful and instantaneous conviction of lightning shooting from sky to ground.

That's how they regrew now, too, lengthening even as the Void ate them down. But it must have been no less torturous than getting eaten alive by wild dogs, over and over and over without end.

This was the closest thing Bittercress had to a singular reality, an unvarnished truth. This was the poisonous bulb beneath every lily. A cave without sunlight. Self-repairing magic branches constantly getting fed to the Void. A Queen without a face—she'd shrink-wrapped herself so as not to show any suffering.

There were figures in myth who got doomed to an eternity of degrading torment. Political schemers would walk around with sawed-open skulls, evil crows forever pecking their naked brains to goo. Sinful gourmands would be forced to extract their own organs and cook an endless parade of fancy dishes for discerning gods.

This was the closest anyone might ever come to seeing those stories replicated in real life.

I was glad I had no magic. I was so, so glad of it, from my shuddering scalp to my icy toes.

The Void puddled underfoot. It washed past my ankles without leaving a single drop on me or my clothes. It paid no more heed to me than to the rocks of the cavern.

It didn't feel like absolute nothingness. It was a thousand disembodied tongues sliding by me, slimy and warm. The sensation came in such truncated flashes that I couldn't be certain I hadn't imagined it.

Animosity built higher in me, brick by brick. Here it was again, that old ugly impulse. The first and maybe most powerful thing I'd ever felt about Wist.

You aren't allowed to do that.

If anyone hurts her, it's going to be me.

I touched the side of her faceless mask. Its texture bore zero resemblance to human skin. Her lips made minuscule movements beneath it, the twitching of prey snared in a net.

The townspeople had been right, in a sense. My Queen was a living ghost. Every time I met her—even when I ate dinner with her, even when I glowered jealously at the Void healing her, even when I stabbed her—the truest part of her had always been trapped down here in the caverns. The truest part of her had always been busy feeding the Void.

There was something pure and animalistic in the way it ate at her magic. It gnawed on her with the singular focus of a primeval gnawing old bones. With the raw mindless efficiency of locusts stripping crops. As long as her magic kept regenerating, it would keep gorging itself till the end of time.

A blizzard filled my head. I'd found her. But I had no idea what to do with this. I had no idea what to do next.

31

I DIDN'T WEEP over her. She'd done this to herself.

The Void hadn't come slithering out of its cavernous den to kidnap my Wist. If we'd continued our planned vacation in Bittercress, the Void would of course have been drawn to her. But the fact remained that she went to it first. Of her own volition.

She left her bed in the night, without a word to her bondmate. She traveled to Katashiro Caverns to find the Void on her own.

Had she realized she would end up like this? How could anyone willingly walk into that? If she hadn't known what a horrific fate she was making for herself, what in heaven's name had she expected instead?

I can connect the dots. By now I had a basic idea of how that night had unfolded. The night she became the Queen of the Void.

She came away from our first visit to the caves thinking it'd be safest to keep her distance. She must've changed her mind for a reason.

Something tipped her off about the Void. Something convinced her that throwing herself into the Void—transforming herself into this awful amalgamation—was actually preferable to leaving it be.

Who knows what the future holds? Maybe, just a couple years from now, the untamed Void would've broken out of the caverns. Maybe it would have eaten all of Manglesea. Then all of Osmanthus. Then the rest of the continent.

So?

Who gave Wist the right to unilaterally decide to save the world? Who gave her the right to bury herself here like a Cressian sacrifice? Above all, how dare she do it all without me?

I'm not asking for a whole lot, you know. I would've appreciated a minor heads-up.

Like this. *Hey honey, I'm about to go participate in a living ritual slaughter. I'm about to join an eternal feast where I'm the one on the menu. I'm about to enter an existential grappling match with an eldritch cave spirit that may or may not have demolished entire civilizations. And possibly even the original Kraken. Sweet dreams!*

I wanted to punch her in her frozen shellacked joke of a face. Would've been a bit of a letdown after digging through her guts with the Cressian blade, though.

I twisted the sharp-petaled clematis pin stuck to my jacket.

That pin had a smidge of magic attached to it. The Void, however, showed no reaction. Why would it? It already was busy stuffing its—well, it didn't have a face. Whatever. It was busy gorging.

My arms had gone cold and stiff.

The Queen's relationship with the Void was a good deal uglier than expected. But that didn't fundamentally change my options. Or the scant few tools at my disposal.

All this time, I'd failed to notice something crucial.

I had plenty of excuses. The eerie fluttering of her congealed stomach wound as it slowly, slowly repaired itself. The viscous liquid motion of the Void. The laminated veil stretched like the skin of a blister across her face. The cyclical devouring and rebirth of her magic.

With all that going on, I hadn't realized her hands were tangled in the long strap of a small Jacian bag.

My bag. My stupid little bag.

I had not given it one single thought since the Queen turned me into a lantern-herder. I'd forgotten it more thoroughly than my own damn name.

I tried to wrest it from her grasp. Her fingers stayed locked around the strap, as secure as a welded chain.

Fine. I couldn't take the bag away from her. I could still open it and dig through its contents.

You think this is bad?

That was the Queen's voice in my head.

"Excuse me?" I said. I deserved enormous credit for my surface-level calmness.

It was worse before. The Void has slowed its pace.

"Oh, so it learned to take its time. To chew its food. Very healthy."

It was starving when I first took it in. Now it feeds more for pleasure than out of desperation.

"That doesn't really sound like a good thing." I rummaged around at the bottom of the bag. Tissues wouldn't be of much use here. "Need a bandage?"

No, thank you.

Aha. I pulled out the velvet pouch that held my prosthetic eye. Quite a lazy hiding spot. She'd hedged for that by making it extra difficult for me to recall my bag's existence.

I might never have remembered the bag if I hadn't come down here and found myself staring at it. I might never have reached this place if

I hadn't wounded her so badly that she ran out of energy to disguise it.

As I piped my prosthesis out of its pouch, the Void rippled with interest. A motion like wind dimpling water.

"You aren't going to stop me?" I asked.

I'm preoccupied.

Indeed. She had a physical body to knit back together and an insatiable pet to keep feeding.

She had a facade to maintain for the sake of the Void, too. She couldn't long for it to leave her. She couldn't long for it to stop mauling her newly regrown magic. She couldn't pray for that even in the murk at the bottom of her own head. She couldn't give the Void any reason to doubt her.

She could not wish, even for a fraction of a second, for an end to her own pain.

I'd hardly ever ventured that far into her mind, and I was her bondmate. The Void possessed no such decorum. It had already embedded itself as deep as it could go. Once it latched on, it would never relent.

I sanitized my fingers with disinfectant from my bag, then popped my eye in.

"Can I run a theory by you?"

Beneath her taut mask, the Queen waited for me to continue.

"The Void looks real powerful right now. I think that's because it's in a powerful vessel. Am I wrong?"

No.

"Would it kill you to elaborate?"

The Void's power and hunger change to fit its vessel.

"Before you came along, it made the caverns its vessel. Guess it didn't have much choice. It hatched here like a subterranean larva."

After the fall of the Cressians, the Void spent thousands of years in a state of near starvation. It grew together with the growth of its own hunger.

These caves are vast and full of magic and history. Much of it unpleasant. The Void spread to fit them.

Her mental tone was just as naked of emotion as her speaking voice. Perhaps more so.

This entire situation felt ridiculous. Like trying to hold a rational conversation with a gladiator while lions ripped them open, methodically turning them inside out. Like chatting with a fish in the middle of getting filleted.

It was also nothing new. She had already been undergoing this every single time we spoke in the past. She'd experienced it in every second of every bucolic day in Bittercress. Ever since she welcomed the Void.

I unpinned the metal brooch from my jacket and placed it in my mouth. Didn't taste great.

I needed the Void to perceive me. My magical right eye, and the bud of perception-altering magic she'd once planted at the back of my socket, and the magical pin in my mouth—together, they might be enough to render me visible.

But that was only the start.

Back in the bedroom, I'd meant to hijack her magic. I'd meant to make her open a vorpal hole in her own body. Wist had already successfully used one to chase the Void out of the caves and straight into her.

I'd failed miserably. I might be able to hijack my Wist, but I couldn't hijack what she'd become now. I couldn't hijack the Queen. I couldn't use the same trick to scare the Void out of her flesh and into the next nearest living vessel.

Into me.

Besides, it wouldn't work if the Void couldn't see me.

The Queen's butchered abdomen pieced itself back together. The wound I could've fit my fist through had been reduced to a lazy laceration. Despite everything, she'd worked extremely hard to stay alive.

Now she'd have to work harder.

I put my right hand in my pocket. My left hand still rested atop my bag. Near her clenched fists. Near her bloodied torso, and the magical carnage inside it.

Maybe I should've circled behind her. Magic manipulation—whether for healing or for torture—was always easier when you had direct access to the lower back of your patient. Or your victim.

I didn't have that kind of time. A new coldness took hold of me as the vicious aftermath of my stabbing withered down to the equivalent of a careful surgical incision. She was getting stronger. She was restoring herself faster and faster.

With my left hand, I performed a move borrowed straight from the Void. I twisted her magic as if bending a joint the wrong way. Bending it backwards to the point of snapping.

I distorted her magic hard enough and fast enough and cruelly enough to wrench it out of the Void's slobbering intangible maw.

She would've suffered less if I'd stuck my fingers in her gut and squeezed the softness there till it burst like rotten fruit. Her magic branches had already been alight with pain before I came anywhere near them. Ragged and half-eaten, dissolving and regrowing, they spilled out of her at my touch. Messier than wayward viscera.

"You can't die," I warned. Hard to squeeze words out past the pin in my mouth. "But you've got to come as close as possible."

As I elongated her magic branches, dragging them toward me, I removed my right hand from my pocket.

I was fortunate that the Cressian knife didn't need any strength behind it to pierce her.

With one wan thrust, the knife sheathed itself between her ribs as if it had always belonged there. She was already pressed up against the side of her hollowed-out pillar, caught in a cavity with nowhere to flee.

She grasped weakly at my arm when I knifed her. As before, I couldn't tell if she were trying to push the blade out or pull it in deeper. My bag tumbled off her lap, forgotten.

I kept the blade buried in her. I didn't let go of the squelching towel-wrapped hilt.

One-handed, I scooped up her magic branches and stuffed them inside me. They had no power in me. They wouldn't stay long. But I had to pretend.

I wound her churning tendrils around us as if binding our bodies together. Rope to tie a pair of hapless prisoners. I braided other branches with our bond, shaping a bright blazing path right to the heart of me. One that even a simple food-motivated creature like the Void couldn't miss.

The paralyzing membrane on her face began to slough off like snakeskin. Her freed mouth sucked in high dying gasps. Sticky purplish-black ink gouted out of every open part of her.

The Void didn't want to cross the distance between us. It pooled and lingered. It nibbled testily at the roots of her unspooling magic, at the tender parts closest to her brilliant core. It wasn't convinced.

So I stabbed her again.

Come on, I urged the Void. (A true prayer to emptiness.) Your host is dying. *Your host is dying!* Look at all this magic writhing around me. Look at the back of my eye. You've got nowhere else to go. Hurry up and slosh your way inside me, you damn—

Sound shot through my brain like a needle gun, slashing every last thought in half.

I recoiled. The brittle knife came with me, slipping out of her with as little resistance as it had met going in.

That was the sound of a vorpal hole tearing open.

The knife clattered at my feet.

I would've howled at her, shaken her—*No one asked for your help!*—but I couldn't see. The Void gushed out of her, a black waterfall unbound by physics. It filled my view as if I were falling into it, hurled into a pool that had no bottom. It palpitated like a newborn animal.

Then it gathered into a muscular swirl. Precise as a funnel, it poured itself at my artificial eye.

If you sprayed your eyes with a showerhead, most of the water would end up all over your face, in your hair, on the walls.

The Void didn't miss. The Void could fit in any space. It made itself thin as a layer of tears. Without spilling a drop, it quested its way around the sides of my prosthesis.

It sought out the exact spot where the Queen had touched me at the top of a water tower, holding me down to stick her finger in my socket. It spiraled toward the dab of magic she'd placed like a seed in soil.

I have nothing left to give you.

I granted you the ability to see what I see.

That seed of magic had lingered with me even after she severed my memories. That tiny seed had shown me the Void leaking, the dark feathering of Void-filled veins beneath her skin. It let me perceive the Void breaking her magic to heal it, and—here in this chamber—devouring her ever-regenerating magic all the way down to her brilliant core.

The Void curled around that seed at the back of my socket like a fattened bear settling down in its winter den. An entire weightless universe behind my false eye. It had no voice. It had no hostility. It was at once massive and completely insubstantial.

Feeling came back to my fingertips. I'd been hanging onto the edge of the stone cavity as if it were the only thing that would save me. As if fighting not to get swept away in a storm.

I spat the six-pointed brooch from my mouth to the ground. I made my body release Wist's stretched-out threads of magic. They rebounded like a thousand snakes fleeing a cage. Behind my eye, the Void stayed docile.

Wist's branches rushed to hide inside her, badly tangled.

I smelled blood. I tasted panic. "You—you opened a vorpal hole," I stammered. "To chase it out. You—"

"A small one," she said hoarsely. Her head leaned on the stone behind her, as if she lacked the strength to lift it.

"Your wounds...."

She'd already used magic on herself—she'd patched the new gash in her ribs. As soon as the Void crossed over. Even as I clung to her branches, threaded them through the holes in my vertebrae and pretended they were mine.

That wouldn't have been sufficient to stop her. The branches had stayed connected to her all the while, and I hadn't tied them into a hobble. But I couldn't comprehend how she'd found the willpower to activate even a single measly skill. She'd been physically maimed and metaphysically half-eaten.

Nor could I see where she'd opened her vorpal hole. I couldn't spot any obvious missing chunks of this body I knew as well as my own.

"I did as you said." The relief in her voice was so subtle that no one else in the world would've been able to hear it. "I came as close as I could get to dying."

Her fingertips hung languid at her side. She only had to stretch them out a few extra millimeters to graze my thigh.

I forgot whatever I'd been about to say in response. The walls she'd erected around our bond were beginning to crumble and vanish. Every last barrier sloughed off in the same way as the placenta-like wrapping she'd grown to immobilize her face.

"You did well," she told me.

Her hair was still white.

"I'm going to strangle you." I sounded hysterical. "I'll saw your head off with this ancient ritual knife. Just watch me."

"Can't be any worse than feeding myself to the Void."

"I know," I hissed. I ripped off the last few shreds of her disintegrating mask. She closed her eyes and leaned the side of her face into my hand.

32

Wist couldn't walk. Her abdomen looked like the scene of a botched autopsy, with emergency medical magic straining to hold it all in.

But she refused to concentrate solely on repairing the damage I'd done to her. More than anything, she wanted to get out of that cave.

I scrambled to collect my fallen things—my sling bag, my pin, the Cressian knife, the stone light from the inn.

She took my hand and ported us to the lantern graveyard. The backlog of piled-up lanterns hadn't gotten any smaller since our last visit.

Dunno where I expected her to take us. Certainly not here. Guess she considered this a more agreeable part of the caverns.

She summoned her luxury office chair and gingerly lowered herself into it. She winced in a way that would have been more appropriate as a reaction to a mildly stubbed finger than to nearly perishing from multiple stab wounds.

I shrugged off my utility jacket and laid it on the cave floor. It was stained beyond repair. Wist's clothing hadn't fared any better. The safety posters on the back wall would not be pleased to see us tramp in here, sprinkling about biohazards. The best I could do was attempt to stay in one place. I perched on a stool; I spun my clematis pin like a top on the workbench.

I held my tongue.

I figured I'd stay quiet till Wist finished patching herself up as best she could. No point in distracting her.

Medical magic had always been one of her weaknesses (at least in comparison to other fields of magic use). Which explained why so many townspeople had been laid up with slow-healing injuries after the primeval stampede I'd incited.

Although I bet she could've cured them in an instant if she weren't simultaneously dealing with the Void's hunger and other aspects of town maintenance. Like keeping the walls immune to ingress. And twisting the flow of time.

"Do you feel the Void?" Wist asked.

"Not really. No more so than—"

"You can stop there, Clem."

"No more so than wearing a tampon," I finished, undaunted. "How'd you know I was gonna say something unsuitable for the ears of royalty?"

"The look on your face."

"What kind of look did I have?"

"Very pleased with yourself."

"Allow me to rephrase," I said. "For your delicate sensibilities. I can tell it's back there, somehow. Behind my eye. But it's not like having a splinter. Doesn't feel any more out of place than the nails on my fingers or the molars in my gums. Quite a contrast from how it treated you."

She shifted the shreds of her smock to examine the half-closed gashes along her ribcage. "You don't have a magic core to whet its appetite. Its hunger and power have both shrunk to fit you. And it hates changing vessels almost as much as it hates vorpal holes. The Void will be safer in you."

"Just like that, huh?" I'd been endeavoring not to cross-examine her. But this was more than I could bear. "Gosh, sure sounds like it would've been a great idea to let me take the Void in the first place."

"No," Wist said.

If she were any less grievously injured, I'd have thrown one of these mangled lanterns at her head.

"All right," I said. "Tell me why we had to go through all this rigamarole. Tell me why you couldn't have just taken me back to the caverns instead of sneaking off on your own."

"If the Void had to choose between us, it would always choose me."

"Yeah, I can think of several easy solutions for that. Worst case scenario—we'd repeat what we did down in that hollow where you'd cocooned yourself. So what if the Void fled to you first? I could stab you half to death and drape your branches over me like fairy lights. Easy peasy. We'd chase it out of you and into me eventually. We could've skipped this entire charade of life in Bittercress. No need to break the taboo against warping the fabric of time."

She sat back in her chair. The slightest movement seemed to make her breath come short.

"There was meaning in my time holding the Void," she said. "It ate from me long enough to taste a hint of satiation. If it went straight to you first—without feeding on my magic—it would have eaten you dead."

"But I don't have any inherent magic."

"The force of its hunger would've killed you anyway. Without meaning to, and without deriving any satisfaction from it."

"Well, what happens when the Void gets hungry again?"

"Borrow my magic to feed it."

"How generous of you," I said curtly.

"Won't have to be frequent. With you as its vessel, its appetite will diminish."

"Like having a giant pet snake," I said. "Throw it a sacrificial goat every so often."

"Something like that," Wist agreed.

Exhaustion permeated our bond.

She beckoned me closer.

She asked if I could see the vorpal holes she'd opened while I fought to lure out the Void.

"Last chance," she said. "I'm about to close them. After a short break."

I looked her over. Legs stretched out. Cold bare feet. Her tattered smock and loose tail of color-drained hair.

There was an incongruous freshness to her complexion, as if the gruesome mask of organic tissue she'd worn in a tight film over her face had in fact served as a kind of innovative skincare.

I'd long ago lost the ability to tell whether Wist was objectively a beautiful woman. Looks aside, most people would find her attractive by virtue of her sheer power. That complicated things.

I wasn't most people. Without even trying to, she'd reshaped all my ideas of beauty and attraction to match her alone, and magic had nothing to do with it.

Wist waited patiently while I lifted her hair out of the way. I glanced beneath the torn flaps of her artist's smock.

The vorpal holes had to be located on or in her body. Not in the middle of a vital organ, presumably. She'd been barely clinging to life when she opened them: she'd done it after abandoning all pretense of neutrality. A last-ditch effort to help drive out the Void.

Were the holes really someplace I could see with my one good eye? If

I were her, I'd have opened them in a spot that wouldn't sacrifice flesh. Like the empty air in her sinuses.

I touched the outer curve of her ear.

"You're kidding," I said. "That's cheating!"

Wist had pierced ears. But she hadn't worn any earrings in Bittercress. Though as narrow as a needle, the piercing hole in each earlobe appeared as an actual perfect hole now. Not the pinprick dimple in flesh you'd see on most people who hadn't wiggled an earring through in weeks.

She'd opened vorpal holes the size of a pencil lead in her piercings.

"The Void abandoned ship over *these*?"

"You were very enthusiastic about impaling me with your knife," Wist said gravely.

"Was I really that bad?"

"You drove me to the brink of death, just as promised. The Void didn't need much of an extra push to bail out."

Despite her abysmal physical condition, it must've been easier to use magic now that she no longer had to put on a good mental front for the Void. After she closed her nearly microscopic vorpal holes, I pulled up a stool and got to work on detangling her.

Something in me felt ill at ease, and not just because of the portentous scenery. Masses of dead lanterns. Humorless workplace slogans.

It had not been difficult to horribly wound her. Multiple times. Shouldn't I have been more torn up over it? Shouldn't I have had a good cry before going straight for her gut?

Then again, Wist hadn't shed any big tears over our woes, either.

She curled her fingers through my hand and pulled it close. "I trusted you not to hold back."

"You really are a masochist."

Her magic was still wracked with indescribable agony. She'd had no choice but to keep using her magic skills—abusing them, really—even as the Void masticated vast swathes of her branches, even as they simultaneously regrew.

If you had to draw comparisons, the Void's consumption was more along the lines of being dissolved in stomach acid than getting chewed off and swallowed whole.

Burning echoes of that acid would linger in her sensitive magic threads long after the Void had left her body. For all my healing prowess, that wasn't something I could simply finger-comb out of her. She might find herself afflicted by random pangs of empty pain for years to come.

I'd been shocked when I first saw the Void healing her magic. Taking my job from me. That too had been a slice of the truth. But only one slice of it. You couldn't call that the whole story any more than you could claim a single twig was the same as an entire tree.

Yes, the Void had healed her. Ruthlessly, and without any care for her comfort, it kept her magic in good working order. At the same time—somewhere much deeper, far outside my perception—it had also been eating her.

I'm not just saying this to minimize my own sins. The Void had hurt her far worse than my Cressian knife.

This raised certain doubts in me.

Wist was tough, yes. Wist was a habitual martyr—an expert at wordlessly enduring unimaginable horrors. And she was strongest of all when it came to tolerating her own pain. She'd crumple much sooner if others had to suffer in her place.

I had as much faith in the Kraken as anyone. I was her bondmate, for crying out loud. Her incredible mastery over time and space and the town of Bittercress? I could buy that.

Yet she'd worked magic on an epic scale while also locking down every last hint of wayward emotion—even inside her own mind—so as to avoid spooking the Void like a skittish horse.

She'd done all that while the Void eagerly consumed her every-growing branches. While it healed the snarls in her magic, too.

Did it heal her because it understood that she (like any mage) would go berserk without proper treatment? Or had it smoothed out her magic to make it more palatable—as instinctual as a squirrel cracking nuts?

The Void hadn't gone about healing her kindly. That much was certain. It had felt like watching a callous hairdresser rip out entire fistfuls in order to rid some hapless soul of tangles.

Had the Wist who'd rode into Bittercress with me really been capable of emerging from this with her mind in one piece? Could any mage survive ingestion by the Void without melting down after it oozed away and abandoned them?

She didn't seem like an empty shell. She didn't hesitate to take my hand. She responded the way she always would when I sniped at her.

Physical torture—say, getting your fingernails peeled off one after another—would be child's play in comparison to what she'd gone through in the depths of Katashiro Caverns.

Why hadn't it destroyed her?

She could sense my mystification through our bond. I made no effort to hide it. Wist, in turn, made no effort to explain herself.

I didn't push her for answers. It wouldn't feel right.

When would it ever feel right, though?

33

WE HOBBLED out of the caverns. At this point, any further porting would be more draining for Wist than limping around on foot. Even though she hadn't worn shoes.

I offered to go find a rickshaw. She shook her head. She leaned on me harder.

So we hoofed it.

The walls around our bond had come tumbling down, but the walls around town stood unbroken. Every townsperson we walked past still called Wist their Queen. No one took notice of our blood-swamped clothing or soiled skin. No one cast stones at me for wearing a magical prosthesis, either.

Okay, I thought. Let's see what happens tomorrow.

In our room at the inn, I helped Wist bathe. The fever-hot surface of her forcibly closed wounds kept pulsing and rippling.

She gave me back all the other things I'd forgotten to demand from her. My bond thread. My ironic Church of the Kraken keychain (the one that formed a matching set with hers). My extra transceiver pins.

Her bond thread had made itself visible on her wrist again. For a time, I idly toyed with it as crickets and autumn frogs sang to us through open windows.

"You were a jealous Queen," I informed her.

"Don't know what you mean," she said wearily.

"I specifically asked you to make me Lester's manager."

"A hermit does not need a talent agent."

"Ah, I'm just kidding. But why'd you turn me into a part-time housekeeper?"

"Guess."

"To get back at me for my attempt at arson?"

Wist made a little noise of satisfaction.

I fell asleep with an arm around her, my face buried in her upper back. Tomorrow would finally—finally—be the day of the equinox.

Tomorrow was not, in fact, the fall equinox.

I squirmed out of bed on my own that morning, leaving Wist sleeping alone. She could use the extra rest.

I scampered downstairs, then outside. I bounded over to the innkeeper as soon as I saw her glimmering fishhooks. I jovially asked her what day it was.

Perplexed, she stopped sweeping the path out front. She gave me the same answer as always.

It was still the day before the equinox.

I slunk sheepishly back up to our room.

Shouldn't have been surprised, really. Unwinding complex magic could be a laborious and hazardous process. Just like how demolishing an urban skyscraper and clearing the debris was no simple matter. It would require meticulous planning, step by step.

Wist could've instantly cut off all the magic she'd woven into Bittercress. But she would only have done that if she cared nothing for what became of the town, or its people, or its primevals, or us.

I gave her time. I did my best not to rush her. It'd be smarter to wait and see how the Void behaved in me before heading off to more populated regions, anyhow.

Thus far, the Void had done nothing of interest. I was a vessel without magic. It became as harmless in me as it had been awful in Wist. No worse than a dormant tapeworm. Almost disappointingly passive.

All in all, learning to live with the Void was much less of an adjustment than losing my eye.

As predicted, once it took root in me, it lost all interest in leaving. Even with a Kraken-class mage—its former vessel—lying next to me.

I believed what Wist had said about how this peaceful coexistence was only possible because she'd tempered the Void with her pain. Her days and nights of anguish had been a means to an end. A way to slowly rein in the wild Void by slowly slaking its centuries of pent-up thirst.

No one else could have faced it on equal footing. But her sheer quantity of magic made it more ravenous. The more she satisfied it, the more she egged on its appetite. The very same Kraken-class power that allowed her to survive the untamed Void was also what drove the engine of her own torture.

"What would you have done if no one took the Void from you?" I asked.

She didn't have a good answer for that. She would've lived forever inside the walls of Bittercress, I guess.

She'd bet everything on my ability to figure things out. To make the right move based on a hunch and a prayer. Or maybe she'd been counting on the fact that if she became Queen of this closed world, I would inevitably get the urge to overthrow her.

She'd been willing to kick me out, all the same. She would've let me go. She would've stayed behind. Alone with the Void.

She was still obviously unwell. I had to restrain myself from grabbing her by the shoulders and shaking her damn head off. My anger peaked and crashed like waves on a stony shore. Nowhere to go except back into the same unsettled pool.

Wist promised to visit specialists back in Osmanthus—professionals devoted to the study of medical magic. If nothing else, they could help check her physical self-repair work.

In the meantime, she spent long hours napping. When she felt up to it, we drank rosehip tea with the innkeeper.

My role in town was the subject of much confusion. Some remembered me as a lantern-herder and housecleaner, others as a foreign tourist. No one scheduled me for any shifts. I chose to regard myself as exempt from my usual work.

Instead I helped the mortician tidy up around the graveyard. Her recovery had accelerated dramatically: she'd stopped using crutches. Wist had prioritized the old injuries of the citizenry over her own near-fatal stab wounds.

Just about every day was the same sort of lovely fall day.

On one such lovely fall day, it occurred to me that I was now the creepiest being in town. I had an ineffable Void tucked behind my artificial right eye. It didn't do much anymore, to be fair, but its very existence was abominable.

Maybe that's why Bittercress began to seem harmless. No more eerie writing smeared on windows. No fingernails scratching frenetically at the tavern walls. No smoking paper wards or milk-dripping doorknobs or sunburnt leather furniture shedding sheets of human skin. No sickly sweet clouds of scent without an obvious origin—except for the one that followed the mortician. I'm pretty sure that was just her perfume.

I wanted to give Lester back his rusty Cressian knife. It had saved my ass more than once. Hopefully I wouldn't need it going forward.

Wist kept stopping me.

"I'll go when you're sleeping," I said, puzzled. "You won't even notice me gone."

What was her problem with Lester? She hadn't objected to me helping the mortician or hanging out with hostlers.

She just shook her head and pulled me back into bed.

The Void gave me strange dreams. Dreams of a sky with an unfamiliar taste to it, and wings, and elder aerials, and unknown languages, and murdered mages. So many murdered mages.

No guarantee that these were true dreams of Cressian times, as opposed to something made up by my Void-addled subconscious. No scholar would accept them as a primary source. Still, I would've liked to tell Lester the hermit. The content of my dreams would mean more to him than they did to me.

For now, I held back. After all Wist and I had been through, I wasn't eager to flit off on my own. Not so long as she wanted me close by her side.

The town walls continued to cast an imposing gray-green shadow over the weeds below. The equinox stubbornly refused to arrive.

Wist, though easily fatigued, managed to get to the point where she could take one good long walk every couple of days. The riverside paths would've been perfect for this, but she preferred the long hill crowned with empty mansions.

Maybe it was just that she didn't want to run into chatty acquaintances. The one time we went together to the river, she made me turn back as soon as we heard familiar accordion music drifting out across the evening water.

There was nearly always a wind blowing through town. The air, at least, never felt stagnant. Today it riffled at the ends of Wist's half-braided ponytail. I'd started plaiting her hair out of boredom, then tired of it and abandoned the effort partway through.

We took frequent breaks on our way up the slope. At the top, we stopped under a wooden pergola. We were in a garden by one of the mansions (not one of the few I'd tried to burn down). An ordinary garden shaped by physical labor—no magic, which made it very different from the wealthiest estates back in Osmanthus.

The foreign owners must have found these grounds to be pleasantly rustic. Homespun, you might say. Although no outsiders would be able to check up on their property so long as Wist remained Queen.

A meadow of vigorous cosmos surrounded the pergola, blocking our view with masses of light feathery leaves. They grew taller than the top of my head. Some were even taller than Wist.

I passed her a water canteen to sip from. Cosmos flowers swayed in the breeze all around us, a capricious mix of purple and pink and white and dark gold. They bowed under the weight of fuzzy black bees the size of my thumb.

"I brought you to Manglesea so you couldn't use magic," I said as she drank. "So much for our vacation."

"Might need a vacation from our vacation."

I snorted. "Am I allowed to do the planning again?"

"Better you than me."

I rubbed my right eye. The Void could have occupied any part of my body it pleased, but it still liked the liminal space around the hidden edges of my socket.

Wist theorized that it had poured itself in behind my prosthesis because the magic on the eye was so strong and multilayered. Much stronger than the cuttings grafted to the pin I'd held in my mouth. Easier to mistake for part of me than the armfuls of magic branches I'd dragged out of her, clumsily trying to pretend they belonged in me. Plus, there was the extra scrap of magic she'd planted in my socket. A perfect little target.

The Void didn't devour any of it—neither the seed nor my false eye. With Wist as its vessel, it had savored an all-you-can-eat buffet of branches rooted in her core. I myself had no core and no native branches. Planted in fallow fields, the Void hibernated. It was the sort of predator with no interest scavenging severed cuttings.

Under Wist's continued influence as the Queen, no one took exception to magic use. Just so long as it was her magic. That's why they overlooked the presence of my prosthetic eye.

After a couple days of wearing it, my memory of life before Bittercress steadily regained clarity.

I avoided picking fights over touchier subjects. Like why we were still here. But my patience began to wear terribly thin.

Beneath it all coursed a kind of ceaseless pumping anxiety. Because she was still violating the taboo against messing with time. We didn't know what the consequences would be, or when they might come for us. What if each circulating day made those future consequences worse? Why would she go out of her way to prolong her violation?

I knew it would take time to dismantle the complicated magical infrastructure she'd set up all over Bittercress, from its air to its soil to the minds of its people. I knew her possession of the Void had sickened her in ways I couldn't begin to understand.

As far as I could tell, though, she hadn't taken any steps to abdicate as Queen yet. The world-warping magic on town remained wholly intact. She wasn't even trying to unravel it.

"Wist," I said in the pergola, "it's time to bring the walls down."

She picked up the canteen again and turned it in her hands. She eyed it as though it were a shaken snow globe.

"Isn't the worst already over?" I demanded.

"I hope so."

"You put yourself through inhuman degrees of torture. You experienced something so unspeakable that other mages won't ever fully grasp it." I paused to catch my breath. "What're you delaying for? No matter what's waiting for us out there, it can't be as bad as when you swallowed the Void."

"No," she concurred, as expressionless as always.

I threw up my hands. "Did the continent blow up while we were busy mucking around with the caverns and the Void? Is there still a world left outside Bittercress? Are we going to be stranded in prehistoric times? Are we going to have to travel back a million years and become the very first Cressians? What aren't you telling me? Obviously it's a hell of a lot!"

"A million years ago would be long before the age of the Cressians," Wist said neutrally.

I fixed her with a look of ill-contained fury. She set the canteen down on the bench. Then she leaned over and plopped the length of her ponytail in my hands. As if asking me to weigh it.

"Explain," I said through my teeth.

"It's white."

"I noticed."

"Why?"

"I could hardly help noticing—you mean, why is it white?"

This tripped me up. Not all magical side effects had a rational explanation. I'd lose my mind if I started questioning every surreal quirk of Bittercress. Wist's hair changing from black to white in one night was the least of it.

"What do you expect me to say?" I asked. "I dunno what caused it—the stress of hosting the Void?"

She pulled back without answering. Cosmos flowers danced to and fro in the wind. A flash of black and red—a six-spot moth—veered past her ear.

Whether or not she'd made her hair go white on purpose, leaving it that way must have been a deliberate choice. She could turn it any color she liked. That sort of magic wouldn't take much out of her. Making it go black again would've been the easiest option.

"You left it white as a clue," I said.

She drew her ponytail through her hands, studying it as though it were something mysterious to her. "Why does hair turn white?"

"When you get a terrible shock?" I guessed. "To stand out? To look cool?"

I hate to admit it, but if that was the goal, then mission accomplished.

"What else?"

"From age," I said without thinking.

Then I looked at the Queen anew.

This was a Wist who, if she tried, could imbue her speech with somewhat more emotion than a fallen log. She was a Wist who didn't slouch to hide her height.

This was a Wist I couldn't hijack. Or even hobble. She had access to a whole new range of magic skills I'd never seen or heard of in my life. Many of the skills she'd deployed across town were so discreet in their power that even I—who could normally brag of sharpshooter-level magic perception—failed to notice them going off.

She'd mastered time-breaking taboo magic.

Above all, this was a Wist who could pick herself up again and act human after getting eaten alive by the Void. On and on, without respite. While I obliviously herded lanterns and dined at the tavern and basked in the fresh countryside air and perfect fall temperatures.

Nevertheless, she was undeniably Wisteria Shien. My bondmate.

But there was a reason it had been so easy to think of her as a relative stranger. As the Queen of the Void.

I'd attributed all such changes in her to the Void's mystical influence.

Maybe I'd been giving the Void too much credit.

"You...."

I had a sense of what she'd done. I just couldn't articulate it. I pushed my thoughts at her through the bond instead. A sticky glob of wordless concepts.

Wist nodded.

"Why didn't you tell me!?"

She traced lines on her palm as she spoke. As if reminding herself not to go off-script. "Not knowing is a choice, too," she said heavily. "The more I explain, the greater the risk of leading you on."

"What?"

She appeared to struggle for words. "I won't usher you to a predestined conclusion. Wherever you go, you should lead the way yourself."

"No idea what you're going on about," I said, "but that sounds patronizing as hell. I figured out the gist of it, didn't I? You already led me there with your stupid talk about hair. Just spit it out. Are you a time traveler or what?"

"Not exactly."

"Wonderful. Clear as tomato soup."

"I didn't travel here from the future. But—"

"Is that the kind of statement you can attach a *but* to?"

She laid a calm hand on my upper back. I bristled.

"I'll talk," she said, "if you'll listen."

34

"It started after..." Wist looked at the right side of my face. "After what I did to your eye."

"That was more than a year ago," I protested. "That couldn't possibly have anything to do with the Void."

"My magic gouged your eye out. You learned how to hijack me, how to use me like a puppet. And you weren't the only one."

She wore a long, loose cable-knit hoodie. It was an off-white hue tinged with gray, darker than her hair.

"The greater my power, the deadlier my vulnerabilities." She smoothed the front of the knit over all the places where I'd stuck my knife in her. "I felt that keenly. Every time I saw your missing eye."

"Sounds like just another way to guilt yourself. No one can completely get rid of their weaknesses."

"About that," Wist said.

"Huh?"

"I wanted to try."

"You arrogant—"

"I would've done anything to guarantee I'd never hurt you like that again. I wanted to craft my own last resort."

I glanced at the open slats of the pergola roof. Dim sunlight fell across us in weak, fuzzy-edged stripes. My righteous indignation blazed so hot and so fast that it collapsed in on itself, burning out, before I could yell at her. All that remained was smoking wreckage and a cold intellectual curiosity.

"You began working on something in secret," I stated. "You've been working on it for years now. Fascinating. Always a smart idea to keep more secrets from your bondmate. That's always served us well, hasn't it?"

My sarcasm rolled right off her.

"Complex new skills take a long time to invent."

"We went to school together, for heaven's sake. You don't need to lecture me about the intricacies of magical R&D. What'd you come up with?"

"I pulled my future self forwards—backwards?—into my current self. I transposed—"

"You switched places with your future self?"

"Is that what *transposed* means?"

"Er, kind of. It could mean that."

"No," she said. "I didn't rewrite myself. I didn't replace myself with a future personality. I reached ahead—I borrowed knowledge and magic skills, mastery and mental fortitude that would have taken decades or more to cultivate."

"You cheated, basically."

"Basically."

"You threw hard work out the window. You found yourself at the peak of your future power, and you brought that power back to the present. Or—you made yourself grow into it in the blink of an eye. Skipping long years of study and labor."

"More like that," she said. "Like a child growing instantly into an adult."

Annoying people is my specialty. But sometimes—okay, pretty frequently—I end up annoying myself instead.

Right now, for example.

My first thought: oh, that's clever. Could she do the same for me? I'm not a mage, though—and most mages don't have the potential to keep growing like she does. My older self might be more crotchety, but not more powerful in any meaningful way. Not like her. Although if I could gift my present self all my future knowledge and experience, then maybe—

I forced myself to stop fantasizing.

"I get you," I told her. "I've rubbed off on you in all the wrong ways. You were looking for a loophole, weren't you? How to access the height of your powers ahead of schedule. Without literal time travel. But how can you be sure this doesn't count as breaking the taboo?"

"I can't be sure."

"Oh. Well then."

She turned sideways and stretched out on the bench as if planning to sleep there. Her ponytail dangled off, brushing the ground. I scooped it up and draped it over her shoulder. No need to thank me.

"That's what made it a last resort," Wist said. "If all went well, I would never have used it. I wasn't planning on using it when I went to see the Void. Then I actually touched the Void—"

"And it was too much for you," I finished. "It would have surpassed you. Rather—it would have surpassed the you who originally came to Bittercress. Without your future skill set. Your hard-won future expertise."

She'd essentially done the equivalent of calling in reinforcements. Even as the only living Kraken, she wasn't a match for something so old and so alien.

So she whipped out her last resort. She instantaneously evolved into a future version of herself who *was* a match for the Void. And she might have broken one of the great taboos in the process.

This did explain a lot. Not everything, but a lot. Like how the Queen had been able to flood a whole town in sophisticated time-bending and mind-bending magic—while preventing me from directly perceiving it. How she'd felt so familiar and unfamiliar at the same time. Her imperviousness to my attempts at hobbling and hijacking her.

In essence, I'd been confronting a Wist who'd already had untold years to practice resisting me.

I'd gotten things backwards. Swallowing the Void hadn't made her more powerful. She'd become more powerful all on her own.

I paced in circles around the pergola. "You claim you didn't use time travel per se. Mental, physical, or otherwise. You didn't import your future self into your current body. You collapsed decades of intellectual and magical growth into the space of a nanosecond. You accelerated your development into that supremely powerful future version of you. I get that much. But that's a matter of semantics, isn't it? One way or another, you became your future self. That's the simple version."

Her eyes followed me as I walked.

"How old are you?" I asked.

"Hm?"

"How old is this future self of yours? How many decades were supposed to pass before you reached the real peak of your power?"

I halted. The field of cosmos tossed in a restless wind.

"Maybe we're not even talking decades," I amended. "The first Kraken could've lived for centuries, if we believe all the stories. Maybe you will, too. So how far in the future are we talking here? Am I still alive? Am I still with you? Have you already dealt with the consequences of breaking the taboo about time?"

She turned gradually onto her back, one knee raised. She held out a hand. I gave her my fingertips.

"Do you think you stayed?" she asked evenly.

This person she had become did seem more jaded than the Wist who had first arrived in Bittercress. There was probably a reason for that.

Ask anyone else on the continent if they'd still be alive centuries from now, and naturally the answer would be a resounding no. I wasn't so wildly optimistic as to imagine that the answer might be any different for me.

And yet—

I contemplated the notion of Wist left on her own for hundreds and hundreds of years to come.

I wasn't one to get existential shivers. Didn't see much point in contemplating my mortality. Still, when I thought of Wist aging alone like that, there was a part of me that did understand the appeal of an unchanging autumnal eternity. I could forgive her reluctance to leave this final fortress, this little time-walled town in rural Manglesea.

"I don't know," Wist said quietly.

"Come again?"

"I didn't bring over any memories of future events."

"You left them out on purpose?" I said, baffled.

"To skirt around the taboo against twisting up time."

"So much for that. You ended up violating it in much more obvious ways later. You're still violating it right now. You've got to let those poor spider lilies bloom someday."

"The ones you tried to poison me with?"

"If you ever let them flower, we can admire them together. It'll be a lovely walk. They're budding all over town. They're only supposed to last a few days, anyway. That's what makes them a sign of the equinox. That's what makes them special."

I pushed her legs out of the way and sat back down on the bench.

"Did you really have to hide so much?" I said. "Have we not grown at all since I first got out on parole? Or since you first broke one of the great taboos?"

No matter what I threw at her, my Wist's face might not have changed. But I would've sensed her reaction through the bond. I would've felt my blows land home.

This Wist didn't flinch. I didn't know how to hurt her. After the Void, my pitiful cries of displeasure might have no more power to shake her than old coins tossed in a dried-up fountain.

I pulled at the hem of her hoodie until she pushed herself up to face me.

I opened my sling bag and took out the Cressian knife.

I didn't point it at her. I held it by the blade. The handle—the part that used to be a handle, many eons ago—was wrapped in layers of bandage-like gauze.

"You've left a lot unsaid."

"Have I?" she inquired.

"Oh, don't give me that. This knife, for instance." I brandished it. "You didn't seem surprised by how deep it cut you."

"Do I ever seem surprised?"

"You know what I mean."

"I was too busy getting impaled to exclaim in shock."

"No," I snapped. "You already knew what it was. You'd seen it before. You had an inkling of what it could do."

She didn't contradict me.

"Well?" I pressed.

"Finish explaining your theory."

I shook the blade for emphasis. It looked as though the slightest force might snap it like a breadstick. Yet somehow it held together.

"How'd our local hermit get a hold of this? Did you sneak it to him? Plant it on him? Did you set me up?"

If there's one thing I hate, it's having my actions massaged and manipulated without knowing it. Losing the option to make my own conscious choices. Getting maneuvered into doing all this crap for the sake of someone else's grand plan. A plan I never even got the chance to vet.

Finally it leapt out at me—the source of my extreme irritation. Someone must have planned this.

Not merely my convenient discovery of Lester's Cressian knife. All of it. Starting with Wist's sudden about-face. How she'd gone from avoiding the Void to sneaking out on her own to confront it.

Wist might have been capable of such orchestration. That is, if she were already at the height of her power, with a lifetime's worth of wiliness. But she'd only become that far-off version of herself *after* meeting the Void.

What, then, had sent her to the Void in the first place?

Something else.

Someone else.

I stuffed the knife in my bag. The walls of tall cosmos flowers were beginning to make me claustrophobic. The top of the pergola had the look of a cage.

"Wist," I said, glaring. "Who are you covering for? Whose bright idea was all this?"

She took a halting breath.

"Wist, I swear—"

She curled her fingers into a loose fist. She looked intensely at the backs of her knuckles. Her eyes remained dark and steady and utterly unrevealing.

She opened her hand again. She pointed at me.

The tip of her finger came to rest on my sternum, light as a wasp.

"You," she said gently. "It was you."

35

I DIDN'T WASTE TIME proclaiming my innocence. I didn't screech at her. I sat like an insect in amber.

I didn't feel the bench under me. I didn't feel sun-warmed strands of wind wafting between us. I felt only the quiet forgiving touch of her finger on my breastbone.

I pictured the stranger I'd seen with Wist. In the garden by the inn. Out on the balcony. They'd been of indeterminate gender, and quite short. Which didn't narrow it down at all—every adult townsperson was just about that short.

And so was I.

She'd claimed that her visitor came in a mask. But Bittercress was rife with such masks. The innkeeper and I had schlepped around boxes full of them in preparation for the equinox.

They'd been wearing a distinctive jacket, too. Black, with six stark red circles marking their back. Like a life-size version of the six-spot seal. We'd noticed a jacket with the same design hanging in a local shop window. At some point it had vanished.

"I'm going to scream," I said.

Wist, keeping eye contact, put her hands over her ears.

I didn't scream. My heart felt like a goddamn time bomb, ticking faster and faster toward a fatal explosion.

"Or maybe," I said, "maybe I'll be sick."

Wist wordlessly lifted the generous hem of her hoodie, holding it out as though inviting me to retch in her lap. I declined.

"Take me—take me away from here," I said blindly.

"Where?"

"Somewhere higher. Not one of your blighted towers. The wall," I decided. "Take me back up the wall."

She hesitated.

"Bad memories?" I sneered. "What a shame. Don't want me to leap off the side again? Don't want me to stab you? I'll take your opinion into due consideration. No promises."

Her magic substituted the top of the town wall for the pergola. Parapets—intact once more—replaced the garden of frilly quivering cosmos.

After she ported us, I sank down on the boardwalk. I put my head between my knees and listened to the sound of the water.

I could feel the softness of Wist's knit on my left; she sat with me. I wound my hand in her sleeve. She was the last person I ought to lash out at. If I understood this right, then everything I wanted to rage about was simply the result of my own instructions.

I was the mastermind. As usual, I was turning out to be my own nemesis.

I raised my head. "It already happened," I said. "But it also hasn't happened yet."

"Yes."

"After all we've been through, this is what I do next. I ask you to make *me* the time traveler. I ask you to send me back to visit your old self in the past. I was the one pestering you in the garden. I was the one pestering you on the balcony."

Wist didn't make a sound. She neither nodded nor shook her head.

I watched the false river go streaming past. It never sped up and never slowed down. Some distance away, a posse of hundred-eye ducks paddled tirelessly against the current.

The shadow of a terrifyingly huge aerial crossed the wall at its leisure.

"Probably did a few other things along the way." I patted my bag. "I made Lester hang on to this knife, didn't I? I told him to keep an eye out for us. To help me if I ever came to him. Bet I warned him to keep his mouth shut, too. To not tell me anything unnecessary. To act like we'd never met."

Abruptly and vividly, I recalled seeing him on our second day in Bittercress. He'd gaped at us as if we were a pair of ghosts.

"Those merchants who ditched us overnight ... I suppose I'm the one who scared them into fleeing town. Damn it. Every single problem I wanted to bitch about comes right back to me in the end, doesn't it?"

"Letting the merchants escape was a good deed."

"Hmph."

It was easier to breathe up here, with nothing but flocks of aerials between us and the sky. I leaned my head back against the chilly parapet.

"This is all annoyingly believable," I said. "I do like playing the mastermind, don't I? There's just one major problem."

Wist tilted her head like an inquisitive pet.

"I'm not a save-the-world type of person. That's more of a you thing."

"That doesn't sound like a compliment."

"It's not a compliment or an insult. It's a neutral statement of fact.

Given the choice, you *would* sacrifice yourself to rescue the rest of the continent, or humanity, or whatever."

Wist obliged me by asking the pertinent question. "And you?"

"Me? It depends. Don't think I'd go out of my way to shoulder the burden of an ambiguous threat like the Void. Left alone, someday it might menace us all the way over in Osmanthus. But *someday* is an abstract concept."

"Someday it would have," Wist said. "I can promise that."

"It might not happen anytime soon, right? It's not operating on a strict schedule. As long as we live—as long as I live, anyway—the Void might never have done anything worse than spiriting away and devouring the occasional unfortunate mage."

"Unlucky for them," Wist said dryly.

"The world is full of tragedies. Some have nothing to do with magic. Is it really worth assuming responsibility for the Void for the rest of our natural lives? Besides, what happens when I die? Future generations might have to deal with the Void regardless."

"Guess you'd better not ever die."

She said this in such a matter-of-fact tone that I swallowed my response. Best not to check if she were joking.

"What happens next?" I asked. "In order for things to unfold as they already have. Will you convince me to keep playing out the script of this farce for the sake of some nebulous greater good?"

I laughed. It felt sharp as a cough in my chest. "I can come up with all the diabolical plans I want, but I never swore an oath to stick to them. I never promised I'd be consistent. I never agreed to politely go along with the schemes of some know-it-all edition of me from—what, a couple more hours from now? A few extra days in the future?"

This was threatening to give me a headache. "Where's the line between me and her? When do I become the near-future me who goes back in time to harass you? Who says I still have to become her, anyway? I'll do anything I want. I'll rip her to-do list to shreds."

I got up with renewed vigor. Tremors went through the wood of the boardwalk. "You know what? Her plan sucks. It's absolute garbage. Look at what it made you endure. It wasn't exactly pleasant for me, either!"

My deepest muscles panged with another errant memory of getting spiked. Wist had erased that mortal damage much more effectively than she'd treated her own knife wounds, come to think of it. Probably due to a major gap in motivation, although the nature of the mage-killing knife might also have something to do with her current difficulties. Whatever the case, she'd always been least adept at curing herself.

"What happens if I decide not to go back in time?" I said. "I know I already went, in a way. If you look at things chronologically. But it can't happen if I don't go. Maybe chronological order isn't the only order that matters. Especially now that you've stirred up the timeline with magic."

"I don't know everything." This was as close as Wist would ever get to sounding apologetic.

"Then take a guess. You're the ultimate version of yourself, aren't you? Use your brain."

She gazed out at the swirling patterns of afternoon aerials. "The course of time is already more tangled than my branches," she said. "You do have a choice."

"Damn right I do."

"You can choose not to visit me in the past. By not visiting me, you can choose to undo this. To shed the burden of the Void. To leave it roiling in the caves. One day it might fully awaken—it might overflow its container. To the detriment of Manglesea, and all the rest of the continent."

"No one knows if or when that day will come."

"It will come," said Wist. "I can tell. You're right that it might not be tomorrow. It might not come for a very, very long time."

"Let's say we leave Bittercress." I pointed at the landscape on the other side of the wall. "Without any more weird time travel shenanigans. Let's say we step off this wall together. Or rappel down. Or port away. Whichever you prefer. Would we vanish in a rising fog? Would it feel like dying? Like fainting?"

She raised both hands. A muted gesture of surrender. "We might wake up in our bed at the inn," she said.

"Together in bed. On the morning of the equinox. Both having slept soundly through the night. No Void at the back of my eye."

"We won't remember anything."

"Because nothing will have happened," I concluded. "No one will have changed. I'll never have met you as the Queen of the Void."

For the briefest of seconds, I had the illusion that Wist looked faintly amused. But of course it was just an illusion.

"Even if we never get entangled with the Void, time will bring you to me in the end," she said. "It's just a matter of when."

We walked slowly upstream. The path itself remained flat. I turned my head to watch the other silver river, the one flowing endlessly from one side of town to the other.

"Might not sound like it," I said to Wist, "but I *am* taking this seriously. Tell me more about the dangers of ignoring the Void."

A small aerial in the shape of a flat ribbon swirled near her, ignoring me. Like an eel, or a flying worm.

As it looped ever-tightening circles around Wist's neck, I momentarily became afraid it would choke her. But it flew off before ever quite touching skin.

"We speculated about the Void before I went back to meet it."

"Before I knew what to call it," I added. "Just knew it as the thing that scared you out of the caverns."

"We told ourselves that it was different from an active volcano. That it wouldn't erupt without provocation."

"Were we wrong?"

"Yes," she said. "I only understood that after letting the Void in."

"After letting the Void in, I understand nothing," I griped.

Wist didn't contest this.

"Even after cheating, as you put it—"

"I meant that as a compliment," I said quickly.

"—I barely succeeded in containing the Void."

"Even with the full strength of your older self."

"Even then."

"It's a foe that scales to your power. Would've been a struggle regardless, no? Unless you first feed it the feast of a lifetime. Then convince it to enter someone with all the magical prowess of a roadside pebble." I pointed at myself.

"Without a living vessel to contain it, the Void would inevitably erupt," Wist continued.

"Eventually."

"The caves are wide and deep. Without intervention, it would only grow stronger and hungrier on its own."

I sighed. "You mean that even if we didn't want it to be any of our business, it would eventually become our business in the worst possible way."

She drew an equals sign on the air with her finger. "Don't have any equations to prove it."

I believed her. I believed her completely.

That did not, however, make the choice any easier or more obvious.

Fluffy seeds floated past us, riding the breeze up and over the looming wall. Actual seeds of ordinary roadside grass, not minuscule aerials. I was impressed with them for getting so high in the air.

When presented with a set path, my first instinct was to rebel. Even against myself.

That alone would have been too petty a reason to ruin my own plan. There were much better reasons not to go back in time.

If I never appeared before Wist, if I never convinced her to put the Void in her body, she wouldn't need to unleash her last resort. She wouldn't need to reach across time and rapidly mature into her most powerful self.

She wouldn't raise the walls of Bittercress or make time keep sidestepping the autumn equinox, all in the name of containing the Void inside her. All in the name of protecting the outside world from what she and the Void might become in the end.

She wouldn't offer to send me back in time as a messenger, either.

In other words: I still had the ability to prevent her from breaking any time-related taboos.

She'd already broken them, in a sense. Even if we went ahead and undid her actions, that wouldn't guarantee a total lack of consequences.

But wasn't it worth a try? Besides, the unknown consequences of violating that taboo might very well be a hundred thousand times more dire than any havoc the Void could wreak on its own.

Yes, the Void could grow up to ravage all we loved. So, in theory, could the fate that might await us after breaking one of the greatest taboos. Anything we could do to reduce or eliminate those repercussions might be more than worth the risk of letting a boundlessly hungry Void sprawl free below Manglesea.

There was another factor, too. I wouldn't mention it to the Wist walking beside me. She had already borne the Void. She had already suffered its abuse in full.

My life in Bittercress had felt like it lasted a few weeks. Or maybe months. Or maybe years. Or maybe decades. With time never truly moving forward, it was all one and the same.

The part of Wist that had been entangled with the Void in the depths of the caves—the part of her that had never seen the light above Bittercress … her torment might have kept turning and turning like a waterwheel for just as long as—or much longer than—the length of time I'd personally experienced here.

I could still spare my Wist in the past. By not going back, I could make it so that every moment she'd spent getting devoured alive had never happened in the first place. All that pain would vanish like bubbles in water, ephemeral, as time collapsed in on itself. As time corrected its course.

Truth be told, I didn't know what to do. And I hated it. I'm usually very sure of myself—to a fault, really.

As long as I failed to make a decision one way or the other, we would by default keep lingering in Bittercress. Safe inside these walls. I understood all too well why Wist had been in no big rush to depart.

36

NOT THAT I would accuse Wist of malingering, but her recovery did seem to gain speed once I clearly understood the choice before me.

As long as we were here in Bittercress, I figured I might as well make myself useful. Now that Wist could comfortably leave the inn and wander around town for long stretches, we spent our afternoons collecting lanterns. Or otherwise pitching in.

No one would expect the Queen to participate in menial labor. By the same token, no one would attempt to dissuade her, either.

At the graveyard, we borrowed brooms and swept the area around the open gate. The purple-blue plumbago that cascaded about both sides of the entrance kept dropping old petals on the ground even as it bloomed anew, over and over. It seemed like it might never stop flowering.

The flannel-clad mortician stumped over to survey our work. She crossed her arms and made approving noises.

"Care for a coffin?" she asked.

"A coffee?"

"A coffin."

"Er," I said. "Kinda hoping we won't need one."

"A wedding coffin," she said impatiently. "For the Queen and her consort."

Is that what I was? The Queen's consort? I shot Wist a look. She gazed determinedly at the lush plumbago.

"We aren't ready for a full ceremony just yet," I told the mortician.

She insisted on bringing us back to her workplace (the pastel yellow building next to the graveyard that served half as a hair salon and half as a mortuary). She showed us a heavily padded coffin about the width of a single bed. It did look rather cozy.

The exterior was all lacquerware, brilliant red and black, with a pattern like starving eyes staring out of a dark forest. Or a dark cave. No wonder these wedding coffins cost so much.

I had a feeling that, if asked, Wist would happily have made a down payment. But no townsperson would request such hefty monetary compensation from their Queen.

"If we ever come back to Manglesea, we'll consider it," I said before dragging Wist away.

The mortician wouldn't have known what I meant. To her, we had always been here, and always would be. The Queen was eternal.

Technically, I had no deadline. Thanks to my sheer weakness as a vessel, the Void remained well-behaved inside me. Lazy as an old cat. I checked myself in the mirror but noticed no hint of darkly glowing veins. I opened my mouth wide but failed to see the Void lapping away at my tonsils.

Any pressure I felt to hurry up and decide was purely self-imposed. It grew heavier with each new day, which was never truly a brand new day.

The innkeeper showed more awareness of my malaise than most other locals. She'd also regained some understanding of the fact that Wist and I hadn't always lived here. Perhaps because of how often she saw us—dining at her tavern, wandering up and down the stairs of her inn.

The next time she offered to read my fortune, I accepted. She'd called herself the priestess of the past and the priestess of the future. If nothing else, she sounded qualified to offer advice.

She asked if I had a preferred method of divination. "I can interpret the currents in running water. The flight paths of mangle rays. The dung of primevals. The bones of river deer."

"Whatever's easiest for you," I said. "Maybe not the dung one."

I thought she might bring us to some special secret divination room, but she did it right by the sunken hearth of the inn.

Wist, who was not an active participant, lounged in a corner. She flipped back and forth through a book of Manglelander folklore.

It was one of those bizarrely bright and sunny days when the wind stormed all on its own, moaning outside like a parade of mourners. I felt weirdly grateful to Wist for letting the weather vary in mood. Helped stave off cabin fever.

The innkeeper donned a cloth mask. It had the same six-spot pattern as the stacks of masks she'd been saving for the equinox. She tossed one to me (and Wist, too, for good measure). It smelled clean, if a tad dusty.

Conventional fortune telling was neither magic nor any other sort of science. At this point, though, I would take whatever guidance I could get.

It wasn't a binding contract, at any rate. No matter what she suggested or prophesied, my actions—and any ensuing fallout—would be all mine.

The innkeeper brought over a capacious stainless steel mixing bowl.

She carried it in both arms; it was full of sloshing water. After setting her bowl down, she took out a bottle of cooking oil and a bundle of metal hooks strung on short lengths of fishing line.

The fishhooks were all different shapes and sizes, as varied as the ones hanging from her hair twists. Some single, some double, some treble. Some shaped like an open J, and others that nearly curled into a complete circle.

After covering the hooks with a cloth, the innkeeper asked me to select six lines.

She sprinkled tasty-smelling oil over the surface of the water. She took my chosen fishhooks and dipped them one by one, stirring, scrutinizing the patterns of broken-up oil they left in their wake.

"See anything interesting?" I asked, unable to keep my mouth shut for long.

She leaned back with a hiss of air through her teeth, as if only now feeling the strain of bending over her bowl. She rested her hands on her pregnant belly.

She explained in great detail the meaning ascribed to each pattern.

My main takeaways: I should show caution when lighting fires. I should be scrupulous about taking care of my teeth (always good advice). For the sake of purification, I should burn one piece of old clothing per year. I should stop dying my hair.

Avoid train crossings, she said, and give more to charity, and spend more time visiting islands.

"Islands," I repeated. "That'd be pretty tough advice for a Manglelander."

She polished each of her divining fishhooks, rubbing off traces of oil. "For us, it might mean walking out to a rock in the middle of the river."

"Huh. Nice and flexible."

The innkeeper picked up her bottle of cooking oil. I hurriedly rose and lifted the steel bowl of water, so she wouldn't have to carry it all the way back by herself.

"It's difficult to tell the fortune of someone with a bondmate," she confided. "Bonded pairs are very rare in Manglesea."

"Because mages are rare in general?"

"Mm. The traditional readings don't apply neatly to bondmates."

"I only asked for my own fortune, though."

"Do you live only for yourself?" she asked. "Is your fortune solely your own?"

I didn't answer. The innkeeper didn't seem to expect a response.

She told Wist and me that we could keep our cloth masks. We'd need them for the equinox.

"I'm excited for your festival," I said. "Feels like I've been looking forward to it forever."

The innkeeper chuckled. The fishhooks in her hair trembled cheerfully. "It'll come soon enough."

Up in our room, I loosened the knots in Wist's magic until she turned and slid her thigh between my legs.

Her expression hadn't become any sweeter. No matter. I would have known what she wanted even if we hadn't been touching at all.

I'd been very gentle with her lately. I'd been downright ladylike, in fact. I'd completely refrained from groping her at odd hours and in odd places.

It was the least I could do, honestly, after using the knife on her multiple times. But Wist didn't always seek gentleness.

Like the Void, I found myself both satiated and unsatiated. There was a hard root of affection in me that had formed, drip by drip, slow as those columns of glistening pale rock down in the caves.

Every time I became aware of how much I loved her, it almost enraged me. After all these years, how dare she grow her presence in me? How dare she make me want even more of her than the bottomless Void?

To put it succinctly: I was in a snit. Wist embraced me, bad mood and all. The end result—I'd worn her out quite thoroughly. She lay half-asleep on my shoulder, legs curled so her feet wouldn't stick off the end of the bed.

I wiggled free, settling her on our shared heap of pale green pillows, and went to remove my prosthesis.

When I returned, Wist had opened her eyes. She watched me climb back into bed.

I lay facing her. I stretched my empty right eyelid as wide open as it would go.

"Can you see the Void?" I asked.

"It's not really a thing one can see."

"But you sense it there. With or without my prosthetic eye in front of it."

"I know it's in you." Her tone could have meant anything.

"It doesn't frighten you? It doesn't repulse you?"

"It was in me before."

"Exactly," I said. "It was inside you. However much it afflicted you, you didn't have to look it in the face. You didn't have to make eye contact. You didn't have to make love to it."

She ran a light hand down my side. Once, then twice. Three times. Stalling while she thought of how to answer.

"I feel the Void," Wist said. "But the Void isn't you. No more so than your underwear, or your prosthesis. It doesn't make me shudder. Should I prove it?"

"How?"

"I'll do anything to reassure you." She wasn't joking. "I'll lick it."

"You'll—"

"I'll stick my tongue in your eye socket and taste the Void."

"As thrillingly romantic as that sounds, I think I'll pass."

I rolled onto my back. The wards on the walls and ceiling—all marked with the so-called Eyes of the Queen—looked very crisp. Brand spanking new. To do penance for the batch we'd inadvertently smoked into nothingness, we'd spent an afternoon pasting up a full set of replacements.

Crickets sang throatily. They sounded so close that I wouldn't have been surprised to find them arrayed like a tiny orchestra on the floor of our balcony.

Is your fortune solely your own?

"Wist," I said. "What should I do?"

I waited for her response. I began to suspect that I might end up waiting forever. I reached over and started pinching her.

She seemed reluctant to open her mouth. No doubt she only cracked because she knew for a fact that I would've pinched her till dawn. "I don't want to steer you one way or another. I don't want to make you—"

"You of all people should know that you can't make me do anything. I'm just asking your opinion. Good grief."

The crickets bravely kept playing their symphony. The show must go on.

At last she said: "I think...."

"Say that again. Louder."

"I think you should go back. Complete the circle. Tie the knot connecting this present to that past."

"Why?"

"So we don't lose custody of the Void."

My hand found the small of her back. "You're the one who's suffered for it."

I could still observe the aftereffects in her magic. Her branches hid amongst themselves like fish crowding into shoals for safety. They willfully tangled together as if to build a semblance of shelter from vengeful eyes. They interlaced into taut blockages like beaver dams. Slender tendrils balked when I moved to heal her, recoiling, too raw to let anything touch them.

Wist would submit without complaint, pulling her shirt up to show me her back. But her magic remembered the shapeless encroaching maw of the Void.

"We defanged it," she said. "Better to carry it around with us than to face it out in the wild one day. In a future we won't even know to prepare for."

"Might be a very distant future."

"Whether we fought the Void a year later, or five years later, or twenty years later, or much longer—our odds would be much worse."

She gave me one of those looks that suggested she could see right through me. In Wist's case, that didn't always mean much. It was the default set of her face—an impression of penetrating insight, with eyes that offered nothing in exchange.

"I already broke the taboo about meddling with time," she told me. "Don't look for loopholes."

"Can you blame me for trying? Loopholes are kind of my thing."

"We won't escape the eventual consequences even if the fact of my violation gets washed away in a tide of changed causality. If we forget about it, we won't even know to watch our backs."

I let this sink in.

"The more I think about it, the less sense that'll make," I remarked.

The croaking of hidden creatures outside didn't do much except underline my existential confusion.

I sat up. No use harping on it. "I hear you. I'll go back in time. I'll become the mysterious stranger."

Wist was silent. I nudged her. "No words of encouragement?"

"Thought you would need more time to decide."

"I've already taken ages, haven't I?" I hugged my knees. "Let's put it this way. When it comes to matters of conscience, I trust you more than I trust myself. I'm more worried about the fact that your past self apparently swallowed everything I had to say. Talk about gullible."

"Would you rather I didn't listen?"

"I'm just saying that you really shouldn't trust me to recommend the right course of action. In a moral sense. My track record isn't great!"

Wist made a singularly peculiar noise against her pillow. I took it for a sob of despair before realizing it must be closer to laughter.

When she raised her face, she was perfectly calm. "My track record isn't anything to boast about, either. This is my second time breaking one of the previous Kraken's taboos."

"This time I made you do it," I countered. "That's the fundamental difference. I can't disavow responsibility. Can't pretend you decided it all on your own."

"Look—you said I was free to reject going back in time. Free to deviate from the course set by the past. That's true. You were afraid to take that from me. You were afraid of influencing my choice. Of making it not a real choice at all."

"Not everything is predetermined," Wist said. "But the scales have been tipped. Didn't want to tip them any further."

"Your efforts were wasted," I said tartly. "Of course you would influence me. You're the only person capable of influencing any decision I ever make."

She met my eyes—my good eye and my empty eye. I tugged fondly at the ends of her hair. The aura of the bedside lights made it downright pearlescent.

"It doesn't only go one way," I went on. "You trusted me in the past when I came to you like a visiting angel—or a visiting devil—and talked you into confronting the Void. You trusted me against your most powerful instincts, your own best judgment."

She'd been desperate to get away from the caverns. At the time, I'd struggled to imagine any threat or temptation strong enough to change her mind. What in heaven or earth could have impelled her back there?

The answer was laughably easy. Me. Of course it could only be me.

"You trusted me then," I said, "with all your heart. I'll trust you now. You know the Void better than I do. If you think it's safest with us—if you think keeping it is the right thing to do—I'll gladly make it happen. Still my own choice. Spare me your moral angst, all right?"

She got up little by little and slid out of bed. She had on a satiny button-up nightshirt, except right now none of the buttons were doing their job. She glanced down and fastened them one by one, maddeningly slow.

Wist did have something of a mischievous streak, but I doubt she was drawing out this reverse striptease on purpose. She'd probably just gotten lost in thought.

"Wait," I said as she turned.

"I was going to get something."

"Well, hold on. Answer this for me."

"Having second thoughts?"

"No, you fatalist. Listen. The branch skills needed to send me backwards through time. Those definitely aren't something you developed on your own over these past few years. You couldn't possibly have been juggling multiple secret projects. I'm not that unobservant."

"No," Wist said, as though unsure where I was going with this.

"You borrowed those skills from your future self."

"Yes...?"

"There's one thing I still don't get," I said. "Think of all you've done to violate the natural flow of time. How is it inherently different from the other taboo you broke?"

Once in her life—long, long ago—she'd resurrected the dead. An entire world had paid the price.

But wasn't resurrection theoretically a type of time travel? She'd restored the dead to a prior state of existence. A living state. Or else she'd rewound time back to before the death ever took place. If resurrection and time-warping were essentially the same taboo, wouldn't she invoke the same consequences?

If she made the same mistake again, wouldn't it break another world?

Wouldn't it break her?

Wist looked at the ward-plastered wall as if it were something far in the distance.

"It's difficult to explain," she said.

"Please try."

"Pour a glass of water and a glass of rice wine, and they might look the same. They're both clear."

She regarded me as though she considered this to be a complete explanation.

"Keep going," I said.

"A rose sculpted from sugar could be made to resemble a rose sculpted from glass. The same degree of translucence, the same coloration. You'd have to taste it to know the difference."

"You're saying that resurrection is a rose sculpted from sugar, and time modification is a rose sculpted from glass?"

She tried again. "A gem produced through artificial means—physical or magical—might end up as a perfect copy of a natural gem. An indistinguishable twin. But the processes that crafted each of them would've been fundamentally different."

I had a go at translating this. "The means by which you broke each taboo are different enough that you're confident the consequences will be different, too. For better or for worse. No—not just that."

The muddiness that had been fouling up my head finally lifted. I was already committed to going back and bamboozling myself in the past. I'd do so with joy. But right until this moment, something in me had continued to struggle with Wist's willingness to break a second taboo.

"Borrowing strength from your future self was a borderline act at best," I said. "I still don't know if that counts as crossing the line. As tainting the flow of time."

"Can't prove it either way."

"Yeah. On the other hand, the skills you needed to freeze time inside the walls here—those all came from the future. So did the skills you'll need to send me back. They came from your greatest self."

Finally it made sense to me. "You didn't steal any actual knowledge of the future from her. But she must understand the consequences for stirring up the river of time. She must've already faced them, or at least started facing them. She must've learned for a fact that the brunt of it would land on her. On you. That it wouldn't be another case where the rest of humanity has to pay the price instead.

"She wouldn't work to invent the skills needed for mucking around with time—not unless she already knew for sure that the price would not be paid by others. She wouldn't develop those skills just to go along with causal obligations established in the distant past."

Wist took a pained breath. "You think my future self saw and dealt with the worst repercussions of time travel. Before originating the skills needed to facilitate time travel in the first place."

"And you think so, too, or else you wouldn't be going along with any of this," I said balefully. "That's what time travel's all about, baby. Ugh."

Better stop dwelling on it before my brain dissolved like collagen in bone broth.

Wist went over to the closet. She half-disappeared as she leaned far inside.

When she emerged, she held a single hanger.

A hanger with a generously sized black jacket.

"You might need this," she said.

She turned it around. Six huge red circles decorated the back. From here, each looked to be about the size of a decent dinner plate.

"Wait—was that in the closet all along?"

"Uh-huh."

"Since before you became Queen?"

"I made it difficult to notice," Wist said modestly.

"You mean you hid it with magic, you conniving—" I choked on my own spit. "That's why it disappeared from the shop window. You tiptoed back there behind my back and—you didn't steal it, did you? Or claim it through some sort of bogus civil forfeiture process? I was never a big fan of tyrannies."

"I paid good money for it," Wist said. I'd offended her.

"When? It was already close to evening when we first saw it for sale. By the next morning, you were gone."

"Made a deal with the shopkeeper over dinner."

"At the tavern? While everyone hollered and sang at us?"

Oh—I did remember her slipping away and abandoning me during the raucous Ballad of Ninny the Hostler.

I slipped the jacket off its hanger and tried it on. I did have a soft spot for oversized clothing. Sometimes it's nice to get totally swallowed up by your outerwear.

I reinserted my prosthetic eye. I put on the cloth mask that the innkeeper had told me to keep after our fortune-telling session, too. A flawless match for my new jacket.

"Look at me," I said. "What a genius disguise."

Wist brushed a bit of fuzz off the outer edge of my mask. "We finally meet again."

"So how does this work? Can you send me back right now? I'll need to make multiple trips."

"You'll have to tell me when and where you want to go."

It was still fairly early in the evening. "You know what," I said, "go put some pants on. We'd better get this all written down."

37

I BORROWED scrap paper and a pen from the innkeeper. Wist went out in search of a meal we could eat in our room.

By the time she came back, I'd sketched a rough timeline of our first three days in Bittercress.

Given everything that had happened since, I'd feared my memory would fail me. But the novelty of vacationing in a new town in a new country had given those early days more mental sticking power than much of what came after.

I distinctly recalled how it had felt to sit in the carriage on our way to the caverns. And how Lester the hired hermit had gaped the first time he saw us. And my puzzled fascination with the innkeeper's deadly-looking fishhooks.

Wist returned bearing an assortment of canned food—typical—as well as stone-roasted autumn sweet potatoes and cheap end-of-day goods from the bakery. The long potatoes had deep maroon skin and golden flesh, and they were hot enough to fill our entire room with their scent.

I complained my fingers would get sticky. Wist held my sweet potato for me like an ice cream cone. She scrupulously peeled off strips of skin, then moved it toward my mouth whenever I mewled about wanting another bite.

Once I worked out a detailed plan of action, Wist's magic would shift me around in time like a token on a game board.

In technical terms, she'd be utilizing an advanced combination of multiple branch skills. All borrowed from her future self, as we'd discussed. Which made sense. Skills capable of sending someone swimming upstream through time, physically defying its current, would take years or decades to devise from scratch.

Besides, Wist the Kraken was the only person in the past couple millennia who could meaningfully conceptualize such taboo-breaking skills. She'd have been forced to invent and imprint them with little reference to past research. And quite possibly without any plans to activate them ever again.

It would have been a rather thankless labor: toiling on and on across an untold number of years to originate some of the most complex and ingenious magic ever conceived of by any human mage. Not for glory or acclaim (although Wist had never valued accolades, anyway). Not even necessarily for her own use. Just so when her past self strained across time to grow stronger, the time-twisting skills needed by that past self would already be there.

Her abilities nevertheless had limits. She could only send me back to times and places where she herself had been in the past. The time-related part of that was a particularly hard boundary. She wouldn't be able to drop me in Bittercress the day before we'd originally arrived.

On the other hand, her location-related restrictions seemed somewhat more flexible. She couldn't send me all the way over to Katashiro Caverns at a time when she herself had been back in Bittercress. But if I were visiting a time when she'd been near the caverns, she could deposit me most anywhere inside the sprawling cave system. If I were visiting a time when she'd been in Bittercress, she could place me wherever I wanted in town.

I could work with this.

Once we'd put enough in our stomachs to avoid getting distracted by hunger pangs, Wist took my face in her hands. She made me hold still while she scrutinized my prosthetic eye. After a few minutes (I'd started squirming), she took a slender cutting from one of her branches and grafted it to the prosthesis.

Focus hard enough, and I could always detect the intensity of the cuttings she'd previously applied there. Magic perception was not strictly reliant on physical vision. I didn't need a real eye to feel the magic filling my socket.

No matter how much she layered on, it'd never be enough to illuminate all corners of the lurking Void.

"I added a transceiver skill," Wist said.

"So I can speak to you from the past? Tell you when I'm ready to move on?"

"It's similar to the cuttings on your pins."

I chortled. "Yeah, real similar."

She released the lock she'd placed on my eye's most important function: its ability to summon her from anywhere in the world. Ironically, she also attached a cutting that would prevent onlookers from noticing any magic on it. Thoughtful of her, considering that I'd be going back to a time before Bittercress had a Queen. A time when all human magic remained verboten. No exceptions.

Wist was moderately more clothed than before, but she still wore her satin nightshirt on top. It was a dusky rose color that she wouldn't have picked out for herself. I might've chosen this one, come to think of it. The loose-hanging fabric became cold very easily, cold enough to startle me when I brushed her.

She ported her office chair in out of—out of somewhere. Did she normally leave it stranded in the caves? Stashed in some poor forsaken water tower?

"Been wondering where you got that from," I said.

"I made it."

Was it my imagination, or did she sound ever so slightly embarrassed?

"Didn't realize you were a chairsmith."

"It's a magical imitation of fancy office chairs I've seen in the past." She took a seat and made a clear effort to pretend this line of discussion had come to a premature end.

I let it go. I could always bug her later. Sending me to the past would demand fierce concentration and exceedingly complicated parallel processing. Few other mages could use multiple high-level skills at the same time. None could simultaneously deploy as many as Wist.

I prepared to talk her through my plan. "In total, how many times did I visit you from the future? Wait—let me guess."

She waited.

"Once out on the bedroom balcony. On our first night in Bittercress." I tapped the paper where I'd drawn my heavily annotated timeline of events. "Once in the garden by the inn. On the afternoon of our second day in Bittercress."

My past self had witnessed both of those visitations. And no others. But there had to be more. At least one more, I thought.

"Did I go with you?" I said. "When you slipped out and went back to the caves again. During our second night in Bittercress."

Knowing what she was setting herself up for, knowing what she'd be walking into, I couldn't imagine myself sending her off to meet the Void alone.

Wist gave me a nod. She opened her mouth. Closed it. Then opened it again.

"Want to know what you said to me?" she asked. "How you persuaded me?"

I'd already considered making her tell me. More information was usually better than less. At the same time—it might take multiple tries, but if my argument had any merit, I'd be able to convince Wist to revisit the caverns without relying on a prewritten script.

I'd chosen to follow the rails I'd unknowingly laid down for myself. That didn't make me an automaton. I'd find my own way to securely link this present and that past.

"No need," I said breezily. "I'll wing it."

To avoid confusion, we decided to go through my stops in the past from oldest to newest.

"First I've got to give this to Lester the hermit." I smacked my bag. Inside lay the Cressian knife, all wrapped up in a hand towel. "The best time for that is the day we came to Bittercress. Right around when we pulled up to town. Think I could find him in his grotto?"

She blinked slowly at me.

"What?" I prompted.

"He was on duty that first day. He mentioned it the following day. In the carriage."

"The carriage," I repeated.

"On the way to Katashiro Caverns."

"Lester wasn't in the carriage with...."

I stopped talking. I drew a mental image of the guard who'd accompanied us to the caverns. The talkative guard, fresh-faced and hale, who liked playing the accordion in his spare time.

I pictured taciturn Lester, clad in a hermit's ragged habit, a false beard and excess eyebrow hair pasted to his incongruously youthful face with spirit gum.

Being a hermit was very much a paid role for him. His comportment when in costume might have little to do with his real personality. Although I had to believe that his enthusiasm for ancient history and literature came from the heart.

Most everyone in Bittercress had multiple roles to play. Multiple jobs. The innkeeper told fortunes. The mortician ran a hair salon. I'd experienced this myself when I alternated lantern-herding with mansion maintenance.

Why shouldn't the town hermit also take on a side hustle as a town guard?

"None of the townspeople were trying to hide it," Wist said. "When he's in character, they pay their respects by treating him as his character."

"When did *you* find out?" I demanded.

Okay, maybe I didn't always pay super close attention to how men looked. Unless they were beautiful enough to leave a lasting impression. Still, I'd never considered myself less observant than Wisteria Shien.

"I wondered about him in the carriage," she replied. "Didn't know for sure till I became Queen."

I was extremely disgruntled to be the last person in Bittercress to learn about Lester's double identity. On the other hand, this didn't fundamentally change what I needed to do next.

"All right," I said. "I stand corrected. He won't be a hermit when I visit him. He'll be on guard duty. Same difference. Hope you know which tower to plunk me down in."

She did. Great. Moving on.

"That night—the first night—you can drop me on our balcony. I'll call you out to talk. Next comes..." I traced a finger along my timeline.

"The second day. Mid-afternoon. Could you arrange for me to run into the mortician? Gotta set her up to drag me off to the cemetery. While she's got my past self hostage, I'll go see you again in the garden."

Wist seemed to be following along.

"On the night of the second day, put me in the merchants' room," I said. "Gotta scare them out of town before everything changes. Last, on the same night—I'll join you at the caves."

Over dinner, I'd made a copy of my cheat sheet for her to keep. Her eyes went back and forth as she familiarized herself with the flow of events.

I did still have the option of going straight to my past self. I could visit her in person. I could even visit her multiple times. I could tell her everything that was about to unfold.

I was under no illusion, however, that we'd become great friends. I knew myself way too well. I wouldn't swallow my own story so easily. I wouldn't do just as planned.

I'm quite capable of being my own worst enemy. I usually think I'm smarter than everyone around me—in this case, including myself. I'd question the necessity of breaking another taboo. And the necessity of making Wist absorb the Void, too. Once I heard how grueling it'd be, I'd fight tooth and nail to spare her.

If I lied to myself, hiding the uglier aspects of our future, it would only serve to make my past self doubly suspicious. She'd go out of her way to mess things up.

So I wouldn't change that part of the past. I would continue to leave myself in the dark.

We went over the details once more. Wist asked if I were ready.

"You've got to do all the hard work," I said. "Are you ready?"

She motioned for me to take her hand.

"Is this the first step of your magic?"

"It's not mandatory."

"More like holding hands while getting blood drawn, then," I suggested. "For comfort."

She sat on her would-be throne with her legs crossed, shining magic branches fanning all the way out to her extremities. She had merciless black eyes, though her lack of mercy was mainly for herself. She did look very much like my ideal evil queen.

I was much shorter, and physically weaker, and I had no magic, and I would never be anyone's Queen. But anytime I told Wist to get off her chair and kneel, she would kneel for me.

38

It DIDN'T FEEL at all like regular porting. My mind stretched sideways like a piece of gum. It stretched until it snapped.

I was very glad to be holding Wist's hand. Until I wasn't.

I wasn't holding anything.

I still had my new jacket, and my cloth mask, and the small bag slung across my body.

The air tasted different. I was in a cramped, green-tinted room. Large windows. No curtains.

I deduced that I must have landed in the water tower painted to resemble a melon. I deduced this primarily because the walls were covered in wavy, sun-faded posters of disconcertingly luscious muskmelons—which were now sadly out of season. Wist and I had just missed the last harvest.

There was a utilitarian table, too plain to call a desk. There was a rifle mounted on a simple rack. There was a well-polished metal horn for playing at the appointed times of day. It rested on an elegant display stand.

And there was a familiar guard in his uniform, holding a book much thicker than your average dictionary. In the first instant he saw me, I worried that he might throw it like a stone at a sinner.

His eyes darted in a triangle from me to his horn to his rifle.

"Sorry for intruding," I said. "My name is Clematis. Your name is Lester. We haven't met yet."

I took the bundled-up knife from my bag and held it out to him. Good thing it didn't look like a regular sharp blade. If he were jumpy, he might've shot me on the spot.

"It's not a bomb," I added, quite unnecessarily.

At that point, he would've been justified in hurling it out the window. But curiosity seemed to win out. He took the rolled-up towel and gingerly opened it to reveal the carcass of a Cressian knife.

"Can you tell what this is?" I asked.

His eyes got bigger and bigger. His fingertips became tremulous.

"Please don't have a stroke," I said.

Before I arrived, he had been entirely absorbed by his reading. Now he pored over the knife instead.

Guard duties in Bittercress must've been a largely symbolic affair. A mangle ray could've fallen outside the window, and he wouldn't have noticed.

He stammered questions. Predictable questions. Who are you? Where'd you get this? How'd you get up here? That sort of thing.

I tossed out vague responses, pretending I'd climbed up the ladder outside. Luckily, he'd been too busy reading to witness the moment when I materialized out of nothingness.

Then I got to the point.

"I'll give you that blade," I told him. "It's yours now. But in the future, if I ever ask to borrow it, you've got to let me have it for a while. Okay? I'll return it afterward. That's a promise."

More of the same questions. I raised my voice and kept going. "I know. It sounds like the first step of some sort of pyramid scheme. If you want a chance to study that knife more closely, though, you'd better trust me. You like ancient mysteries and stuff, right? Don't demand all the answers at once."

When he wasn't working as a guard, he lived alone as a paid hermit. As far as I could tell, he'd played that role for quite some time. I figured he'd be open to unusual schemes.

For that matter, everyone in town did things that didn't make a whole lot of sense. All in the name of getting along. Like herding lanterns. Maintaining extra water towers that no longer had a purpose. Letting wild primevals run the place, dropping dung wherever they pleased.

"I knew there were travelers coming to town," said Lester the guard. "Two of you. Arriving today."

"You all gossiped about us before we showed up, huh?" No big surprise there. "Tomorrow you'll see us outside the inn. You'll take us on a ride to Katashiro Caverns. Don't mention any of this. I won't recognize you, either."

"You want me to—"

"Think of this as another acting gig," I said. "A paid acting gig. Just like being a hermit. Play your part, and you'll be rewarded."

I looked meaningfully at the Cressian knife. He cradled it as if holding a newborn kitten. "No one else in town has any true interest in Cressian artifacts, do they? Would you want this getting tossed in a storeroom together with old trumpets? Archaeologists in the big city might not appreciate you having it, but once it's yours for good, you can decide what to do with it. At least you know its real value."

"But its provenance—"

"One day I'll tell you everything," I lied.

Our friendly chitchat on the ride to the caverns must not have been quite so friendly on his end. On the inside he must've been anxious, rapidly choosing his words, at a loss for how to figure us out. I suppose eventually he got used to me acting like we'd never met before.

I took this opportunity to make a couple more small requests. When you meet me as a hermit, I said, don't mention being a guard.

If I'd known he was a guard, I might never have asked him to play an old spare horn at the wrong time, and thus incite the primevals to riot. If I'd known he was a guard, I might have assumed he'd say no. Perhaps I'd have expected him to rip off his hermit garb—revealing a full guard uniform beneath—and promptly arrest me for my audacity.

"Don't act like you know me," I continued. "But if you can, try to commit me to memory. Me and my—me and the mage I'm staying with. You've got a better memory than anyone else in town."

It took a lot more back and forth (along with numerous questions about the knife that I really couldn't answer) before he agreed to my terms. The blade, which looked about as impressive as a mass of dried mud, would not have had this hypnotic effect on anyone else.

I left through the door leading outside. There was a tiny platform, then nothing but exposed ladder rungs all the way down the side of the tower.

I yanked the door shut in Lester's face so he couldn't try to watch me climb down. He rattled the knob—puzzled, but not yet using all his strength to force it open.

I raised my other hand to touch the tender skin at the corner of my right eye.

Time for stage two, I told Wist in the future.

On the other side of the door, Lester would abruptly stop sensing resistance. He'd pull it wide open and stick his head out into the sunlit breeze. He'd look down past the shoebox-sized platform, straining to make out more of the ladder beneath. He'd see green-painted rungs marching on and on toward the ground like train tracks. But he wouldn't see me.

I'd already leapt to a different time and place. Late at night on that same day, our first day in Bittercress. Out on the balcony by our room. It had a fresh, vegetal scent.

Inside, the curtains were closed. I put my ear near the cold glass. I could hear nothing but the usual tireless mallet bugs and bell crickets.

I backed all the way up to the balcony railing. I reached for my artificial eye and, for the first time ever, completed the full ritual to summon my bondmate.

39

DON'T KEEP ME WAITING, SNOOKUMS, I thought resentfully. Look—I didn't have a choice. The magic required that exact phrase.

Next I reached up and rotated my right eye in its socket as if trying to churn the Void like butter.

Something pillowy hit my face. To wit: Wist, forcibly ported from her bed to the balcony, collided with me—with sufficient force to make the railing creak. We grappled in a kind of baffled embrace.

She extricated herself. She backpedaled to a distance that would've been perfect for starting a fistfight. Her shoulders moved as she breathed. Her gaze remained glued to the right half of my face.

"You know it's me," I said.

The world might end before Wist let out a cry of surprise. She hung back by the sliding door and observed me as one might observe a single-file line of ants crossing the street. But—and I'd be hard-pressed to describe how—I could tell she was shaken to her core.

No question of whether she'd recognized me in the dark, mask and all. I'd given myself away by calling her with my eye.

She turned toward the room as if she could see straight through closed curtains.

You know it's me, I whispered through our bond.

She jerked as though I'd shot her.

I flapped my hand at her till she drew closer. Her hair was blacker than anything else in the night. She wore a familiar belted robe: the type that the inn gave out to guests.

I remembered coming out here on the balcony to question who she'd been talking to. I remembered finding her alone.

Suddenly, devastatingly, I forgot everything I'd meant to say. All my clever hint-laden lines, my sly inside jokes, my deliberately mysterious turns of phrase that would only make sense to her once we were together again in the future.

Pathetic though it might sound, I'd relished this rare chance to be the mystical one. To bewilder her. To astonish her. It could've been fun. When would I get another chance to show up out of nowhere like an angelic oracle and prophesize the future?

But how could I tell her to go deep in the caverns and conquer the Void? How could I tell her, knowing what would transpire after she let it inside?

"Clematis?" she said.

At least she didn't turn back and yell for my other self to wake up. Understandably so. Dealing with two of us at once would be the stuff of nightmares. It'd end with my jealous past self raring to tie me up and perform an interrogation.

At last I found my voice. I would have other chances to speak with her. For now—

"You're going to Katashiro Caverns tomorrow."

She waited to see what I'd say next.

"You'll sense something disturbing. Something that makes you want to flee. It's okay to turn your back. It's okay to run away.

"But first—endure it as long as you can. Every step shows your bravery. You're on the right track. You're right to wonder about what's down there. Don't be afraid of the caves. Tomorrow, nothing will happen."

Wist repeated this under her breath—*Tomorrow, nothing will happen*—as if trying to parse a secret message hidden in the space between words.

I lifted her hand to my right eye. Her fingertips had already lost all their languorous bedtime warmth.

She'd made this eye for me. Not to restore my vision, but to protect me. She would know her own work, even if it now carried extra magic that my black-haired Wist had never seen or used before in her life.

"You're from...."

She stopped. She swallowed.

"Another time," I said.

Her fingers curled into a fist against my eye socket. She'd figured it out before I confirmed it.

I still felt the drowning weight of those words in her. I may as well have tied her to a concrete block and tossed her in Osmanthus Bay.

"I broke another taboo." She lowered her hand. She raised her head. "Did you come back here to stop me?"

"There's no stopping what's already happened," I said. "Well—no, that's wrong. The taboo is broken. No point in fretting over it. But you still have a choice. You don't have to listen to me."

I mimed lobbing a ball out into the night. "You can chuck me right off this balcony. Cancel your visit to the caverns. Wash your hands of this whole mess." I pointed at the glass door. "That other me won't mind."

An animal howled loud enough to tingle the back of my neck. Not out in the wilderness, but from somewhere in town.

This was what had woken me up. This was when I'd noticed Wist missing.

"She'll be suspicious." I nodded at the curtains. "Tell her that I was … uh, a passing cleaner. Just stopping by to sweep the balcony."

"At this time of night?"

"You're free to make up any excuse you like," I said with dignity.

Wist shifted to stand more fully in front of me. Her face never changed. In her stillness, I could sense her fighting to decide what to say.

"Will you appear again later?"

I touched her sleep-disheveled black ponytail, chilly from the night air.

"Twice more," I replied. "Look forward to it."

Linger any longer, and I'd make eye contact with my skulking past self. I told my future Wist to get me out of here.

Next came the mortician. I jumped to the afternoon of the following day and found her doing paperwork in her salon.

The door wasn't locked, but it had a Closed sign out front. Guiding us around town that morning and tending to the cemetery must've kept her too busy to offer haircuts.

In situations like this, it helps to be shameless. I let myself in and began selling her a long-winded story.

Took me a while to get there, but in the end I said: "So it's almost my birthday—it'll come just a bit after the equinox."

"Congratulations," the mortician said mirthlessly.

"I think my partner is planning a surprise."

"How lovely for you."

I glanced at the square clock on the wall. "I'd like to give her some space. To prepare, you know. But I don't want her to realize I've caught on. Could you help get me out of the way? If you can, come fetch me about half an hour from now. I'll be in the garden by the inn. Near the hammock."

The salon reeked of her signature melon perfume. I was sort of glad to be wearing a mask over my nose and mouth.

From the start, I didn't try to pretend I was anyone other than myself. The mask only covered part of my face. The hood of my jacket would only disguise me from behind, or from a distance.

Unlike my past self, the mortician knew her fellow townspeople much too well to ever think I might be one of them. And once you eliminated the locals, there were a limited number of strangers in town. So I took a more straightforward approach.

"Hustle me out of there and try to keep me away from the inn. Doesn't have to be so long. Maybe until the next horn plays. I'll act like I don't understand what's going on, but that's purely for show." I leaned closer and added confidingly: "We're actually really interested in your wedding coffins."

Now that got her interest. Like Lester and most others in town, I'd reckoned the mortician would be fairly willing to look past the eccentricities of a foreign stranger. Just had to find the right angle to hook her.

Next: back to my black-haired Wist over by the inn. I found her curled in a garden hammock.

She startled violently when I appeared by her head. She came dangerously close to flipping out of the hammock like a hapless canoer.

I put my hood up. My past self would start snooping around in a matter of minutes.

As soon as Wist extracted herself from the hammock, I took her arm and led her deeper into the shade of the garden. We passed a sign warning of killer hornets.

The largest hornets were most likely to sting people in black clothing. Such as my lovely new jacket. Hopefully Wist would do something to defend us if we came under attack. Although at this time, she had yet to break the law of the land. She had yet to use any magic.

"You'll see this jacket up for sale later today," I said. "The one I'm wearing right now is the same one you'll spot hanging in a shop window."

Wist wasn't listening. "That thing in the caves." Her arm tightened in mine. "What is it?"

Before I could formulate an answer, she tensed further. She stared at something far past my shoulder. Probably not a killer hornet.

"Is it me?" I asked. I didn't turn my head. "No worries. The mortician will help babysit her till the next horn plays. You'll find her over in the graveyard."

"Not in a grave," Wist said tautly.

"No. I'm not a ghost."

As I'd predicted, the mortician and her crew got my past self out of the way. Good riddance, I say. (If she had any idea what was going on, she'd definitely feel the same way about me.)

There in the cooling shadows of the garden, I told Wist everything I knew about the Void. Including the fact that I now possessed it.

I would never risk giving myself any hints about future events, but I felt safe telling Wist. Unlike me, she wouldn't alter her behavior out of petty defiance. Even if she could see it coming, she wouldn't swerve merely to avoid suffering. If she still chose to act differently, despite everything, I would accept it.

I described—more explicitly than I had ever described anything in all my life—what would become of her if she went to claim the Void. And what she'd feared would happen if she didn't.

"You aren't obligated to go through with it," I said. "Escaping has its virtues, too."

She had her knuckles pressed to her mouth. She spoke a fraction more rigidly than usual. "If you didn't want me to go through with it, you wouldn't have come here."

"If that's a future you choose to reject, no one will blame you. I certainly can't. In the end, no one will even know you rejected it."

"Except me. I'll remember this."

I shrugged. "Will you? When time irons itself together, this moment might fade like an old stain. It might never have happened at all."

"You said I'd already broken the taboo about time. You said there was no reversing that."

"No one knows that for a fact."

"Are you here to persuade me or to talk me out of it?" she asked.

I was starting to get a little confused about that myself.

As we meandered about the garden, I came very close to idly kicking out at what I'd assumed were enormous decorative boulders. Oddly placed, but not without a certain slapdash charm.

On second glance, they turned out to be sleeping primevals. Wist steered me to a safe distance before my boot had a chance to strike home.

I pointed a finger at my mask. "Before I showed up, there was only one path visible before you. Never go near the caverns again. Never approach the Void.

"I came to show you the invisible place where the road divides. You can still take either path. But there *is* a future where you swallowed and survived the Void. I've been there. I'm here to stand with you as you look down that fork in the road."

I laced fingers with her just like how I always would on private walks. No special reason, no deeper thought behind it.

She stared at our joined hands. Maybe she was experiencing a fragment of what I'd felt when I first met the Queen. That troubling combination of soul-deep recognition and irreconcilable strangeness.

"If you choose my future," I said, "if you walk back in the caves—at least you won't have to walk back in there alone."

Only as those words left my lips did I realize this was the whole truth of it. Forget about logic and proper causality. This was my reason for being here. I couldn't bear to send her off to the Void like a judge delivering a sentence.

If she went back in the caves, I'd go with her.

I'd known I would feel this way. I'd known I would visit her once more, for that very reason. Before wading here against the current of time, I'd thought of that additional visit as a small bonus. A way to wrap up a few extra loose ends.

I'd been looking at it all wrong.

In my tour through the past, my final stop would be by far the most important. (Maybe not when viewed rationally. But damn everything else—I would've clawed my way back through time solely to be there with her in the last fearful moments before she became a vessel to the Void.)

A laughably large hornet buzzed through the trees on our left. We turned our heads in unison to follow its flight path.

At last Wist looked back at me. "I would have gone to the Void alone," she said.

"I know, you idiot. Better not ask the other me to come along. But you could at least have tried asking *me*."

"I didn't need to." She didn't smile, but an unusual warmth suffused her voice.

I stifled my urge to tell her to back out. Don't do this to yourself. Don't submit to carrying shadows cast by others—long-dead civilizations, the imperialistic first Kraken, and whoever else might have buried eons of magical ugliness down in those caverns. Why should you have to bend to the point of breaking under the weight of their sins? Why should you have to forcibly remake yourself just to endure other people's garbage?

I kept these thoughts to myself. Wist would be able to sense some aspect of them through the bond, anyway.

In the future and the past, I'd already said my piece. Here in the garden, she'd believed my stories of the Void with all her heart. Whatever happened tonight, I'd honor her choice just as she'd honored mine. Regardless of how it might reverberate on and on across time.

40

ONE LAST TASK remained before my final visit to Wist. I had to sneak back in the inn and scare off some innocent merchants.

On the night of our second day in Bittercress, I materialized in their room like an unholy apparition.

I'd made arrangements with Wist (the one in the future) to help set the scene.

I didn't want to explain anything. I didn't want them to recognize me as one of the women staying down the hall. I just wanted to galvanize them to get the hell out of town. Before Wist reached out to the Void, and the walls rose to glorious new heights, and it became impossible for anyone to leave.

I told my co-conspirator that she didn't have to come up with anything new. I listed off the greatest hits from our time in Bittercress. Clouds of flies swarming indoors, blood on the walls, blades growing from the ceiling with a screech of metal like a rusty bicycle, feral cats screaming all around the building, floorboards cracking under the weight of an unseen intruder. Among other things.

The spectacle worked. I didn't have to say much. After a few portentous words of warning, the merchants scrambled to flee. Didn't even stop to change out of their sleeping robes. The innkeeper would have to figure out a way to bill them for those later.

They left the room stinking of urine, too. Every good deed has its price.

Next, I shifted laterally through space and time. When I landed, only a few extra minutes had passed.

It was after midnight. We were at the entrance to Katashiro Caverns. The original entrance, from back when the caves had been a respectable distance from Bittercress. We stood by the illegible wooden sign that pointed the way inside.

Magical light in the shape of a firebird rode on Wist's shoulder. She had her hair in a sleepy black braid, which would have gone up in flames if the bird were made of real fire.

At this point in time, she'd only used magic twice since setting foot in Manglesea. Once to port herself from the inn to this signpost. Once to make light.

Wherever we stepped, the grass underfoot emitted the biting odor of horseradish. Just like last time. I rubbed my arms. My new jacket blocked the wind, but it wasn't especially warm.

Wist led the way in. The caves were still wondrous. After my extensive lantern-herding career, however, some of the novelty had admittedly begun to wear off.

I told her not to port us any further—better for her to conserve her magical strength for the Void. We wove between alabaster pillars. We twisted to dodge pointed growths of stone that curved out like long ivory tusks. Wist barely said a word.

There was just one thing I'd asked her to tell me in the future. One thing I couldn't bluster my way out of with rapid chatter or empty threats.

I'd taken the Cressian blade from the future and given it to Lester in the past. But that knife hadn't come out of nowhere. It hadn't originated in the future. We still needed to discover it here in the caverns.

Thanks to white-haired Wist, I knew exactly where to look.

I made us stop once we reached the cave of lost objects. The cave with a dead end marked by a humongous six-sided door.

Pebbles of broken pottery kept getting stuck in the tread of my shoes. I wasn't going out of my way to step on precious artifacts—they were nigh impossible to avoid.

"I have to find something," I said, "and bring it to the future. It'll be somewhere in that hole."

A cartoonish stuffed primeval guarded the wall. It wasn't that much smaller than your average townsperson. I tackled it out of the way to reveal a narrow horizontal shaft. A kind of crawlspace.

"You're not going in there," Wist said.

"One of us has to. You won't fit."

"I can—"

"Don't waste magic. Save your resources for the Void."

She didn't argue. Her petite firebird flew past me, all the way to the apparent end of the shaft. The main cave went dark. A feeble orange-yellow glow flickered like candlelight from the depths of the hole in the wall.

I took off my jacket and my bag. I got to crawling.

It was a tight fit, but not so dreadful as to induce an immediate panic attack. I had room to maneuver. Thankfully, the bottom turned out to be made of regular rock and gravel. Painful, but preferable to a path of potsherds or broken glass.

The back of the shaft opened up into what might once have been a tomb. Here I could stand, though I had to hunch my shoulders and bend my knees.

The firebird flitted worriedly around my head, shedding a kaleidoscope of changing shadows.

I wasn't knowledgeable enough to recognize most of what I saw. Large sealed jars, many toppled over. Imposing stone boxes that may or may not have been coffins. Loose beads of some sky-colored gem that struck me as being neither turquoise nor jade.

And weapons. So many weapons. If I tripped and fell, I might very well cut my own head off.

Most were in shockingly good shape, still recognizable as swords or daggers or axes or what have you. (My armament-related vocabulary dried up somewhere between halberds and switchblades.)

Unlike the mage-killing knife, these looked as though they might actually be able to gut me like a fish. Must've been made of different material. Or maybe the rust-encrusted knife was simply that much older than all the rest.

I sifted through the piles of weapons with extreme care. Many bordered on being too heavy to lift. I dragged them out of the way, trying not to start an avalanche.

I recognized the mage-killer as soon as I saw it. After all, it was the least impressive object in the entire tomb.

Exiting hurt my arms and legs more than entering. I escaped mostly unscathed, Wist's firebird lighting my way. After I stashed the Cressian knife in my bag, Wist insisted on applying First Aid magic to my scraped-up palms.

I'd promised to give the knife back to Lester for good. In the future, I'd do just that. Leave it here, and the same knife would continue existing in two places simultaneously. In the hidden tomb, and in Lester's possession. The universe hadn't collapsed yet, but something about that made my skin creep.

"Remember this for me," I said to Wist. I described the exact spot in the tomb where I'd uncovered the knife.

She nodded mutely. Now that I had my personal business out of the way, it gradually dawned on me that Wist was nervous.

No—much worse than nervous.

We crunched our way past ballpoint pens and primeval scales. Decorative seashells from far-off lands. Woolly mittens and fraying shoelaces. A belt with a broken buckle. Half a bicycle. Cooking chopsticks. A sheepskin rug. All this detritus washed up against the six-sided door on the far end of the chamber. As if cast up by an invisible tide.

"These can't all have belonged to vanished mages," I said. "It's a bit much, isn't it?"

"For some mages ... perhaps the Void only siphoned off their belongings. Instead of taking them whole, body and soul."

"They'd have left Manglesea complaining about a boring vacation and a pair of lost socks." I snorted. "Little did they know."

"Others might not have been sucked away into thin air," Wist said. "The Void might have lured them to walk into the wilderness. To come here on their own two feet. Maybe a few stopped in this room. Maybe they resisted the call of the door."

I tried not to look around for old bones.

"This isn't a door you cross by opening it," Wist stated.

"Whatever it takes, I'll go in with you."

For a long second, she was silent. Without meaning to, we inhaled at the same time. The air here, infused with the scents wafting off all these old forgotten things, had more of a human essence to it than anywhere else in the caverns.

"You can't," she said.

"I can do whatever I—"

"You shouldn't." She indicated my false eye. "The Void might be on the other side of that door. But it's also inside you. We shouldn't bring them together."

I couldn't protest. Whatever I'd been meaning to say—it got clogged up in the narrowest part of my throat. Because of me, there were currently two Cressian knives coexisting in the same slice of time. Because of me, there were also two Voids.

I started to apologize.

Wist looked me in the eye and said, without any attempt to hide it: "Clem, I'm scared."

I'd never heard her utter those words in that order before. Never. My chest squeezed inward like a collapsing star. Her myriad threads of magic swayed restlessly, probing the confines of her body for an escape hatch. Her firebird pecked intangibly at the curve of her jaw.

I'd excise my heart from between my lungs and juice it for her, if drinking it could lend her strength. But I had nothing tangible to give her. Nothing of value.

I caught her hand. I stepped up on a rocky outcrop, one just high enough to make me an inch or two taller. I pulled her in. She came with zero resistance.

Now—for once—she didn't have to bend at all for me to hold her. It was her breath soft and hot against my neck, her hair tickling my cheek.

Our bond felt more like a single brilliant point of light than a stretched-out binding strand. It sparked in every spot we touched.

"Close your eyes." My voice came out rough. "Imagine yourself in a—in a throne."

"A throne?"

Quizzical was better than terrified, but she didn't exactly sound inspired. Jewel-encrusted thrones would never do much for her.

"Picture something more modern, then. The sort of chair a CEO would sit in. Or the head of a mage clan, ready to do business. Heck—picture the most expensive office chair in the continent. Comfortable. Subtle. Tasteful. The sort of furniture I'd tell you to purchase in order to look the part of the Kraken."

I had a sinking feeling that I was making Wist increasingly confused. I tightened my arms around her. "Think of how viscerally the Void frightens you," I said. "Like nothing we've ever encountered before. The Void itself is equally frightened of vorpal holes. You won't be standing there pleading with it to enter you. You won't be wringing your hands, trying to strike a bargain with the devil.

"You'll rip open a vorpal hole. You'll wait for the Void to crawl on its knees to take refuge in you. You'll watch it approach like a petitioner groveling before a cruel queen, begging for its life. You'll think of yourself in your invincible chair. You'll withstand it. I've seen you on the other side.

"But you don't have to." My voice cracked. "You can still turn around. You can—"

Wist lifted me off the outcrop and put me back on level ground. She stretched her arms toward the ceiling, one at a time. When she finished, she stood nearly as tall and straight as she had in the guise of the Queen.

She looked down at me without blinking. She briefly leaned forward to breathe from the top of my head, burying her face in my hair.

"You're being weird," I said.

"I can be weirder."

"So can I, I guess."

"Will I still be myself?" she asked suddenly. "No matter what I ... will you still know it's me?"

I used my forefinger and thumb to widen the lid of my right eye, as if inviting a doctor to shine a light in it. "I've got the Void right now," I said. "Nothing like what you'll be facing. But it's there. It's bottomless. Am I still your Clematis?"

She blew out a forceful breath, emptying her lungs of old waste. She said *yes* somewhere below the level of speech, somewhere in the brief space between our bodies where our bond connected us like an ephemeral tightrope.

We went up to the door together. Wist made me release her hand. She transferred her firebird to my shoulder.

"I'll see you in the future," I said.

The six eyes carved into the door regarded us without comment. Wist touched the coppery stone with the backs of her knuckles, an idle knock that made no sound.

The door shivered like a struck gong. When it stilled, she had vanished.

Her firebird winked out. Plunged into darkness, I could neither see nor move. I thought I couldn't hear, either, until a bone-shattering screech sheared through me.

A vorpal hole had begun opening. Right on the other side of that door.

Wist—!

Without meaning to, I thought it at both of them. The Wist here in the caves, and the Wist in the future. A sharp cry that I should've kept to myself. My right eye socket ached as if it were on the verge of imploding.

41

IN THE FUTURE, at our room in the inn, Wist was very unhappy. I knew this not from her stiff body language or the impenetrable look on her face or the way her voice dropped, but because the first words out of her mouth were: "You forgot to call for me."

I flopped into bed. She didn't. "I may have gotten a little caught up in the moment."

She held up the paper I'd left with her as if it were a test with all the wrong answers. "You made this plan."

"Sure did."

She jabbed the end of the timeline. Hard enough to poke a hole in it.

"It would all be for nothing," she said, "if you lingered long enough to get caught up in my devouring of the Void. And its devouring of me. I needed that signal from you to extract you. All you had to do was—"

I got up and pried the paper from her fingers. It almost ripped in two along the way. I folded it and tucked it in my bag.

"I can accept criticism," I said. "I waited too long to give you a signal, yeah. But you got me out of there anyway. We're here. We're alive."

She rubbed a spot to the left of her sternum as if her heart had cramped from strain. "You were right about one thing."

"Only one?"

"We need a vacation."

"Yep. Much more so than when we first came here."

I pushed Wist's chair over to a corner by the balcony doors. It rolled as smoothly as if the floor were made of ice. I tossed my clothes on it, grabbed a T-shirt to sleep in, and chased her to bed.

We were too wired to sleep and too frazzled to do much of anything else.

"Now what?" I asked.

"You locked in the past," Wist answered.

"Give yourself some credit, too. So we can go home?"

"We can go anywhere."

"I'd like to stay for the equinox," I said. "After all that anticipation, I'd be rather crushed to miss it."

"The equinox will be tomorrow."

"I'll have an epic fit if it isn't." I snuggled up to her side. "Did you ever close the vorpal hole you opened in the last cavern?"

"Of course."

"Not right away, I assume."

"Took a while to find the necessary ... presence of mind. It's closed now."

"Whew. It'd be a real shame if a bunch of vorpal beasts moved in to supplant the Void."

"I caught a couple wandering the caves," Wist admitted.

"All gone now?"

I felt her nod.

I had no memory of falling asleep. Between garbled dreams of flying and falling and dying, I blinked blearily and saw her sitting in her chair in the corner. Moonlight leaked around the sides of the curtains to light her, but her interlacing veins of magic were a thousand times deeper and brighter.

In one of those moments, something fundamental shifted beneath me. Beneath the whole building. Like the world turned ninety degrees and then snapped cleanly into place. It had always belonged that way.

Nothing actually moved. Not the mattress, and not the moon, and not Wist in her chair. It had been an earthquake of the mind alone.

The following morning, I woke to the sound of chickens screeching. I rocketed out of bed, yanked on a pair of pants, and barreled downstairs to find the innkeeper.

I caught her kneeling by the hearth. "What day is it?" I demanded. "Is it the equinox?"

She laughed. Fishhooks shook in the air by her neck. "Even children don't get this excited for festivals. Yes—today is the equinox."

"Excellent," I said. "Perfect. Thanks!"

I'd gotten halfway up the stairs when I realized she was no longer pregnant. To be more precise: she no longer looked remotely pregnant. Every other time I'd seen her, she'd appeared long overdue for delivery. True or not, and despite the fact that she was pushing sixty, people in town claimed she'd been carrying for years.

"It's the equinox," I said to Wist. I closed the bedroom door behind me. "What'd you do?"

"I took down the walls."

"You did more than take down the walls." I told her about the innkeeper.

Then, distracted once more, I did another double-take. "You changed your hair back."

It was black again, through and through. Just like mine when I dyed it.

"I left it white as a clue for you," Wist said. "It served its purpose."

"Went right over my head. But thanks for trying." I surveyed her from various angles. "Hm. Well, I like your hair in any color."

Wist didn't have a solid answer about the innkeeper. She did have a theory, though.

The Queen's influence on Bittercress had not been a phenomenon isolated to any given present moment. Her grip on reality had been formidable enough and relentless enough to send hairline cracks racing far into the past.

For example—take the fact that in recent times, there had only been one or two mage disappearances per decade. It used to be considerably more frequent. That reduction had been a positive distortion caused by the gravitational pull of the Queen's power.

Other aspects of life here may have gotten thrown off, too. Was the innkeeper a natural medical miracle? Was she really supposed to have been pregnant so long? Was she still supposed to be pregnant now?

I wasn't so tactless as to ask her. But I wondered.

No one called Wist their Queen. No one would let us help set up for the festival, either. We were honored guests once more. Foreigners. Permanent outsiders.

Fewer aerials circled in the sky. Fewer primevals prowled the streets. The human population felt smaller, too.

That morning, we walked from one end of town to the other. We opted to go on our own feet rather than take a rickshaw. We marveled at how the view had changed when the walls came down.

I saw child-sized unicycles rusting in someone's yard. No children ran out to play with them. In fact, for all that it was supposed to be a day of family festivities, I scarcely noticed any children at all.

I plucked at Wist's shirt. "The mage kids I saw running around—you said they were basically ghosts. What about all the other kids?"

Her black ponytail flapped like a flag in the wind. "A lot of magic I performed as the Queen was done in broad strokes. There was too much of it—all at once—to consciously regulate every fine detail. The shape of the town, its texture, its quirks—much of that came from the desires and fears of those living here."

"So I shouldn't blame you for that time I saw the mortician shedding maggots. You're saying the blame lies with her?"

"You can and should blame me for everything," Wist said stoically. "I was the Queen. But if the town felt busier back then, if you remember seeing more children, it's because that's the sort of town they longed for it to become. At least some of them."

Maybe the innkeeper had desperately wanted to be pregnant. Or to stay pregnant. For as long as she possibly could, well past the point of credulity.

I thought of the grave stelae, tall and short, covered in names I couldn't read. Then I strove not to think too much about anything at all. If she were fortunate, she might not remember her unduly long pregnancy. Or it might seem like something that had happened long ago, far away, to a different person altogether.

There were still mansions on the hill. They were a lot duller than I recalled, and at least one looked downright dilapidated. When we asked a gardener about it, he chuckled and said the owners had stopped paying for maintenance.

The equinox festival lasted multiple days.

The ubiquitous lantern plants began rapidly fading to brown lacy husks.

Spider lilies, scarlet and white, bloomed all over the graveyard and the riverbank and along the wreckage of the ancient walls.

We all wore six-spot masks. We hung flashy necklaces of imitation coins around our necks. Ceremonial ropes studded with woven eyes and iron thorns stretched across the river, crisscrossing between bridges. The oldest folk in town marched in a slow yet determined parade, hoisting up colorful banners, zigzagging from one bridge to another.

Middle-aged merrymakers poured us cup after cup of mead, and pear cider, and every conceivable combination of the two.

In deference to the innkeeper's fortune-telling, I tossed my bloody utility jacket on a public bonfire meant for ritually burning old possessions. At night, we silently watched glowing lanterns bob their way down the water. Just a couple at a time.

In this reality—in this town without a Queen—lantern-herding was a dying profession. The town itself, too, felt just a bit like a dying town.

As for other changes: Katashiro Caverns had gone back where they belonged. The water towers appeared shorter and squatter, not to mention rather fewer in number.

When local primevals wandered off to graze in the hills, all they had to do was step past the tall fluffy maiden grass that waved incessantly along the ruins of the wall.

Wist and I packed to leave. We hadn't brought much with us, so there was plenty of space for the souvenirs we'd gotten to give away in Osmanthus. Mead and honeycomb, beechnut butter and rosehip jam and pomegranate syrup from the inn, skincare products made with beeswax and royal jelly, sweet preserved chestnuts and figs.

I kind of wished we could take home one or two stone lights, too. I'd become rather fond of their bedtime glow. But before going to haggle with the innkeeper, I remembered her telling us how they needed to be fed and cared for like houseplants. Not the best choice for me, then.

Maybe the ones rooted in the caverns had gotten most of their needed nutrition from the rock around them.

A couple days after the equinox, my birthday passed without incident. Just the way I liked it.

(We did have a very nice candlelit dinner, right in the same private room where I'd once fed Wist spider lily salad. This time, we managed to get all the way to the dessert course without any deliberate acts of poisoning.)

For every item we bought to gift friends in Osmanthus, Wist got a duplicate for me to hoard for myself.

After all that build-up, the short-lived spider lilies began to wilt and crumple only a week or so after the equinox.

We stayed long enough to watch the festival decorations come down again, though not long enough for all the six-spot burnet moths to vanish for winter. At the afterparty in the tavern, I recited traditional Bittercress nursery rhymes to tremendous applause.

The sky ships sail from land to land, across the mangled sea.

The crossroads are bitter, the crossroads are sweet. The sky ships sail for me.

I nodded sympathetically when the innkeeper muttered about how she needed to get the storeroom locks changed. Someone had used her key, though no one seemed to know what was missing.

The day before our departure, I paid one final visit to Lester.

He'd helped escort the march of elders on the equinox, merrily playing his accordion as they paraded from bridge to bridge. Now he was back in hermit mode, tattered and somber. I caught him on the verge of disappearing inside his grotto. I passed him the Cressian knife, this time packaged in an inappropriately colorful gift bag.

"See?" I said as he held the bag open to peek dubiously inside. "I kept my promise. It wasn't a scam."

He lifted his head slowly, like a man in a dream.

It wasn't just makeup that made his eyes baggy and his cheeks sunken. He was still one of the younger adults in town, but he'd become genuinely haggard. He suited his role much too well. A hermit was neither a jester nor a bard, after all. A hermit needed a reason to retire from society.

He spoke haltingly.

He did remember my promise to give him the knife for good.

He also remembered parts of the Queen's reign. Parts that everyone else had long forgotten. Like playing the old horn I'd given him. Causing a primeval stampede. Other townspeople told him no such thing had ever happened. At least not anytime in the past few decades. But he still had the horn stashed guiltily in his grotto.

I tried to follow through with my end of the bargain. As best I could recall, I told him about the contents of the tomb in the caverns. The place where Wist and I had discovered this blade he so treasured.

He pointed out the fact that I'd popped up in the melon tower and given him the knife an entire day before he took us to the caverns.

"Did I?" I scratched my head, feigning bewilderment. "You sure about that? Doesn't make any sense, does it?"

Lester deflated.

"My point," I said more strongly, "is that Wist—the Kraken—says it's safe to go deeper in the caves. As deep as you wish. Go live your dreams, young hermit. Go dig up all those Cressian dregs. Or don't. It's up to you. Do try to get permission first."

A cold fall wind rustled his dying herb garden, his neglected tea bushes, his stubby pomegranate trees. He turned his walking stick in his hands as if boring a hole for planting.

As much as he'd helped me—as much as I'd set him up to help me, rather—I didn't really know him. The chipper guard who'd shown us to the caves struck me as being just another role. No closer to his true personality than the taciturn hermit. His guard self would commute back and forth from a house or dormitory that had nothing to do with this decaying grotto. His guard self performed on a different stage.

Either way, that uncanny memory of his was not necessarily a blessing. He would keep doubting himself and his reality for a long time to come.

I could've asked Wist to get in there and perform some restorative mental surgery. To at least make his understanding of the past match up with everyone else around him.

That didn't quite seem like the right thing to do, either.

"Will you be okay?" I asked without context.

As soon as I said it, I wished I hadn't. What was the point? To salve my bruised conscience?

If he said no, what could I do but wish him well and briskly tromp away into the sunset?

"I'm used to ambiguity." He kept turning and turning his stick to drill new dents in the ground. The gift bag hung from his wrist, rocking back and forth, the knife still tucked inside it. At last he came to a stop.

"History is made of contradictions. Deep history is characterized by a lack of answers. It's a long, long void with occasional sparks of discovery. But no two people see those sparks the same way. Very rarely can you get anyone to agree on what they mean."

"Hm," I said. I was not a historian.

For whatever it's worth, that wasn't the last time I saw him. In guard uniform, he helped wrestle Wist's conjured office chair into the stagecoach that would transport us back to the border.

Since Wist could no longer get away with bending everyone to her will, she was making an effort not to break the law again. No porting allowed. She paid handsomely to have the chair carted out of town with us. She paid enough, I think, to keep anyone from questioning where in the world it had come from.

The mortician gruffly offered to perform a ceremonial coffin marriage before we left. "Won't be legally binding," she said in a tone of apology.

We declined. "Maybe next time!" I said brightly.

A smattering of acquaintances gathered to see us off. We'd squeezed into the stagecoach together with Wist's office chair, but it was an extremely tight fit. I had to crane my neck by the window to see mangle rays coasting grandly through a blustery blue-gray sky.

"Don't be lost," said the mortician.

"Don't be lost," said Lester the guard.

"Don't be lost," said the innkeeper.

"Don't be lost," chorused hostlers, and beekeepers, and the baker, and the blacksmith, and lantern-herders, and tavern regulars, and a single lonely large-eyed child. The inn's hatchet-shaped door handles steadily retreated from sight.

High above and far away, the noontime horn began to play as we pulled down the road. It sounded weaker than ever before. A loud conversation would've been enough to erase it.

Wild primevals ambled in and out of town beside us, their scales and stringy hairs almost rubbing up against the sides of the stagecoach. They stepped without hesitation on the foundation of the old forgotten wall.

42

THE STAGECOACH was precisely as uncomfortable as it had been the first time around. No, worse: now we had an incredibly unwieldy chair to contend with.

Since I couldn't lean over to sleep on Wist's shoulder, I instead occupied myself by needling her.

"Congratulations," I said. "The rest of your life will be in easy mode."

Wist gave me a look that could have only meant *What?*

"You were already the Kraken. Now you're at the height of your power. Way ahead of schedule. You've peaked—all you've got to do is stay there."

"Peaked," Wist repeated. "That usually isn't a good thing."

"Easy. Just stay on top. Problem solved. If nothing else, your usual duties should be a lot less draining. No?"

I hadn't been too worried about the coachman overhearing us. No one would have any idea what we were talking about.

Wist was more cautious. *Some aspects of my new power will fade over time*, she said through our bond. *Now that my time has begun moving forward.*

"What? Why?"

I borrowed many, many future magic skills that I haven't actually developed yet.

I massaged my temples. "You won't forget about the experience of borrowing those skills?"

"No."

"So you'll end up serving as your own inspiration when you invent or reinvent them in years to come. A self-completing cycle. Like a phoenix."

"Should we change my title?" she asked. "Should I be a phoenix-class mage?"

"Very funny."

The stagecoach relentlessly bounced along. It had a padded seat that made my butt feel like it was getting pummeled by boxing gloves. Sick of trying to see Wist past the bulk of the chair between us, I looked out the window.

Some Manglelanders thought human magic fed a curse embedded deep in their land. They weren't wrong—careless magic use would've helped feed the Void.

To the end, we'd never get a textbook answer about its origins. We didn't know whether it had formed naturally, before the Cressians, or only in response to their practice of mage sacrifice. We didn't know whether or not they had fed the Void on purpose.

We didn't even know if the first Kraken had really gone down in the caverns to face it.

Wist feared that the Void might represent the final fate of the previous Kraken. And eventually her. Like the darkness after the death of a star.

After all, they did share certain characteristics. Compare the first Kraken's drive to conquer to the Void's insatiable hunger.

Last night I'd burrowed next to Wist with my leg wedged over her leg. "Can't promise it isn't what you'll become in the end," I said into her shoulder. "But normal people wonder and worry about death, too. Everyone has a void in their future. A world collapses every time someone dies. The rest of us keep going. Well, for the most part.

"Consider the fact that the first Kraken warned Manglelanders to stop using magic. To stop feeding the curse. Would she have been able to come back and warn them if she'd succumbed to the Void? Or if she'd become it in death? Those tales suggest that she met the Void and survived it. Although they might all be apocryphal."

"Are you trying to comfort me or not?" Wist asked dourly.

Occasionally I brought up the fact that if the Void were going to be stuck in me for the rest of my life, we might as well run experiments to find a use for it.

Wist expressed trepidation. To put it mildly. Wouldn't stop me from pitching ideas, though.

On a similar note, I regretted relinquishing the Cressian blade. Couldn't imagine a better weapon for self-defense against mages. The materials and processes they'd used to craft their tools of sacrifice seemed like a long-lost art. I might never get my hands on anything comparable.

"Part of you relished stabbing me," Wist said as I lay in bed and rubbed her stomach. "Don't think I couldn't tell."

"I was a serf rising up against a queen," I said virtuously. "I won't do it again. Unless..."

"No."

"All right, no more stabbing. Unless you become a tyrant."

"Same goes for you," Wist muttered.

"Who? Little old me?"

"You're the Queen of the Void now."

I laughed, startled. "Not quite the same, is it? I'd consider myself more of a custodian. A pet sitter."

"The Pet Sitter of the Void," Wist said woodenly.

"Doesn't have quite the same ring, huh."

As we left the country, we would carry the Void away with us. If they wanted to, Manglelanders—and visiting travelers—could safely use magic now. This could in theory revolutionize their entire society.

In reality, nothing changed. Wist made no claims about having exorcised a curse from their land. She didn't bless Manglesea, telling its citizens to toss old laws out, to go forth and live new lives suffused with magic.

Some people would have believed her. There were always people willing to believe the word of the Kraken. But in truth, we didn't have any way to prove it.

Neighboring countries, such as our native Osmanthus, would frown on anything that might politically or militarily strengthen (or weaken) tiny Manglesea. Making such radical assertions would be considered an act of incitement.

Manglelanders would be violently split between those eager to throw out older cultural practices and those who preferred to preserve their country as the only nation on the continent unburdened by magic and its complications. Berserking mages, power struggles, random vorpal holes....

With the Void gone, Manglesea might see its first significant new vorpal holes in centuries. For that reason alone, we knew one day we'd come back. One day they'd need the Kraken to save them.

Before our departure, Wist did make one formal statement as the Kraken. She thanked the townspeople for their hospitality and reported on her visit to Katashiro Caverns. She declared firmly that the caves no longer posed any danger—no more so than any similar cave system. She encouraged the town to invest more in research and exploration. She left a hefty donation to get them started.

(I ghostwrote this statement for her, by the way. I struggled to stifle my laughter whenever people called the Kraken well-spoken.)

As the primeval-drawn stagecoach rattled us closer and closer to the border cities, we stopped seeing mangle rays, sky nettles, and most other aerials. All that remained were one or two forlorn-looking birds, gliding high and slow.

Something less tangible hung over our heads instead, sharp and too heavy to measure.

"Can you take a guess at the consequences?" I asked. Didn't need to specify that I meant the consequences for breaking another ancient taboo.

Wist half-shook her head. "We'll face them one day. Hopefully not for a long time."

"I hope so, too," I said. "But hope isn't good for much. Bank on it all you like. Won't pay any interest. I like my investments to give me dividends."

"Do you even know what a dividend is?"

"Do you?"

"Vaguely," Wist murmured.

We stayed a night in one of the border cities. I wore an eyepatch again, my false eyeball tucked safely in my Jacian bag. Just in case.

Our purchased gifts made it safely through customs. So did the Void, for that matter, although I didn't declare it. What would I list as its monetary value? Its quantity? Its weight?

In Osmanthus, Wist came tottering back to her tower after a dizzying slew of meetings with an onslaught of government officials. From their perspective, our trip had been nothing unusual: just about as long as we'd originally promised. The day before the equinox had only lasted for a single day. And then it was over.

The prairie outside the tower grew as blue as ever, with hints of deep-sea green shuddering through it when the wind blew at certain angles.

Manglesea didn't have an exclusive patent on natural beauty, that's for sure.

I'd never confess to being homesick for Osmanthus, but I did have a soft spot for this tower and its sprawling isolation. Its improbable architecture. The way every last part of it felt like sinking into a hot bottomless bath of Wist's magic.

Wist found me entertaining myself by hissing at her cat. She stood back and watched us for quite a while before interrupting.

"Need more time?" she asked.

I hissed at her, too, for good measure.

She claimed she had two things to show me. I followed her to a sunroom full of miraculously still-living plants.

A set of white wicker furniture had been pushed off to one side. In its place, in the sunniest part of the room, rested a lacquerware wedding coffin. The one the mortician had offered us.

"I get it," I grumbled. "This is why you were so determined to pack that stupid chair in the stagecoach. To throw me off the scent. Well done."

She must've made secret arrangements with the mortician to send the coffin by international courier. My brain balked when I tried to run a mental simulation of the total cost.

I blinked and rubbed my left eye. "Wait—is this your way of proposing?"

"Coffin marriage holds no weight in Osmanthus," Wist said mildly.

She'd always been way more sentimental than me on the inside.

Marriage in general still seemed superfluous to me, compared to the permanence of healer-mage bonding.

I ran a hand over the red-and-black lacquered flank of the coffin. It looked like the final resting spot for some profoundly evil entity. Not a romantic love nest.

The craftsmanship, however, was undeniable. Wouldn't want to get up to anything too wild in here, but maybe it would be comfortable for warm winter naps.

Wist reached in the coffin and pulled out a black bundle of straps.

"Did being Queen of the Void awaken new interests in you?" I asked politely. "Looks like a bondage thing."

"Would that be a new interest?"

"Huh. Guess not."

She slipped the straps around the backs of her shoulders. "It's a posture corrector. Remember your promise?"

I looked innocently off at the panes of glass between us and the autumn sky. "I dunno, Wist. You really did a number on my memory back in Bittercress. All that mental manipulation—no real consent—so cruel."

"You do remember, then."

"You can't hold me to promises I made days before you turned around and brainwashed me," I said self-righteously. "Plus the entire rest of the town, to boot. Sure, you had to deceive the Void. And yourself. Sure, you had a reasonable excuse for it. Doesn't change the fact that—"

"You set that entire sequence of events in motion." Wist remained impassive, the extra straps of her posture corrector hanging loose around her upper back. "You chose to go to the past."

"Just don't do it again. Not even if I'm the one giving you orders. Directly or otherwise." I turned her around and started tightening the straps.

"Will you lift weights with me? Like you said you would?"

"You've got to keep your cat from getting underfoot while we do it. That was part of the deal, too. But sure. Fine. Whatever you want, darling."

She winced. Either at the endearment, or because I'd pulled her straps too viciously. Maybe both.

"You've grafted magic to this," I observed. "Trying to take shortcuts?"

"The magic isn't for my posture," she said. "It's to help resist the Void."

"Like ... a chastity belt?"

"What an unpleasant analogy."

"Sorry," I said, unrepentant.

A tremor went through her otherwise peaceable branches. One so slight that no one but her bondmate could've noticed.

"The Void will begin to stir soon." She looked over her shoulder at me, as outwardly composed as ever. "You'll know when it gets hungry."

I lowered my hands from the straps cinching her back tall and straight. Just like how she'd stood as the Queen.

Wearing it all the time could be just as harmful as not wearing one at all. After years spent training herself to look smaller, though, she could use a little help with learning other ways to stand.

"Wist," I said. In a rare event for me—and against my better judgment—it came out sounding utterly serious. "Are you afraid of me?"

I'd asked her that before. I'd asked if she feared the Void in me. She'd avoided giving a direct answer. At the time, I hadn't been pitiless enough to dig deeper.

She started to turn around. Then, changing course, she stepped out of her house slippers and climbed in the coffin. She lay on her back and held her arms out.

I joined her. The coffin was naturally a lot less springy than a mattress.

To me that made it feel like home. I had something of a predilection for floor beds.

I rubbed my chilly feet on her warm bare ankles. Wist locked her arms around me and asked, in turn: "Are you afraid of me?"

"No," I said. "You won't hurt me."

Laughter vibrated her ribcage. It was not a happy laugh. "That's a strange thing to hear coming from you. I've hurt you in ways I can never make up for. More than once. Even in Bittercress—"

She cut herself short. "That's not what I'm trying to say."

"Then try again," I said briskly. "Try as much as you want. We've got time."

"Is it reasonable for a deer to fear a wolf?" she asked.

"The wolves in Manglesea have flat teeth," I said. "But I suppose I see what you're getting at."

"It's only logical to be wary of a loaded gun. For those without magic to tread lightly around those who have it. For other mages to desperately curry favor with the Kraken. I've seen that fear in your eyes, Clem. Both as the Queen, and as nothing more than myself."

"Now you feel it, too," I said slowly. "Because I have the Void in me. Now you know what it's like."

On an intellectual level, she'd understood that I could hobble her and hijack her magic. None of that could compare to her memories of being consumed alive, on and on, by a Void whose thirst would never be slaked.

She had diminished the Void with her sacrifice, pouring water on its fire. But that primal dread of predation had burned itself into her body and every last thread of her magic. It had changed her just as much as the experience of prematurely growing into a scarred and distant future self.

There would be no such thing as returning to normal. Not from being the Queen, and not from eating the Void, and not from meeting her own terror of total consumption.

"You know," I said, "if you need more time and space to start getting used to—"

Wist squeezed me until I coughed.

"This is how you've always felt beside me, isn't it?" she said. "I like knowing how you feel."

"Were you always such an optimist?" I inquired.

"Maybe you've had a positive influence."

"Hah! Good one."

She was right in the sense that I never forgot Wist was the Kraken. Whether at home or in the city. In Osmanthus or foreign lands. In her arms or outside them. The sheer mass of her power was impossible to ignore.

If she felt like it, she could permanently stop the flow of time. She could kill anyone or everyone, and get away with it. Hell—given sufficient opportunity to prepare, she could flip the entire continent upside down. She could open a vorpal hole large enough to swallow the world.

The human mind wasn't equipped to appropriately digest that kind of threat. Even if you knew her to be loving, compassionate, self-sacrificing, an incorrigible softy beneath her shell.

But just as I never forgot she was the Kraken, I also never forgot she was mine.

The future would not be all sweetness and sunshine. The Queen she'd grown into had not been crushed by the weight of her burdens. Nor did it seem as though her burdens had lightened. Her acts of time manipulation would ultimately bring karmic retribution down on our heads, though no one could say what or how or when. Even if she never dabbled in time-traveling magic again.

There was nevertheless a future out there waiting to be grasped. By reaching forward to a much older self across an untold span of time, Wist had inadvertently proven that.

I closed both eyelids—I might have dozed off for a bit—then opened them. I rubbed the itchy skin around my prosthetic. This sunlit coffin was turning out to be a lovely spot to cuddle.

Wist's warm scent mingled with the foreign fragrance of the bedding in the coffin and the vibrant lacquer outside it. Beneath an unbroken sky so blue that it edged on purple—a sky that had never known aerials— I began mentally sketching out a plan for our next vacation.

A Note from the Author

I LOVED jumping back into the main Clem & Wist series. I hope you did, too! I'm enormously thankful to everyone who has read and rated past entries in the series (and this one as well). Thanks so much for your kind support!

I already had this story percolating at the back of my head while I wrote previous Clem & Wist novels (as well as my standalone books set in Jace: *The First and Last Demon* and *The Forest at the Heart of Her Mage*). I've been looking forward to it for years—but until recently, I didn't feel ready. Some books just need more time to brew.

Maybe that's why I feel a curious sense of gratitude toward *Clematis and the Queen of the Void*. Even as I published multiple other stories, the essential concept of this novel stayed with me like a guiding star. It gave me something to anticipate. More importantly, it gave me a reason to strive to grow as a writer—in hopes that I could one day do it justice.

By now I've got several other future story ideas that I'm sure I'll find similarly challenging. Can't wait to start tackling them!

One last note: for the record, *Clematis and the Queen of the Void* takes place prior to both Jace books. If you enjoyed it, you might also have a great time reading *The First and Last Demon*.

Follow my Author Page for future updates if you'd like to see more:
https://amazon.com/author/hiyodori

Hope to see you again next time!

– Hiyodori

Novels by Hiyodori

The Clem & Wist Series

Book 1: The Lowest Healer and the Highest Mage

Book 2: The Reverse Healer Case Files

Book 3: Clematis and the Queen of the Void

Prequel: No One Else Could Heal Her

Set in the World of Clem & Wist

The First and Last Demon (Standalone)

The Forest at the Heart of Her Mage (Standalone)